PLAYBOY PRINCE

CRYSTAL KASWELL

Copyright

This is a work of fiction. Similarities to real people, places, or events are entirely coincidental.

Also by Crystal Kaswell

Pierce Family

Broken Beast - Adam

Playboy Prince - Liam

Ruthless Rival - Simon - coming soon

Dirty Rich

Dirty Deal - Blake

Dirty Boss - Nick

Dirty Husband - Shep

Dirty Desires - Ian

Dirty Wedding - Ty

Dirty Secret - Cam

Inked Hearts

Tempting - Brendon

Hooking Up - Walker

Pretend You're Mine - Ryan

Hating You, Loving You - Dean

Breaking the Rules - Hunter

Losing It - Wes

Accidental Husband - Griffin

The Baby Bargain - Chase

Inked Love

Sign up for the Crystal Kaswell mailing list

Chapter One

LIAM

"You're like a son to me."

Shit.

Bad news.

No one follows *you're like a son to me* with *this party is going to be off the chain. Let's celebrate with the fine scotch I've been saving.*

Not that I want the scotch.

I know, I know. I'm a spoiled rich kid. I'm supposed to wear designer suits, smoke cigars, sip scotch.

I've got the suit down, but the rest?

Cigars are nasty.

Scotch is bitter.

I'll take a mixed drink any day. The more embarrassing, the better. I love the look I get when I sip a cosmo or an appletini.

Men roll their eyes.

Women giggle. Ask for a sip. Fall into my fucking arms.

Easy peasy.

"Sit," Preston continues. "Have a drink with me." He

motions to the leather armchair across from him. Pulls out a decanter filled with brown liquor. Two brandy glasses.

"Let me get that." I pick up the bottle. Fill both glasses. Sit in the burgundy armchair across from Preston.

The same way I have a hundred times.

Preston took over as my father figure when my dad died. Whenever I got into trouble (it happened a lot), he sat me down, told me how much he appreciated me. Then…

This.

I'm twelve again.

A helpless kid, waiting for news about his father's surgery. Desperate to hear anything other than *I'm sorry, Liam, but he didn't make it.*

It's the office. The stupid shelf full of economic theory.

The oak walls.

The hardwood floors.

The leather chairs.

It's too familiar.

"You're supposed to pour two ounces." He waits for me to settle. "But you've always marched to the beat of your own drum, Liam." He stares into the middle distance with a soft smile. One of those *I'm lost in a memory* smiles.

I appreciate the look on a former fuck. When it's *oh God, do you remember that night in Paris, up against the wall? I've never come that many times before.*

This?

I can't fucking do this.

"Give it a chance." Preston raises his glass. "Cheers."

"Cheers." I raise. Force a smile. Swallow a mouthful.

A little sweet, fruity, the distinct taste of expensive alcohol.

Not my preference. But if I'm having this fucking conversation?

I down half my glass.

Preston sets his on the side table. "How is it?"

"Fucking fantastic." I finish the rest. Refill. Settle into my seat.

Preston holds his gaze. The parental one I know. Only mixed with something I can't place.

Usually, I read people well. It's the key to fucking with them properly.

Right now—

It's bad. I know it's bad.

"Harrison's wedding is going to be great." I swallow another sip. Try to find some other change in subject. Harrison is Preston's son. His only son. This is prime celebration time.

Not prime sitting in the study wistfully time.

But, hey, there's booze. That's the common denominator. Drink to celebrate. Drink to mourn. Drink to numb.

Doesn't matter as long as it's good.

"It will be quite the spectacle." Preston nods. "He's over the moon. He adores her."

"It's good to see him in love." It would be. If his fiancée wasn't as awful as she is gorgeous.

"It is. He's over the moon." His eyes go to his cup of brandy. "I said that, didn't I?"

"Good to hear it twice." My next sip is sweeter. Fruitier. The alcohol is working. Thank fuck.

"I want him to enjoy the festivities without worrying about me."

"We've got a boss bachelor party planned."

"I'm afraid I'm losing my ability to keep up appearances."

Fuck.

"Liam, I mean it. You're like a son to me. Simon and Adam too." He mentions my older brothers. "And Bash…

I still feel that loss. I can't imagine how much you miss him."

No, we're not going there. This conversation is torture enough. We're not adding my kid brother's death to it. "He was unstoppable."

"You've always been my most difficult son." He offers a soft laugh. "The best liar."

I don't like where this is going.

"I need your help now."

"Anything."

"I'm dying."

All the air leaves my lungs at once.

The room stills.

I can hear the hum of the air conditioner, taste the apricot in the brandy, smell the leather and oak.

He just—

I—

Fuck.

"I hate to tell you this way, son. I do." His words are practiced. Sure. "I hate to ask this of you."

What the fuck am I supposed to say to that?

"This is Harrison's time. The happiest in his life. I want him to enjoy his wedding without this specter hanging over his head."

"He'd want to spend time with you."

"He will. After the honeymoon. We're setting up the London office together. For six months. That's longer than… I'll tell him once we're settled."

That sounds like bullshit, but I can't exactly argue. *Hey, dying father figure, take my advice on how to handle your relationship with your son. 'Cause I'm the expert.*

"I know how much I'm asking, Liam. But I need your help."

"How?"

"The symptoms are starting to show. He's going to notice."

"And you need me to cover for you?"

"Like you did for Harrison, when he snuck out to meet his girlfriend."

"You knew about that?"

"Harrison's footsteps woke me up."

He does clomp like a Clydesdale. "Simon? Adam? Your colleagues?"

"You're the only person I've told."

Fuck.

"I know what I'm asking. And I know you're capable."

He's right. I can cover for him. Say we spent the night partying. Drinking too much apricot brandy. Watching the opera.

If anyone doubts me, I'll distract them with a ridiculous claim about dancing on the bar or buying a six-thousand-dollar bottle or bedding a soprano.

It's not hard to deceive people. Not practically speaking.

But the blowback from lying to my friends and family?

My coworkers?

My oldest brother Simon is already the most distrustful person on the planet. Now that he has a year of digging into a suspicious accident…

That's not an easy feat.

"I know it's a lot to ask. Especially with your fiancée here."

My what?

"Briar. She's perfect for you. I never thought I'd see the day. Liam Pierce finally settling down. My son marrying the woman of his dreams. And Adam's found someone too. This isn't easy. But it's easier, knowing my boys are happy."

"I'm—"

"I know. Simon is still closed to love. It's not perfect. But I can see it coming for him. He isn't like you. He wants to love and be loved. He just can't admit it."

"But—"

"I never worry about him. I didn't worry about Adam until the accident. But you, Liam…" He lets out a joyful laugh. It fills the air. Brings color to the room. "I worry about you. You and Harrison. Knowing you've found someone… it's a wish come true."

Fuck.

"If you can't lie to your fiancée, I understand. It's no way to start a marriage. But I can't have anyone looking at me like I'm falling apart. Please. Do me this kindness." He presses his palm into the arm of the chair. Uses it for leverage to push himself up.

All at once, I see it.

The lack of color in his cheeks, the thinning brows, the loose suit.

The man who sees me as a son is dying.

He's disappearing, one piece at a time.

First, the flesh around his middle, the hair, the complexion.

Then the movement, the energy, the spirit.

I've seen it before.

I don't want to see it again.

But he's right.

It's his call.

And I owe him more than this.

"Will you help me, Liam?" He offers his hand. "Please?"

"Of course." I shake. Promise to lie to my friends. My family.

And to my father figure too.

Briar isn't my fiancée.

She isn't my girlfriend.

She's not even a fuck buddy.

And, somehow, I've got to convince her to play my paramour for the next two weeks.

Chapter Two

BRIAR

"**A**re you with the bride or the groom?" A man in a suit shoots me a coy smile. "No. Let me guess."

How fun.

"You seem like a creative type." He's not subtle about looking me up and down. From my short, purple hair to my tight black dress to my heeled combat boots. Then back to the dress. The chest portion of the dress, specifically.

I'm not especially gifted in this area, but Suit Guy is perfectly pleased. He stares at my cleavage like his life depends on guessing my bra size.

"You must be friends with Lee."

No one is friends with Lee. She makes Regina George look sweet and misunderstood. Lee is the mean girl to end all mean girls.

How she ended up with someone as down to Earth and caring as Harrison, I don't know. But whatever, sure, I'm friends with Lee. She's an artist. I have purple hair and tattoos. Match made in heaven.

Or something.

"Have you seen her dress? She's a vision." I swallow my last sip of my grapefruit martini.

"Oh yeah. A babe, all right. Harrison is lucky." Somehow, his stare intensifies.

I pop an ice-cube in my mouth. Switch my drink to my left hand. Hold it up with my engagement ring on full display. A very large, very fake rock designed to deter douchebags from flirting.

Usually, I reserve it for business functions. But when Liam asked me to play wing woman at his friend's pre-wedding party, I had a feeling I'd need it.

There's something about weddings. Men think single women are easy picking. They think we're all sitting around swooning over the gown, wishing we were the ones wearing white.

And, well—

I won't lie. As much as I hate to admit it, Lee looks fantastic in her dress. All those layers of tulle. A modern princess. A dream.

I wouldn't mind rocking the gown, the heels, the fancy updo even.

But walking down the aisle, standing under the altar, saying I do?

No thanks.

Marriage is a trap. Especially for women. Look at my mom. Still wed to an asshole who thinks fidelity is exclusively for audio quality.

My father is a cheater. He apologizes every time he ends the affair, begs her to forgive him, promises to change.

Then he finds a new younger woman.

"When are you getting married?" Suit Guy's voice remains equal parts *I'm a happy party goer* and *I'd like to fuck you.* "People say it's just men who want to sow their wild oats—"

Ew.

"—but I've known a lot of women who get the same urge."

Where the fuck is Liam? He's supposed to hold up his end of the bargain. Not leave me trapped in conversations with horny douchebags.

Ah. There he is.

The Playboy Prince himself.

Liam steps out of the hallway, frustrated look on his face. Then he shakes his head and it's gone. Replaced by his usual carefree smile.

I've worked with the CFO for long enough to know he does, in fact, get frustrated. But the glimpses of sincerity are rare. Usually, he's all troublemaker all the time.

Everyone at work calls him Playboy Prince because he inherited his fortune and he mows through pretty, young women like it's going out of style.

He's got money, connections, movie star good looks.

Of course, he acts like a spoiled prince.

He scans the room. Finds me.

I mouth *help.*

He nods and makes a *drink* motion.

I hold up my empty glass.

He nods *got it* and heads to the bar.

Suit Guy follows my gaze. "Your fiancé?"

"Uh-huh." I suck on another ice cube. Try to absorb as much gin as possible. This conversation needs to go faster.

"How is it you know Lee?" he asks.

"Work." It's true, even if it's not accurate. I know Liam through work—he's my boss, lucky me. And I know the bride and groom through Liam. Close enough.

"Weddings always make me emotional."

Here it goes.

"What about you? I think about what is and what could be. And how I want to find love one day."

"I'm happy."

"Do you have a date?"

"We're going to elope."

"You know, most people think Las Vegas is the wedding capital of the US, but it's actually Maui."

"Fascinating." A beach in Maui. Warm water. Soft sun. A handsome man in a Speedo. What a happy place.

Only the handsome man in my traitorous brain is Liam.

All tall and broad and tan and hard—

Fuck.

"Hey, baby." Finally, Liam arrives. "I have this." He looks to Suit Guy. "Do me a favor. Take that for her." He motions to my empty drink.

Like so many people before him, Suit Guy falls under Liam's spell immediately. "Sure."

I push my drink into his hands. Take my replacement from Liam.

He slides his arm around my waist. Pulls my body into his. "Thanks for keeping my fiancée company. I'm Liam Pierce." He holds up his cup in lieu of shaking.

"The Liam Pierce?" the guy asks.

"The one and only."

"It's an honor." His eyes go to Liam's bright green drink. "Is that—"

"An appletini, yeah." Liam takes a long sip. Lets out a soft sigh. "My favorite."

It is his favorite. He orders so-called girly drinks to fuck with people.

It works too. Messes with the equilibrium somehow. And it's obscene how well it attracts women.

But then Liam doesn't really need a colorful drink to attract women. He's gorgeous. Equal parts Prince Charming and Olympic swimmer.

Blue eyes, sandy hair, winning smile.

Broad shoulders, built arms, lean torso.

And those thighs—

That ass—

Not that I stare. I just notice how well his suit hugs his butt. It's impossible to not notice.

And when he changes into running gear on his way out of the office.

Or at the pool party last summer, in a royal blue Speedo, smiling as women stared at his crotch.

Not that I contemplated how well he filled out his swimsuit.

What does that matter?

I mean, even if I did care about dick size—and I would never suggest such a thing in front of Liam—the Speedo tells little.

He might be all show and no grow.

Even if the show is quite—

Uh—

I swallow a sip. It's strong. The perfect mix of tart citrus and herbaceous gin.

"Good?" Liam's eyes flit to my lips.

"Huh?"

"Your drink? Is it to your liking, baby?"

"Absolutely… sweetheart." I work with what I have. "In fact, I was just telling…" The guy has a name, but I can't remember it at the moment—"my new friend about how we're going to elope."

"In Maui, I hope," the guy says.

"If you promise to wear your black bikini." He slips into his role effortlessly. "It was great meeting you, but we need to talk."

"About the wedding," I add.

The guy nods *of course*. The second Liam turns, he motions *call me*.

Yuck.

Liam presses his palm into my lower back.

"Where are we—"

"Somewhere quiet."

There's nowhere quiet. We're at a party. A rich people soiree, sure. It's soft orchestra and trays of hors d'oeuvres, not loud pop and potato chips, but the idea is the same.

There are a lot of people in a small space and they're all laughing, talking, flirting.

Liam leads me into the hallway—we're in the living room of a massive Upper West Side apartment—then up the stairs, down another hallway, into an empty bedroom.

He presses the door closed.

"What do you think is happening here?" I swallow another sip and set my drink on the oak dresser.

This room is huge. By New York City standards, it's obscene. The size of my entire apartment with a big bed, a wall full of framed photos, an oak desk, an old-school book shelf.

This must be the groom's room. It's all earth tones and leather.

"I'm gonna fuck you. Take off your panties and get on the bed, baby." Liam shoots me a *get real* look.

"Oh, because you've never offered to fuck me?"

"You think I'm not good for it?"

"I know you're good for it."

He chuckles, but it's not with his usual joie de vivre.

"What happened?"

"Talked with Preston."

The groom's father. The man who's like a father to Liam. Not that he'd ever admit it. "Is he okay?"

"Yeah. Just a little mix-up."

"What kind of mix-up?"

"You know how you wear that ring everywhere?"

"Only when there are stock bros to avoid."

"So everywhere."

Okay, yes, there are a lot of stock bros to avoid in the Financial District. And the rest of Manhattan. And most of Brooklyn. "I do."

"And how you're here as my date."

"Your colleague."

"Yeah. But when the Ogle McGee over there was staring at your tits, you were happy to call in your fake fiancé. And I'm happy to play my role. Even if I can't blame him for looking." He motions to my chest. "You look fucking fantastic in that dress."

"Is that your idea of a compliment?"

"I said you looking fucking fantastic."

"It was about a jackass staring at my tits."

"They're on display."

"They are not."

He raises a brow *really*.

"A little." It's a party. I'm dressing festively. Men don't have to deal with this bullshit. They can rock a suit from work to dinner to the damn clubs.

Women have to ride the line between professional yet formal. Wear a suit skirt to a party and everyone will think you're uptight.

Show too much cleavage or upper thigh and you're a whore.

It's lose-lose.

Usually, I don't worry about looking "professional." That's one of the things I like about Liam. He encourages me to express my personality with my clothes.

All right, maybe he likes that my personality includes tight black pants and sheer blouses. His motives aren't noble.

But I don't have to wear a suit. The ends justify the means.

"You had a point?" I fold my hands over my chest.

His eyes meet mine. "I need a favor."

"You should write that on your forehead."

"I'll make it worth your while."

Of course he will. What is it about men with money? They think they can buy anything and everything.

"You work for me."

"I'm aware," I say.

"Because I'm smart."

"You hide it well."

He nods *obviously*. "Because you want to learn from me when you launch your start-up."

Yes. Of course. I wouldn't work for Liam—seriously, he is the most annoying person on the planet—if he wasn't also brilliant in the area where I need the most help: finance. "Are you going to repeat things I know?"

"What if I help you?"

"Aren't you doing that?"

"Real help. Seed money. Access to my team. Advice. Everything."

Everything. As in him funding my start-up? As in me launching my mental illness support app in the next six months? That's exactly what I want and he knows it.

"I'll keep you on salary for the next year. I only want ten percent."

"What happened to it being a favor?"

"It's going to take mid-six figures."

"But—"

"If you raise funds with a venture capital firm, you'll have to give away sixty percent."

Yes, that's true. And, sure, I only know it's true because I've learned it from Liam, but—"How is it a favor if you get a percentage?"

He shoots me that same *really* look.

Ten percent *is* a lot less than sixty, but it's too much for a favor. "Five."

"Nine."

"Seven."

"Seven and a half."

That's a good deal. I offer my hand. "What do you need?"

"Two weeks."

"Two weeks of…"

"Two weeks of active work. Then a few where you need to… keep a secret."

"What is it, Liam?"

"You know the engagement ring you're wearing?"

"Yes."

"And how you act as my date at these events."

"Yes."

"Because I'm introducing you to people you want to meet—"

"Because you need to show up with someone respectable—"

He motions *kinda*. "That's all it is."

"What?"

He runs his finger over the ring on my left hand. "That's it. Two weeks. Two weeks of keeping up this ruse."

"What ruse?"

"That we're engaged."

"What—"

"I need you to play my fiancée."

Chapter Three

BRIAR

N o.

Hell no.

No way in a million years.

How many ways can I say no?

I still remember Spanish (it's no, pretty easy). French. German.

Which language best expresses my distaste for this idea?

Liam Pierce, as my platonic date, is bad enough.

Liam Pierce as my fake fiancée?

The list of reasons to say no is a mile long.

He's a player.

He's my boss.

He takes nothing seriously.

He's way, way, way too handsome.

"People already think we're fucking," he says.

"Is that supposed to entice me?"

"Yeah. They'll think more of you if we tell them we've been dating secretly."

"People will think that's how I got my job."

"This is how you're getting your job."

"Liam!"

"They already think it." His voice stays strong. "I agree. It's bullshit. You should be able to fuck whoever you want. Including me."

Ugh.

"People shouldn't judge you for having your tits on display. Or sleeping with the hottest guy at the office."

"I haven't slept with anyone at the office." Or anyone. In a long time. Liam keeps me way too busy.

"Neither have I."

I copy his *really* look.

He returns it. "I'm good at my job."

"Unfortunately true."

"I know the lines. I don't fuck with them. I wouldn't ask if it wasn't important."

"Then why are you asking?"

"Because it's important."

"But why?"

Frustration fills his blue eyes. Then he blinks and it's gone. Back to his version of a poker face. *I'm Liam Pierce and I'm a troublemaker. Who knows what I'm thinking?* "Preston's moving to London after this. To set up their UK branch."

Okay…

"He won't feel good leaving me alone in New York unless I've settled down."

"Really?"

"Yeah. Really. The guy's practically my dad."

His dad died when he was a kid. Not that Liam ever talks about it.

"And you know what parents are like," he says. "They think marriage is some magical cure all."

Not untrue.

"I want him off my back."

"That's it?"

"What do you mean, that's it? He's like a father and I want him to rest easy. That's a fucking lot." His voice rises.

It's unlike him.

"There's shit going on, okay? I can't talk about it. Just trust me on this," he says. "I need your help. You want to fund your company. Is it really so bad pretending you like me for two weeks?"

"Only two weeks?"

"He's leaving after the wedding."

"And when he comes back for Thanksgiving?"

"He won't." Liam's eyes darken.

"Christmas?"

"He won't," Liam says again.

"How do you know?"

"He's moving to London."

"But Harrison isn't. He'll still come to visit you. Do I have to dust off the engagement ring every time he's in town?"

"For six months. Then we'll fake a breakup."

"I pick the reason."

"You pick. But I have veto power."

"Two entire weeks?" I ask.

"Until after the wedding."

Fourteen days pretending I'm Liam's fiancée. And all the damage to my reputation that comes with it.

There are perks to a tech executive as a fake fiancé.

But unless Liam is promising to fund all of my future endeavors, there are big downsides too. No one takes the girl who sleeps with investors seriously.

I don't want to be that girl.

"Liam, I—"

A knock on the door steals my attention. "Is that you, son?"

All the color drains from Liam's face.

"I won't interrupt. But I'll send everyone home if you've had enough celebrating," the man says.

Liam motions to my purse.

"What?" I whisper.

"Drop it," he whispers back. "And take those off." He points to my shoes.

"They're boots."

He nods *fine*. Then his hands are on my hips. And he's pushing me onto the bed.

What the fuck?

I fall onto the down comforter.

"Oh shit, you're allergic to feathers, aren't you, baby?" Liam offers me his hand. Motions *play along*.

"I am allergic to feathers." It's not a joke. It's a huge pain in the ass when we travel. Every nice hotel in the world has down bedding. And they only remember to switch to hypoallergenic bedding half the time I request it.

"Five minutes," he whispers back.

"Six percent," I say.

"Seven."

"And a raise."

He nods *fine*.

I take his hand.

"Sorry." He turns to the door right as Mr. Charles enters. Preston.

I've only met the man a few times. I don't know him well, but I know he's a great guy. He always goes out of his way to help me, even with little things, like finding my favorite tea. He's kind, funny, smart. The perfect father figure.

Even now, the smile he offers Liam is warm and knowing. *Ah, Liam, that lovable scamp*. Then he looks at me like I'm holding his heart in my hands.

Like he trusts me with the most valuable, precious thing in his possession—his almost son.

"Briar." His smile widens. "It's lovely to see you again."

"You too, sir. I mean, Preston," I say.

"I see Liam is his usual self."

"You know me." Liam shrugs. "Can't help myself. Especially when I need to get out of my head."

Huh?

Liam and Preston exchange a knowing look.

Liam forces a smile. Preston lets out a sigh.

Something is going on.

Something strange.

"There's silk bedding in the spare room," Preston says. "But I don't know if Harrison would appreciate it."

"Isn't this your house?" I ask.

"Now," Preston says.

"But he's gifting it to Harrison. Wedding present. So it will be Harrison's soon," Liam explains.

"I wish my dad was that generous," I say.

"Yeah. And in the spirit of generosity, I've got to take my girl home, and show her the true meaning—"

"Please stop," I say.

"Baby, you're going to eat those words," Liam says.

Preston chuckles. "He wants everyone to know he's difficult."

"Tell me about it." I try to hold his gaze, but I can't. He's too warm, too paternal, too happy to see me.

Everything my father isn't.

Everything a father is supposed to be.

How can I lie to someone so honest and open?

"But that is a good idea, Liam. Leaving. We have a big day tomorrow," I say.

"On Saturday?" Preston asks.

"We have very busy Saturdays." Liam winks.

"And we are leaving. Thank you for inviting us to this…" What did they call it? Some made up pre-wedding ritual. "Party. It was lovely." I grab my purse. "I can't wait to see you for the next… wedding thing."

"How about brunch Sunday?" he asks. "The three of us."

"Absolutely," Liam says. "I'll find someplace that works for all of us. Right, baby?"

"Right."

He takes my hand.

Preston steps into the hallway. Motions *after you*.

He watches us leave. Stays there, upstairs.

I guess it's his house. And he's older. I'm twenty-four and I'm already partied out.

But then, a lot of that is Liam.

The most difficult man in the world escorts me through the party. He nods goodbye to friends and family, gathers our coats, leads me straight to the ride share he summoned for the two of us.

"You're not coming up," I say.

Liam chuckles. "I didn't think I was."

"You're going home after this?"

"Yeah." Liam nods to the driver. "Two stops. It's a thing now."

"And you're trying to save?"

"I'm a gentleman."

"You are not," I say.

"When have I ever not been a gentleman?"

"When you told Mr. Charles you were going to show me the meaning of generosity. Five minutes ago."

Liam chuckles *true*, but it's still missing something. He's not his usual impossible to ruffle self.

The car pulls onto Broadway. We drive past the lights of Times Square, the quiet skyscrapers of midtown, the

NYU flags lining the village, the closing storefronts of Chinatown.

All the way to the Financial District. To the very expensive building where I live in a very small apartment.

"You should stay at my place," Liam says. "There's plenty of room. And if Preston drops by…"

"I haven't said yes."

"You shook."

"That was before I saw Preston." And all the hope in his eyes. "I don't know if I can lie to him."

Liam's face deflates. There's something there. Something more than him wanting his mentor to move in peace. "Sleep on it. That's all I ask."

"Really? That's all you ask?"

"Scout's honor."

This time, I laugh. "I know how that one goes."

"Simon is the kinky one."

"But you still know your way around a knot."

"Whatever you want, baby. You know that." He winks. It's charming, but it's missing his usual spark. "I aim to please. Ask anyone."

"Any random person?"

"Yeah. They know."

"I probably have a one in three. If I ask a random woman in the city."

"One in two." He opens the door. Helps me out. Motions *one minute* to the driver and walks me to the door. "Whatever you want… name it. I'll make it happen."

Chapter Four

BRIAR

Ah, home sweet home.

All four hundred square feet.

I leave my boots by the door. Walk past the bathroom—attached to the hallway—and the kitchen—actually in the hallway—to the tiny main room.

Bed on the left. Desk on the right. Just enough floor space for a yoga mat between them.

And the balcony, a little bigger than a yoga mat, with a view of the other side of Wall Street. If I step outside, and really strain, I can see the water.

The sky is dark. Well, dark by New York City standards. It isn't like home. Even with all the light pollution of Los Angeles—I grew up in the scorching hot suburbs—the sky was dark at night. Blue-black. Deep enough to see stars.

I had to go out to the desert to see a sky full of them, but on an average night, I could sit on my bed, stare out the window, find Orion's Belt, imagine the other constellations.

There was something comforting about the stars. A

grandness to the universe. This knowledge there was life out there, somewhere. Different people, different thoughts, different values.

A world where parents didn't fight. And moms didn't lock themselves in their bedrooms to cry. And dads didn't make weak excuses about business trips and working weekends.

What would my father say if he heard I was getting married?

Would he congratulate me? Or warn me to run the other way, because all men are cheating bastards like him?

I sit on my twin bed. Fall onto the cool cotton comforter. It's spring now. The weather is unpredictable. Some days, the sky is heavy with dark clouds. Others, it's light and clear.

Thankfully, my apartment is well insulated. We didn't have air-conditioning when I was a kid. All summer, the house was sweltering. All summer, I waited for the sun to fall and the sky to darken. The temperature swings wildly in Southern California.

Here, the humidity holds in the heat. Summer nights offer relief from the rays of the sun, sure, but there's no drop in temperature.

Only my sweet air conditioner.

And sometimes a little too much gin at a rooftop bar.

My eyes close. My thumb goes to the ring on my left hand. My thoughts go to Liam. The night last August. The work party. Everyone else left—I'm his assistant, so I stay as long as he does—and we were tired and hot.

He dared me to jump into the rooftop pool.

I dared him back.

Of course he did. He took off his watch, left his cell on a high table, and he jumped into the water in his suit.

The pants alone cost two grand. How could I make the

excuse of saving my thirty dollar H&M blouse, even if it's worth about the same to me as two grand is to him?

I didn't care about the blouse. I cared about the temptation of diving into the water with him. Getting wet and cool and messy and running out of excuses for not touching him.

He's difficult and bossy and obnoxious and extremely handsome.

I undress, run the shower, move into the small space.

It's too small for two, but that's still where my head goes. Liam here with me, his hands on my skin, his lips on my neck, his voice in my ears.

How can I actually touch him and kiss him and hold him and survive?

How can I lie to someone like Preston?

How can I say no?

This is the best opportunity I'll ever have. Liam is a difficult boss. And this job isn't what I want to do.

I'm not complaining. It's a great opportunity. With my English degree, and my unwillingness to ask my parents—especially my father—for help, I'm glad I have a job with a reasonable salary.

New York is expensive.

I don't mind the minutiae of work—the emails, the rude executives, the coffee fetching—but it's not what I want to do with my life.

I want to reach people. Help them when they're struggling. With normal stress and sadness. Or the riptide of depression.

That horrible feeling of being pulled out to sea, helpless, and floundering the more you struggle.

It's not as simple as a riptide. There isn't a clear path to shore—swim parallel, out of the riptide, then to the beach—but there's help.

People need it.

Mom needed it.

I've needed it.

Maybe this company isn't going to change the entire world. Maybe, even with Liam's money and help, it's going to fail.

In the meantime, I'm going to help people.

I can't turn that down.

Even if it kills me.

———

BLUE SKY.

White sand.

A soft breeze against my skin.

A tall, tan man in a Speedo. A cocky grin on his face. His hands on his hips.

His swimsuit on the ground.

And he's knocking.

Again.

Louder and louder.

Shit.

My eyes open. My gaze goes to the clean white ceiling. It's not a tropical paradise, but at least I'm not dreaming about Liam naked.

"Briar—" Like he was conjured by my subconscious, Liam knocks on my door again. "I have coffee."

I roll over. Check the watch on my left wrist. "It's early. Go away."

"It's ten."

"On a Saturday." I pull my comforter over my head. Close my eyes. Will my dream island to return, sans Liam, but it doesn't. "You said I could sleep on it."

"Yeah."

Ugh.

"You want to launch your company or not?"

Double ugh. I push myself up. Take a deep breath. Try to inhale peace and exhale calm. "Stop yelling in the hall."

"I'll consider that."

"If management asks me to leave, you're paying for my move."

"Deal."

I let out a low groan. It's impossible to ask rich people to change their behavior. They throw money at all their problems. "And the first six months of rent."

"Done."

"Then keep yelling. I want a separate office."

That stops him, of course.

I roll out of bed. Find my glasses. Then the bathroom. I go through my usual routine. Find a sweater to throw over my tank top. I'm still in impossibly short shorts—I run hot—but at least my boobs aren't on display.

I open the door for Liam.

He holds up a coffee. A coffee carrier with two drinks, more specifically.

"You know how to fetch your own latte?" I ask.

He makes a finger gun, aims at an imaginary target, blows imaginary smoke. "That was a good one."

"You're supposed to be offended."

"You know me better than that."

I do. Most of the time, Liam is impossible to rattle. He's especially hard to offend. He loves when people make jokes at his expense. The more cutting, the better.

"Game appreciates game."

"No one says that anymore."

He shrugs *go figure*. Motions to the drink on the right. "Your favorite."

"You know my favorite?"

"You drink the same thing every day, twice a day."

"I get it."

"You don't believe me?"

I do drink the same thing every day, twice a day. When I can. Most coffee shops don't make a London Fog. And asking them to try is an exercise in disappointment.

They pour hot water over a tea bag then add milk right away. It's a weak, pathetic mess.

"See." He motions *go on*. "If I didn't get it, I agree to all your terms. If I did—"

"No deal." I take the drink and bring it to my lips. The sweet scent of Bergamot fills my nose. Tea. Milk. Citrus. Just enough honey.

And lavender.

He went to the place with lavender Earl Grey.

How did he know? There's only one coffee shop in the Financial District that makes this perfect London Fog and it's out of the way.

He made an effort.

An actual effort.

"I pay attention to what you put in your mouth," he says.

I flip him off.

He smiles, victorious.

"Traditionally, when you tell someone they can sleep on it, you let them wake on their own," I say. "You don't show up at their apartment before noon."

"Traditionally, maybe." He sips his coffee. Sets the carrier on the counter. Motions to the main room.

Liam wants to enter my apartment.

Okay, technically, he's in my apartment right now. But this is a studio. This tiny room is my bedroom. The place where I sleep, dream, undress, fuck myself.

It's private.

Personal.

"I don't have a couch." It's the only thing I can think to say.

"I went to college. I know how this goes. You have a desk?"

"Yeah."

"You want the desk chair or the bed?"

"Bed." There's no way I can let him into my bed. That's a can of worms I will not open.

He motions *after you*.

It's three steps to my bed. I kick a discarded bra under the frame, but I'm too slow.

He notices. Raises a brow. Sits at my Ikea desk. "Nice place."

"We don't—"

"I'm being sincere."

"You're capable?"

"Rarely." He looks around the room carefully, noting the star decals and string lights, the wine red sheets, the black desk. "It's you."

"What does that mean?"

"It feels like a place you'd live." He motions to a shelf on the wall packed with literary fiction. "Down to the depressing books."

"They're not depressing." Okay, they're a little depressing.

His eyes flit to my exposed thighs. His pupils dilate.

Is he thinking about how easy it would be to lay me on the bed, peel my shorts to my ankles, pry my legs apart?

Or am I projecting?

Ahem.

"My lawyer's at the office," he says.

"I didn't agree."

"You did, actually. And a verbal contract is—"

"Isn't valid for a deal with this high a price tag."

"Damn. Taught you too well." He shakes his head. Sips his coffee. "Hit me. Whatever you want. I'm not leaving until we have a deal."

"Will you tell me why?"

"I did."

"You left something out."

His gaze goes to the sky. "For a reason."

"Which is?"

"You're better off not knowing." His lip corners turn down. "Trust me."

Trust Liam? That's a terrifying thought. "You really have good intentions?"

"For the first time in my life." He looks back to me with a half-smile. It's like last night. Missing his usual spark. "I do."

"The seed funding for the app in exchange for seven percent." I try to recall all the negotiating tips Liam has taught me. I'm still waking up. The tea isn't working fast enough.

"As agreed."

"And I'm there for a year. With my current salary. Plus twenty percent."

"That's a substantial raise."

"And a signing bonus." I want that better apartment. Or at least a nice vacation. "I think thirty percent is fair."

"Of your yearly salary?"

"My new yearly salary."

"Anything else?"

"What am I agreeing to, exactly?"

"You're my fiancée until Preston leaves. We'll hug, dance, act like we love each other."

"Do I have to pretend to like you?"

"No one would believe that." His eyes meet mine. "Tell them you're using me for my body."

A laugh spills from my lips. "That is plausible."

"I know."

"We have to kiss?"

"That's what couples do."

They do.

"And you're staying at my place for the two weeks."

"Not in your bed."

"I have a spare room."

"What do you need a spare room for?"

"It was for Adam." Adam was in the accident that killed Liam's kid brother, Bash. Adam survived, but barely. He spent a lot of time recovering at the mansion where the boys grew up.

"Doesn't he have his own apartment?"

"Yeah, but…" He doesn't say *but I wanted to keep an eye on him*, but it's there. "It's for whoever and it's got a queen bed, not that tiny thing."

A queen bed is tempting.

"Counter if you like. But I'm not giving you the bonus unless you stay with me."

"Why do you care?"

"Because I do."

"Anything else?"

"You're my fiancée. You need to look the part."

My cheeks flame.

"You're fucking gorgeous, Briar. It's not that."

"What is it—"

"The price tags."

"Why can't your fiancée wear cheap clothes?"

He shoots me a *get real* look. "You ever meet a rich guy with a girlfriend in cheap clothes?"

"A few times."

"And…"

"She was always a sugar baby." A new one, too. Rich guys get off on buying young women clothes, for some reason. And escorts know to look the part. "Okay, fine. But you don't get a say. And you pay for them."

He nods *obviously*. "I've already got an account for you at a department store in midtown. And an appointment at three. That should give you enough time to find shit before dinner."

"Dinner?"

"With Adam and Danielle." His brother and his brother's girlfriend.

But—"They know us."

"Yes."

"They know we're not engaged."

"It's practice."

Okay…

"We tell them we've been fucking secretly."

"Liam—"

"And you're finally making an honest man out of me. 'Cause you don't want anyone else touching me."

"That's half true."

He smiles. "We both know you get jealous."

Sometimes. More than I like to admit. Especially when he flirts.

"That's it. We'll sign in"—he checks his watch—"forty-five minutes. You'll pack your shit. My team will move it. You'll get your dresses, get all dolled up for dinner, in whatever combat boots you like. I'll pick you up at the department store. We'll practice."

"Practice?"

"Our couple face."

Kissing. Touching. Looking madly in love.

Or madly in lust.

I can do that.

Maybe.

In theory.

"We gotta move fast, Bri. Preston wants to do brunch at ten tomorrow. We need to be camera ready in twenty-four hours."

"I don't know if I can—"

"I know you can."

"What if I screw it up? Give something away?"

"How?"

"I don't know. How I'm acting."

"You won't."

"What if I do?"

"You won't."

"And you're sure you won't?"

"Yeah."

"You've never had a girlfriend before."

"I'm aware." He takes another sip. Stands. Motions to the hallway. "Get dressed. I'll call my lawyer. Update the terms. I'll meet you downstairs in ten." He offers his hand to shake.

I take it.

"We have a deal."

A deal with the devil.

Chapter Five

LIAM

"This is excessive." Briar runs her fingers over the expensive pen. Stares at the dotted line like her life depends on it. "Even for you."

"Even for me? Is that a category?"

"A rare one." She reads the last paragraph again. Takes a deep breath. Pushes an exhale through her nose.

Then she signs and places the fountain pen in my palm.

She's right. This is excessive. I fuck with people for fun, but I never mix it with work. I don't cross the line with coworkers. I don't talk business with fuck buddies.

A sixteen page contract isn't a normal part of my personal life.

I work with my brothers. Business and personal is a tangle. But business and sex?

Uh-uh.

No way.

Not ever.

I've made plenty of mistakes, including sexual partners, but never with a coworker.

Now, I'm asking my assistant to play my fiancée.

To stand close enough, I smell her honey shampoo.

To smile and stare into my eyes and bring her lips to mine.

Fuck, those lips. They're painted wine red today. A gorgeous dark hue that complements her hair and screams of sex.

She's not wearing it to torture me—Briar is a punk rock princess, whether I'm here or not—but she's doing a good job of it anyway.

What do those lips taste like?

How would they feel on my skin?

And when she comes, are they parting with a sigh?

Or pressed together with a groan?

Fuck. I close my eyes. Try to picture anything else. Fail miserably.

My cock whines.

Briar. Now.

In those heeled boots of hers, she's nearly as tall as I am. It would be so easy to bring my hands to her curvy hips, pull her soft body into mine, taste her wine red lips.

When she groans *Liam* now it's irritation.

But if she said my name like it was the only thing she needed—

Fuck.

Not the time.

Not the place.

Not a possibility.

I force my eyes to the paper. This is it. Two weeks of lying to the guy who taught me everything I know.

My last gift to him.

It's not even close to enough.

I can't fuck it up.

I sign. Set the paper on the desk. Give my lawyer room to collect it.

He reminds us about some of the finer points, then he says goodbye and heads to the elevator.

Briar looks around the empty office. The frosted glass walls of my suite. The clear windows letting in the light of the city.

It's a beautiful day. Bright blue sky. Puffy white clouds. Lemon yellow sun.

I can see half the Financial District, the Hudson, Staten Island. Even the outline of the Statue of Liberty.

A babe in a sheet. It doesn't get better than that. But it's not just the French hottie. Or even the vision of an ideal America.

I know liberty isn't the same thing as freedom. Let's be honest. I've never wanted for liberty.

But freedom?

The second I broke out of my parents' house, I let freedom rule every one of my decisions. From starting this company to staying single.

People think I'm a slut. I get around, sure, but I don't count the notches on my bedpost.

I'm a man. I have needs. I fill them in a way that hurts as few people as possible.

I've tried other arrangements. Fuck buddies. Friends with benefits. Four-week flings.

They never work.

Women get the wrong idea about me. Think I'll fall in love. Stick around. Become their happily ever after.

No matter how sure they are they want casual at the beginning, they have a different idea after two weeks of sex.

They don't get it.

Sometimes, I develop feelings. Sometimes, I don't want

to say goodbye. Sometimes, I'm tempted to extend our arrangement.

But I don't.

No matter how much I want someone, I want freedom more.

Coupled people are half a partnership and I'm not ready to compromise. I want my personal life to be mine.

Maybe if I met someone like Briar. Who got me. Who didn't try to make me into someone I'm not.

I follow her rules. Respect her boundaries. All that important shit.

All right, maybe I'm not acing the boundaries test, being her boss and asking her to kiss me, but at least I'm aware of it.

I trust her, respect her, want the best for her.

And she's straight with me. Yeah, that's usually her calling me a fucking asshole, but, hey—

I am a fucking asshole sometimes.

"I think I'm going to throw up." She holds her stomach. "Is there food here? That was too much tea on an empty stomach."

"In the kitchen, yeah—"

Someone rounds the corner. Steps into the lobby of the office.

My oldest brother, Simon. He stares at us, picking us apart. Picking me apart.

I motion to him. "Get out while there's still time."

"He's not that bad."

"He's worse." I check my watch. "I'll send a car for your appointment."

"My appointment?"

"At the department store."

"Is that really—"

"Do you want free clothes or not?"

"Good point." She looks to me. "Are *you* okay?"

"No. Simon's about to give me shit." I motion *go*. "You've got twenty seconds until you're screwed."

"How will I—"

"Take the stairs."

She nods *right*. "And we're convincing him too?"

"Yeah."

"So I guess this is, uh…" She looks at me awkwardly for a second, then she throws her arms around me.

I pull her closer reflexively. She's warm and soft and safe. It's strange.

A feeling I've never had before.

Not with a woman.

Not with anyone.

"Shit, we look so awkward. You're right." She presses her lips to my cheek. "We have to practice. Good luck." She releases me. Nods goodbye to Simon on her way out.

He stands there, in his fancy designer suit, staring at me the way he always does. *What have you done now, Liam?*

But I don't care the way I usually do.

I'm too tuned to Briar.

"Nice to see you too." I stretch my arms over my head. Let out a yawn. I didn't sleep for shit last night. How could I when the *Preston Charles is dying* neon sign kept flashing in my head?

"What are you doing here?"

I motion to my desk.

"You fucked your assistant on your desk?"

"If I did, do you really think I'd let it go unsaid?"

He nods *probably not*. "What are you doing here?"

"Work."

"It's Saturday."

"You're here."

Yeah, I don't have an argument. Only *I'm not in the mood for your attitude*. "Do you want something?"

"To say hello before I go to my office."

Right. I'm being an asshole. But he's always an asshole. So we're even. "Hey."

He scans the space suspiciously. Notes the raised blinds, the clear desk, the quiet computer. "What was Briar doing here?"

"She works with me."

"Her lipstick is on your cheek."

"It is." There's a smart way to play this. It's not telling him we're engaged.

Or even admitting we're dating.

He wants to uncover the truth himself. It's an obsession of his.

And he thinks I'm an arrogant playboy.

He's already judging me for fucking Briar. I haven't. I even told him that.

Not that he believes me. If anything, he's more convinced when I denied it.

A real lose-lose situation under normal circumstances. Or it would be, if I gave a fuck about Simon's opinion.

Don't get me wrong. I love my brother. I'd do anything for him.

But the man is a bitter asshole.

His take on relationships? Not worth a second thought.

And with this wedding—

Well, it's not hard to guess why he's in an extra shitty mood.

"It's a new thing I'm trying." I turn to show off the hue. "What do you think? Is red my color?"

"That's Bordeaux. And no."

"Harsh."

He doesn't laugh. "It's too dark for your complexion."

"What should I wear?"

"Mauve."

"Where did you learn this?"

"I live with a teenage girl." Our half-sister. Long story.

"Be honest. You let her give you makeovers."

"Are you volunteering to take my place?"

"Sure. Bring her to dinner. We're meeting Adam and Danielle tonight."

His blue eyes—the same shade as Adam's and Dad's—stay suspicious.

"It's a thing where you sit and eat with people you like. Sometimes there's wine."

"You drink wine?"

"Sometimes there's a Sex on the Beach."

"A Fuzzy Navel?"

"Exactly."

He stands there, in the doorframe, expert poker face. Or maybe that's his normal face. I can't tell anymore.

"I'm going to get to work. But I'll text you those details. If you decide you want to join the human race."

He gives me another once-over. "Don't fuck the help."

"We're colleagues."

He shakes his head *Liam, what a disappointment*, turns, leaves.

I wait until he's in his office—thankfully at the opposite corner of the building—then I close the door, shut the blinds, take to the old leather couch.

I don't expect to fall asleep, but I do.

There's no rest. Only memories of my late brother, Bash. My dad's funeral. Preston saying *you're like a son to me* again and again.

———

I wake sweaty and tired. Rush home. Shower. Change. Take a cab to the department store.

I'm late. But Briar doesn't have an eye on the time. She's standing in the middle of the enormous dressing room, in a long silver gown and heels, her attention on her reflection.

She's a vision, already. The silver brings out the luster of her purple hair and the deep red of her lips.

Bordeaux.

I need to drink it immediately.

I hate wine, but I need to drink it immediately.

I need to drink every fucking ounce of her.

"Hey." I slip my hands into my pockets. It's strange. I don't get nervous. Not when it comes to women.

She turns to me with a smile. Holds the sides of her dress. Twirls.

Her gown spins with her. The skirt is straight. It hugs her ample hips and just barely flares at the knee.

She stops. Raises an eyebrow, challenging me.

"You clean up nice."

"Don't worry," she says to the woman helping her pull dresses, "that's his idea of a compliment."

The woman, Bree, our long-time stylist, shoots me a warm smile. "I've known Liam a long time."

"How unfortunate for you," Briar says.

"Do you need me to pull a tie, Mr. Pierce?" She looks to me.

Briar raises a brow. *Really, off your game today.*

She's right. I forgot to put on a fucking tie. How is that possible? I've got ten years of boarding school training. Another half a dozen of corporate career.

Some guys complain about the monkey suit, but I don't mind. It's not as comfortable as jeans, but it serves its purpose in crafting an image.

Perception is everything.

I know that.

I know how to do this. I know how to convince people I'm a certain person who wants certain things.

Why is my heart thudding against my chest?

"Are you wearing that tonight, Ms. West?" she asks.

"Do I need something this fancy?" Briar asks me.

"If you want to outdress Adam and Danielle," I say.

Briar shakes her head. "I want to convince her to go dancing." She turns to Bree. "The short ivory dress. Since I can't wear it to the wedding festivities."

"Ah, I know just the tie." Bree beams. "I'll give you two a minute. Fifteen, to be specific." She winks at me. *Use them wisely* slash *make it fast if you're fucking because I don't want to walk in on that*.

She exits quietly.

Leaving the two of us alone.

Briar holds out her hand, asking me to help her off the podium. "I could do it in my boots. But these—" she pulls up the dress with her free hand, showing off a pair of silver sandals.

Her fingers brush my palm. Her hand closes around mine.

I try to hold her steady, but she still stumbles.

Lands in my arms.

She looks up at me awkwardly. "I guess we should get used to this."

"We should." She swallows. "And we still have fourteen minutes."

Right. "We need to practice."

"We do."

"Are you ready? Or do you need a minute?"

Chapter Six

LIAM

B riar's grey eyes fix on me. Her fingers curl into my suit jacket.

Her nails are that same shade of wine red.

I still want to drink every drop. Feel her hands on my cheek. My back. My cock.

Shit.

The mental image refuses to leave my brain.

Blood rushes south.

Not the time.

So not the time.

I tell my cock to cool it. But the motherfucker doesn't listen to me.

"Let me change first." She releases me. Steps backward. Motions to the dressing room. "I'll be two minutes."

"Only leaves twelve."

"I need eleven to convince myself you're not the most annoying person of all time."

"It's going to be a challenge, yeah." I push an exhale through my teeth. Channel cooling thoughts.

"Actually." Briar turns so her back is to me. "Can you unzip me?"

Fuck me. "Sure."

"Thanks." She rolls her shoulders. Brushes a purple strand behind her ears. Her hair is cropped short. At the nape of her neck.

One of those trendy styles that follows the line of her jaw. Keeps her long neck on display.

"How many times have you done this?" She presses a hand to her chest, holding her dress in place.

I find the zipper. Pull it down her back as gently as possible. The sides of the dress spill apart. Leave her long, elegant back on display.

"Thanks." She steps into the dressing room.

The lock clicks.

Her dress hits the floor.

She slips out of her silver sandals. Into the boots she was wearing this morning. The heeled combat boots she wears everywhere.

The image forms in my mind immediately: Briar, against the wall, her legs wrapped around my waist, her wine red nails digging into my skin.

Fuck.

I scan the room for something, anything, to distract me. Mirrors. Closed doors. Ivory walls. Pink details.

All feminine and sweet. The opposite of Briar's style. Of her room. There's nothing soft and sweet about the wine red sheets on her twin bed.

Fuck, I need to see her naked in those sheets.

Tangled in my sheets.

The white cotton. The black silk. That perfect shade of wine.

That's what I need. New sheets. For her. Only her.

My thoughts evaporate as Briar steps out of the dressing room.

She's in a snug white dress. A one-shoulder thing, cut just above her knees, hugging her lush hips like it was made for her.

"You look fucking amazing," I say.

"That's one of your better compliments." She takes another step toward me.

"You like it?"

"The dress? I picked it out."

"Wearing designer?"

"It's a local designer." She smooths the stiff fabric. "Still out of my normal price range. But not—"

"Clashing with your ethics?"

"You pay attention."

"I like watching your lips move."

She half-smiles. "You don't fool me."

"I don't?"

She nods. "You're nervous."

"I am?"

"You are." She half-smiles. "I don't know if I've seen you nervous before."

"What about the pitch in Toronto?"

"A little. But this… Liam Pierce is blushing."

Shit, is that why my cheeks are warm?

"I kind of like it."

"I'm nervous for you."

"For me?"

"My skills are immense."

"Your kissing skills?"

"Yeah." I pull my hands from my pockets. Immediately wanting them on her skin. "I don't want to overwhelm you."

"Catch me if I faint." She calls my bluff.

I answer it. Take a step toward her. "You don't have to ask."

"Just in case." Her hand goes to my chest. The wool of my suit jacket. "When did you last kiss someone?"

"Don't remember."

"Really?"

"I don't keep a running total."

"Well, you *can* only count to ten."

"If that."

Her fingers brush my neck. "What's the last kiss you remember?"

I try to find memories of other women, but it's impossible. "Nothing special. You?"

"My last kiss?"

"Yeah." My stomach churns with an unfamiliar sensation. Envy. No wonder Simon's such an asshole. It's awful.

"You met my boyfriend. Ex-boyfriend."

"John." His name is bitter on my tongue. The guy was unworthy of Briar. Pretentious and smug and not nearly as funny as he thought. He wasn't a bad guy, but I still despise the asshole for having her, losing her, hurting her.

"We were at the Cloisters. He took me there for my birthday. He had this picnic set up. Wine and cheese and a beautiful view. It was the first time, in a long time, I felt the way I did when we met; like he saw me as someone special. Then he put his hand on my cheek, and he stared into my eyes, and he kissed me like he wanted to give me everything he had."

My stomach churns.

"I hadn't felt that in a long time."

"Is that why you broke up? Because it stopped?"

She nods. "And because I stopped wanting it. I stopped wanting to give him more of me. It's hard to explain to someone who's never been in a relationship. It feels good to have someone there. Warm. But when their love fades, it's cold. Lonely. Much lonelier than being alone."

"He's an asshole."

Her eyes stay fixed to mine. "Sometimes. We all are."

I still hate him. "He didn't deserve you."

"Is that a compliment?"

"Of course. You're way hotter than he is."

She half-smiles. "You say stupid shit when you're nervous."

"I always say stupid shit."

"True." Her fingers curl into my neck. "But there's a certain kind of stupid…"

"I told you. I'm nervous for you."

"Then be gentle this first time. For me."

"You're ready?"

"I am." She stares at me with those gorgeous grey eyes.

Then her eyelids flutter closed.

Her hand finds the back of my head.

Her lips brush mine. It's soft. A hint of a kiss.

But I feel it everywhere.

My entire body is buzzing.

"You okay?" Her fingers skim my chin.

"Yeah." I'm dizzy. I'm floating. I have to pull her closer to stay on the ground.

"You're blushing."

"It's embarrassing bringing up my skill. I'm a humble guy."

"Of course." She smiles *you're so full of it*, but she doesn't call me on it. "I do appreciate you going easy on me."

"Sure thing."

"You can turn it up this time."

"In an engaged kind of way?"

"We are engaged," she says.

"I'm more used to an *I'm going to take your clothes off* kind of way."

"I can lead." Her eyes meet mine. "If you don't know what that looks like."

"You're using me for my body, right?"

"I am."

"So we could do it my way."

"Let's try it this way first."

"Go for it," I say.

She doesn't buy my bravado. She looks me over carefully. Like she sees every crack.

No one else looks at me like this.

My brothers look for cracks, sure. Adam does it with concern. Simon does it with suspicion.

Briar is all curiosity. She's trying to see me as I am. See every part of me.

It's terrifying.

Intoxicating.

"I'd look at you like this." She slides her arm around my waist. Stares into my eyes with hazy affection. "Hey."

"Hey."

"You look nice tonight."

"You look hot as fuck."

She smiles in that *Liam is difficult and I like it* way. "I know." Her hand goes to my cheek. Her hips melt into mine. "I'm trying to torture you."

"It's working."

Her fingers curl into my waist.

Her eyes close.

Her lips meet mine.

Softly at first.

Then harder.

Her lips part.

Her tongue slips into my mouth. Dances with mine. Not the aggressive *I've got to fuck you now* song I know.

Something slower. More tender.

Infinitely more inviting.

She pulls back with a low, deep sigh. "Good?"

"Fucking fantastic."

"One more?"

I'm not going to survive one more. I'm going to dissolve. Or throw her against the wall and fuck her right here.

Those are the only two possibilities.

But I need to do this.

For Preston.

And for me.

Because I want to give this to him. Because I want to convince him I'm the kind of man he wants me to be.

The kind of man Briar deserves.

I swallow hard. Then I get my head in the game.

I wrap my arms around her, pull her body into mine, bring my lips to hers.

The softness overwhelms me.

Honey shampoo.

Lemon soap.

The mint of her lipstick.

And Briar.

My hand finds her ass.

Her hand knots in my hair.

She kisses back with that same fervor. Groans as my cock brushes her stomach.

I'm too fucking hard.

And I don't fucking care.

I need to have her here. There. Everywhere.

Where the fuck is the zipper on this dress? I need her

clothes gone. I need her naked, under me, groaning my name.

"Mr. Pierce." Bree clears her throat. "I have your tie ready."

Shit.

"And a pocket square. Unless you'd prefer I return later." She shoots me a cutting look. "The room is booked at seven."

Briar blushes as she steps backward. "We were just, uh…"

"You are engaged, aren't you?" she asks.

"Yes. We are," Briar oversells it. "Very engaged. Practically married already."

Bree looks to me. "And you didn't tell me." She raises a brow *I know something else is going on, but I know better than to press*. "I'm disappointed."

"You're the first to know." Kind of.

"In that case, congratulations." She smiles. "How did it happen?"

"Huh?" Briar asks.

"How did he ask?" She looks to Briar. "Or did you ask? I love hearing about women who propose, don't you?"

"I do," Briar says. "But, it was Liam's idea. He, uh—"

"I begged her," I say. "It was pathetic, honestly."

"Yeah. On his knees and everything," she says.

"Both of them? Or just the one?" Bree asks.

"You know me." I wink. "One to start. Then both."

Bree smiles *ah, Liam, what a silly boy*. "The way you talk about her… I've always wondered if there was more." She turns to Briar. "He adores you."

"He says that?" Briar asks.

"In his way." She winks at me. "Really, Liam. Congratulations. Your fiancée is a wonderful woman."

"She is." I try to find my footing. I need to get used to

this. I need to play my part. "And she's got a fantastic ass too."

Bree chuckles, not buying the story I'm selling. "You have five minutes to clear the room." She lays the accessories on a display table and nods goodbye.

"Thanks," I say.

"I got it." Briar folds the pocket square and slips it into my pocket. She looks up at me as she fixes the tie. Slides the knot into place. "I haven't done that in a long time."

Again, my stomach churns. It's ridiculous, but, apparently, my sense of jealousy is as unreasonable as my dick. "You ready?"

"Are we really telling them we're engaged?"

"Yeah."

"What if they don't believe it?"

"They will."

"If they don't?"

"We'll have to convince them." Adam isn't as close to Preston as I am. And he's not suspicious to the degree Simon is.

But he's plenty close and plenty suspicious.

These two will be the easiest to convince—Danielle already believes I'm secretly in love with Briar—but they're still a fucking hurdle.

And they're only the first hurdle.

I try to think up strategy as I call a car, but my thoughts stay tuned to my Briar. Her wine red lips. Her soft skin. Her sharp nails.

The sweet feeling of her body melting into mine.

It's pretend.

I'm not even capable of this kind of affection.

I'm certainly not capable of falling in love.

So why the fuck am I so concerned I'm going to fall in love with her?

Chapter Seven

BRIAR

"That dress is gorgeous." Danielle throws her arms around me. She squeezes tightly, releases me, looks me over slowly.

Not as a friend adoring another friend's style. Not as a concerned future in-law.

As a photographer.

She drifts into artist mode. Focused, dreamy, somehow here and somewhere else at once.

I'm flattered she's considering me as a subject—she's talented—but I'm terrified too.

Danielle mostly photographs naked people.

A few months ago, Adam fell in love with her self-portraits, found her, won her over. He claims he fell for her when they met in person, before he ever saw a picture of her naked, but I'm not buying that story.

Adam spent the last year locked in the Pierce manor. He had plenty of time to search for babes online. He met almost no one.

It's clear which is more likely.

I'm glad he found someone, however he did it. A year ago, he and the youngest Pierce, Bash, were in an accident.

Bash died. Adam was in critical condition.

He spent months in recovery. Then more months locked in the Pierce family manor. He barely left the house. He was too afraid to face the world.

Because he couldn't survive without his brother?

Because he couldn't take the whispers of foul play? Sure, there were rumors, and some people suspected Adam, but no one who knew him like I did. Adam adored Bash. He'd die before he hurt his kid brother.

Maybe it was the physical scars that kept him home.

They're not that bad—soft pink lines on the left side of his face and body—but they're not the Disney prince thing he had going before the accident either.

Danielle says he's more handsome now. That he was attractive before, but in a plain way.

I see what she means. The scars add character. Show he's been through something awful and survived.

"Can I talk you into posing for me?" Danielle asks.

"Depends. How much do you pay?" I ask.

She smiles. "How much do you want?"

"Am I wearing clothes?"

"This." Danielle looks to Liam. "I need something on my cell now." She slips into that photographer trance. "Liam, stand next to Briar."

"I thought we agreed you were taking naked photos of me, Danielle," Liam says.

She smiles, charmed, and motions for him to move next to me.

He looks to me and raises a brow *should we?*

I nod. *We should.*

We're engaged. We're somehow explaining our secret love affair. The one that never happened.

We might as well pose together.

Liam wraps his arm around my waist.

I rest my head on his shoulder.

Danielle snaps a few photos, asks us to embrace, snaps a few more.

"Angel, they're here for dinner," Adam says. "Not a photo shoot."

"One more." She snaps a final pic. "Then I'm putting it away. I swear."

"I've used that one before. I didn't mean it either." Liam winks at her.

She shakes her head in that *silly Liam* way and slips her cell into her pocket.

He's still pressed against me. He's still close and warm and tempting.

Why is he so tempting?

I want to kiss him again.

I want to kiss him forever.

"You want a drink?" Liam motions to the bar. "Or are we ready to sit?"

"We're ready," Danielle says. "Unless you want another angle."

Adam studies her with adoration. He loves everything about her, even her obsession with her camera. Or maybe especially her obsession with her camera. She does use it in *interesting* ways.

He's still the strong, silent type. When he's not around Danielle, he's stoic. Right now, his heart is on his sleeve. He loves her. Everyone in the room can see it.

"Only if I'm naked." Liam hails the hostess in that subtle, rich, guy way. He turns to her. Nods. Catches her attention immediately.

How does he do that?

He knows exactly what to say to everyone. To get whatever he wants.

It's not my strong suit. It's not something I want to do. But it's fascinating, watching him charm the world.

The hostess gathers menus. Leads us to a table next to the window, in the back corner of the room.

Actual privacy. That's why this place is a Pierce family favorite. It's quiet, secluded, expensive enough to offer relief from prying eyes. Adam spends time in the city now, but he still avoids the spotlight.

Liam and Simon don't mind working around their brother's needs. Not that they admit it. They claim love for different reasons—the dessert menu and the whiskey menu respectively—but there are other places with better options.

It's a compromise. One made easier by money, but a compromise all the same.

I can't believe I see it. A year ago, I would have been in awe of this place. Fancy cocktails, spacious oak tables, sweeping views.

Midtown in all its glory. The softer shade of midnight blue. The skyscrapers silver still and yellow light.

But I'm not here to soak up the atmosphere. I'm not here to contemplate Pierce family dynamics.

I'm here to convince Adam and Danielle I'm madly in love with Liam.

Adam pulls out Danielle's chair for her. He's a perfect gentleman. It suits his whole moody prince trapped in his castle vibe.

Liam does the same for me. It's normal. He does this all the time. Childhood training, I guess. The Pierce family is old money.

I don't usually think about it. Today, my head spins.

This is boyfriend territory. He's pretending he's my boyfriend. My fiancé.

I need to get used to this.

"A grapefruit martini?" Adam asks.

"Huh?" I ask.

"Do you want a grapefruit martini?" Liam asks. "The same way Adam and Danielle have theirs."

"As long as it's as tart as your smile," I say.

"Make it four." Liam nods a thank you to the server.

She smiles and disappears. The practiced invisibility of the help. I never got the hang of it.

I guess I don't need to get the hang of it. In two weeks, I'm on the path to greatness. I'm launching my start-up and conquering the world.

"Is there any way I can convince you two to come over and do a wedding set?" Danielle asks. "Clothes on."

"Where's the fun in that?" Liam asks.

"I won't stop you from taking them off." She looks to me. "But I imagine Briar might have other ideas."

"Do you, baby?" Liam turns to me. "Do you have other ideas?"

This is it. A perfect chance to claim him as my fiancé. But I can't find the words. Lying to Preston is hard enough.

Danielle and I are friends.

"For the right price." I need to work up to it. So it feels natural. "I'm thinking four-figures."

"You heard the woman." Liam shrugs, effortless. "She's not doing this for free."

Adam chuckles.

Danielle smiles. "I'm a humble artist. I can't do four."

"Be careful. She's a shrewd negotiator," Liam says. "Learned from the best."

"Simon did give me a few tips." There. This is our

normal rapport. I tease Liam. He teases back. We're here to be normal. Not weird and secretive.

"Briar, baby, you're killing me." Liam mimes being stabbed in the gut. "Next thing I know you're going to tell me you want to pose with him."

"Is he naked?" I ask.

"If you talk him into it," Liam says.

"I'd pay to see that," Danielle says.

"Really?" Adam raises a brow. "Maybe I can arrange something."

She laughs. "To see Briar negotiate Simon's modeling session."

"You don't have to pretend, Danielle. We know you want to photograph the entire world naked," Liam says. "Starting with the best." He taps his chest. "But if you can't have the best…"

"You only offer to pose every time you see her," I say.

"I have a generous spirit," he says.

"Go on," Danielle says.

"Don't encourage him," Adam says.

"He's going to go on whether I encourage him or not," Danielle says.

Liam chuckles. He swats the air, playing sheepish. Or maybe he's actually sheepish. I can't tell anymore.

"I'm not sure with you, Liam. You talk big talk. Do you really live up to it?" Curiosity fills Danielle's dark eyes. "Could anyone live up to your talk?"

"Danielle, you know you're baiting me," Liam says.

"Baiting you to do what?" she asks.

"Throw Briar on the table and push her dress to her waist," he says.

This is where I object. If we're friends. Boss and employee. Coworkers.

But we're engaged.

I still need to object. I don't want Liam eating me out at this very public restaurant.

In private, in his corner office.

Or my tiny twin bed.

His dining room table. I've never seen it. I've never been to his apartment.

But the image still fills my head. Some massive oak table. Liam's hands on the inside of my knees. His lips on my thigh. His name rolling off my tongue again and again.

Is he good with his mouth?

Danielle is right. He talks big talk. Can he really live up to it?

"Baby, should I go right now?" Liam asks. "You know I'm insatiable."

My cheeks flush.

Danielle's eyes fix on me.

She already thinks we're fucking. Liam is right. Everyone thinks we're fucking.

That's the only lie I really need to sell.

And it's only half a lie. We kissed. I want to fuck him. I'm not going to fuck him, sure, but I'm already moving in that direction.

My head is already filling with beautiful mental images of his head between my legs.

Is Liam generous?

I have no idea.

But I want to find out.

I really, really want to find out.

"You okay, baby?" Liam reaches for my hand. "Or do you need mouth-to-mouth resuscitation?"

I take his hand. For our ruse. For moral support. So I won't put my hand someplace it shouldn't go. "I need…" I try to find the worlds to explain this. It's simple. We're engaged.

Now that we're engaged…
Check out my giant rock…
Speaking of massive things…
Something.

But my mouth is dry. Sticky.

I look to Liam for help.

God, those blue eyes.

I lean forward. Let my eyelids flutter together. Let my hand find his neck.

Let my lips find his lips.

He kisses back with everything he has.

We're here with his brother.

We're doing this for our ruse.

We're pretending.

But everything inside me screams *real, real, real.*

Chapter Eight

BRIAR

"Are you…" Danielle's eyes fix on mine. Not with doubt or suspicion. With the support of a friend who wants to make sure her friend is dating a guy worth her time.

"Are you fucking?" Adam asks.

"You know I'm not going to answer that." Liam shrugs, playing cool. His usual MO.

It's smart. He's doing this as Liam. The guy his brothers know well.

That guy is aloof. That's who people think he is.

Who do people think I am?

I have the purple hair and combat boots, yes. A few tattoos. Deep lipstick. Acerbic wit.

That's what I need. My wit.

"It's much worse than that," I say.

Danielle's face lights up.

Adam's eyes perk.

"Is this worse?" Liam asks.

"Sex is one thing," I say. "We can all understand the appeal of your body."

He nods. "It's pretty fucking nice."

"But the personality… it ruins the whole thing," I say.

Liam nods *true*. "I had to take off a lot of clothes to get you to look past it."

"Most of them."

"Is that really how it happened?" Danielle leans forward. "When? Where? How long?"

"Nine inches. Three hours," Liam says.

"Only nine?" Danielle asks.

"Only? Do I need to whip it out?" Liam says.

"Shouldn't you call a doctor at that point?" Adam asks.

"Four hours," Liam says.

"You would know." Adam chuckles.

"It's important to keep track of these things." Liam nods.

"How did it actually happen?" Danielle asks.

"Well, first, I took off her—"

"I'm not going to stop you from offering details," Danielle says. "But your fiancée looks horrified."

Am I as red as I feel?

"All right. I'll spare her. For now." Liam winks. "We were in Toronto. After a pitch. Celebrating with the hotel's signature drink."

We were in Toronto, sipping berry martinis.

Five, six months ago.

It was freezing outside. Scorching hot in the hotel.

And I got so drunk, Liam had to put me to bed. It's fuzzy. I barely remember. But I remember his lips.

Why do I remember his lips?

"You remember those?" Liam motions *play along*.

Right. I was drunk. But I remember. I remember him laying me in bed, whispering *good night*, coming so, so close to kissing me. "It was bright red. Perfect for Liam."

"More of a raspberry," he says.

"Strawberry. A strawberry martini," I say.

"We had a few too many," he says.

"He walked me back to my room. He was going on about how we had to get up early, to get poutine, so I said, 'I don't want to hear another word. If you want to make your mouth useful…'"

"And I did." Liam reaches for me under the table. "The rest is history." He taps my hand. My ring finger.

Right. I raise my left hand. Show off the dazzling rock. It's the same one I wear to ward off douchebags, but it's huge enough to pass as a Liam selection. And it's nice too. A simple solitaire in a Tiffany setting, white gold, sparkling enough, it outshines the real thing.

Danielle studies the ring for a moment, then she smiles. "Did it just happen?"

"Pretty recently," Liam says.

"How did it go?" she asks. "Where were you? Did you get on one knee and everything?"

"Oh yeah." Liam is faster with the story this time. Practiced. "I dropped to one knee, and I begged. It was pathetic, honestly."

I nod. "I took pity on him."

"No. That wasn't it. It was when I took off my shirt." He shrugs, once again cool and aloof. "I figured it worked once…"

"The abs really distract from the personality."

"And the tattoos," he says.

The tattoos. The ones he hides under his suit. No, hide isn't the right word. This is Liam.

He only hides his intentions.

Everything else is on display.

The waitress interrupts with our drinks. None of us

have looked at the menu, but we've been here enough times we know what we like.

We order.

The waitress disappears.

Danielle's attention returns to me. "When was Toronto?"

"Which time?" Adam raises a brow.

"Last time," Liam says.

"You've been fucking for the last six months?" Adam asks.

"I told you, Adam. I don't call you every time I fuck someone," Liam says. "But I can. Expect a very detailed call tonight. I've got plans for after this."

Adam half-smiles.

"What's that?" Liam draws a circle around his brother's face. "Is Adam Pierce, the most miserable man in the mansion. Props to Danielle for giving me that one." He nods to her. "Is the most miserable man in the mansion actually happy about something?"

"I never thought I'd see the day." Adam's eyes flit to me. "She's too smart for you."

"Don't tell her." Liam shakes his head *jeez*. "This is why no one ever wanted you as a wingman."

"Liam is smarter than he looks," Danielle says. "And he has other appealing traits."

"Hey, you dissing my girl?" Liam asks.

"I'm complimenting you." She laughs. "And her too. Her taste." Danielle raises her glass. "To love."

I turn to Liam as if I'm madly in love with him. "To you knowing where to put your mouth."

He smiles that charming smile of his, raises his glass, taps it against mine. "Anytime."

"Really? Anytime?"

"Yeah."

"In the middle of a board meeting?" I ask.

"Hell yeah. If you don't mind the audience," he says.

"What if I want privacy?" I ask.

"I'll clear the table. But you've seen the conference room." He looks to Danielle. "Glass walls. Good for people who like being watched." He winks at her.

She blushes. I think. It's hard to tell with her skin tone.

"Congratulations." Adam raises his glass.

We all toast.

I take a long sip. Mmm. Grapefruit, gin, Saint Germaine. The perfect mix of herbaceous, tart, sweet.

Liam takes a long sip. "How can a drink this pink be this tart?"

"Have you never tasted a grapefruit?" I ask.

"What was that about tasting?" he asks. "That's why you like me, isn't it?"

"Who says I like you?"

"My skill at cunnilingus."

My cheeks flush.

Adam chuckles. "Why do you spell it out? We all knew what you meant."

"You know how it is. Bird's gotta fly. Fish gotta swim." Liam motions *take it*.

"Liam Pierce has to brag about his sexual skills," I say.

"Hell yeah." He raises his glass. "To you loving men with fat bank accounts and big dicks."

My cheeks flush.

Danielle nearly spits out her drink.

"What happened to cunnilingus?" Adam teases.

"Hey, I'm not one of those guys who thinks a big dick is enough," Liam says. "I use all the tools at my disposal."

Danielle laughs. "What do you think, Briar? Does he?"

"I can't complain," I say.

"You sure? Because I could have a lot of fun answering those complaints," Liam says.

Her laugh gets louder. Deeper. She nearly drops her drink on the table. Brings her hand to her chest. "Liam…" She barely gets out the words. "You're so full of shit."

Adam nods *you are*.

"Pretending it's all about sex. You don't ask someone to marry you because of sex," she says.

"Really? 'Cause I know this artist who will make you reconsider that stance." He pulls out his cell. "Maybe you've seen her photos. Goes by Broken Beauty. Believe her real name is Danielle Bellamy." He throws out the bait.

She bites immediately. "They're not about sex. They're about honesty, intimacy, vulnerability. What you reveal to other people."

"What you reveal?" Liam raises a brow.

"Emotionally," she says.

"And physically."

"It's a metaphor! The pictures in lingerie, sure, that's sexual. But nudity isn't always sexual. We're born naked. We shower naked. We swim naked."

"You swim naked?" Liam looks to Adam. "And you're not taking her to Tahiti right now?"

Adam returns Liam's look. Some mix of curiosity, brotherly concern, skepticism.

Danielle wants to believe we're in love. She's wanted to believe it since she met us.

Adam knows his brother well. Well enough to doubt his ability to commit.

He isn't buying our story. Not yet.

We need something to convince him. Something more. Something better.

Liam ignores his brother's doubt. Turns to me, like this is any other Saturday night. "Do you swim naked too?"

"Only in private," I say.

"So if I rent a private beach…" He raises a brow.

"I'll consider it," I say.

"What about our pool?" he asks.

"It's spring," I say.

"I can wait until summer," he says.

"The pool at the mansion?" Danielle asks. "Have you seen it?"

"Only pictures," I say.

"Really?" Danielle whispers something in Adam's ear. When he nods, she turns to us with a smile. "Then you two have to stay over one weekend. Or wait until the wedding. We're hosting the rehearsal dinner. Everyone is going to be there."

"Everyone? Meaning Simon and the rest of the bridal party?" Liam asks.

"He doesn't mind," Adam says.

"And you believe him?" Liam asks.

Danielle looks to her fiancé for a clue.

"The bride's sister is Simon's ex-girlfriend," Adam says.

"The one who crushed his heart?" Danielle asks.

"One woman hurts him and he never loves again." Liam rolls his eyes. "It's been a decade. Get over it."

"Are you the expert now?" Adam asks.

"Isn't Briar your first girlfriend?" Danielle asks. "Wait, if it's been six months—"

"Five," Adam corrects.

"Then you've been together the whole time I knew you." Danielle's eyes light up.

"It was just sex at first," Liam says. "She was trying to keep it that way. But the skills… she had to nail that down."

Danielle laughs. "Of course."

"Plus the money," Liam says. "You know what it's like. Mr. Rich Broodypants over here is loaded."

She swats the air. "Tech billionaires are a dime a dozen in this city."

"I'm not the first rich man to fall in love with you." Adam's words are loaded with history. A history I don't know.

He's secretive.

Maybe that's all it is. People who keep secrets, who lie, who hide their feelings believe everyone else does the same.

The same way honest people believe other people are honest.

"It's like Marylin Monroe says in *Gentlemen Prefer Blondes*," Danielle says.

"Isn't that from the fifties?" Liam asks.

"It's still true. Money for men is like beauty for women. It's not the only reason you marry someone, but it doesn't hurt," she says.

"You're a babe. He's loaded. Story checks out," Liam says. "What do you think, Briar? You like what's in my pants?"

"Not if you mean your wallet." I shrug as if I can't help admitting the truth.

"Oh?" Danielle asks.

"You were right before," I say. "It's sex."

"Told you." Liam turns to me with a smile. "To knowing your partner."

It's true. We're partners now. Not in love, sure, but in business. And that's as intimate as any relationship. "To knowing your partner."

We toast. Sip. Smile. Slip into our usual rapport.

As if this is any other Saturday night dinner. And it just happens to be the Saturday night after we got engaged.

And we just happen to be ready to go public with our relationship.

We're the same Briar and Liam. That's the story. But it's not true.

I still see my annoying boss when I look at Liam. But I see something else too, a man I really, really want to kiss again.

Chapter Nine

LIAM

Briar steps inside my apartment.

I follow her, close the door, take her coat.

My usual routine. Manners I've practiced my entire life.

But this isn't usual.

She's in my space.

My apartment. My home. My life.

My heart beats faster. My limbs grow lighter.

I invite plenty of women home. Why not? This is a fantastic apartment.

Amazing view. Enormous bed. Soft sheets.

Then there are all the other places to fuck: The leather couch in the main room. The long dining table on its left. The clean white wall behind the TV.

The kitchen counters on our right.

The shower in the hallway bathroom. The tub in the master.

And those are the places I've used. There must be another dozen I haven't touched.

There have been a lot of women in this apartment. Too many, probably.

But I can't picture a single one. I can't remember a name on my lips, a head of hair in my hands, a dress on the floor.

The memories form, but I don't see the women I invited to my bed.

I see Briar.

Her long legs wrapped around my waist. Her grey eyes wracked with bliss. Her head falling back as she comes.

On the fucking floor in the kitchen, because we can't wait to get to the bed.

What the fuck is wrong with me? I'm a slut, sure, but I'm a grown-ass man. I have some self-control.

"You want a drink?" I ask.

"Are you having one?"

"If you are."

"Always a gentleman?" She turns to me with a soft smile. The one I recognize. *You're Liam Pierce and you're ridiculous and I like it.*

"You're the one who disagrees."

"You offered to eat me out in front of your brother."

"I'm not following the logic."

Briar lets out a soft laugh. "Of course not." She takes a step toward me. "Are you really going to fix me a drink?"

"Why wouldn't I?"

"You're a billionaire."

"With manners."

"Still." She takes another step toward me. "Usually, I'm the one fetching your drinks."

"Enjoy the role reversal."

"I will. Thank you." Her smile widens. "Do you know how to make a drink?"

"Gin and grapefruit?"

She nods.

"It's a complicated recipe, but I think I'll get it."

She laughs. It's different than her normal *you're ridiculous* laugh. Softer. More intimate.

Or maybe that's the space.

She's in my apartment.

I only invite women to my apartment for one reason.

I have friends. I throw parties. But if I'm offering plus ones, I host at a public space.

Too much security risk otherwise.

Too many opportunities for failure.

Parental training? Or running a cyber security company? I'm not sure anymore. I'm not a tech guy. I know enough to do my job, but I'm not passionate about computers or software.

Numbers are more my speed. Nobody could believe it when I started acing math tests in middle school. I was a troublemaking kid. I didn't take anything seriously. I didn't even do my homework.

Math made sense. I was good at it, and I enjoyed my expertise, but it wasn't until I started studying money that I fell in love.

Money is fascinating. A piece of paper with arbitrary value. And people do anything to get it.

Easy for me to say. I have a lot. But I see wealthy CEOs make mistakes all the time. Overpay for a company to spite an enemy. Or undervalue an employee who annoys them. Attempt to trade cash for respect.

Look at me, offering Briar a massive amount of start-up cash to play this game with me.

Yes, I want to invest in her company. Yes, I believe in her success.

But there's no monetary value to our ruse.

What is it worth, making a dying man happy?

There's no financial benefit. I'm not expecting any inheritance, or a leg up, or the chance to buy Preston's business.

There's no gain at the end of this transaction.

Only loss.

But maybe there is something in between. Some need for respect, love, closure. A need to prove myself, to prove I'm the kind of guy Preston believes I can be.

I move into the kitchen. Fill two lowball glasses with ice, grapefruit, gin. I even find triple sec.

Briar is standing at the window, staring at the skyline. "You really live here?"

I don't know what she means. "No, I broke into some guy's apartment. Thank fuck, he has your brand."

"You have my brand?"

"Yeah."

"You said gin tastes like Pine-Sol."

"It does."

She motions *explain*.

"Some women prefer gin. You drink enough of it to know—"

She flips me off.

I smile.

It's normal. Our usual back and forth.

Then she looks out the window and it's different again.

This shit with Preston is fucking with me. I'm off my game.

Maybe that's it.

Maybe she's the same. Maybe we're the same.

Maybe kissing her didn't change anything.

I hold up her drink. "You want to go to the balcony?"

"You have a balcony?"

"A terrace."

Her eyes go wide. "And you're just telling me now?"

"It's been ten minutes."

"Ten entire minutes."

My lips curl into a smile. She's adorable. How can such a tough badass be so fucking adorable?

I grab our drinks. Lead her to the balcony.

She opens the sliding glass door. Steps outside. "This is yours?" She turns the corner, walks along the other edge, to the open space at the end. "All yours?"

"All mine."

"You don't owe the bank?"

"Bought it with cash."

"I thought that was a dumb investment."

"I was outbidding an asshole."

"Liam Pierce, as petty as the rest of us."

"Our secret."

She mimes zipping her lips. "Do I know him?"

"Who?"

"The asshole."

"The tech guy from San Francisco."

"The one tech guy from San Francisco?"

"The one with the hipster glasses."

She shoots me a *really* look. "That barely narrows it down."

"He tried to poach you."

Her eyes light up. "He tried to fuck me."

"That too."

Her eyes meet mine. "You were jealous?"

"He was an asshole."

"You were jealous."

"Nobody steals my fucking assistant."

"Your assistant…" She brings her drink to her lips. "You didn't want him to steal your assistant."

I didn't want him to touch her. But what was I going to

say? No, Briar, don't fuck this douche. So what if he's rich and hot and incredibly interested in wooing you.

I don't have a claim to her. I can't tell her to keep her pants zipped.

Yeah, I haven't dropped mine in a while. Since that night in Toronto. It hasn't felt right.

But I can't have her.

I'm not going to be that asshole who tells her not to fuck someone else just because it makes me sick.

She's a grown woman. She can do what she wants.

No matter how much I hate it.

"He treated you like shit," I say.

"He was really sweet, actually."

I hate his stupid face and his hipster haircut. "Still hate him."

She smiles. "This place is new?"

"That was a year ago."

"A year is new."

"It was time to upgrade. Especially with shit with Adam. I wanted space for him here. Didn't know he'd lock himself in the mansion."

"You didn't have room for him before?"

"Not enough."

"Only a thousand square feet for him?"

"That spare bedroom is why you're not sleeping in my bed."

She smiles. "And where are you sleeping in this scenario?"

I see it immediately. Briar in my bed, in only the white sheets, her soft body melting into mine.

The two of us locked together.

It's absurd. I don't cuddle.

I don't kick women out of bed. I'm a gentleman. I fix breakfast; I pour coffee; I hail a cab; I kiss goodbye.

I don't mind the morning routine—especially if it comes with a round two—but I don't linger in it.

I certainly don't dream about holding someone close. Smelling her shampoo. Tasting her lemon soap.

That's relationship shit. And I'm not capable.

My brain is confused. All this shit with Preston. This ruse. That's it. It's too much.

"Liam? Are you okay?" she asks.

Fuck, what are we talking about? Sleeping arrangements. Not helping my cock cool it, but I'm a grown man. I can take it. "The bed. We're engaged."

"The floor," she corrects.

"Whatever gets you off."

"Really? If I said it would get me off if you slept on the floor, you'd do it?"

"If I get to watch."

She shakes her head *you're ridiculous*, takes a long sip, turns her attention to the view. "Did you buy the place to piss off the tech douche?"

"My first bid was to piss him off. Then I fell in love."

"I can see all the way up to midtown. And the water. The view is better than your office."

I nod.

"You've never mentioned the view."

"I'm used to it."

"I don't know if I'd ever get used to it. I've been in New York since I was eighteen, but it still amazes me." She turns to me. Brushes a purple hair behind her ear. "How long has it been for you?"

"In the city? Since college." I've always loved the city. The life, the energy, the people. It's a million times more vibrant than the still mansion where I grew up. Or the secluded boarding school I attended.

But it's so much better through her eyes.

Bigger.

Bolder.

More brilliant.

"This isn't what I expected of you. It's elegant. Understated."

"I'm not?" I ask.

"You offered to eat me out in front of your brother."

"You said that already."

"Yet it needed to be said again."

"It was a legitimate offer."

Her cheeks flush. "Was it?" She brings her drink to her lips.

We're on the north side of the building. Facing the lights of the Financial District and Midtown beyond it. "You don't think I'm good for it?"

"I can't tell when you're kidding sometimes."

Me either, honestly. "You'd never say yes."

"If I did?"

"Adam would stop us."

"Not Danielle?"

"Are you kidding? You've seen her pictures."

"We've looked at them together."

"Exactly."

She lets out a soft laugh. "She'd pull out her camera."

"Could be hot."

"Not my thing."

"No? Never took pictures with someone?"

"No," she says.

"You wouldn't?"

"I wouldn't ask a third party to take them." She turns to me. "She'll probably want to shoot us now that she thinks we're engaged."

"With clothes."

She shoots me that same *get real* look.

"She'll ask, sure. I'm game, but if you're not—"

"Liam!" Her voice rises to a girlish squeal. "Your sister-in-law is not taking nude pictures of me."

"She's not my sister-in-law yet."

"Was that really the salient point?"

"Was it not?"

She laughs *you're ridiculous*. "Would you really pose for Danielle?"

"Fuck yeah. Can you imagine the look on Adam's face?"

"He has the same look on his face at all times."

"To the untrained eye, sure. But I can tell when he's pissed."

"And that's it? You'd do it to piss off your brother?"

"I offered to piss him off. If she wants to do it, why not?"

"You'd let her post them publicly?"

"Once I'm officially single again. If I'm on the market, I might as well advertise the goods."

She lets out a soft laugh. "And it has nothing to do with helping her?"

"Fringe benefit."

"You just want women to look at your dick that badly?"

"It deserves to be looked at."

"Uh-huh." Her eyes flit to my crotch. "No one's stopping you."

"Stopping me from what?"

"Leaking nudes. Claiming you were hacked."

"I'm CFO of a cyber security company. Not a good look."

She nods *true*. "Finding another photographer, then. Saying it's for art."

"Before, maybe. But I can't do that to Danielle."

"Uh-huh."

"I promised."

"Did you really?"

"Of course," I say.

She lets out a soft laugh. "How did that go? Danielle, I know you're my brother's girlfriend, but I don't care. You shouldn't be defined by a man. You should be defined by your tits."

"Everyone's seen them."

She continues. "And by your talent too. Your talent at capturing the beauty of your tits. Have I mentioned how much I enjoy your naked images yet?"

"It's relevant. They're self-portraits."

"Yes, Danielle. It's the artistry I appreciate. Not the beauty of your tits."

"Don't forget the ass."

"The whole package. You have it all." She turns to me. Imitates my posture. "I so appreciate your talent that I promise I won't allow any other woman to photograph me naked."

"Not for art."

She drops the Liam voice. "Is that really how it went?"

"I offered. She said she'd think about it. Didn't want it to be weird."

"Yeah, how could that be weird?"

"I know."

Briar laughs so hard her tits shake.

Not that I'm staring.

Fuck.

"I told her I was ready." I clear my throat. "Ready whenever she was. And I'd wait until she was."

"What if you ask for special permission? Since she said no?"

"She'll come around."

"You really think so?"

I have no idea.

"And you'd really do it?"

"I would."

"I believe that." She stares at the Empire State Building. "I don't think I would."

"Now? Or if you were a man?"

"Now. If I was a man… I'm sure I'd be as obnoxious as other men."

"There are men out there more obnoxious than I am?"

"Of course not." She smiles. "You're at the top."

"Thank fuck."

"But you have some stiff competition."

If she keeps talking about posing naked, I'm going to have something stiff. Fuck. That's not even a good joke.

And it's not a joke.

Blood is fleeing my brain at an alarming rate.

The booze isn't helping. It's a bulldozer to my inhibitions.

"I don't even want to imagine being a man." She smooths her dress. "It's funny. I can see all the downsides to being a woman. All the ways it makes my life harder." She raises a foot. "These shoes."

"You said they're comfortable."

"They are. But I bet yours are more comfortable."

"Let's trade."

She laughs. "They won't fit."

"Buy me some that will."

"You think I won't?"

"You think I won't wear them?"

She nods *good point*. "The shoes, the strapless bra, the dress. Having to pick out a dress for dinner. You can wear that suit all day."

"I have to wear it all day."

"It's easier."

"It's easy, yeah. But it doesn't leave a lot of room for sartorial expression."

"Sartorial?"

"Fashion."

"I know what it means. I just didn't expect to hear you say it."

"I'm full of surprises."

She nods *you are*. "I guess I didn't think of that. It's a pain in the ass, picking out a dress for dinner. Spending the money on another item of clothing. But it does offer me a lot more freedom to express myself."

"And that matters to you." I brush a purple strand behind her ear.

Her eyes flutter closed as my finger skims her jawline. "It does."

I need to touch her. I can't touch her. "It suits you."

"I know." Her eyes open. Meet mine. She stares up at me for a moment. Considering the possibility. Then her eyes flit to my tie. "You're not drinking."

I'm not.

"You didn't have to drink the same thing I did."

"Couldn't remember two recipes at once."

"You don't like it?"

I bring the glass to my lips. Take a long sip of cold liquid. The tartness of the grapefruit. That hint of juniper that screams of gin and Christmas. It's not bad, really. "It's no appletini."

"What is?"

The taste of her lips. Her skin. Her cunt.

Fuck.

What the fuck are we talking about?

Clothes.

Some shit about clothes. Men wearing suits. The short hemline of her dress. Her long legs on display.

"You do make an effort." Her eyes flit to my pocket square. "To bring a little flair to your style."

"I am Liam Pierce."

"Do you really feel like it's not enough?"

"I don't think about it."

"If you do."

"Sometimes." I take another sip. Try to ignore the mental image of her lips on mine. "It's easier. You're right."

"And you don't have to worry about wearing something too sexy. No one taking you seriously."

"Is that really a concern?"

"Is that an actual question?"

"Not the sex." I'm not an idiot. I see the way men treat her. Most are respectful. But most isn't enough. "Do you really want to be a serious guy in a suit? You could wear a suit every day now."

"No."

"You go to a lot of effort to dye your hair."

"It's easier than it looks."

"Keep it in that neat line." I trace it without thinking.

She shudders as my fingers brush her neck.

"Paint your lips wine."

"I make an effort, sure."

Now how about I wear off that fucking lipstick. "You look fucking fantastic."

"I know."

"You could do less if you wanted. Still more than some guy would have to do, but less."

"I could."

"I get what you mean."

"You do?" Her eyes fill with incredulity.

"Yeah. It's easier for men. We can wear a suit every day without any implication. You could wear a suit every day, but people would think you're stuck up."

"Yeah."

"It's not as simple as that. There's a real dick measuring contest in business. Men judging each other's ties and watches. But that's about money, power, status."

"People take you seriously by default."

They do.

"Even if you posed for Danielle. People would call it a bold move. If a woman in your position did the same thing…"

"The world is a sexist mess."

"Yeah. I just. Uh… even though it is, I'm still glad I'm a woman. Even though I wouldn't have to worry about my skirt length or my makeup if I was a man. Even though I'd go further, faster in my career. I love being a woman. I'd never want to be a man."

"Isn't that how most people feel?"

"I don't know. I haven't asked." She looks up at me. "But, uh, as it is now, being a woman in business, I wouldn't pose for Danielle."

"If she kept the pictures private?"

"Maybe."

"You don't trust her?"

"I don't know what I need with artistic nudes of myself."

"I can take them off your hands."

Her voice softens. "What would you do with them?"

Chapter Ten

LIAM

This is it.

An invitation.

I can say some stupid shit. The way I normally do.

Or tell her the truth.

I want to kiss her again. I want to carry her to my bed. I want to dive between her legs and never come up for air.

We're twelve hours into our ruse and I'm already losing my shit.

And losing interest in holding on to it.

Why pretend?

Why not make her come?

That makes sense.

It's the only thing that makes sense.

Her grey eyes are still glued to mine. She's still there, at the precipice, waiting for my answer.

I want to respond with gusto, with every fucking thing I have.

But I can't.

"When we go to the house, I'll show you the spare room," I say. "The way Danielle decorated it. I'd do that."

"Hang them in your spare room?"

"Fuck no. My bedroom."

"What would you tell the women you bring home?"

"That's a later problem."

She laughs. "Of course."

"They might be into it."

"Into pictures of other women?"

"You've never gotten hot off a picture of another woman?"

She makes that *hmm, that's a good point* noise.

"Plenty of babes are like Danielle. Exhibitionists."

"Or voyeurs."

"Exactly."

"And you aim to please. That is what you always say."

"I do." What gets her off? What's the best way to push every one of her buttons? I want to know. I have to know.

Briar smiles *silly Liam* and finishes her drink. She pops an ice cube in her mouth. Sucks hard.

The way she'd—

Fuck.

Not going there.

She bites the thing in half.

That's the mental image I need. Sharp teeth a place they shouldn't be.

Or a place they should.

My neck. My chest. My thighs.

Briar lets out a soft sigh. "That was good. Thanks, Liam."

The sincere compliment feels strange. My sincere, "You're welcome," feels stranger.

It's not us.

Not me. Not her.

We're awkward now.

I want her too much. Her smile, her laugh, her touch.

I've always wanted Briar.

Because she's gorgeous and funny and smart.

This is different. Harder to handle. Tinted with the taste of her lips.

"I forget, sometimes." She gives me a slow once-over. She's checking me out, yeah, but there's something else too. Something deeper. "You're such a charming guy. You ask for what you want in this way… it feels like you're doing someone a favor by asking them for a drink."

"I'm charming?"

"You know you're charming."

"I don't know you think I'm charming."

"Really?"

"Not the way you're saying it now."

"How am I saying it now?"

"It's hard to explain."

"I'm here. You're here." She taps my glass. "We have alcohol." Her eyes flit to my chest. Stomach. Crotch.

She wants to fuck me.

I want to fuck her.

We're both tipsy enough to do it.

It's a bad idea.

A really fucking bad idea. I don't do serious. She doesn't do casual. I'm not throwing away our relationship for one night.

Even if it would be the best night of my fucking life.

Now what the fuck are we talking about?

Me. Charming her. Annoying her with my bullshit.

I try to find my normal tone. "You laugh at my jokes. You smile at my stupid shit. But when I bring you to a work dinner, and I'm schmoozing some asshole, you get this look. Like you can't believe I'm actually making an effort to win over this douchebag."

Her lips curl into a smile. "I do?"

"Usually." I hold up my drink. "Especially after a few."

"They are douchebags."

"Absolutely."

She takes a long sip. "It's not that I think less of you."

I raise a brow *really?*

She nods *really*. "It's more I have no idea how you do it. I couldn't. I was ready to stab that guy who was staring at my boobs with my shrimp fork."

"You've played nice at plenty of dinners."

"I have?"

"Last month. The guy with the clothing empire. He barely looked up from your tits."

"I was scowling the whole time."

"He couldn't tell. He wasn't looking at your face."

A laugh spills from her lips. "True."

"You had them out. He couldn't help it."

"I was wearing reasonable dinner attire. It's ridiculous. If I cover up, I'm uptight. If I show too much skin, I'm a slut."

"No one thinks you're a slut."

"But you—"

"I get your point. It is bullshit."

"It's the world." She turns to me, her back to the view. "I could have chosen a different field."

"A less attention grabbing hairstyle."

"If it grabs so much attention, why are guys staring at my boobs?"

"That's a good point."

She motions *see*.

"But if I may speak for people who enjoy breasts—"

"Can I stop you?"

"Yours are really fucking nice."

"How do you know?"

My eyes flit to her chest. "I know."

"You haven't seen them."

"Is that an offer?"

She doesn't tell me to fuck off the way she normally does. She blushes. Looks to the door. "In your dreams."

"Hopefully."

It hangs there in the air.

The offer.

Her blush.

My blood rushing to my cock.

Baseball. People think about baseball. But I don't know shit about baseball.

Simon's disapproval.

Adam's concern.

The pride on Preston's face.

The tone of his voice. *I'm dying.*

It's miserable, but it doesn't help. I want to touch her more. To soak in the warmth of her skin and the sweetness of her lips.

The vibrancy of life.

Some primal urge to make more.

I need to get the fuck out of here. But this is my apartment. And Briar *is* a guest. I can't abandon her on the balcony.

I can't stand here and smell her shampoo.

There's only one place that leads. I need to do something—

That's it.

I swallow my drink in one gulp. Take her empty glass. "Another round?"

"No. I'm wiped. I'm going to hit the hay." Her eyes flit to the hallway. "Is my stuff really here?"

"Yeah." I lead her inside. To the second door on the right. The spare bedroom.

She steps into the space. Notes the clean white sheets, the mahogany dresser, the leather armchair.

Her bright purple duffel sitting in front of the burgundy leather.

"Have I ever clashed so much?" She whips her hair forward. It doesn't suit the room.

She doesn't belong in the room. It's all old money masculine bullshit.

She's not soft and feminine in the way people usually describe it. She's not powder pink and lace.

But she has her own feminine energy. Magenta and sheer mesh and heeled boots.

Punk rock sex appeal.

And the understated side of her. The side she doesn't show to anyone.

I swallow hard. "It's for Adam."

"The decorator nailed him."

"She did." I'm not sure how, since she never met the guy, but she really did capture my brother's energy.

"And you?" She turns to me. "Did she capture you?"

"You've seen the rest."

"Your bedroom?"

"You want to see my bedroom?"

Her cheeks flush. "To see the decorations."

"Only one reason why I invite women into my bedroom."

"Is that a requirement? Really?"

It's an inevitability. "I can make an exception for you, but I can't make any promises about the results."

She looks at me like she can't tell if I'm joking or not. Then she shakes her head. "Maybe tomorrow." She presses her lips to my cheek. "Good night, Liam."

"Good night." I step into the hallway. Pull the door closed. Stare at the handle for too long.

Am I joking?

I can't fucking tell anymore.

———

My concentration is shot. I try to focus on the TV show I'm watching. Some action thriller with drama and explosions and a plot that requires no brain power. But the female lead makes me think of Briar.

She has the same sharp nose and take no shit energy.

She's not as tall or curvy. Not as compelling. She's too typical. Long blond hair, bright blue eyes, tight leather.

She's hot, sure, but in a plain way. A vanilla latte.

Briar would kill me if she heard me comparing a woman to a drink. *That's objectifying, Liam. Women aren't beverages. How'd you like it if I said you were a vanilla latte?*

Then she'd roll her eyes when I'd say some stupid shit about being any flavor she likes.

Or not caring as long as it means she wants to drink me.

I don't have a type. I enjoy all sorts of women. Or I did.

Until that night in Toronto. The night we almost kissed, and I started comparing every woman I met to Briar.

No one compares.

I give up on TV, take another shower, change into my pajamas.

I'm not an insomniac. I work hard; I play hard; I come home exhausted.

Not last night. Not with that news.

And not tonight.

Fucking nap.

I toss and turn, trying to push my thoughts away from the matter-of-fact tone of Preston's voice.

My head goes straight to the curiosity in Briar's eyes.

That's all I can think about.

Death and sex.

I'm as fucked up as Adam.

There's only one way I'm falling asleep. One thing that works like a charm.

It's not a good idea.

After another hour, I don't care.

I close my eyes, ditch my boxers, try to push my thoughts to my last fuck.

Someone.

Anyone.

As long as it's not the woman sleeping in the other room—

For a second, I have it. The blonde from the TV show. Her long hair falling over her perky tits. Her fire engine nails on my chest.

Then they're Briar's wine red nails.

Her short purple hair.

Her lips parting with a groan.

I'm hard in an instant.

I give in to the mental image.

Briar's thighs against my cheeks, her hands in my hair, my name rolling off her lips again and again.

It can't happen.

It's fucked up.

But it's so fucking beautiful to picture it.

Chapter Eleven

BRIAR

W arm sun. Soft sheets. The gentle hum of the air conditioner.

The smell of leather and wood.

I roll to my side. Open my eyes. Take in the view.

The deep blue Hudson. The bright sky. The sun bouncing off steel and glass. Raising the temperature of my skin.

It's beautiful, and comfortable, but it's not my room.

It's Liam's spare room.

Not mine. Nothing like my room.

For one, it's a bedroom, with plenty of space to spare, not a cramped studio apartment.

And it's masculine. Old school. Perfect for Liam's brother, but nothing like me.

For a second, I soak in the warmth of the sun on my skin. No complicated plan. No kissing my boss. No wondering if he really wants to invite me to his bed.

Only the beautiful blue sky and the buildings surrounding us.

Simple pleasures.

Then I rise, I use the bathroom in the hallway, wash my hands, brush my teeth, find Liam in the kitchen.

In a towel.

Only a towel.

He's at the counter, pouring water into the French Press, his back to me.

And he's dripping wet, his hair sticking to his forehead, the cerulean cotton slung low around his hips.

It's barely hanging on.

If that cinch fails and he turns—

I swallow hard. "Good morning."

"Hey." He turns to me and gives me a quick once-over. "You sleep in that?"

Right. I'm in a tank top and boxers. A very thin tank top. I do run hot. Only in here, with the air-conditioning on high—

Shit.

"What should I sleep in?" I ask.

"Nothing." He smiles that charming smile of his, but there's something off, the way there was after the party.

"Are you okay?"

"Bree didn't send you home with pajamas?"

"I didn't look." I was exhausted last night. Not that it helped me fall asleep. I kept thinking about the taste of Liam's lips. The feel of his hands on my skin. How badly I want to feel his hands on my skin again.

"She has a set she likes."

"How do you know?"

He shrugs and turns to his coffee. "I had a phase."

"A phase of dressing women you fucked?"

"Longer arrangements."

"Two nights instead of one?" I try to say it with my usual tone, but there's judgment in my voice.

Liam pauses. He notices, but he shrugs it off, stays that

easy-going, impossible to ruffle version of himself. "An entire week once."

"That's an eternity for you." There. Normal voice. Teasing. Fun teasing. Not *I'm judging you for being a slut* teasing. He is a slut. Or he was. But that's his business. As long as he's safe, why should I judge?

When I started college, I—

Well, I certainly didn't compete with Liam's numbers, but I had my moments. Hookups at parties. Friends with benefits. A fling with an older man even.

I wanted to prove I wasn't a sucker like my mom. I wanted to prove I wouldn't give up my freedom or my self-respect and commit to a man.

But I over-corrected. I didn't like meaningless hookups. They were, well, meaningless. Even when they were good —and some were really good—they were empty.

Then I over-corrected again. Started dating John because he was stable and committed. He was an asshole sometimes, but usually he was an asshole for me.

Did I love him? I thought so, at the time. Now, I don't know.

He never made my heart race or my stomach flutter. Not the way Liam does.

I didn't trust him the way I trust Liam.

Not that I trust Liam.

It's just—

It's complicated.

"Weeks sometimes," he says. "Months even."

"Really?"

"Six months, once."

"You were with the same woman for six months?"

"I'm capable." He reaches for something in the cabinet. "London Fog?"

"You know how to make one?"

He nods. "Looked it up last night."

"Last night?"

"Couldn't sleep."

"You either?" Shit. I bite my tongue. I might as well add *oh, were you thinking about fucking me the way I was thinking about fucking you?* That's a good idea. Totally a good idea.

"Yeah."

I couldn't stop thinking about your lips. Was it the same for you? "What time is brunch?"

"In an hour."

"Shouldn't we wait?"

"I've seen what happens when you don't have your tea."

"Because you've woken me up."

"You overslept."

"Only once," I say.

"And when you found out they didn't have coffee or tea at the meeting…" He turns to me with a smile. "The scowl on your face put Simon to shame."

"Who doesn't serve drinks at a meeting?"

"They had water."

"It was eight thirty! They should have tea."

"Yeah." He chuckles. "You were cranky all morning. The look on your face when we finally left. And you told me to pull over at the first place we could find. I never thought I'd see you so excited to drink Starbucks."

"Their Earl Grey is solid."

"High compliments."

"Less talk. More tea."

"Yes, mistress." He winks.

I almost believe things are normal. I almost believe we're normal.

But we're not.

And he's not.

There's something going on with him.

"Are you sure you're okay?" I ask.

He grabs milk from the fridge. Fills a cup halfway. "You like it creamy?"

"Half milk, yeah."

He nods. Slips the cup into the microwave. Returns the milk to the fridge.

"Liam?"

"You should get ready. It's a quick drive."

"We're not taking the subway?"

"When do I ever take the subway?"

"It's faster." I smooth my shorts. "Usually."

"Not on a Sunday going uptown."

That's true. "You're wearing a towel."

"Yeah. But it's like you said. Takes longer for women to get ready."

"What if I go in this?"

He turns to me. Gives me a long, slow once-over. "I'm not going to object."

"Did you really buy me pajamas?"

"The only instructions I gave Bree were 'buy her whatever she wants.'"

"That's it?"

"I may have told her to put up a fight if you complained about high price tags."

"Liam Pierce needs a fiancée with expensive tastes?" I ask.

"How long have you worked for me?"

"Two years." Give or take.

"How many men in my position have you met?"

"Executives? A lot."

"And how do their wives dress?"

"I know." I don't know where to put my hands. I need

to put them somewhere. Not his shoulders. Or his back. Or that cotton towel. "I'm just… It's weird."

"It is." The timer beeps. He grabs the mug of milk. Pours the brewed tea into it. "It was weird the first time I sent someone to Bree."

"Why did you?"

"She was a friend from college," he says. "An artist. She didn't come from money. She wasn't part of this world. She thought it would be like college."

"Keg stands and beer pong?"

He chuckles. "You see me drinking beer?"

"Appletini pong?" I suggest.

"Now that sounds like a game I'd play."

"You'd be wasted after three rounds."

"All the better." He holds up my mug, beckoning me.

Right. I'm drinking this tea. My normal morning routine.

No, my normal breakfast—eggs and toast—is nowhere to be seen. No doubt, there's some fancy rich people's version on the way.

Poached eggs. Scones. Rose petal jam.

I appreciate the free food. The fancy free food. And I'd kill for Liam's apartment.

But I'd rather be in my tiny studio, spreading Trader Joe's Raspberry Jam on cheap bread, reading a book alone.

No ruse. No lies. No struggling to tear my eyes away from the towel barely covering Liam's ass.

Okay. Maybe I don't mind that so much. Or I wouldn't. If I could touch him without ruining everything.

If I could press him against the counter, push the towel off his hips, wrap my hand around his cock.

"Your tea is getting cold." Liam's eyes flit to my bare legs. The ends of my boxers. "Those belong to your ex-boyfriend?"

"If I'm wearing them, they belong to me."

"Were they his?"

"Probably."

"You still wear his stuff?"

"It's comfortable."

His lips curl into a frown. An actual frown, not his usual over-the-top put-on. "You should lose them."

"Why?"

"If someone stops by, they'll see you lounging in your ex's boxers. That doesn't look good."

"How would they know they belonged to my ex?"

His eyes flit to the shorts. "Mine don't look like that."

"But how would anyone know?"

"I don't like it. You can wear whatever you want as long as it didn't belong to your ex."

"And you have nothing here left by other women?"

"I don't."

"What about your six-month fling?"

"It was a long time ago. A year after school," he says. "And it wasn't serious. She came over after work to fuck me and left when we were finished."

"Then why did she need clothes?"

"I'm a gentleman."

"You offered to eat her out in front of your brother too?"

"We went to dinner. Events. She was my date, the way you are now."

Not the way I am now. We're not having sex. But I don't want to say that out loud for some reason.

"She was a designer at a small firm. She knew expectations were different than they were in school, but she didn't know business. She didn't know people would judge her for wearing flat shoes and a sweater to dinner. In school, guys didn't care if a girl came from money. The scholarship students and the rich kids went to the same parties. Everyone wore sweat pants after all-nighters. There was judgment, but it was about how cute or funny someone was, not how much they spent on their shoes."

Liam spent six months fucking a down-to-earth artist from school.

Why does that bother me?

I don't think about his one-night stands. I don't ask myself if he's screwing models or sweet girl-next-door types.

I don't like it. I don't like imagining some other woman touching him. But I've had meaningless sex before.

It's meaningless.

This.

A girl from school. A girl he actually liked.

I hate it.

"She felt out of place at events," he says. "She didn't want to show up as my date. I should have listened. Instead, I sent her to Bree for new attire. She liked the lingerie, the cocktail dresses even. We could go out to nice places, alone, stay away from assholes. When other people were there… She tried. But she hated the bullshit. And she hated me for asking her to do it."

"She ended things?"

"It was more like they melted down, but yeah."

"And you've reflected enough to see your mistake."

"Am I not capable of growth?"

"I don't know. What did it teach you?"

His eyes flit to my cup. "I'm not an expert, but I'm pretty sure you're supposed to drink that, not hold it."

Right. I take a small sip. Bergamot. Tea. Milk. Honey. "This is good."

"Don't sound so surprised."

"Thanks, Liam."

"I'm capable of fixing tea too."

"Tea and cocktails."

"What was that about cock?" He smiles. This time, he nails it. That dazzling *I'm Liam Pierce and I'm ridiculous* smile.

It lights up the entire room.

Makes my stomach flutter.

Raises my pulse.

He's too handsome.

Why is he so handsome?

It's not fair.

"What did you learn?" *What was that about cock? I'd like to sit on yours. Now. Thanks.* "From your fling?"

"Mandy."

"What did you learn from your fling with Mandy?"

"To be clear about what I want. And what someone else wants. She was always trying to tell me she didn't want to be part of this world. But I thought it was humility. Or some shit like that. I thought she'd be disappointed if I took her to the place she liked in Chinatown instead of the expensive restaurant in Midtown."

"But she was a down-to-earth girl who liked down to Earth things?"

"And authentic Cantonese food."

"And you thought she wanted nice things. You thought that was part of the Liam Pierce package."

"Fuck. Never thought about it that way, but yeah, I guess I did."

"Other women?"

"People know who I am. Or they learn fast."

"And they do want the Liam Pierce package?"

"They want the package, yeah—"

"You're nervous again," I say.

His voice softens. "For a while, I did the whole expensive lingerie and fine dining thing. Then I stopped the longer arrangements."

"Do you like it better that way?"

"No." He must notice my surprise, because he explains right away. "I'd rather fuck someone for a while. I get to know them, what they like, how to make them come."

He prefers longer arrangements?

"Women, even the more sexually aggressive ones… they don't trust me right away. I'm not as good the first fuck as I am the tenth."

"It's always awkward the first time."

"Yeah. Sometimes the novelty overcomes it. Or the thrill of a one-night thing. But there isn't that same…"

"Intimacy?"

"Yeah. Intimacy. Trust."

Liam wants intimacy and trust?

"But I learned the hard way… Most women, they don't do things halfway. That intimacy, the trust, it's not just sexual. It becomes more. They want more."

"They fall for you?"

"Maybe not all the way, but enough they want a relationship."

"You don't?"

"There were a few women I really liked, who I wanted to see more often. I thought about trying the boyfriend thing. It was tempting."

My stomach churns.

"But I was never willing to give up my freedom. I've known that since I was fifteen." His eyes meet mine. "You've been in a relationship."

"Only the one serious one."

"You loved him?"

"I thought I did."

"You enjoyed his company?"

"For a long time."

"The sex was good?"

"It was okay," I admit.

"No? Small dick?"

"Why do men think everything is about dick size?"

"I'm not hearing no."

"His dick was fine."

"Well, if it was fine…"

"It wasn't about his dick." My cheeks flush. I take another sip. Try to think of a response. Think of the citrus scent of his soap instead.

Oranges.

Why does he smell like oranges? Oranges and pine, yes, but oranges.

Why am I so desperate to taste his skin?

"What was it about?" he asks.

"He wasn't a very creative guy. And he was… inhibited. But it wasn't just him. I was too."

"You needed someone like me."

I need you, specifically. Lose the towel. Pin me to the wall. Let's go right now.

"Someone shameless."

"Maybe."

He turns all the way around. So his front is to me. "I'm surprised."

"Huh?" My eyes refuse my command. They trace a line down his body. The broad shoulders. The rose tattoo on his chest. The Latin quote on his ribs. Something for his brother. Those v-lines.

The cerulean towel begging for my hands.

Begging for release.

"You don't seem inhibited," he says.

"I never thought I was. But the first time I told him what I liked, he made me feel awkward. And I just… I didn't try again."

"Was it that freaky?"

"No."

He raises a brow *really*.

My eyes return to his hipbones. "You're not getting it out of me sober."

"Maybe you are uptight."

"Compared to you."

He catches me staring. Smiles. Smug. Victorious. Interested.

I'm not imagining things.

It's written all over his face.

He wants me too.

And I need to leave before I do away with that towel. "I should get ready."

"Lose your ex's boxers."

"I'm not—"

"For yourself. You're better than wearing his clothes, Bri."

"And if that means I walk around in my panties, so be it?"

"Yeah. So be it."

I flip him off.

"I'll ask Bree to send over pajamas if she didn't pack any."

"I don't need your pajamas."

"Have you ever worn silk pajamas?"

"I'll give you one guess."

He chuckles. That *I love your sass* chuckle of his. "Don't knock them till you try them."

"She has my sizes."

"I'll have her send them over."

"What if she packed them?"

"Can't hurt to have more." He motions to the hallway. "Go. Before I trash those boxers."

He isn't saying *go, before I fuck you senseless*.

But he's saying something close.

Something really fucking close.

Chapter Twelve

BRIAR

Everything on our drive from the Financial District to Columbus Circle is bustling.

The second we turn onto Park Ave, the city quiets.

The street outside Preston's building is empty. There are parked cars, sure, but there isn't a single person walking past apartments or smoking on a stoop.

I check my lipstick one more time, smooth my emerald green sundress, take a deep breath.

I can do this.

I can absolutely do this.

Liam opens the door for me. Offers his hand.

I let him pull me to my feet.

He pulls too close. Or I land too close. My hands are on his chest. My legs are pressed against his.

My lips are close to his lips.

In my wedge sandals, I'm eye to eye with him.

And, god, those deep blue eyes—

I want to stare into them forever. Watch them fill with wonder, joy, bliss.

"He's probably not watching." Liam brings his hand to the small of my back.

This dress is thin and soft, sure, but it's not enough. There's too much fabric between us.

"But you can see the street from the living room. And from Preston's bedroom." He pulls me closer.

"How do you know?"

"Are you kidding? I know every angle of every window." Liam brushes my hair behind my ear. "I spent a few weeks here every summer. Had to know how to get out unseen."

"Of course."

"My motives were pure. I was trying to help Harrison."

"Uh-huh."

"Yeah. The guy had no game. Still doesn't."

"That's why he ended up with someone so…"

"Physically attractive."

I bring my lips to his ear. "You hate her too?"

"I don't think about her enough to hate her."

"But you recognize her…" I try to find a euphemism.

"Horrific personality? Yeah."

"She tries to hide it."

"She says some snide shit about your outfit every time she sees you."

She does. But I didn't think he noticed.

"I told her to fuck off."

"You did?"

"The way I do."

"As a joke?" It's smart, really. Defuses the tension. But that's Liam. He always knows exactly what to say.

"Yeah. She pretended like it was all compliments. But I'm not an idiot. I may not know style, but I know *wow, you're so brave to wear something like that to a party* isn't a fucking compliment."

"You stood up for me?"

"Of course." His lips skim my ear. "The only person who's allowed to give you shit is me."

Fuck, his breath is warm on my ear. It feels good. Too good. Even in my breezy dress, I'm overheating. "Aren't you hot in that suit?"

"Baby, I'm hot in everything." He drops the sincerity. Back to shit-stirring Liam.

It's what he does when he's nervous.

But is it about kissing me again? Or is about Preston?

There's something he isn't saying. Something wearing on him. I can't believe I can see it in his posture, but I can.

Liam releases me and leads me to the door. "You ready?"

No. But when is anyone ready to convince their boss's surrogate dad of their fiancée status? "I'm starving."

He smiles, but it's missing something. Whatever it is that's weighing on him. Then he shakes his head, shakes it off, leads me inside.

Preston's place is a brownstone. Four stories, long rooms, half a dozen bedrooms and just as many bathrooms.

Eight figures of Upper East Side real estate. Elegant and old money. The opposite of Liam's modern apartment. Maybe not the exact opposite. It's still a building in Manhattan. Everything is efficient. Close together.

We walk through the first floor. A sort of living room/lobby mix. The party was here—and on the second floor—but the space looks different in the morning light.

Hardwood floors. Cream couches. Wood coffee tables. White walls adorned with art.

"The dining room's on the second floor," Liam says. "There's a bathroom down here if you need it. It's nicer than the one on that floor."

"I remember."

"Right. You were just here." He shakes his head *obviously*. "Shoulda had more coffee."

"Stopped at Dunkin' on the way?"

"Ordered some hazelnut vanilla thing with a hundred grams of sugar." He nods. "Sounds refreshing."

"Refreshing coffee?"

"Iced."

"Should I fetch you an iced latte?"

His eye corners turn down. "Bet you won't miss that."

Is he sad I'm not going to be his assistant? Or is it something else? "I won't miss working under the most difficult man in the world, no."

"Working side by side is better?"

"I'm waiting for the sex joke."

"I'm game for anything, Bri. You know that."

"I do."

"But side by side… not as good. Unless you're talking sixty-nine. And even then…" The lightness returns to his voice. "We can try tonight." He motions to the stairs. The footsteps on the second floor. He's telling me Preston is here. Listening. "But I'd rather you sit on my face."

"If it will shut you up."

"Is there a better way?" His smile widens. Brightens his eyes.

It's real. Authentic. The teasing Liam I know well.

"Is that you, Liam?" Preston calls.

Liam's smile disappears. "Just some guy who's going to fuck his fiancée on your couch."

"How am I supposed to sit on your face on the couch?"

"Do you need a live demo?"

"I'm starving," I say loudly.

"See, I was thinking I want to eat too—"

"You did not just say that."

"I did."

"It's not sexy."

"I didn't tell you to get on the dining table because that's where I eat all my meals."

"Did you hear that in a bad porno?"

"Opal read it in some book."

"Why are you talking to your teenage sister about bad dirty talk?"

"Someone needs to teach her about finding the right men."

"And you're that someone?"

"Who knows men's bullshit better?" he asks.

That's not a bad point. But this is Liam. He's probably full of shit. "You didn't really—"

"I did."

"Promise you'll never say it again."

"I'm not sure I can do that."

"Women aren't meals."

"Women? I'm not thinking about women—"

"My—" Oh my god, I can't say this with Preston in earshot. "This"—I draw a circle around my pelvis—"is not a meal."

"I didn't suggest it was."

"But you—"

"Said I want to eat you out, yeah. Last time I checked, you didn't have a problem with that language."

"Is he this ridiculous when he thinks no one is listening?" Preston calls.

My cheeks flame. He can hear us. That's why Liam is doing it.

He's such a nice, respectable man. And he's listening to Liam discuss dirty talk.

It's not dirty talk we're actually using.

But it's still—

Ugh.

I'm going to die of embarrassment. I really am.

"But if you'd prefer, 'I want to taste your cunt.' Or 'I need you to come on my face—"

"Liam!"

He smiles. It's pure joy. Pure evil *I love making you blush* joy.

"Let's go upstairs."

"I've been waiting for you to say that."

"To breakfast."

"Do I have to say the thing about the table?" he asks.

"Do you want a chance at doing *that*?"

"Baby, are you really asking me that question?"

"Then don't say it." I offer my hand.

He shakes.

"If you offer to eat me out in front of another family member, friend, or coworker, I'm leaving."

"You're a coworker."

"Another coworker."

"I'll be good." He holds up four fingers. "Scout's honor."

"Uh-huh."

He takes my hand and leads me up the stairs.

Preston is standing in front of an oval dining table. He's dressed exactly as Liam is. A three-piece suit, only his is navy, and his tie is burnt orange.

The orange isn't his color. It makes him look a little sickly. But I'm not here to give the guy fashion tips. Besides, he looks stylish in that understated rich guy way.

"I feel a little outclassed," I admit.

"If your dress is upsetting you and you need to take it off, I… well, I don't want you to be upset." Liam shoots me a *got ya* look.

Preston laughs *ah, silly Liam*. "You look beautiful, Briar. You put both of us to shame."

That's not true. They both look fantastic. Sure, Preston isn't brimming with youthful vigor the way Liam is. And his designer suit is a little big for him.

But he's in a designer suit.

I'm in a sundress and sandals.

And this is from my new closet. My bought by Liam closet.

Not that I'm complaining about the free clothes. I'm earning the fuck out of them. And I, uh…

"Thank you." That's the appropriate reply to a compliment.

Liam pulls out my chair.

I smooth my dress as I take a seat.

"You do," Liam says. "Beautiful. Classy. And hot as fuck."

"Oh my god." My cheeks flame.

Preston chuckles. "Don't worry. I know Liam and his need for attention."

"He's incorrigible," I say.

"I love when you use big words," Liam says. "Makes me hard."

Preston motions *see*. "What would you like to drink, Briar? Champagne? Coffee? A Bloody Mary, maybe."

"Tea. Earl Grey if you have it," I say.

"I'll check." He steps into the attached kitchen. Semi-attached, I guess. There's a wall separating the two rooms. It ends just past the table. Leaves a wide open space. A line separating the hardwood and the tile.

"Whatever is fine," I say.

"Don't believe the lies. She's picky," Liam calls.

"How picky can I be if I'm with you?" I ask.

"Do you really want me to expand on that here?"

Liam's eyes meet mine. He raises a brow with his usual *I dare you* energy.

It actually feels normal.

Are we normal?

I don't know. But it's not like we've ever been normal. Not the way people usually say it.

We're both weird in our own ways.

"Ah. Here it is. Smith Tea," Preston calls. "A pyramid bag."

"Perfect," I say.

"How do you take it?" he asks.

"Plain is fine." A London Fog is complicated. I have to brew the tea double strength, then add warm milk. And I need to start with a particularly robust Earl Grey. Most are too light. They lack the body for milk. "Or a little honey."

Preston mumbles an okay. He moves ceramic in the kitchen. Fills a kettle.

"Let me help." Liam doesn't wait for an answer. He jumps out of his seat and moves into the kitchen.

He and Preston trade whispers. They seem friendly, but I can't make out the tone.

I stay busy checking my phone. The usual sale alerts from clothing companies and work emails that can wait until Monday. A text from my kid sister asking about my next visit home. A friend from college throwing a party next weekend.

A coworker who wants to know the status of Liam Pierce and me.

I know you work with him, but is that all it is? There's a rumor going around the office.

It's been a day and a half. How is this already circling the office?

I text Danielle to ask.

Briar: Did you tell anyone about Liam and me?

120

Danielle: Is it a secret?

Briar: No, but we don't want to upstage the bride and groom.

That's a plausible explanation, but it's not enough.

Briar: And I want to explain it to people at the office. I don't want people to think I got my job on my knees.

Danielle: That would be an interesting role play.

Briar: Speaking from experience?

Danielle: Oh god, I sound like Remy, don't I? Sorry.

Briar: You're only a three on the Liam scale.

Danielle: He's a ten?

Briar: An eleven.

Danielle: He'd like that.

He would.

Danielle: Adam and I haven't left the apartment.

Briar: Ah?

Danielle: It's not TMI?

Briar: If you don't mind me picturing you and your boy toy naked?

Danielle: Adam as a boy toy. I like that.

It is absurd. Adam isn't in any way a boy. He's mature, stoic, serious.

And he's chiseled in a masculine, adult way.

Liam is all boyish charm and youthful energy. He's boyishly handsome too. He'd look good in a newsboy cap.

Adam would look silly.

Briar: Is your boy toy up to your standards?

Danielle: We've been busy.

Briar: That is barely any information.

Danielle: Now, you sound like Liam.

Briar: I guess that happens.

Danielle: I thought you two were perfect for each other the moment I met you.

She did?

Danielle: You had that energy. Like you knew each other's bodies.

Like you'd already fucked.

That's our story. That we were already screwing. But it's not true. Did Danielle imagine it? Or was there something between us?

Briar: Guilty. Where's my information?

Danielle: I did get ideas about the bridal shoot. Convinced Adam to create them with me.

Briar: With his clothes on?

Danielle: At first.

Briar: Can I see?

Danielle: When they're ready.

Briar: And he signs off?

Danielle: That's part of getting them ready.

"Earl Grey. As promised." Liam drops off my tea. A milky mug of coffee. He motions *one minute*, heads to the kitchen, returns with waters and another cup of Joe.

"I'm not a master chef." Preston enters holding a tray of French toast. "But Sunday is Jacinta's day off." He presents the silver tray with pride.

"That looks amazing. Thank you, Preston." It really does. Thick bread. Powdered sugar. Sliced strawberries. Maple syrup.

I'm not usually one for sweets first thing, but I haven't had French toast in years. Since I woke up early to make it for my kid sister on the weekends.

We were never close, really, but I always tried to take care of her when Dad was busy screwing around and Mom was too hurt to be present.

We fought a lot. We still fight a lot.

She doesn't see our parents' marriage the way I do. She thinks it's great they're committed and working through their problems.

Ugh, why am I riling myself up?

I'm not here to complain about the ills of marriage. Or

the difficulty of family. I'm here to play Liam's fiancée. To convince Preston I'm making an honest man out of his surrogate son.

Besides, a cheating father and a well-intentioned yet absent mother are nothing compared to what Liam's been through.

He was so young when his mom died he barely remembers her. And he was only a kid when his dad died.

Then last year, his brothers were in that awful accident, and Bash died.

Liam spent two weeks out of the office. Came back as if nothing had happened. Mostly. I saw the weight on his shoulders, the tiredness in his eyes, the lack of enthusiasm in his gestures.

It's the same now.

The slumped posture he corrects the second he notices. The brief frowns. The not quite there teasing.

There *is* something going on here.

But maybe it's just the wedding. Maybe there's something I don't know about Liam and Preston and Harrison and Lee.

Maybe Liam had a secret affair with Lee.

Or Harrison.

Who knows? I've never heard him express same-sex desires. But I wouldn't be remotely surprised if Liam told me he was open to anyone with a pulse.

And now I'm imagining Liam fooling around with Harrison on the dining table.

And then Harrison disappears from my mental image. And it's me. The two of us, his slacks unzipped, my panties on the floor, his thick cock driving into me again and again.

Fuck.

I take a long sip of my tea. It's a little weak, but it's

good. The rich flavor of black tea and the hint of bergamot.

"I used to make French toast with my sister," I say. "We were in love with the dish at this fancy French restaurant."

"Pain perdu?" Preston asks.

"That's it. French toast stuffed with mascarpone and orange marmalade. I tried to make it at home, but I never got it quite right," I say.

"We have orange marmalade." Preston places a ceramic plate in front of me. "We might have mascarpone."

"This is great. Thank you," I say.

Preston beams with pride. He wants to take care of Liam. To take care of Liam's future wife.

He already likes me so much. Even though I wear thick eyeliner and dye my hair purple and absolutely don't fit into his old money, Upper East Side life.

But maybe he's not that person anymore. Maybe he never was. Maybe he inherited the place from his father and he's horrified when he's compared to the man.

The way I am.

Everyone tells me how much I look like my dad. Remind them of my dad. We have the same grey eyes and intense stare.

He's a smart man. Successful. People who don't know about his affairs mean well with the comparison, but it still makes me sick.

Preston finishes passing out plates, then he sits, turns to me, and says, "I know I won't get a straight answer from Liam."

"I'm sure," I say.

"So tell me. How did the most obnoxious man in Manhattan win over someone as beautiful and charming as you?"

Chapter Thirteen

BRIAR

"What did Liam tell you?" I arrange the sliced strawberries on my toast. Cover them in maple syrup. The rich comfort food is a perfect distraction. I can focus on the sugar to bread ratio, not the lie.

Liam didn't win my hand the way Preston means, but he did win me over.

When I first met Liam, I hated his cocky smile and his confident swagger. I hated how everything fell into his lap and how casually he handled it.

Then I saw the guy under all the bullshit.

I realized the bullshit was well-intentioned.

I started looking forward to seeing him at the office. I started laughing at his jokes and savoring our alone time.

"You know Liam. He can't answer a direct question to save his life," Preston says. "But he talks about you."

"He does?" I ask.

"He thinks I don't notice the way his voice rises. The way his hands go to his cufflinks." Preston models the gesture. "The first time he mentioned you, he lit up."

"What did he say?" I ask.

"He'd hired this woman with purple hair to piss off Simon," Preston says.

I shoot Liam a *really* look.

He shrugs *guilty as charged*.

Preston continues, "he was in awe of your wit. He thought it meant you'd be tough enough to put up with him."

"I was right," Liam says.

"And it drove you crazy." Preston chuckles. "He already liked you. I could tell."

"I always liked you," Liam says.

"You never tried anything," I say.

"You had a boyfriend."

"Really? That stopped you?"

Liam's expression gets sheepish. "No. I didn't care."

"What was it then?" I ask.

"I don't mix sex and work," Liam says. "Not usually."

"Why'd you do it this time?" I ask.

His eyes flit to my chest. "Is that a real question?"

"Yes." I'm not sure what I'm asking. What convinced him to ask me to play this role? Or maybe why he wanted me? Why he wants me as the woman on his arm, maybe?

Is it another way to fuck with people?

Liam turns to me. "I had every intention of staying on my best behavior."

"Oh?" I ask.

"But that night in Toronto." He reaches for his coffee. Swallows hard. Blushes. "It wasn't just the berry martinis."

"They helped," I say.

"Yeah. But I'd been dreaming about kissing you forever." His eyes meet mine. "I tried to stop thinking about you, I did, but I couldn't. I couldn't work, couldn't sleep, couldn't find interest in other women."

"For how long?"

"Five months," he says.

"Five months?"

"Five months before we first kissed," he says.

That night in Toronto when we almost kissed. It was five months ago.

Has he really gone five months not touching anyone else?

It doesn't matter. This is pretend. He might want me. I certainly want him.

But we're not crossing the line.

So it doesn't matter whether or not he spent the last five months dreaming about my lips—

Falling asleep thinking about the feel of my skin—

And it doesn't matter that I'm desperate to kiss him again. That I want to climb into his lap and tear his clothes off and feel every inch of him against every inch of me.

"I tried," he says. "Believe me, I tried. I was in the utility closet with this babe at a conference. She was on her fucking knees about to unzip me, but I couldn't—"

"Liam, if I may offer some fatherly advice," Preston interrupts.

Liam snaps out of his trance. Slips into his usual aloof role. "Shoot."

"I understand your generation is more modern in your attitudes about sex," he says. "If I'm wrong, correct me."

Oh Lord.

"But I imagine your fiancée doesn't want to hear about your encounters with another woman in lurid detail." Preston turns to me. "Or is it some sort of kink?"

My entire face flames.

"What do people call it? Cuckolding?" Preston asks.

Liam's eyes meet mine. He raises a brow.

Somehow, my blush deepens.

Liam chuckles. "Cuckolding is the other way. Man who gets off on his woman with another man."

"Ah." Preston nods.

"Not sure there's a name for this one," Liam says. "Have had a few women ask for it though."

"Was Briar one of them?" Preston asks.

Liam notices my blush. Smiles, charmed and victorious. "No."

"Then stop while you're behind," Preston says.

"This is why I need you. Smart advice," Liam says. "I never know when to shut up."

"I'll second that," I say.

Preston chuckles. "We're weak, aren't we?" He sips his coffee. "Men who have everything throw it all away for sex."

"Not me." Liam turns to me. "Only love."

"Is that right?" I ask.

"Yeah. Never crossed the line before." He holds up four fingers. "Scout's honor."

"Do you trust him?" Preston asks.

"To be faithful?" I swallow hard. Liam is loyal to me, yes, but it's a different kind of loyalty. "I do."

"I know what matters," Liam says.

"I'm not sure fidelity earns you bragging rights, son," Preston says.

"Five months is a long time for me. Five months without a fuck. Can't I brag about that?" He looks to Preston. "It was before we were together." Something drips into his voice.

He means it.

Or I'm imagining things.

I'm out of my mind. My blood is in my cheeks. My sense of embarrassment is draining my reasoning abilities.

"It doesn't appear to impress your fiancée," Preston says.

"Fuck. I guess whipping it out is off the table, huh?" He looks to me. Raises a brow. "Proving I know how to satisfy."

"Please don't," I say.

He smiles. "I can wait."

"You still haven't told me"—Preston looks to me —"how Liam won you over."

"I, uh… I need some strength after that assault on my, uh…" Something.

Preston motions *go ahead*.

I cut a slice of French toast. Mmm. Warm, eggy bread. Rich maple syrup. Fresh strawberries. "This is really great. Thank you."

"French toast is Liam's favorite," he says.

"It is? I never see you order it," I say.

"Not appropriate for morning meetings," he says.

"It was a Pierce family tradition. Every Sunday," Preston says. "I took it over after Liam's father passed. I hope you two will continue it once you marry."

Liam's eye corners turn down.

That thing that's weighing on him? Or his father's death?

I have no idea, but I know I want to soothe him. I want to wrap my arms around him, hold him close, whisper *it's going to be okay* in his ear.

But I can't promise that.

I have no idea if it's going to be okay. And I hate empty promises.

What can I say that's true? I don't know anymore. I care about Liam. I have for a long time. But where does it end? I don't love him. Not the way Preston thinks I do.

As a friend, maybe.

And I want him. I really, really want to ride him until we're both spent and sweaty.

But, I, uh…

"Bri sleeps in," Liam says. "We don't do a lot of weekend breakfasts."

"You're always at the gym when I wake up." Or just back from the gym. The one time I slept over. But, hey, that does fit the definition of always. "And I need to catch up on sleep. My difficult boss never lets me have any rest."

"Not for long," he says.

"Oh? You won't be working together any longer?" Preston asks.

"We will. But as partners," I say. "Liam is funding my start-up."

"That's wonderful." He smiles. "The two of you are going to create a splash."

"Oh?" I ask.

He nods. "You'll be on the cover of Forbes."

"I think he means Page Six," Liam says.

"The Playboy Prince Finally Finds His Princess," I say. "I see that."

"Playboy Prince?" Liam asks.

"You haven't seen it in the tabloids?" I ask.

"Of course." He sips his coffee. "Didn't know you had."

"Well, uh… it's your nickname. At the office," I say. "I thought you knew?"

"Of course." He slices his toast. Takes a bite. "My idea."

"Really?" I ask.

He nods. "Yeah. Complained about myself to some intern who mistook me for Simon. Thought it would annoy Simon."

"Did it work?" I ask.

"Fuck yeah. Everything annoys him." Liam looks to Preston. "You know how he is."

"I know how you are," Preston says.

"Busted," I say.

Liam shrugs *so what if I am?* "You still didn't tell him."

"Tell him what?" I ask.

"How I won you over." Liam's eyes meet mine. Fill with that trouble-making spark. He's closer to a hundred percent, but he isn't quite there. "I'd like to know myself."

"You didn't," I say. "We're not married yet."

"Fuck, still time to fail." He mimes being stabbed in the gut.

"It's all, uh… it's all sex." My cheeks flush. "At least, that was how it started."

Preston chuckles. "Say no more."

"Then he took me for drinks on the balcony, and he made me breakfast, and he tried to help me launch my business. He's annoying and bossy and difficult." I look into his blue eyes. "But he's sweet too."

"He hides it well," Preston says.

"I didn't want something serious. I tried it once, but I didn't like it. I was afraid of ending up like my mom." I swallow hard. "My parents are still together, but he isn't faithful to her. She pretends she doesn't notice. Or maybe she puts up with it for the money. Or for me and my sister. I don't know."

"I'm sorry," Preston says. "Ella and I had our issues, but we tried to keep them from Harrison."

His ex-wife. Harrison's mom. "I had to take care of my mom when my dad was MIA. And I had to take care of my sister when my mom locked herself in her bedroom to cry. She tried to hide it, but…" Fuck, this is way too much information. "I never wanted to get married. I'm still not sure. But when Liam took my hand and looked up at me—"

"And begged," Liam says.

"I saw something in his eyes," I say. "This need I wanted to fill. So I said yes, but I'm still not sure." I bite my tongue. This isn't proper fake fiancée talk.

But Preston nods with understanding. "Some people are like Liam. They only have two modes: zero and a hundred percent."

That is Liam.

Preston smiles. "I can tell he feels that way about you."

He can?

"It's not easy for everyone," he says. "It takes courage to admit that. To be honest."

"Honest. Yeah," I say. "I'm always honest with Liam."

"And I'm always honest with Briar." He says it with sincerity. He means it.

He's always honest with me.

I believe him. I shouldn't believe him—I'm helping him craft an elaborate lie, after all—but I do.

"It's mostly the sex though," I say.

Preston's laugh is big and hearty. "You are perfect for each other." Something calls his attention. A noise downstairs.

The door opening.

"Dad?" someone calls. Harrison, I guess.

"You're early." Preston pushes himself up. Slowly stands straight. "Liam and Briar are still here."

Harrison steps onto our floor. He surveys the room carefully.

He's a quiet guy. The type who keeps everything to himself. He's always kind and helpful, but that's all I really know about him.

He looks his father over. Checks the table. The floor. "Is everything all right?"

"Fuck yeah. You're exactly who I need to see." Liam jumps to his feet. "I have bachelor party questions. And you're not going to want to answer them in front of your dad."

No, no, no. I can't stay here with Preston on my own. I can't keep up this lie myself. "Liam—"

"We'll be ten minutes. That's it. We can pick up some mascarpone," he says.

"I don't want mascarpone."

"Then we'll go upstairs. Talk about girls in our sleeping bags like we used to." Liam pats Harrison on the back. "Ten minutes, okay?" He looks to me with a *please* in his eyes.

"Ten minutes." I can keep up a lie for ten minutes without his help.

Can't I?

Chapter Fourteen

LIAM

"What are you doing here, Liam?" Harrison pulls out his desk chair. Motions for me to sit.

"You still have the shit here?" I ask.

"What shit?"

"Used to keep a bottle back in the bottom drawer." I motion to the dresser. "I finished it a few times."

"It's barely noon."

"And we're talking bachelor party," I say.

Harrison frowns exactly the way his father does. His eyes are lighter. His skin is darker. And he's not fading the way Preston is.

But he still looks so much like my memory of Preston. The guy who sat me down to tell me my father died.

It's fucking weird. Harrison looks like his dad. And he looks like himself. Like the guy who begged me to help him sneak out so we could go to a party and meet girls.

Not girls. A girl he liked.

He's always been a die-hard romantic. Always wanted

to find the one. Something about his parents' divorce. His need to prove he was different than his dad.

At the end of the day, we're all the same: rich assholes trying to prove we're doing better than our parents.

Only he's about to lose his dad.

I'm losing my father figure, yeah, but he's losing his actual father.

He's losing his father and I can't let on.

"You haven't been here in years," he says. "Why are you having brunch with Dad?"

"I was here Friday," I say. "For your party."

"I don't mean parties." He pulls open the bottom drawer. Finds an ancient bottle of Maker's Mark. "This is from college."

"Aged."

"It stops aging when you open it." He sets the bottle on the desk. Motions *go ahead*.

"How about a glass?"

"What are you doing here, Liam?"

"Your dad invited me."

He stares at me. It's not quite Simon level of suspicion, but it's a lot.

"I know Lee is a blonde, but is that your preference for the party? Might be more fun to have a taste of what you'll never have again," I say.

"Liam."

"I can't plan my buddy's party now?"

He folds his arms. "Aren't strippers a little obvious for you?"

"There's a twist."

He rolls his eyes.

"I can't tell you. It will ruin the surprise."

"If you're not going to tell me why you're here—"

I have to say something. "Two reasons."

He motions *go on*.

"You want the good news or the bad news?"

"You know the answer to that."

I do. He's a bad news first kinda guy. But, hey, might as well give him a choice? Maybe he's in a mood.

No, he is in a mood.

An *I don't want to deal with Liam on top of whatever is going on with my father* mood.

Preston is obviously fading. I can see it. Even Briar can see it. She looked at him with concern the second she saw him. Maybe it was *I want this guy to approve of me* concern, but since when does Briar give a shit about anyone approving of her?

I need to distract Harrison.

Thank fuck this is my wheelhouse.

"What the fuck is wrong with you?" I ask. "Accepting the invite to the house?"

"I can't say no," he says.

"You can tell your fiancée to ask her sister to stay home," I say.

"Really? I can tell my bride to ask the maid of honor to skip the rehearsal dinner?"

"It's your wedding. You can do whatever you want."

"Is this about Simon and Vanessa?"

"No shit."

He doesn't buy it. "It's been a long time. He's over it."

"Uh-huh."

"I asked him," he says.

"He's got no self-awareness."

"They're high school rivals, not sworn enemies," Harrison says. "Maybe you should treat him like an adult. An adult who can spend time with someone he dislikes without causing a scene."

"Maybe you should meet Simon."

"He's not—"

"He is." I wasn't going to make this argument. Harrison is right. This won't upstage the wedding. Simon and Vanessa are rivals, sure, but she's as stoic as he is. Even if she does find him as annoying as I do, she won't say shit. He'll stare like he wants to fuck her —and he really does—but he'll keep it to himself. There's no reason to fret. They see each other at holidays and events and stay civil. But I need to pretend I care if I want to convince him I'm here for a reason. "We can change the bachelor party. Take the whole weekend."

"We can?"

"Yeah. Let the ladies party at the Pierce place."

"Adam is the one who invited us," he says.

"Adam can stay."

Harrison shoots me a *really* look.

Yeah, pointless argument. But I have to put up a fight or he won't believe this is why I'm here. "Think about it. Think about how whatever shit goes down between Simon and Vanessa is going to snowball and explode at your wedding. How is Lee going to feel about that?"

"Will you drop it if I promise to think about it?"

"Yeah. But if you think about it, you'll see I'm right."

He folds his arms, not buying my shit.

He doesn't think I'm right. But he thinks I'm here to convince him.

"What's the good news?" he asks.

"You're gonna want to sit down." I motion to the bed. "Trust me."

"It's good news."

"Do you trust me?"

"As far as I can throw you."

"You work out. That's gotta be a few feet."

A chuckle breaks his frown. "All right." He sits. Motions *go on*.

"Me and Bri. We're engaged."

His eyes go wide. "No."

"Yeah."

"Since when?"

"Not long."

"Dad knows?"

I nod.

"You said you weren't sleeping with her," he says.

"I wasn't. The first time you asked."

"For how long?"

"Five months."

"You went five months without bragging about sex?"

"It shocked me too."

He chuckles. "That can't be right. At the charity gala last month—"

"I was there with her." That is true.

"Why didn't you say anything?"

"She wanted to keep it on the down low."

"I'd be embarrassed to sleep with you too."

"Yeah, it's low for her. To let her physical needs overtake her mental ones."

He chuckles. "Did you just brag about your dick and pretend it was humility?"

"I did, didn't I?"

He shakes his head *silly Liam*. "You're really engaged?"

"Yeah."

"As in you're going to get married."

"That's the plan. But I'm not sure she's sold yet."

"She's wearing a ring?"

"Yeah."

"And you two are in a monogamous relationship?" he asks. "Really?"

"I'm not fucking anyone else."

"She isn't either?"

"Not that I know about."

"Shit. Liam Pierce engaged." He shakes his head. "I can't believe it. Really."

"I know."

"You asked her?"

"Begged her."

"She didn't want to say yes?"

"Her parents have a fucked-up marriage. She's a cynic."

"You're the romantic in the relationship?"

"Have you met Briar?" I ask.

He chuckles *true*. "She's the only woman who's put up with your shit this long."

"Tell me about it."

"And she's cute," he says. "But not the kinda of girl you usually go for."

"Since when am I picky?"

He raises a brow *really*. "You think I don't remember high school?"

"We went to an all-boys school."

"And all summer you went after Prom Queen types."

"This is because I hit on Lee the first time I met her, isn't it?" I ask.

"That might be skewing my memory," he admits. "But I don't remember seeing you with an alternative chick."

"I don't like her because she has purple hair."

"So you won't mind if I want a purple-haired dancer at the party?"

"You're finally pro-stripper?" I ask.

"If I am?"

"You ask my fiancée for a lap dance, I kill you."

"If I ask your fiancée for a lap dance, we're even."

That might be true. "If you touch her, I kill you."

His lips curl into a wide smile. One at my expense.

"What the fuck is that?"

"You're jealous."

Shit, I am. Again. I can see the image. Briar, here, in some hot as fuck black lingerie set, sliding onto his lap in this bed, tugging at his tie, whispering *this is my wedding present* in his ear as she does away with her bra.

It would be fucking hot if it wasn't so fucked up.

"Don't fucking touch her." I try to keep my voice even. Fail miserably. "Please."

"Will you tell me what you're actually planning for the bachelor party?" he asks.

"Fuck no." I'm not the best man. But he did delegate this particular task to me. "Is purple hair your final answer?"

"No strippers."

"But if you had to have one…"

"Someone Jimmy will like."

"Smart. Keep them both distracted."

"He'll probably pay her for sex."

I shrug. "Girl's gotta make a living somehow."

"Nothing illegal. I mean it, Liam."

"Scout's honor."

He shoots me a *please* look.

"You know I don't have honor I can swear on."

"Promise anyway."

"I can only promise for myself. Not Jimmy." The guy is pretty wild.

Harrison nods *fair*. "Is this your first time leaving her alone with Dad?"

"Since we told him, yeah."

"Are you telling everyone?"

"Only immediate family. Don't want to upstage your wedding."

"You could have waited to propose," he says.

"The moment struck me."

"Of course." He shakes his head the way he did when we were kids. "You should get back there. Before he tells her where the bodies are buried."

Preston knows a lot of embarrassing shit about me, yeah. Usually, I don't care. But I don't want Briar thinking less of me.

I want her to look at me the way she does in front of Preston.

Like she loves how ridiculous I am.

Like she sees every part of me.

Like she wants me so much she ignores reason.

But that isn't why I need to get back.

It's because she's too honest. She might spill the truth by accident.

I need to stop her.

And kiss her.

I really fucking need to kiss her.

Chapter Fifteen

BRIAR

Thank goodness for parental pride. And parental desire to embarrass. Preston is still responding to my *what do you think Liam wouldn't want you to tell me* question.

So far, I've learned about the gelatin in the pool prank that nearly got Liam kicked out of boarding school.

The time Preston caught him sneaking a girl into Harrison's room.

The time—and this is one Liam doesn't know Preston knows—Liam set up a legitimate Cyrano De Bergerac situation, and told Harrison exactly how to flirt with a girl.

They were in high school, sure, but it's still horrible for the poor girl, who must have been so confused by quiet, mild Harrison suddenly saying outlandish Liam-like things.

And it's so like Liam to go out of his way to help his friends.

I'm not saying I approve of him lying to this poor girl. But I can see the good intentions there somewhere.

And, really, who am I to judge someone for lying? I

may not tell any actual, factual lies today, but I'm deceiving Preston.

"Can I ask the same thing?" Preston smiles warmly. "What would Liam not want me knowing?"

Besides this big lie? "He's trying to talk Harrison out of hosting the rehearsal dinner at the Pierce manor."

Preston nods. "I told him the same thing. Simon…"

Simon and the maid of honor are exes, yes, but —"That's only part of it."

"Oh?"

"Liam would be horrified if anyone knew he worries about Simon."

Preston chuckles. "Yes."

"He's afraid to stay in the house too."

Preston's eyes turn down. "He told you?"

"No. He didn't have to. Before Bash died, the guys would meet there once a quarter. They'd spend long weekends. He'd take women sometimes, especially in the summer…" My cheeks flame. Some mix of embarrassment and envy. That was a long time ago, when I was with John. I have no right to be upset Liam was sleeping with other women. I was sleeping with another man.

Only the one.

But, uh, after I broke up with John—

I did the same thing I did when I first got to college. Tried to prove I wanted to be free by sleeping around.

"I didn't know him that well then," I say. "And after Bash… it was strange. He was out of the office when he got the news. He told me in an email. It was so matter-of-fact. 'Sebastian and Adam were in an accident. Sebastian died. Adam is in the hospital. I'll be with him for the next two weeks. Clear my calendar. Schedule meetings with investors next month. We need to convince them we're steering the ship.'"

144

"He was thinking about the company?"

"I don't know. Maybe he was in shock. Sometimes, it's easier to focus on work. On things that make sense."

Preston nods with understanding.

"It's what I do when I'm overwhelmed." Or depressed. But, hey, I've already told Preston about my parents' fucked-up marriage. No need to share my mental health woes too. "I called him to make sure he was okay. Maybe not okay. Of course, he wasn't okay. But if he needed something…" What could I have done? Held him, maybe. But that would have been inappropriate. We weren't close then. Not the way we are now. "He only said a few words to me. Something about how he'd call when he had news. I'd never heard him like that. Terrified. Vulnerable."

"We were scared."

"I was too. I didn't know Adam well, I still don't, but he seems like a great guy."

"He is," Preston says. "Have you lost anyone?"

"My grandma. But we weren't close."

"Death is strange. This specter hanging over everything we do. The knowledge we're mortal. Most of us don't engage until we lose someone. For me, it was my father. This strong man, as strong as an ox, then, all of a sudden, he was gone."

"I'm sorry."

"Thank you." His eyes get dreamy. "It's a strange thing, losing a parent. You're never ready, no matter how old you are. This part of you splinters. Every time you lose someone, you break in another place. Eventually, you start to understand the scenes in movies, where someone is ready to go. You understand they'd rather be with everyone they've lost and why they're holding on. How could I ever say goodbye to my son? For the last time? But I will, one day."

Fuck.

"I'm sorry. You're not here to listen to an old man discuss grief. You're here to celebrate your engagement."

"It's okay. I, uh…" I have no idea what to say. "I'm sorry."

"Thank you." He smiles warmly, but there's a sadness to it. "Does he talk about Sebastian?"

"Liam? No. After he came back to work… I started to see the signs of wear. It was strange, like I finally knew who he was."

"He was too tired to keep up his usual facade."

Maybe that's it.

"Grief is exhausting. Physical. I hate to say you'll see, but it's the price we pay for love. The loss on the other side."

Is he contemplating love because of his son's wedding? His own failed marriage?

The ghost of Bash's death?

Or something else?

I don't know.

"He is different now," Preston says. "Liam."

"He is."

"Have you heard of Kintsugi?"

"The *Death Cab for Cutie* album?"

"The Japanese art of filling cracks in pottery with gold."

That sounds familiar. "Maybe. Tell me anyway."

"Grief is similar. The loss cracks your heart. It's up to you to fill the space, grow stronger."

"What if you don't?"

"You find a way."

Or you fall apart.

Fuck, I'm not going there. Not now. Not when I'm doing so well.

"I hope you can help Liam do that," he says. "I know it's not your job to look after his mental well-being. It's a burden that falls on women too often."

"It does." I swallow a sip of cold tea. "But I'm not good at it. I can barely take care of myself."

"Maybe. But you are there for him. I can tell."

How?

"That's all you need to do. Be there when he needs you, tell him when you need him." He chuckles. "Listen to me. An old man telling young people about love. What do I know? I've been divorced for a decade."

"Failure is the best teacher."

His laugh is sad. "You're so young. You have your entire lives ahead of you. Hold on to that. Remember the beautiful things."

"Live, laugh, love?"

He looks at me, confused.

"It's a poster people put on their kitchen wall. My sister has one. I call it a 'mom quote.'"

"Is she a mother?"

"Not yet," I say. "She and her wife are looking for a donor. They want to know the guy. It's complicated."

"Just hope she doesn't ask Liam."

"She'd hate him."

He smiles. "A mom quote. I suppose it is. It's cliché, but it's true. It's easy to lose yourself in pursuit of money."

"You did all right."

"My father's company," he says. "I never loved the work, but I wanted to make him proud. Now, Harrison… he forged his own path. I'm proud of him."

"Are you going to tell me money won't make me happy?"

"I suspect you know that already."

I nod.

"But no one wants to hear a rich man say money isn't everything. It's like hearing a beautiful woman say looks don't matter."

He means me. My cheeks flush, even though it's not true. I'm cute, sure, but I'm not beautiful.

My hips are too wide. My chest is too small. My nose is too long.

I don't mind my unique features. I appreciate the hints of blue and green in my grey eyes. I appreciate the sharp angle of my chin. Hell, I even appreciate the way my ample ass fills out a pair of jeans.

I don't care I'm not a New York Ten.

But I'm aware of it.

"Not a fan of compliments?" he asks.

"Liam enjoys them enough for both of us."

He smiles. "You two are perfect for each other. You both hide behind your wit, but you have this sincerity to your eyes."

"My eyeliner isn't obscuring it?"

"The eyeliner gives you away."

"It does?"

He nods. "You want the world to know you don't want to belong."

"Is it the hair?"

"Isn't that part of it?"

"Not exactly."

"Liam hides his rebellion," he says.

"What do you mean?"

"The tattoos." He chuckles. "Does he think I don't know?"

"Probably."

"It's good for boys to have secrets. Especially from their fathers. I know I'm not his father, but…"

"He looks up to you," I say. "Your approval means a lot to him, even if he wouldn't admit it."

"You too."

The door on the next floor opens. Footsteps move down the stairs. "Briar, baby, I'm pretty sure Harrison wants you to give him a lap dance."

"Pass. No offense, Harrison," I say.

"Have you heard what he's offering?" Liam asks.

"You'd approve?" I ask.

"Maybe I'm into cuckolding."

"Since when?"

"Or maybe I'm green with envy and I need to show him you're mine." He rushes to me. Takes my hands. Pulls me into his arms.

His lips find mine.

His kiss is hard and deep, hungry for some part of me, something I don't usually give.

Fuck, he tastes good. Like Liam and mint. Did he brush his teeth upstairs? Did he get ready for this?

When he pulls back, I'm dizzy.

"Sorry, Preston, but we gotta go." He nods. "I gotta undo the damage you've wrecked."

Preston chuckles. "I'll see you Friday?"

"Fuck yeah." Liam slides his arm around my waist. "You ready, baby? Or you need something?"

"My purse." I grab it. "And the bathroom."

Preston gives directions.

Liam insists he'll call a car.

They whisper to each other as I walk down the hallway.

Is Preston offering Liam fatherly wisdom?

Or is it something else?

———

CRYSTAL KASWELL

Liam keeps up his playboy smile until we're in a car, heading back to his penthouse apartment.

He rests his head on the door, loosens his tie, closes his eyes. "Fuck, what time is it?"

"You're wearing a watch."

He brings his wrist to his eyeline. "That was only two hours?"

"Was it that exhausting?"

"Aren't you tired? Pretending you like me for two solid hours?"

"It took a lot."

He lets out a low yawn. Stretches his arms over his head. "You want to stop for coffee? Cold brew happy hour. Two bucks for twenty-four ounces."

"And you really need to save."

"Never too rich for a good deal."

"If you want. You know I—"

"Will drink cold brew but prefer iced tea."

"Yeah."

Liam shakes his head. "I'll get something at home."

"Are you okay?"

His eyes go to the window. "No."

"Something Harrison said?"

"This thing with Simon and Vanessa. It's going to be a headache."

"And you'll be stuck at the house."

"Exactly."

And he hates being there now. Not that he'll admit it. I want to ask him. I want to comfort him. I want this to feel less complicated. "We can spend the weekend in the pool."

He perks up. Just barely, but he does. "You're bringing a black bikini?"

"If I have one."

He pulls out his cell. Brandishes his text chain with Bree. "Your new pj's are already at the apartment."

"That was fast."

"Money talks." He taps a reply to her. "What's your bra size?"

"None of your business."

"She needs it," he says.

"She has it."

He shakes his head. Shows me the phone. It says it, right there.

Bree: Does Ms. West have her bra size handy? I can send a few options if she isn't sure.

"She sent me home with new bras," I say. "This is a plant."

"She's not at the store."

"You're bothering her at home?"

"You want the bikini or not?"

"I'm not telling you my bra size," I say.

"Fuck, Bri, I'm not asking to see your tits. What's it matter if I know your size? I'll give you a measurement in inches if it makes you feel better."

"I couldn't trust a self-report."

"You want to be the one to measure?"

"Yes, of course, I've been dreaming about the chance to hold a ruler next to your dick. It's my greatest sexual fantasy." I roll my eyes.

He smiles, charmed by my quip, desperate to reply with his own.

He's hiding his exhaustion well, but it's there. The heaviness in his shoulders. The frustration in his eyes.

Then he blinks and he almost fools me. I almost believe he's an obnoxious playboy who doesn't give a fuck about anything.

"I can do it now," he says. "Or wait until we're home."

I flip him off.

Again, he smiles.

Again, he doesn't quite sell it.

He's upset. He doesn't want to talk about it. He wants easy.

I guess that's fine. We're not really engaged. He's not really my life partner. He can keep secrets if he wants.

I don't like it. But maybe it's better. Maybe we need this line between real and pretend.

"It's hot today," he says. "You want to go for a swim?"

"Where?"

"I'll find a place. Somewhere private."

"How?"

"Event planner friend. She does corporate shit. There's always something free on weekends."

"Just the two of us?"

He nods *just the two of us*.

"Is this an elaborate scheme to get my bra size?"

"How'd you know?"

"Give her my number. I'll tell her."

"I can guess."

"You cannot. Cups are tied to band. So you can't just say I look like a c-cup. A 30c and a 36c are vastly different sizes."

"You're a c-cup."

"None of your business."

"I had a vision," he says. "When Harrison said he wanted a stripper with purple hair."

"He really said that?"

"He was fucking with me, trying to make me jealous."

"Did it?"

He doesn't answer the question. Describes his vision instead. "He's sitting on his bed. The lights are all red purple. You come through the door in this black bra and panty set. Some sheer mesh that makes him rock-hard in an instant."

"Where are you going with this?"

"Fuck, I'm supposed to go somewhere?"

"You told the story for a reason, I assume."

"Your tits. They were in my vision."

Honestly, his story is too absurd to annoy me. And maybe I want my boobs in his vision. Maybe I want him thinking about how badly he wants me.

He taps something into his phone. Shows it to me.

My bra size.

He's close. My sister's size.

"One cup up. One band down," I say.

"Damn. Was hoping you'd have to swim topless."

"Ha-ha."

"Where's the joke?" He smiles, effortless, charming, fraying at the edges.

"You sure you want to go swimming?"

"It's eighty and humid."

"Your place is air-conditioned."

"If you don't want to go, I'll drop you off."

"No, I want to go."

"Perfect. You're good with topless, right?"

I flip him off.

He smiles. I see it for a second. That aloof version of Liam I know well.

And the one who showed up at his office two weeks after his brother's death.

Tired and burdened.

But with what?

What is it he won't tell me?

Chapter Sixteen

LIAM

"Why did I doubt you?" Briar looks up from her spot on the lounge chair. She takes in my blue Speedo with a soft smile.

"'Cause there's no one here to see me."

"True."

"Can't even brag about my dick."

Her eyes flit to the area in question. "Are you really going swimming?"

"Yeah. And I'm going to pull you into the pool in that dress if you don't change."

"You are?"

"Why do you say that like it's a question?"

"You're different today."

"How's that?" I ask.

"Something happened. With Preston."

"Yeah."

"Are you going to tell me?"

"Are you going to put on your swimsuit?"

"You're working hard to see me in a bikini."

"What did you say about hard?"

She laughs in that *Liam, you're too much* way. That *Liam, I'm playing coy, hell yes* way.

Or maybe my dick is trying to push my brain out of the driver's seat. This is already a stupid idea. It's hard enough not touching her when we're in our clothes.

And I find an empty pool?

I should call Simon. Invite him here to cock-block me.

It's Sunday. Are Adam and Danielle still in the city? Fuck knows she'll enjoy a new place to take pictures.

But then she might want to take pictures of us. Pictures of us without our clothes on. It's what she does.

Fish gotta swim. Birds gotta fly. Danielle Bellamy has to take photos of naked people.

"You promise you'll tell me?" She pushes herself up, presses her knees together, smooths her dress. "Really?"

"Promise."

She looks to the bar inside. The bartender is still there.

The only witness. I don't know if I want to curse him for keeping her clothes on or thank him for keeping my pants on.

Well, swimsuit on. The pants are long gone.

But, hey, as long as my dick is covered—

That's something.

"Order me a drink," I say.

"I have to put my swimsuit on!"

"While you're in the changing room."

"It's early."

"It's the weekend."

"Okay, but I pick the drink."

"No fucking way. You'll order straight gin."

"It's not bad."

It's worse. It tastes like her lips. "Appletini."

She shakes her head.

"Something in a martini glass."

"I could order a dirty martini. With gin."

That's a good point. "Appletini."

"I'll pick something you like."

"No gin."

"Yes gin." She stands. Shakes her head *ridiculous Liam*. Moves inside.

This is a nice place. I have to give it to my friend. Thankfully, I never fucked her or this could be even more awkward.

Gel plans business events all over the city. She knows every private party venue and whether or not it's rented. This was one of three private pools.

The best, she said.

The same one I dragged Briar into last summer. Well, she jumped. I dared her, but she made the choice to jump.

I can still see her soaking wet, her sheer blouse sticking to her skin, her chest heaving with her inhale.

That's where we should be. In this pool. Out of our clothes. Her soft body pressed against mine.

My hand between her legs.

Her groan in my ear.

That makes sense.

I need something that makes sense.

I need to get the fuck out of here. Before I do something exceptionally stupid.

Too late.

Briar steps through the sheer curtain dividing the pool and the bar. She's in a black bikini and she's holding two martini glasses.

They're red-purple. An alcoholic version of her hair and lipstick.

"Berry martini." She takes a step toward me.

My eyes go right to her tits. Fuck, she looks divine in that swimsuit.

Long, curvy legs. Lush hips. Narrow waist.

Her tits aren't huge, sure, but they're the perfect size for my hands.

And those thick thighs—

I want to dive between them.

I want to die between them.

Is there a better way to go?

"Liam?" She laughs, reveling in her upper hand.

My eyes stay on her hips. "You have a tattoo there."

"And?"

"I didn't know that."

"You don't know everything." She motions to something, but my eyes refuse to follow. "Three seconds and I'm dropping it."

Right. My fingers brush hers as I take the drink. It's a tiny touch. I kissed her an hour ago. The brush of our fingers shouldn't mean anything, but it does.

It's electric.

She ordered these on purpose.

Maybe to celebrate. Maybe to fuck with me. Maybe to comfort me.

I don't know.

I liked them in Toronto.

I like them now.

"There's a lot I'd like to know about your body." I bring the drink to my lips. Sweet, tart, the hint of alcohol. The taste of her lips. "We can start with the tattoos."

"Maybe we should start with yours." Her eyes flit to my chest. "Does that really say danger is sweet?"

"In Latin."

"Isn't that obvious?"

"Coming from the woman with *she flies by her own wings* on her ribs."

"In Latin," she returns.

"Latin didn't save mine."

Her cheeks flush. "You don't like it?"

"Did I say I didn't like it?"

"I don't care if you like it."

"Then why'd you ask?"

She takes a sip. Motions to the pool. "Are you going in?"

"After you." I offer to hold her drink.

She gives it to me. "You won't say anything about my smudged makeup."

"Isn't it waterproof?"

"If it smudges."

"Can I say it looks hot?"

"Can I stop you?"

I shake my head.

She smiles.

For a second, it feels normal. Like it did last year. The first time I felt normal after Bash died.

Or at least, I thought I did.

Now—

I try not to think about it. He's gone. I can't bring him back. I don't want to be like Adam, locking himself in his castle, lost to grief.

He almost died.

He needed time to heal.

And he was closer to Bash. Closer than anyone.

But it wasn't fair. Adam took all the space. I didn't have any. Simon didn't have any.

It wasn't fair to Bash either. He wouldn't have wanted Adam miserable.

He'd want me here, coaxing Briar out of her bikini, demanding she come on my face.

He'd want the details later.

He'd want to prove he could one-up me. Be even more

ridiculous.

He couldn't, but he tried.

We had some sort of younger brother agreement. I tortured Simon. He tortured Adam.

Only it didn't work that way. Adam loved mentoring Bash, even when Bash drove him crazy.

Simon can't stand me. Yeah, he loves me. We *are* brothers. But he can't stand me, especially when I drive him crazy.

And now it's Simon and Adam against me. The serious older brothers against the ridiculous younger brothers.

But I don't have backup. Only this feeling everyone is keeping secrets.

And now I've lost my fucking high horse too.

How am I going to give Simon and Adam shit for whispering about Bash's death when I'm lying about Preston's?

He's not in the ground yet.

Fuck.

"Are you sure you're okay?" Briar's voice is soft. "No. I know you aren't. I know something happened." She takes another step toward me. Until she's close enough to touch. "But if you want to talk about it…"

"I want to see you dripping wet."

She raises a brow, daring me to expand.

I don't have it in me. I'm too fucking tired. If she kisses me, I'm kissing back. I'm not doing the smart thing and stopping her.

I'm not stopping until I'm completely spent.

"You'll tell me what Preston said?" she asks.

"I promised." I take another sip of my martini. It's enough to make my head spin.

Briar gives me a long once-over, then she turns and dives into the pool.

She does it with grace. The practice of a girl who grew up with Southern California summers.

She was on the swim team when she was a kid. She quit in high school. She didn't want to get up early.

I played water polo and swam competitively until I hit college.

I finish my drink, set hers on the edge of the pool, dive in after her.

Cool water surrounds me. That familiar feeling. Safe and dangerous. Warm and cold. Enclosed and free.

I surface. Take a deep breath.

"You're still pretty good." She swims to the edge. Looks to my empty glass.

"You too."

"I know." She turns to me. "What happened?"

"Preston."

She motions *go on*.

"He really likes you, that's all."

"And that upsets you?"

Fuck, how can I explain it without betraying his secret? "He said he hopes we get married soon. So he can walk us down the aisle."

"Why soon?"

Shit. I'm too tired. I'm not bringing my A game. "'Cause he's moving to London. Remember?"

She doesn't buy it.

"'Cause Simon is gonna kill me this weekend, when he has to watch his high school crush make out with her date. So, we better get to the courthouse by Friday."

"He won't."

"You sure about that?"

"He might kill you, but it won't be for that."

"No?"

"No." She moves closer. "He plays fair."

"You sure about that?"

"He'll only kill you if you've earned it."

"I've definitely earned it."

"Twenty-seven years of torturing him? Yeah. You're screwed." She moves closer. Close enough, her fingers brush my chest. "Would you let him walk you down the aisle?"

"Are you proposing?"

"Hypothetically."

"Who else will do it?"

"Trish." She mentions our housekeeper.

"Both of them maybe." Trish was like a mom to me.

"I always thought… well, I never thought you'd get married, but if you did, I figured Simon would be the one."

"Simon would walk me down the aisle?"

"He is your older brother."

"Thank fuck I'm not getting married."

"Ever?"

"You know me."

"You appreciate your freedom, yeah." She smiles. "But then Preston was right too. You do things a hundred percent. One day, you'll meet someone, fall in love, marry her the next day."

"Maybe."

"How do you think it will go?"

"My wedding?" I ask.

"Yeah."

"It won't," I say. "I'd have to meet someone like you."

"With purple hair and a cliché tattoo?"

"The hair, I'm negotiable, but the cliché tattoo, absolutely."

"You two could get *love conquers all* together." She smiles softly. "Right here." She draws a line just above her bikini bottoms.

"Perfect."

"Then…"

"Someone who gets me."

"I get you?" she asks.

"You don't ask me to be someone else."

"Isn't that love?"

"Are you really asking me?"

"It's not like I know."

"Better than me."

Her eyes fix on mine. All that curiosity and need. She wants to know me. Every part of me.

It's terrifying.

And exhilarating.

I have to be careful. I can't give this away. "I thought you loved John."

"I did. But not the way I wanted to love my husband," she says. "Not enough to spend my life with him or give up my freedom for him."

"It's not just about getting laid."

"I didn't say it was."

Right. I'm defensive. Tired. Stupid.

She smells so fucking good. Like chlorine and Briar.

I bet she tastes like it too.

I bet she tastes divine.

"Is that why you're upset? Because you don't want to get married?" she asks.

It's a good excuse, but I can't sell it. "No."

"Then what was it he said?" She rests her back against the wall. Looks to the clear blue sky. "Was it about Bash?"

"What?" Why the fuck is she talking about Bash?

"He was asking me. Or maybe I was asking him. About

how you handled it. About losing people. I guess he's in a contemplative mood, seeing his son get married."

That's a part of it, sure, but it's not enough.

I have to talk to him. Tell him to keep his mouth shut if he wants to keep his secret close.

"You never talk about him," she says. "Your brother."

"What's there to say?"

"I don't know. I haven't lost anyone. Not like that." Under the water, her hand finds mine. "Do you remember the last time we were here?"

Of course. "Remind me."

"It was August, I think. July maybe. Hotter than this. You were in a three-piece suit. I was in this cheap polyester blouse. It was thin, but it trapped all the heat."

"That sheer black one?"

"You remember?"

"I could see your bra."

"I was wearing a camisole under it."

"All right, I could see your camisole."

She smiles. "You dared me to jump into the pool. Then you took off your watch and your shoes, took your cell phone out of your slacks, and you did it. You dove into the pool in a, what, five-thousand-dollar suit?"

"Probably."

"The water felt so good. Even better than it did today. And the space was ours. All ours." She turns to me. "Only it was dark. And there were string lights everywhere. Like something in a movie."

"I remember."

Her eyes meet mine. "You laughed. And there was something about it. This warmth. This depth. I realized it was the first time you'd really laughed since Bash died."

"I laugh all the time."

She nods. "But not like this, with this… abandon. I

realized I knew you. I knew when you had your mask on. And when you let your guard down. Seeing you with it down..." Her eyes flit to my lips. "I'd never felt that special."

"Being the only person who sees through my bullshit?"

She doesn't take the bait. She stays close. Sincere. "Yeah." She brushes my wet hair from my forehead. "After that, I saw that guy more and more. Glimpses of him. Moments. Then minutes. Hours even. I feel the same thing every time. This need to get to the bottom of the mystery. Who is Liam Pierce? I want to know." Her fingers skim my chin. "Do you want to tell me?"

Chapter Seventeen

LIAM

Do *you want to tell me?*

It's a fair question.

But it's so much more than that.

It's an invitation to offer everything I have.

A promise. A kiss. A touch. A fuck.

She wants me to kiss her.

I want to kiss her.

I want to sit here on the concrete, roll her bikini bottoms to her ankles, lick her until she's groaning my name.

But that can't happen.

I need to stop before I ruin everything.

"There's nothing to know." I push off the pool floor. Move toward the other edge. "Liam Pierce exists in the shallow end."

"You literally just went into the deep end."

"I'm bad at metaphors."

She notices the change in posture. The refusal. The denial.

Her eyes turn down.

Her lips curl into a frown.

She still wants to kiss me.

I still want to kiss her.

But we can't. And she knows.

Or maybe I'm imagining shit. Maybe I can't handle the idea of her not wanting to fuck me, so I have this complicated explanation.

My ego isn't easily bruised. Not by rejection. Whatever the situation, there's some other opportunity.

Another woman at the bar.

Another investor searching for a company.

Another programmer in need of a job.

But that isn't the case here.

There's no other Briar. Only one.

She dives under the water. Surfaces without a care. Or pretending.

I can't fucking tell anymore.

She speaks in her normal tone. As if we aren't half-naked and ready to fuck each other. As if we're not part of this elaborate ruse. "Preston was talking about Kintsugi. Have you heard of it?"

"Sounds Japanese."

"Yeah. The Japanese art of repairing pottery with gold." She follows me into the deep end. "He made it sound beautiful. To break and put yourself together. To become better because of what you've been through. He was talking about you. After Bash. And how I must have helped. He didn't know we're not really…"

"Yeah."

"But that sounded beautiful, too. Helping someone you love repair themselves. Or maybe finding the strength you need to repair yourself in their love. I don't know. I think that's love. Trusting someone to see your cracks. Trusting them with your broken pieces."

It's beautiful on her lips.

"I never had that. I never trusted John with my broken pieces. I never wanted him to see the cracks." She pushes her hair from her eyes. "I did love him. And he loved me. But we… we were wading, not diving into the ocean."

"And that's why you ended things?"

"Because I didn't want to follow him deeper. Or maybe I didn't want to lead him deeper."

"Because of him?"

"Because of both of us. I didn't trust him to see me. I wasn't ready to show him. I thought it was about freedom. Maybe that was part of it. But I was scared too."

"Takes guts to admit that."

"Maybe." Her eyes meet mine. "It would be gutsier to dive in headfirst. But it's not easy for everyone."

"You think I'm different?"

"I don't know. You do things full force."

"I don't love anyone."

"Never? Even when you were a kid?"

"You've asked before."

"You've been full of shit before."

And I answered with my default no, but I was telling her the truth. "I've had feelings, yeah, but never love. Now, Bash… he fell headfirst. A ton of times. The woman he was seeing when he died… I don't know what happened to her, if she ever got the news. I guess she must have. Fuck, maybe she was at the funeral, I don't know."

"What was it like?"

"What was my brother's funeral like?"

"It's a legitimate question."

"Why are you asking it?"

She moves closer. "Because I want to know."

Are these really my only two options? Sex and death.

They're everywhere lately.

I'm not sure which will destroy me faster, fucking Briar or focusing on Preston's imminent demise.

"It's okay if you don't want to talk about it," she says. "I'm sure it's hard. I don't really know. But I… the way Preston talked about it, about how I could be there for you after your brother… it really felt like love. Like what I would want, if I had someone."

If she had me. If I was her someone.

"I know we're not really together, but we're friends."

"I'm your boss."

"Not for long. And you're my friend too."

"Horrifying for you."

She notices my attempt at distraction. Ignores it. "You too. Being friends with me."

"No, gives me credibility with women, to have such a badass punk rock boss as my friend."

"Uh-uh."

"Yeah-huh."

"Won't they think I'm your ex-fiancée?"

"Guess it's complicated now."

She nods.

"But maybe for good. They'll think I'm still in love with you. Know better than to get attached."

"Or fall faster because you're emotionally unavailable."

"Why does that happen?"

"I don't know. Self-sabotage? Daddy issues?"

"I have plenty of those."

She laughs. "Me too."

"Do I need to keep an eye out? For emotionally unavailable guys who might win your heart?"

"Only if they're especially handsome."

"That's it? Handsome?"

"Funny."

"Handsome and funny?" I ask.

"And they don't take themselves too seriously."

"No software douche nozzles who want to invent a new cryptocurrency?"

"Absolutely not," she says.

"And we're not getting more specific with handsome?"

"Handsome is handsome." Her eyes pass over me slowly. Stop at the tattoo on my ribs. "I do like some tattoos."

"Oh?"

"Shows commitment."

"I have them."

"Even so."

"Be honest. It's the pain tolerance."

"You got me." She laughs. "I need a man with a high pain tolerance."

"I knew it," I say.

She laughs the way she always does—like she loves that I'm an idiot—but there's something else there. Something deeper.

That offer filling the air.

I want to fuck her.

I want more. Everything.

"Was there something else?" she asks. "About Bash?"

"Yeah. The way he loved… You know how my dick gets me into trouble?"

"Does it?"

I motion *kinda*. "When I was younger."

"You have a story?"

"That's classified shit."

"Since when?"

Since I started caring what she thinks about me. "There was a friend with a hot sister. That was probably the biggest mistake."

"What happened?"

"It was before I knew how to make things clear. I broke her heart. I didn't mean to, but…"

"She fell for the emotionally unavailable bad boy?"

"Are you stereotyping me?"

She nods.

"What does that make you?"

"The punk rock poor girl who thinks she's too good for rich assholes."

"Your parents have money."

"Not Pierce money."

"Enough."

"You wear a suit and have surprising depth."

"Isn't that the fantasy? The guy who's mean to you because he's so broken inside?"

She laughs. "Where did you learn that?"

"Opal."

"She knows better than to fall for that?"

"We watched *Gilmore Girls* together."

"You did not."

"The first few seasons."

She smiles. "You're fucking with me."

"Scout's honor."

"You weren't a scout."

"And you want to be the one to tie me up, huh?"

Her cheeks flush. "If it would get you out of my hair, maybe, but I've never had that fantasy."

"Never?"

"Have you?" she asks.

"Tried it?"

She nods.

"Of course."

"Really? With who?"

"A woman."

"And…"

"And what?"

"Did you like it?"

My brain tries to sound the *shut the fuck up* alarm, but it's running out of blood. "I liked how much she liked it."

"Only one woman?"

I nod.

"Why only one?"

"She got weird after."

"Weird how?"

"Started asking me to call her mommy."

"No, she didn't."

"I swear to god."

Briar laughs so hard she has to swim to the edge of the pool. "Oh my god, when she was naked or…"

"Except for her heels."

"Oh my god." She slaps the concrete. "Did you?"

"Of course."

Her laugh deepens. "And?"

"Instant deflate."

"No."

"Yeah."

"Were you embarrassed?"

"To lose a hard-on?"

"Yeah." Her eyes flit to my crotch, but she can't see anything with the water in the way. "Some guys get weird."

"It was already pretty fucking weird."

"But you didn't…"

"I was relieved I didn't get off on mom role play."

"That was it? No… disappointment?"

"Maybe."

"Liam Pierce gets insecure?"

"Not the way you mean."

"How do I mean?" she asks.

"It wasn't that I failed to rise to the occasion."

"No?"

"No. Not a problem unless I've had too many."

"How many?"

"Enough I'm slurring my words."

She nods, making a mental note.

"But it did hit my self-image. I thought I was down for anything. And here was this woman with a pretty mild kink, in the world of freaky, and I couldn't do it."

"No shame in having limits."

"I guess not."

"Has there been anything else? Anything you couldn't do?"

"Hardcore shit."

She raises a brow.

"One woman wanted me to wear a ski mask, take her at knife point."

"Did you try it?"

"I put on the ski mask."

"Really?"

"Yeah. But I wasn't feeling it."

She smiles. "You're pretty vanilla."

"Oh? You taking guys at knife point?"

"Is there any other way to have sex?"

My smile widens. "That's the real reason you dumped Johnny boy? Too vanilla."

"He was game for the knife. But when I wanted to get a gun…"

"Can you imagine?"

"I really can't." She laughs. "I've never even touched a gun."

"What about those?"

"Huh?"

I motion to her biceps. "Those are pretty serious guns."

174

"Well, of course I have these, yeah." She laughs. Looks to my arms. "And those too."

"You haven't touched them."

"I have."

"I'd remember."

She holds my gaze for a moment. Fights a blush. "I always imagined you as being game for anything."

"Me too."

"John was… well, we never broke out the ski masks, but he would shut down anything out of the ordinary."

"How out of the ordinary?"

"That's uh… that's not information I'm going to share at this time."

"Other guys?"

"Huh?"

"You do anything weird with other guys?"

"Nothing too weird."

"What's too weird?" I ask.

"Well… There was a guy who wanted me to call him daddy."

"You lecture him about fidelity?"

Her eyes go to the water. "I never told you that."

"You did, just not in those words."

She pushes herself out of the pool. "He's always screwing around on my mom. A new woman every few months. Just because… I don't know. I don't think he loves the other women. I think he just wants a new place to put his dick."

"He's an asshole."

"Yeah, but she stays. I don't want to be like that. I don't want to be stupid."

"Is she happy?"

"How could she be?"

It's a good question. One I can't answer. I only know I want to comfort her. Wipe the frustration from her eyes.

It's not like me.

It's out of the question.

"Is that why you don't do relationships anymore?" I ask.

She nods. "Probably why I never trusted John."

"Or maybe he wasn't the guy."

"Maybe."

"Bash… fuck, I wish you knew him better. When he was in love, the whole world knew. He was effervescent."

Her eyes meet mine.

"You're not open that way."

"You either."

"I like that about you." Fuck, what am I saying? I'm too stuck on *I like you*. I like her.

It's not just a desire to fuck her.

It's not just a need to make sense of something.

It's more.

"Do you remember that party before the accident? He popped a bottle of champagne. Went around telling everyone he was celebrating new love."

"I do." Her voice is quiet. "He was vibrant."

"He was proud he loved someone. Proud of her. Proud of himself. Proud of the concept of love. He couldn't keep it to himself."

"Why would he?"

"She was married."

"Oh."

"Yeah." I meet her at the edge of the pool. "He didn't care that she was married. Not really. Not the way you would."

"Is my stare that judgmental?"

"You're hiding it well."

She swallows hard.

"He said she was miserable. Hated her husband. Maybe it was true. Maybe it was bullshit. I don't know. But I knew Bash, and he loved her with his whole heart. He needed to share it. He couldn't stop himself."

"Beautiful adultery. Sorry. I shouldn't—"

"It was fucked up. His death doesn't change that."

"But he—"

"You don't have to approve. I didn't."

"Really?"

"Yeah. He went on about how her husband was an asshole and she deserved better and she was going to leave him. I told him that's what people say, but he didn't listen. He believed her. He didn't care what happened next week or next month. He loved her and he wanted whatever he could have, even if it was an affair, even if it was stolen moments and afternoons in hotel rooms."

"It sounds romantic, that way."

"I don't expect you to excuse him."

She watches her feet as she kicks the water. "He was so in love. You're right. I saw it on him. I just… you didn't make excuses for him? With her husband?"

"I don't even know her name."

She nods. "I'm sorry. Really, Liam. I'm sorry you lost him."

"Sorry you lost the chance to tell him off?"

"No… maybe." She forces a smile. "It would have been normal in its own way."

It would. "I miss fighting with him."

"You do?"

"Yeah. I miss everything." I need to get the fuck out of here. Or think about something else.

"I really killed the mood, huh?"

"The mood's been dead."

177

She smiles. "You hide it well."

"I do my best."

She motions to the bar. "You want to go?"

"We have another hour here."

She studies me for a long time. "I think you do love."

"I do?"

"Your brothers. It's not the same, I know, but you're close. Closer than I am with my sister."

"Adam and Simon don't tell me shit."

"Maybe. But they love you. And they trust you. And they give you attitude because they worry."

"They don't trust me. They're always whispering shit." Shit about Bash, but I can't go back to that subject. I'm about to burst already. "They keep secrets."

"Have you asked for answers?"

"No." I take a deep breath. "I don't know if I want them. Sometimes, the truth fucking hurts and I… I've had enough truth for a while."

"Sometimes, you need to hurt."

"I knew you were into that."

Again, she notices me shifting the subject. Notices me jumping to sex.

This time, she stays there, in this awkward transition.

Not jumping with me.

Not calling me on my bullshit.

Just here.

It fills the air.

I can't deal with my shit.

I can't talk about death.

I can't talk about sex.

Even the berry martinis are loaded.

She doesn't break the silence with words. Instead, she dives into the pool.

She looks good under water. Too good.

The sight is too familiar. Takes me back to swim meets —the rare co-ed ones—and summers at the house.

Talking women into diving into our pool.

Skinny dipping late at night.

Fucking in the solarium.

Most swims didn't end that way. But some did.

I enjoy sex. Especially good sex. But I'm not the player people think I am. When I invite a woman to the pool, I want to swim, laugh, have fun.

If that involves making her come, all the better.

If not, that's fine.

But now, with Briar here, in that tiny black bikini—

It's all I see. The two of us at the house, sneaking out late, stripping out of our party attire to jump into the pool naked.

Dripping wet, out of breath, pressed against each other.

That makes sense.

It's the only fucking thing that makes sense.

A life raft in the middle of the ocean.

And, somehow, I have to keep myself from grabbing it.

Chapter Eighteen

BRIAR

W e stay the entire hour.

I change in the dressing room. Wipe my smudged eye makeup. Apply another coat of lipstick.

There. I don't look great, but I look presentable.

Even with my hair more silver than purple. Chlorine fades the color like it's going out of style.

I can touch it up tonight.

Only I'm not going back to my apartment. I'm going to Liam's place and I don't have my hair dye handy.

Or maybe that's another thing he anticipated. Maybe I can text Bree and ask her to send something over.

What would Liam do? Send me, probably.

I wouldn't mind the task, really. I'd enjoy the time out of the office. The excuse to browse a local shop. Is there anything punk rock left at Saint Mark's? Or should I go straight to Ulta?

Fashion colors aren't as big as they were a few years ago, but they aren't the rarity they were when I first tried to dye my hair pink in middle school.

I'd watched *Eternal Sunshine of the Spotless Mind* so many times I couldn't get the idea out of my head.

I loved the movie before I understood what it meant. Before I understood the idea of loving someone so much it hurt. Of wanting to erase that memory, but knowing, deep down, I'd lose some part of myself.

But then I don't think of John.

I think of erasing every happy memory with my dad.

The day he pulled us out of school and took us to Six Flags. The birthday we made carrot cake from scratch. The summer trip to the city, where we stood in the middle of Times Square and soaked in the wonder.

It's almost embarrassing to think about now. How could I, a certified New Yorker, stare at the most cliché site in the city with stars in my eyes?

Worse, I still love the flashy billboards and throngs of tourists.

I tell myself it's ironic. The symbols of capitalism and all its ills. A knowledge of its place in society.

That's true, but there's more too.

The little girl, in awe of the Coke billboard, asking Dad for a piggy-back ride, begging for real New York pizza.

At that moment, I knew I wanted to move to the city. I knew I wanted to be three thousand miles from home.

Did I know, somewhere deep down, that Dad wasn't a great guy?

That he was part of the reason Mom locked herself in the bedroom all weekend?

It wasn't just him. It was more too. The brain chemistry she passed on to me and my sister.

But if he was there, if he was what she needed—

It would have been easier for her. Wouldn't it?

I've always hated the women who took up with him. I

tried to keep the blame on him. He's the one who broke his vows.

But he's my dad too. For all the fucked-up shit, he's still the guy who taught me to swim and fixed my favorite dinner every Friday and took me to the movies every weekend.

He kept me busy, kept me from spinning out of control, when Mom pulled away.

Bash was the other man.

He wasn't perfect. I didn't know him well enough to judge him, but I knew he was a guy who made mistakes.

He just…

He was always such a romantic.

How could he toss aside her vows?

Maybe it was different. Maybe her husband was an asshole who mistreated her.

Maybe he cheated first.

She was still married.

How could he?

What can I say now?

He's gone.

Liam didn't excuse him.

Besides, we're not a real couple. It's none of my business, no matter how much it nags at me.

I comb my fingers through my hair until it's presentable. Then I take the elevator to the lobby.

Liam is there, at the hotel bar, talking to another man in a suit.

They're talking like work friends, but ones with a long history.

The other man is familiar, but I can't quite place him. He's not a typical New York rich dude.

He's tall and Black and nearly as laid-back as Liam.

Well, as laid-back as Liam pretends to be.

Despite the scorching temperature outside, they're both wearing suits. Liam is in the same one he was wearing this morning. The other guy is wearing a fuchsia tie.

It's familiar.

I've seen him somewhere. Seen his tie somewhere. Noticed how well it complements Liam's appletini.

Even noticed the way the guy's lime garnish complements Liam's appletini.

Liam turns to me. All at once, his picture-perfect smile fades into some mix of frustration and exhaustion.

Tired of me?

Or tired and able to let his guard down with me?

I'm not sure. The last two days have been strange. Extremely strange.

"You coming over here?" Liam calls. "I'm trying to explain to my friend that I like you for your wit, but he's not buying it."

"It sounds like bollocks." The man speaks with a British accent.

He's not an investor.

He's a competitor.

But what the fuck is his name?

"Do I need to take you home?" Liam says to me. "Put you to bed?"

The guy chuckles in that *ah, of course, Liam is ridiculous* way.

Liam motions *come here* again.

Right. I'm his fiancée. I'm wearing the ring. I'm playing the loving paramour.

Random friend at hotel lobby isn't a specific part of the deal, but this will go faster if I say hello and head home.

I nod a *hey* and meet the men at the bar.

Liam slips out of his chair. Pulls me into a kiss.

He tastes like chlorine and apple liqueur. It shouldn't be an intoxicating combination, but it is.

"Briar, you know Ian?" He introduces me to his friend.

"I don't think so." I offer my hand. "Briar West."

"Ian Hunt." He shakes.

Hunt. He's on the board of another company. Him and his brothers. Or one brother maybe. It's all fuzzy right now.

He's British. The company is big in the UK and the rest of Europe. They aren't direct competitors, exactly. You could even argue we make each other better—they find information whereas we hide it—but you could also argue our goals are in direct opposition.

No ring. He's not married.

He's older than Liam, but I can't tell by how much. And he's handsome too. Dark skin, dark eyes, charming smile.

Almost as charming as Liam's.

"Have you really not met?" Liam asks.

"I'd remember," I say.

The guy, Ian, I guess, nods. "I'd remember meeting you, Briar."

"Hey, turn down the charm. Don't you see the ring?" Liam makes a show of objecting.

Ian looks to my left hand. Notes the engagement ring. "Is that why we've never met? You couldn't introduce your fiancée to someone more handsome than you are?"

"What did I say about the charm?" Liam chuckles. "Do you have a level below ten?"

"Absolutely not," he says.

"He's got a girlfriend. Don't get ideas, baby." Liam wraps his arm around me. Is he actually jealous? Or does he just want to touch me?

That's his third drink in two hours.

Or maybe four. I haven't been counting. I have no idea if he was drinking with Harrison.

"You're his type though." Liam brushes a hair behind my ear. "His girlfriend has teal hair and tattoos."

"Those are her defining traits, yes." Ian chuckles.

"He's an idiot," I say. "He can't help it."

"She's smart too." Liam turns to me. "Not as smart as you, obviously, since you're with me."

"That was one of my dumber moves, actually," I say.

Liam smiles. "See? What did I tell you? Witty."

"I should get him home," I say.

"It's not your job to babysit him," Ian says. "Let him get himself home."

"It is, tragically. Or it was. I was Liam's assistant," I say.

"My condolences."

"We're partners now." I explain my start-up in as few words as possible. "Liam. Let's go."

"Are we going to bed?" he asks.

"It's early," I say.

"Not that kind of bed," he says.

"We're not doing it here."

"This is a hotel. We could do it here," Liam says.

I don't have the patience for drunk Liam. "I'm leaving. You can stay here with Ian. Or come with me."

"If I'm gonna come, it's going to be with you." Liam nods goodbye to his friend. Reaches for his wallet.

Ian stops him. "You can get drinks next time."

Liam doesn't engage in the usual *no, I'm paying* pissing contest rich guys love. "Bring your girlfriend next time. She and Bri can talk circles around us."

"She'd like that." He nods goodbye to me. "It was nice to meet you, Briar. Good luck. Liam isn't easy to handle."

"There is a lot to handle, yeah." Liam winks.

So much for not engaging in a dick measuring contest.

Thankfully, his friend doesn't bite. He just shakes his head and says goodbye again.

I keep up the smile until I'm in the revolving door.

All at once, the cool of the hotel air-conditioning disappears. Warm air hits me. The noise of the city. The heaviness in my shoulders.

Something is wrong.

Something Liam won't tell me.

Why won't he tell me?

Why am I so desperate to know?

Chapter Nineteen

BRIAR

"I don't need sleep." Liam steps out of his shoes. Shrugs his suit jacket off his shoulders. "I need another drink."

I go to the sink. Fill a glass with water. "I'm your friend. And I'll help you, because I'm your friend. But I'm not going to monitor your drinking or your self-care or your feelings."

He stares at the glass like it did him wrong. "I'm not drunk."

Probably. I've seen Liam drunk. Slurred words, struggling to stand drunk. This is only tipsy for him, but it's enough he's annoying me. "Then why are you saying stupid shit?"

"'Cause I'm Liam Pierce. It's what I do."

"I'm not going to give you shit, because I know you're going through something."

He stares back at me.

"With Preston. And the wedding. And maybe Bash too. I don't know. I'm here, if you want to talk, but I'm not going to be your babysitter."

"I don't need a babysitter."

"Then we're in agreement. I'm going to my apartment to pick up a few things. I'll be back later." Or maybe tomorrow. I don't know. I can't decide if I want to slap him or kiss him.

He's so fucking frustrating.

"Drink your water. Go to bed early. Show up at work tomorrow, rested and ready to hit the week."

"Did you swallow a corporate training book?"

"Would you rather I say 'get your shit together'?"

"Yeah."

"Then get your shit together, Liam. You can talk to me if you want. I'm here." I want to be there. Way too much. "But if you don't talk to me, I don't know how to help you."

"Bri—"

"Whatever it is, it's not getting easier. We have a busy week. A meeting with Simon. Then the party. The wedding. So get your shit together. Okay?"

"You want to talk to me?"

"Not right now."

"You're mad at me?"

"I'm too tired to be mad."

"So if you weren't tired—"

I don't know. I'm confused. Overwhelmed. "It's been a long weekend. I need to touch up my hair and have some time to myself. We'll talk tomorrow."

He nods. "I didn't mean shit with my friend. Just being the guy he expects."

"I know."

"Do you?"

Maybe.

"I wouldn't do that, you know."

"Huh?"

"What Bash did. I wouldn't fuck around."

"Really? All the women you've been with. None of them have been married?"

"I wouldn't fuck around on you."

"We're not really together."

"If we were."

"You don't do relationships."

"You either." He takes a step toward me. Then another. Another. "I wouldn't, Bri. I never have." He wraps his arms around me. "I'll swear on anything." His eyes meet mine. "I'd never hurt you. It would destroy me. And, fuck, Bri… I'm this close to falling apart as it is."

What the fuck am I supposed to say to that?

"I care about you." He moves closer. Close enough to kiss me, touch me, fuck me. "I do. Whatever you believe, believe that."

"I know."

"You sure?"

"I'm sure." And I'm sure I need to go, now, before one of us does something we can't take back. "Good night, Liam."

"It's three o'clock."

"I'll see you in the morning."

———

My apartment is close, but it's not close enough to save me from melting. It's way too fucking hot. It's only May and it's already way too hot.

My weather app claims gloom and rain in the forecast. It's hard to believe the sky will turn grey and cool, but after years in New York, I'm used to the unpredictable spring weather.

I down a glass of ice water to cool off, then I fix a London Fog and change into an old t-shirt and boxers.

John's boxers.

They're clean and comfortable. What does it matter they belonged to John?

I shouldn't care.

I shouldn't hear the possessive edge to Liam's voice.

Does he really have a possessive side? Is it really directed at me?

I shouldn't like it, but I do.

Whatever. They're just clothes. I have others.

I find something all mine—a black tank top and shorts —then I apply purple die to my hair, stream *The Americans*, and sip tea as I wait.

After half an episode, my thoughts turn to Liam. The hurt in his eyes. The heat of his body. The taste of his lips.

I strip in the bathroom. Run the water. Rinse my hair. Soap, shampoo, condition.

The shower is still a happy place for me. A place that's mine. Where I don't have to smile or tell Mom it's okay or keep up appearances.

I close my eyes. Soak in the warm water and the smell of citrus.

Then my thoughts return to Liam.

The tattoo above his hips. The strong thighs. The desire in his stare.

I let myself drift back to the pool. The feel of his body in the water. The things we could have done.

My bikini top on the ground.

My bottoms around my ankles.

Liam's hand between my legs. His lips on my neck. His voice in my ears.

I come fast, but it does nothing to sate my craving.

Even as I dress, work, dine on takeout Indian food, I think of Liam.

Hurt and lost and unwilling to share his feelings with me.

Liam Pierce is not my boyfriend.

He's not my real fiancé.

He's not the kind of guy I can trust with my heart.

I need to remember that.

Chapter Twenty

LIAM

Why is it so fucking bright?

I swallow another sip of water. Close my eyes. Will my head to stop pounding.

No good.

The attention only aggravates my headache.

This annoying throb chanting *don't be an idiot, Liam.*

You fucked up, Liam.

Don't fuck it up worse, Liam.

At least I didn't kiss her. Not when we were alone, anyway.

And, bam, the second the idea returns to my brain, it takes over.

For a moment, it's all I see.

Briar's purple hair in my hands.

Her red lips on mine.

Her soft body pressed against me.

Her groan filling the space.

"Mr. Pierce." A knock on the door interrupts. That's her voice. But what the fuck is she doing calling me Mr. Pierce?

Bri hasn't called me Mr. Pierce in months.

Either I somehow transported to the land of politically incorrect sexual fantasies—aren't they all—or I fucked up worse than I thought.

"You can see he's not in great shape," she says.

"I can," a deep voice replies.

One I know well. Difficult to read with that light hint of judgment.

My oldest brother.

I force my eyes open.

And there she is, Briar standing at the door to my office, in a hot as fuck outfit. A pencil skirt and a button up blouse.

She's wearing her usual lipstick. Her hair is in that neat line.

But she's wearing pumps instead of boots.

Did Bree buy those for her? Or are they something Bri actually owns?

A pencil skirt and pumps.

What the fuck is happening?

"Do we have a meeting today?" I ask.

No one answers.

"Briar. Do we have a meeting today?" I ask.

"We have a meeting every Monday, sir." Intention drips into her voice. Somehow she packs *I'm calling you sir because you fucked shit up and I'm pissed* into the word.

Or I'm imagining shit.

Briar calling me sir.

What the fuck?

If this is the land of fucked-up sexual fantasies, I'm at some newer, deeper, more depraved level.

And the price I pay is my brother's presence.

If that's not fucked up, I don't know what is.

"The meeting is in twenty minutes. Do you need anything first?" she asks.

"He's fine," Simon says again. "There will be coffee at the meeting. Thank you, Ms. West."

Her eyes meet mine. They ask for something, something I'm desperate to give her.

But I don't know how.

How can I ever be the person she needs? I can't even pretend I'm a functional fiancé.

I can't do that shit for real.

"Thank you." I mouth *sorry*.

She shakes her head. *It's fine*. Or *I'll never forgive you*. One of the two, but I'm not sure which.

I haven't seen her all morning. But then I've had the blinds down since I got here. It's cloudy today, but it's still too fucking bright.

Briar leaves for her desk.

Simon closes the door behind us. He doesn't wait for me to offer him a seat. He doesn't take the seat in front of my desk.

He sits on the damn couch. "Were you going to tell me you fucked your assistant?"

"Is that really why you're here?"

"What did you do to her?"

"If you want those details—"

"She's not usually this…"

"Like you?"

"Corporate." He stares at me like he's looking for cracks. "What happened?"

"What are you doing here, Simon? We have a meeting in twenty minutes." Apparently. I'm too fuzzy to remember any of this.

"You're hung over."

"Not an answer."

"It's Monday morning."

"Also not an answer."

"Did Saturday night last that long?"

"If I want to spend my weekends drunk, that's my business."

"You're still my brother." He softens, but barely.

"Is that why you're here? As my brother?"

He sits up straight. "I'm worried about you."

"Why?"

"You've been acting strange."

"I'm always strange."

He doesn't accept this explanation. "Adam tells me you have news you want to share in person."

Fucking Adam. When did he even talk to Simon? He's supposed to be locked in his love nest.

"Bachelor party is all prepped for Thursday," I say. "Then everyone is heading to the house Friday night."

"Everyone?"

"The wedding party," I say.

His shoulders stiffen.

"I tried to talk sense into him. Explain that you're going to meltdown over your desire to screw Vanessa, but…" I'm too tired to pretend I'm worried about this. I shake my head like I just can't believe how unreasonable everyone is being.

But the gesture makes me nauseous.

Simon is right. What the fuck am I doing drinking all day Sunday?

I'm twenty-seven. I'm too old for this shit.

I'm better than this shit.

But I can't tell him the truth. I can't tell him Preston is dying and I'm failing to handle it.

So bullshit it is.

"Why are you talking to Adam anyway?" I ask.

"He's our brother," he says. "Did you forget?"

"You don't talk to me," I say.

"I saw you Saturday morning."

That is true.

"I see you every day. He lives at the house."

"Not for long." Danielle prefers the city. Adam may be smarter than I am, but he's still a man, and he still wants to be where his girlfriend is.

He says love.

I say he wants to fuck her as much as possible.

Tom-ay-toe. To-mah-toe.

"The city is too much for him," Simon says. "He isn't ready."

"Are you here to talk about Adam?"

"No."

"I don't have time for twenty questions. Get to the point or get the fuck out."

Simon's stare is one hundred percent Ice King. He has the blue eyes for it too. Just not the fair skin and blond hair.

"Yes?"

"Did you really ask your assistant to marry you?"

Fuck. I'm not seeing straight. I don't know how to play this. "She's not my assistant."

"She's sitting outside your office."

"She's finding her replacement."

"So you fucked her then fired her? That's going to look good."

"I'm investing in her company."

"The app?"

"Don't say it with that fucking tone, asshole. It's a comparable industry. And it's going to actually help people. Unlike our fucking privacy software."

"Did you come to that conclusion before or after you fucked her?"

"Before."

He raises a brow *really, you expect me to believe that?*

"It's my money. Mind your own fucking business. Is that all?"

"Are you really engaged?"

"Are you really asking?"

"Yes," he says.

"Yeah. We're engaged."

His eyes flit to Bri, sitting at her desk, pretending she's not spying. He turns to me, nods as if to say *there's more to the story, but I'll torture you for that info later.* "When did this happen?"

"Recently."

"And that's what you told Adam?"

"Yeah."

He looks me over. Examining my story, my facade, my fucking outfit even. Then he says the last thing I expect: "Congratulations."

"Thank you."

"How long have you been fucking her?"

"This is the worst fucking congratulations I've ever heard."

"What about your high school graduation?"

Fuck. I can't help but chuckle. "That was up there."

"I'm improving."

I motion *a little.*

"She's an amazing woman."

"I didn't realize you'd noticed."

"Not all of us feel the need to verbalize every thought in our heads."

"I have so few," I say. "I can't help myself."

"You're not very happy for a recently engaged man."

I shrug.

"Cold feet already?"

"No." There's no question. I'm doing this. Playing this part. But that's not what he's asking. I don't know how to answer the question he's asking.

I need to explain my attitude somehow. With something better than *too much booze*.

"We got into a fight." I need an explanation. An excuse.

"Weddings force us to consider our future."

Sure. I'll go with that. "Yeah."

"Is that why you asked?"

"I didn't really plan it out."

"She's wearing a ring."

Right. That's pretty fucking obvious. "Impulse buy."

He chuckles *of course, that's so like you, Liam.*

I know him. I know what he wants to hear. I'm not afraid to throw myself under the bus to convince him.

That's why I'm so good at this shit.

No ego in the way.

I know my strengths and my weaknesses. I know how people see me.

"I'll take you to dinner before the party," he says. "To celebrate."

"She'll be busy getting ready."

"The two of us then."

Fuck. So much for being good at this. "Sure."

"Seven?" he asks.

"I'll meet you in the lobby."

"You'll see me in"—he checks his watch—"five minutes."

"And again, tomorrow."

"It's horrifying for me too."

"Uh-huh."

"It is." He stands. Offers his hand to shake. "Really, Liam. Congratulations."

I stand. Take his hand. "Thanks."

"Don't fuck it up."

"I'll do my best."

He releases me. Opens his mouth, about to say something. Stops.

This is too easy.

He's too willing to believe me.

He's not a cuddly kitten. He's a python, waiting for the right moment to strike, endlessly patient, lethal as hell.

Or maybe my hangover is fucking with my reasoning.

I don't know anymore. I can contemplate Simon's bullshit later. Right now, I need him out of my office.

"Bring your a game for the party," I say. "There will be dancers."

"But…"

"But what?"

"Strippers are cliché for you."

"I'm not going to ruin the surprise."

He nods *uh-uh*. "Will it embarrass Harrison?"

"That's the point."

He chuckles again *silly Liam* then he pulls me into a hug. An actual hug. "I'm proud of you." He pats me on the back. Releases me. Looks at me with paternal affection.

He is my older brother.

He filled in plenty after Dad died.

But he never looks at me like this.

Something is happening.

Something strange.

But I've got an awkward meeting to sit through. A hangover to nurse. And a fake fiancée to—

Something. I don't know.

I can't let shit stay weird and awkward. I need to talk to Bri. To explain.

But what the fuck can I say?

Sorry, I'm avoiding you. It's because I can't stop thinking about your thighs against my cheeks.

Let's go right now. Get it out of our system.

That makes perfect fucking sense.

Doesn't it?

Chapter Twenty-One

LIAM

At the meeting, I slip into my role. The charming finance guy.

Briar stays weird and overly professional.

Simon stays equal parts judgmental and proud.

After, I fix my own fucking coffee, find my own fucking aspirin, distract myself with work.

With my pounding headache, it takes a while to concentrate, but once I slip into the zone, I'm there. I don't look up until Briar knocks on my door.

"I'm about to head to a dance class. Do you need anything before I go?" Her voice is stiff. Awkward. Like she's playing up the professionalism in case anyone is watching.

But it's late. The office is nearly empty.

Simon's light is on, yeah, but he's supposed to believe we're engaged. Either Briar is operating on some other level of meta-game or this is *I know you want to fuck me, stop making it weird* shit.

I reach for something to say to make it normal, to get her calling me Liam, at the very fucking least.

My mouth is too sticky. My throat is too dry.

This is too confusing.

I want her.

I can't have her.

She's the only thing that makes sense.

I have to stop myself from grabbing on to the only thing that makes sense.

"Your hair looks good." I stand. Smooth my slacks.

She tries to hide the confusion in her eyes.

"You touched it up last night, yeah?"

"I did. Thanks."

"I'm sorry if shit got weird."

"It's fine."

"It was… I said something to my friend. Something I shouldn't."

"About us?"

"About Simon keeping secrets."

"Oh?"

My eyes flit to the clock. "What time is your class?"

"Soon."

"You have to change?"

"At the studio."

"Since when do you dance?" I ask.

"Since Danielle invited me."

"She's still here?" I ask. "In the city?"

"Adam went back last night."

"Trouble in paradise?"

"No. She's hanging with her brother."

"Intentionally?"

"Crazy, I know. Who would choose to spend time with a sibling?" she teases.

It's almost normal.

Then my eyes go to her chest.

And her eyes go to my tie.

And it fills the room, the knowledge we're picturing each other naked.

"What, uh… what did you say to your friend?" she asks.

"I asked him if he could find out what he's keeping secret."

"Right. That's what their company does."

"Corporate espionage."

"You make it sound exciting," she says.

"The guy's basically James Bond. He's former Mi6."

"He is not."

"He is."

"And he ran around foreign countries sleeping with beautiful women, drinking his martinis shaken?"

"Gin and tonics, but yeah."

"You're full of shit."

"Ask him."

"I don't need to ask him. If you're saying it, it must be bullshit."

"It's not. And he got with his girlfriend in a real fucked-up way, too."

"Why'd he tell you that?"

"He didn't."

"Who did?"

"Someone who had a little too much to drink," I say.

"How do you know it's true?"

"It's too specific to be made up."

She shoots me that same *bullshit* look.

I press my hand to my heart. "On my hatred of dirty martinis."

"What happened?"

"He was secretly reading her online journal for months. He fell in love with her wit, then, when she confessed she was thinking about selling her virginity…"

"He just happened to fall in love with a hot, young virgin? For her wit? Please. You think I've never met a man before?"

"You're young and hot."

"Three years younger than you are. And I'm not a New York ten."

"Excuse me?"

"Don't bullshit me, Liam. We both know appearances matter."

"I'm sorry? Is feminist icon Briar West judging women on a ten point scale?"

"I'm referring to other people—"

"You're going to lose your card for that."

She laughs. A real, full laugh that fills the room.

A normal fucking laugh.

"There's no card," she says. "But… you might have a point."

"Me? Really?"

"Yes. It is a silly scale… I just mean, I'm not the kind of woman men consider top tier."

"Top tier?"

"You know what I mean!"

"I know you sound like a stock bro."

She flips me off.

"You're hot, Bri. You can claim whatever you want— say the purple hair turns guys off, even though that's bull-shit—but don't try to tell me you aren't hot." My eyes go to her chest. "And don't pull any of that 'my boobs are too small' shit. They're nice."

Her cheeks flush. "Is his girlfriend young and hot?"

"He loved her before he knew what she looked like."

"Uh-huh."

"And she's… she's like you."

"Not a New York ten?"

"I would never rate women. That's terrible."

She flips me off again.

"Sexist trash, really."

"Ha-ha."

"She's not model perfect."

"And she's how much younger?"

"A lot."

She raises a brow.

"Half his age."

"See."

"What are you looking at me for?"

"You've never slept with an eighteen-year-old?"

"I was eighteen once."

"In the last two years?"

Have I? Fuck, I don't know. It's too hard to think about other women with her so close. "I didn't card."

"Exactly."

"He's in love."

"Of course. She probably thinks he's smart and worldly and—"

"He has a British accent."

"Hmm. That's true."

"And rich."

She nods.

"You don't think he's handsome?"

"Do you?"

"Yeah. Of course."

She smiles. "You have an easy time calling another man handsome."

"Why wouldn't I?"

"A lot of guys are weird about it."

"They're insecure."

"Yeah, but I like that you aren't."

"You don't think he's hot? Really?"

"He's hot, yeah."

"So there you go. She's hot and young. He's hot and rich. Everyone wins," I say.

She laughs.

"And maybe… maybe he really does appreciate her intellect. And she adores his—"

"Wallet?"

"Dick."

She laughs.

"Ability to make her come?"

"Well, yeah, if she's a teenager, she probably doesn't know better."

"Do you want to meet her? Explain that?"

Her blush deepens. "That will go well. Hey, friend's girlfriend, let me pull you aside and ask if your hot, rich, older boyfriend gets the job done?"

"Is that not appropriate?"

Again, her laugh fills the room.

Again, it warms every fucking molecule of my body.

I need to make her laugh.

I need to keep her mine.

If it's my friend, so be it. But I need her to be mine. I need to hold on to this.

The way she looks at me. *Oh, Liam, you're an idiot, and I love it.*

"You really don't believe they're in love?" I ask.

"I haven't even met her."

"But you don't?"

"I'm doubtful."

"Do you think anyone is?"

Her eyes fill with surprise. "Huh?"

"Do you believe in any couples you know?"

She swallows hard. "I don't know. I haven't thought about it."

"Adam and Danielle?"

"He adores her."

"She's hot," I say.

"And he isn't?"

"I thought you didn't like the scars."

"That makes me sound awful."

"Yeah. Pretty fucked-up shit, Bri."

"I don't dislike them. I'm just not into them the way she is."

"You think that's all it is? Sex?"

"For now."

"Lee and Harrison?" I ask.

"Is that a real question?" she asks.

"Yeah. She's horrible, but he loves her."

"He does," she admits. "But… I don't know. Maybe that's all relationships. Maybe we always love how we feel with someone. Or the empty spaces they fill."

"It almost sounds romantic."

"Almost." Her fingers skim the doorframe. "What are you asking him to do? Your friend, Ian?"

"Nothing."

"Nothing?"

"I'm thinking about it."

"Thinking about…"

Asking him to find out what the fuck Simon is hiding. "Just checking on Simon."

"Why don't you ask him?"

It's not a bad point. If Simon pulled this shit with me, I'd never let him hear the end of it.

But I've tried.

It's clear he's keeping secrets.

Yeah, I can't talk, but I can't keep looking the other way either.

"I'll see you at home," I say. "Yeah?"

She nods. "Danielle and I are going to get dinner after class."

"Oh."

"But after that…" Her voice softens. "It might be late, but I'll be home after that."

Relief floods my body. She's coming home.

She's not running away.

I haven't fucked things up irrevocably.

"Don't call me Mr. Pierce. Fills my head with dirty role play scenarios," I say.

She smiles. "It's your name."

"Call me sir again, I order you out of your panties. Understand?"

"I do." She takes a step backward. "Good night, Liam."

"Good night." I watch her leave.

My shoulders relax. My chest eases.

For a while, I slip into the zone. I work until I see a light turn off in the other side of the office.

Simon.

He's still hiding something.

And I still have to find out.

I text my friend.

Liam: Does your offer stand?

Then I hit the gym, run until I'm out of energy, go home, shower, fix dinner.

He doesn't reply until I'm on the couch in my pajamas.

Ian: Of course.

Liam: What does this level of intel run?

Ian: Don't be ridiculous. I'm not taking your money.

Liam: I don't want to owe you a favor.

Ian: I'll cash it now.

Liam: You already bought drinks.

Ian: Even so.

Liam: Don't tell me you want a threesome. My girl won't go for it.

Ian: I don't share.

Liam: You just want to watch?

Ian: Not if you're there.

Liam: No deal.

Ian: Isn't your brother screwing a photographer who posts pictures of the two of them having sex?

Liam: Like you don't know.

Ian: Everyone knows.

Liam: Is that the favor? You want the inside scoop?

Ian: What scoop? She's gorgeous and talented. He's thinking with his cock.

Liam: Aren't we all?

Ian: We're idiots.

Liam: I'll drink to that.

Ian: When we meet with the information.

Liam: When?

Ian: If we meet with the information.

Liam: What's the if here?

Ian: I don't know what I'll find. It might not be what you want to see.

Liam: I know.

Ian: Sleep on it. Take the night. Hell, take the week or the month if you need it. This is a line you can't uncross. Be sure you're ready to cross it.

Chapter Twenty-Two

LIAM

As promised, Briar gets home late. She claims exhaustion, wishes me good night, showers, and goes to bed.

Her room stays quiet. Only the hum of the fan.

She's asleep. We're normal. Or as normal as we're going to be.

I try to find a distraction with the TV, but everything is sex and death and secrets.

It's the entire fucking world.

After a few hours, I give up, get ready for bed, fail to find sleep.

I toss and turn forever.

Until I give in to my thoughts of Briar. Her black dress rolled to her waist, her panties at her ankles, her long body bent over my desk.

My name rolling off her lips as she comes.

Is there any better sound in the entire fucking world?

THE DAY IS BUSY. BRIAR AND I DON'T HAVE TIME TO discuss anything other than numbers. All morning and afternoon, we work. Finally, right when I think I'm free, my family arrives to fuck shit up.

My half-sister, Opal, rushes into my office with a smile.

Briar steps in after her. "Ms. Pierce, I don't think—"

"Oh my god, Briar! Don't call me that. It makes me feel a million years old." Opal throws her arms around me. "I can't believe you're finally engaged." She releases me. Turns to Briar. Hugs her like she'll never let go. "I always wanted you two to be together. I love seeing an idiotic man with a smart woman."

"Hey," I claim offense.

Opal ignores me. "And you're just so cool. Oh my god. Am I gushing? I think I'm gushing." She smooths her long, dark hair. "Can I buy you dinner?"

I try to delay her—"We're actually…"

"Not you, Liam. Briar." Opal presses her hands together. "Please."

"Can we do it later?" Briar asks. "I'm totally wiped."

"What if we come over?" Opal asks. "Me and Simon! I know Simon is all"—she drops her voice an octave—"grrr, I'm overprotective and mean. I won't let you have any fun, even though you're an adult woman who is attending college next year." She rolls her eyes. "He's a drag. I know he means well, but he's a serious drag."

Briar laughs. "He is."

"But he's really accommodating about buying ingredients. And I'm a great cook," she says.

"Charm really does run in the family." Briar looks to me. *Is it okay?*

"How did Adam and Simon end up with none then?" I ask.

"'Cause you, me, and Bash took it all! Obviously," Opal

says. "I wish he was here for the wedding. He would have *a lot* to say about Harrison and Lee."

Briar whispers something in Opal's ear.

Opal nods *of course*. "Sorry, Liam. I didn't mean to bring that up. I just—"

"I know he's dead," I say. "You don't have to dance around it."

"I'm not dancing. I'm trying not to ruin the mood." Her brow furrows for a second, then she shakes it off. "He was my brother too."

All right, I'm being an asshole.

I'm too tired for this shit.

"Is there something I don't know?" she asks. "Simon says there's nothing, but he gets all hush-hush whenever Bash's name comes up. And now you're being weird too. Even by Liam standards."

"Nothing I know," I say.

She nods, deciding whether or not she believes me.

Sex, death, and secrets.

My entire fucking life.

I want the truth, yes, but Ian was right. This is a line I can't uncross. Simon might not forgive me.

Mercifully, Briar shifts the subject away from my brother's mysterious death. "Don't you and Simon live uptown?"

"Like *Gossip Girl*." Opal laughs.

"I've never seen it," Briar says.

"No!"

"I've never been a teen soap person."

"Briar West, don't say these things!"

"It's true." She smiles. "I'm more of a reader."

"The show started as a book series."

"Depressing Russian literature," I say. "That was her focus in college."

"Really?" Opal asks. "Those bleak six-hundred-page tomes?"

Briar nods.

"That explains your stamina working with Liam," Opal says.

Briar doubles over laughing.

"That was pretty fucking good," I admit. "Did you set her up for that?"

Opal shakes her head.

"The sense of humor is genetic too," Briar says.

"You make me proud, kid." I pull my sister into a hug.

She hugs back with enthusiasm. She does everything with enthusiasm. It's not just her age—she turned eighteen a few months ago—it's her.

"Don't you have homework?" A judgmental voice interrupts. Simon.

"Hello, I graduated two weeks ago. You were all there... did you forget?" She rolls her eyes.

"Is that a no?" Simon asks.

"Okay, yes, I have homework. But it's an art class. And it's for fun, not credit."

"You should do your homework," he says.

"I still need to eat," she says.

"I'm sorry, Opal, but I'm too tired to head uptown." Briar offers an apologetic smile. "Maybe tomorrow?"

"She has class tomorrow," Simon says.

"What if we come over? I can cook. Or we can order something. Do you like spicy? There's this great Thai place around here. The drunken noodles are amazing. And Simon's favorite too." She looks to Simon. "Please?"

Simon eats greasy Thai food. Since fucking when?

He looks at her and melts. The way Adam always did with Bash.

He sees her as a daughter as much as he sees her as a

sibling. She showed up at his apartment three years ago with a paper that said she was his half-sister.

None of us knew, even though Dad had set up a trust in her name.

Our family has always been a fucked-up mess, but at least I knew my father, knew where I was expected to fit into the world. Opal didn't even know she had siblings until her sixteenth birthday. The same day she found out she was going to inherit a fortune at thirty.

That's another level of fucked up.

"One hour," Simon says. "Then you do your homework."

"Thank you!" She throws her arms around him. "You're my favorite brother. Sorry, Liam."

I chuckle. "Whatever lies you have to tell him."

"Can we go now?" she asks. "Or do you need time?"

"How about I pick up dinner?" Briar asks. "And meet you at home?"

"You're living together?" Simon asks.

I reach for the dirtiest response I can find. "How else are we going to—"

Simon interrupts me. "Not in front of her."

"I know about sex," Opal says. "And I know Liam. He has to brag. It's in his veins or something."

"Yeah, you never do it," I say.

"Not as much as you," she says.

"You have time," I say.

"You're a grown-up. You're supposed to be more mature."

"I thought you were a grown woman?"

Her cheeks turn red. "I am a grown woman. I just… ugh! You know what I mean, Liam!"

I do. But it's fun riling her. Almost too easy.

Simon pulls out his phone. "Opal, why don't you go

with Briar? Pick up the food with her." He taps in his order then hands the phone to her.

"He's trying to get rid of me." She inputs her order. "Bad news for you."

"Tell me about it." I take my turn. Look to Briar. "The usual?"

"Please," she says.

Opal presses her hands together. "You know her usual? That's so romantic. Oh my gosh. I hope I have this kind of love one day. Well, maybe with someone a little less slutty. No offense, Liam. Or Briar. He's the one who's slutty, not you. Or are you?"

"Is anyone compared to Liam?" Briar asks.

Opal laughs. "Was anyone? No. That's true." She looks at me. "Take care of her."

"I will," I say.

"I mean it, Liam! Don't fuck this up. Briar is my favorite future sister-in-law," she says.

"What do you say to Danielle?" Briar asks.

"My favorite future sister-in-law with purple hair," she says.

"She didn't qualify Simon being her favorite," Briar says.

"I noticed that too." I mime being stabbed in the gut. "You're brutal, kid."

Opal smiles. "Liam… you know you're my favorite brother… who's a CFO."

"You really have the Pierce charm." Briar laughs. "I believed that."

"It's true." She turns to Briar. "Will you help me dye my hair purple?"

"You're not dying your hair purple," Simon says.

"I'm an adult," Opal says.

"If you keep bringing it up, you weaken your case," Briar says. "Just do it. He can't stop you once it's done."

Opal taps her chin, taking in the advice. "Smart. Very smart."

"Is this your natural color?" Briar asks.

Opal nods.

"You'll fry it if you bleach it light enough for purple. Even with a lot of TLC."

Opal frowns. "That's what my stylist says."

"It's pretty like this."

"Yeah, but it gets boring, you know?"

"I do." Briar looks at the phone. "Ten minutes. We better go. Good luck with Simon."

"I'll need it," I say.

She kisses me goodbye.

It's fast, for show, but I still feel it everywhere.

Chapter Twenty-Three

LIAM

This is the longest seven block walk of my life.

It's not the grey sky, the fat clouds, the threat of rain.

It's Simon.

He surveys the gloomy sky suspiciously. As if the weather turned from sunny to miserable as some kind of personal affront. "You could have said no."

"Huh?"

"To Opal. She gets her way too often."

"You budge?"

"She knows what buttons to push."

That's hard to imagine. Simon is unflappable. But maybe there's something I'm not seeing. Maybe he's not the guy I imagine. I don't see that guy grabbing takeout with his half-sister. "Since when do you eat Thai food?"

He stops on the sidewalk. Looks at me funny. "Why wouldn't I?"

"Why wouldn't you eat greasy noodles? You're really asking that?"

"Yes."

"You're like Adam."

"Taller than you?"

"Yeah. That's it. Tall people don't eat noodles."

"How am I like Adam?"

I shoot him a *really* look.

"Because I take a few things seriously?"

"You're both brooding bastards."

"Adam isn't a bastard."

A chuckle spills from my lips. "Fuck. Did you just cop to being a bastard?"

"Why wouldn't I?"

I shoot him another *really* look.

"You play your role. I play mine."

"Master of the Universe?"

"I was expecting 'bossy bastard.'"

"Stuck-up suit maybe," I say. "Or control freak."

"Bosshole?"

"Perfect."

Finally, we turn onto my street.

I motion *after you*. Follow Simon inside, into the way too tiny elevator.

He waits until the doors are closed. "You're good at hiding your feelings, but not as good as you think."

What the fuck does that mean?

The elevator arrives at the penthouse with a ding. The doors slide open. Simon motions *after you*. Waits.

Okay, fine. I step into the hallway. Open the door for him.

Again, he motions *after you*. Again, he waits.

Is he not buying this ruse?

Briar and I are a little awkward, sure, but I can fix that perception now.

The shit with Preston—

That's harder.

Simon knows something. He's been walking around like he knows something for weeks, months even.

But is it whatever he whispers to Adam or is it something else?

"Have you talked to Harrison?" I step inside.

He follows. "About the wedding?"

"No, about his favorite color. I'm guessing blue. It's the most popular color. You know what's second?"

"Green."

"Bingo."

He shoots me that *Liam, you're ridiculous* look. "Is it about the wedding?"

"Is what?"

"Whatever it is that's upsetting you?"

"Have you ever heard of boundaries?"

He shoots me the same look.

"As in 'I say something is none of your business, then you respect that and drop it.'"

"I'm familiar with the concept."

"So…" I motion *get with it*.

"Do you really want a conversation with this level of sincerity?"

Hell no. "Do you?"

"I can take more than you can."

Probably. This isn't a fruitful argument. I need to find something better. His weak spot. "You want a drink?"

"What are you having?"

"What do you think?"

"A Blue Hawaiian."

I can't help but laugh. "You'd drink one?"

"I have to do it once."

"Save it for your trip to Tahiti."

"When am I going to Tahiti?"

"On your honeymoon," I say.

"I didn't realize I was engaged."

"What do you want?"

"Whiskey, neat," he says.

"Original choice."

"We can't all drink appletinis."

Am I crazy, or is that respect in his voice? "Don't knock it till you try it."

"Sure."

"Sure?"

"Sure. Fix an appletini."

All right, that's a distraction I need. I find the bottles and lemons in the fridge. Martini glasses in the cabinet.

I fix three drinks worth of appletini, strain them into martini glasses, offer one to Simon.

"Cheers." He raises his glass.

I do the same. "Cheers." Not the greatest appletini in the world but good. Sweet, strong, artificial flavor. An alcohol version of a green apple Jolly Rancher.

"Are you okay?" He says it without judgment.

But it still puts me on edge. "I'm fine."

"You're not. I'll drop it if you ask, but I won't believe you're fine."

How the hell do I play this?

"Is it about Bash?"

"What about him?"

"His death." He says that without judgment too.

But, still, I don't buy it. "He's been dead."

"He was fucking a married woman."

It's a plausible explanation, but there's something about the way he says it. Something I'm missing. "Did he tell you more?"

"More about what?"

"The woman he was fucking."

"The same things he told you."

"How do you know what he told me?" I ask.

"Bash wasn't good at keeping secrets."

That's true. It's missing something, but it is true.

"He told me a lot about the sound of her groan. The way her toes curled when she came. How badly she wanted everything with him."

That sounds like Bash.

"He put you to shame."

I can't help but laugh. "In his dreams."

"Maybe." Simon studies the bright green hue of the drink.

"It's good."

He takes a sip. "Better than I expected."

"I'm a man of many talents."

He finishes half his drink. Sets his glass on the counter.

Mine is better with the next sip. Sweeter, stronger, promising a release from this torture. I can't discuss death for another fucking second. "Is that all he said?"

He doesn't reply.

"Did he tell you her name? Who her husband was? If she was at the funeral?"

He holds my gaze for a moment. "He didn't tell."

Bash didn't tell him.

But he knows now.

That's what he's hiding. Something about the woman Bash was fucking?

But why?

"Is she okay?" I ask.

"I don't know."

"But you know her. Who she is?"

He says nothing. But that says everything.

He knows the woman Bash was fucking.

"What else do you know?" I ask.

"Liam—"

"Tell me the fucking truth."

"Why? What good could come of it?"

"It's the truth."

"You've never kept a secret?"

Guilty as charged. "That's not the point."

"He loved her. He wanted to keep their affair secret."

"He's dead. Doesn't fucking matter what he wanted."

"It does."

Whatever.

"If it was you—"

"I wouldn't give a shit, because I'd be dead."

The door interrupts us. Laughter. My kid sister and my fake fiancée step into the room, each holding a takeout bag, each sopping wet.

"It's raining." Briar takes Opal's bag. Places both on the counter. "Raining really hard."

"Do you have anything I can borrow?" Opal asks.

"Yeah. I have my clothes in the spare room," Briar says.

"Your fiancée sleeps in the spare room?" Simon asks.

"No." Briar stumbles on her explanation.

"She's a closet hog," I say.

She nods. "There's not enough room in Liam's bedroom. So I took the closet in the spare."

Opal nods. "Doesn't he have a walk-in closet? Really, Liam, you should let your fiancée have the bigger closet."

"His clothes are worth more," Briar says.

"But yours are way cooler. You look amazing—" She motions to Briar's short black dress and boots. "He's another guy in a suit."

"I like him in a suit." Briar crosses the room to me. "Though I like you better out of it." She presses her lips to my cheek. Leans in to whisper. "Can we make this fast?"

I brush her hair behind her ear. "I'm trying."

"Thank you." She pulls back. Looks to Opal. "Any preference?"

"As long as it's dry." Opal follows Briar into the spare room.

Their banter fades into the background.

Simon stares intensely.

I try to ignore him as I plate our takeout, bring it to the dining table.

Years of training take over. Simon and I fall into the routine of manners.

He places the silverware.

I place the plates and drinks.

The ladies emerge in dry clothes, and big smiles, but the air stays charged. Simon's expression stays grim.

He shoots me a *we'll talk about this later* look. The same one he had when I was a kid who fucked up.

Then he shifts into loving older brother. Gets Opal talking about her art class, her friends from school, her love of spicy food.

Opal lights up the massive room. Gets Simon smiling and Briar spilling advice on acing classes and avoiding assholes.

They leave right after dinner.

Briar offers to clean up. When I insist I've got it, she wishes me good night, and retires to her room.

The dishes distract me for a while.

I shower, change into pajamas, try to zone out with the TV.

But the thought gets louder every minute. What the fuck is Simon hiding?

A smarter man would let it go.

A better man would confront his brother.

But I'm neither.

I text my friend. Accept his offer to find answers.

I'm tired of being in the dark.

Simon is hiding something. And I'm going to find out what it is.

Chapter Twenty-Four

BRIAR

A h, the fun of alcohol. I fall asleep easily. Wake two hours later with an intense need to pee.

Two drinks and my bladder is screaming. Or maybe it's all the water I drank at dinner. Opal claimed the dish I ordered wasn't "that spicy," but it set my tongue on fire. She's adorable. Okay, maybe she's a little tall to be adorable, but she's full of energy and enthusiasm. Too cute to be a master of spicy food.

That's what I get for making assumptions.

I use the bathroom in the hall. Wash my hands. Brush my teeth. That's one alcohol side-effect down. To handle the other—

I fill a glass in the kitchen. Drink with eager gulps.

The lights are off. The space is quiet.

But there's something different. The door to the balcony is open.

Liam is standing there in the rain, hand around a glass, eyes on the dark sky.

"Are you okay?" It's a stupid question.

He's hiding some heavy secret. Of course he's not okay.

And what am I doing asking anyway?

What the fuck are we doing?

We're soon to be business partners. Once this ruse is over, that's it. Our relationship is strictly professional. Liam's deranged version of strictly professional, but a lot more professional than midnight meetings on the balcony in our pajamas.

My head screams *no, stop, do the smart thing and don't make this more complicated.*

But my feet move anyway.

Liam turns as I step into the doorframe.

At once, the frustration on his face turns to desire. His eyes flit to my bare shoulders. The neckline of my pajama top. My exposed legs.

"Do you like them?" he asks.

"Huh?"

"The silk pajamas."

"I do." They even feel expensive and luxurious. I'm not sure I need six sets, but I am glad I have this tank top and shorts set in black, wine, and green. "How do I look?"

"Is that a real question?"

I nod.

"You look hot, Bri." He gives me a long, slow once-over. "Don't tell me you don't see it."

"There isn't a mirror here."

He half-smiles, but his heart isn't in it.

Whatever it is that's weighing on him is still there. And I want to fix it. I want to soothe him.

I want to crack him open and hold him close.

But I can't say that. So, instead, I talk about the weather. "It's raining."

"It is."

"You're wet."

He raises a brow. "That's a softball."

"And you're too good to swing?"

"You followed through on the sports metaphor."

"Go Dodgers."

He chuckles *sure*.

I take a deep breath. Exhale slowly.

His eyes stay on my chest. This outfit is designed for temperature control. The top is cut low. The shorts are incredibly short. A lot of skin is showing.

Not that I usually think of it that way.

It's my body. If I want to adorn it in barely there shorts, that's my business.

But with Liam's eyes on my skin—

I feel impossibly on display.

And impossibly eager to show him things I shouldn't.

"Do you want an umbrella?" I ask.

"No." His eyes flit to my legs. "Are you going to stay there?"

"I can't convince you to come inside?"

His eyes go to my chest. "You're persuasive."

Yes, come inside, take off all my clothes, then all of yours. Now. Please. "Are you okay?"

"Better now."

"Really, Liam."

His shoulders relax.

"What was that?"

"Thought you were gonna call me Mr. Pierce again."

"Why does that bother you, Mr. Pierce?"

His pupils dilate. His jaw cricks. "Fuck, you're messing with my head."

"I am?"

"Don't know if I'm pissed things are weird or desperate to engage in some dirty role play."

"What role play is that?"

"Bri—"

"Yes?"

"There are bells you can't unring."

"Are there?"

"Call me Mr. Pierce again and you'll find out." The teasing tone drops from his voice. It's not a joke. It's an offer.

I want to do it. I want to tug at his fucking tie and groan *what are you going to do to me, Mr. Pierce?*

I want to touch him, taste him, feel him inside me.

Liam is right.

I need to go. Or I'll do something I can't take back. We'll do something we can't take back.

I can't fuck my boss.

I can't fuck my future business partner.

I can't convince myself to leave.

"Now, you're daring me," I say.

"I know." He looks at the doorframe over my head. "Are you going to stay there?"

Right. I'm not inside. Not outside. I need to commit.

I need to go back to bed, get as much sleep as possible, survive tomorrow.

But I don't.

I step onto the balcony.

Drops fall on my head, shoulders, chest.

It's raining hard. Liam must be soaked.

"How long have you been standing here?" I meet him at the railing. The city is beautiful in the rain—slick and shimmering—but my eyes return to him.

"Awhile."

"Is there a reason?"

"Thinking about shit."

"Do you want to talk about it?"

"No."

"It might help."

"Maybe." He looks at the building across from us. A tall skyscraper, all steel and glass, dark except for a few pockets of yellow light.

"Do you want to not talk?"

"Your dad… are you glad you know about his affairs?"

Huh? That's a weird question. I don't usually think about it. But if an answer will help, I can give him that. "No. I'm not happy about it. It's not a happy thing. But I'd rather know the truth than wonder why my mom locks herself in her room and cries for days at a time."

"Fuck. She does?"

"Depression runs on her side of the family. It's not just the affairs but it's part of it."

"Feeling abandoned. Worthless. Inferior. Fuck. No wonder you don't believe in love."

"And you do?"

"I do." He turns to me. "Despite all evidence to the contrary."

"Liam, what are you talking about?"

"What if he was gone? Your dad? And you didn't know. Do you think it would be better to keep it that way? Or would you want the truth?"

Is this about his late brother? "I don't know. If he was gone, I couldn't do anything. I couldn't tell my mom to leave him. I couldn't confront him about his behavior."

He nods. "You can't fix your relationship anymore. You lose that possibility forever."

"I didn't think about it that way." I place my hand next to his. "Is that how you feel about Bash?"

"Sometimes. We were good. We fought, sometimes, but it wasn't like with Simon. It was… normal."

"Bossy older siblings who keep secrets are normal."

"I guess you'd know."

"I would."

"Does your kid sister ever listen to you?"

"She wouldn't even let me teach her how to draw her eyeliner."

He chuckles. "What about books?"

I shake my head. "She doesn't like to read."

"So nothing?"

"I taught her how to cook. Since Dad was never around. And Mom was…" Absent, I guess.

"No one ever took care of you?"

"Sometimes." I suck a breath through my teeth. "She wasn't always depressed. Sometimes, she was okay. Every time she came through, she took us to this sandwich shop on the way home from school. She'd order the largest sandwich—it was so huge it was absurd—and she ate like she hadn't eaten a proper meal in months."

"Had she?"

"No. She'd stay in her room and eat chips. These horrible salt and vinegar potato chips. They made the whole room smell sour. I still can't stand them." My nose scrunches at the memory. "They had chips at the shop too, but she always got the barbecue. It was this symbol. Or maybe she was sick of salt and vinegar."

"And that was the only thing that got her out of bed?"

"Maybe." My laugh is sad. "Maybe it was that small. And it wasn't this big gesture. I don't know."

"I'm sorry."

"You are?"

"That your parents weren't there. It's fucked up."

"Thanks."

"My parents were gone, but I had Preston. And Trish. And even fucking Simon. He never hugged me and told me I was doing a great job. But I knew he was there. I knew people would help if I needed it. I… Fuck, Bri, I wish I could make it better."

"I can take care of myself."

"I know you can." His eyes meet mine. "I wish you didn't have to. Not all the time."

"Who else would do it?"

"Someone who loves you."

My stomach flutters.

"Isn't that love? Being a shoulder when someone needs it?"

"You're still asking the wrong person."

"I know. I'm just… tired, I guess."

"Me too."

"You should go to bed."

"You too," I say. "Or at least put on something dry."

"You're already wet."

"Did you just say that with a straight face?"

He half-smiles. "Do you want to make it dirty? 'Cause I will."

"Can I stop you?"

"You can try." He turns back to the view. "Would it be better? With your dad? If you knew?"

"I can't imagine not knowing. Not anymore."

"That's fair."

"If I was completely in the dark and had no idea… maybe. But I always had some inkling. Some sense something was wrong. It's not like *The Matrix*. It's not a perfect simulation."

"Did you just reference *The Matrix*?"

"It's a popular film."

"For computer nerds."

"Like my sister."

"Of course."

"She had a huge crush on Trinity too."

"Who didn't?"

"Really?"

"Fuck yeah. That leather get-up? Those fight moves."

"The sex scene in Zion."

"You know the movie pretty well."

I mime zipping my lips.

"Just a supportive sister, huh?"

"That's right."

"What bullshit."

"It's too bad idiotic men ruined the red pill metaphor. It was solid," I say.

"You think about the metaphors."

"Everyone knows about that."

"'Cause you love sci-fi. Briar West, lover of Tolstoy and Wachowski siblings."

"And Keanu Reeves."

"Should we watch *John Wick*?"

"Do I have to?"

"See." His smile widens. "It's the sci-fi."

"You're an idiot."

"You know my favorite part of the movie?"

"I have no idea."

"Adam had this phase. Watched it all the time. You know computer geeks. They get excited about robots taking over the world."

"I see the appeal."

"He was always talking about the metaphors. But the one I remember was my boy Mouse."

"Who?"

"He's the kid who created the woman in the red dress. The one who distracted Neo in the simulation. He tells Neo ignoring our impulses is as good as being a machine."

"I see why you like him."

"And why Adam just—" He makes a *woosh* sound as he makes the *went over his head* gesture. "Not a clue."

"Was he really always like that?"

"You knew him before the accident."

And he was always quiet, in control, hard working. A monk, practically. Except around Bash. Poor guy. He lost his brother in the same accident that nearly killed him.

"He even offers Neo a chance to enjoy a simulation with the woman in the red dress."

"So that's some kind of robot pornography?"

"More like a simulated sex doll."

"Fucked up."

"It's the robot apocalypse." He shrugs *what are you gonna do*. "There's probably no regular porn left."

"Use your imagination."

"Are you looking at me?"

"You're here."

"You think I don't have an imagination?" he asks.

"I think I'll say *bullshit* if you claim you don't look at porn."

"I'm not claiming that."

I raise a brow *see*.

"But it's not my preference. Honest."

"Uh-huh."

"Check my browser history."

"You run a cyber security company. You know about Incognito Mode."

He chuckles. "I look, yeah, but I prefer memories. There's something real about them. Something porn is lacking. Even the classy shit Danielle makes."

"She'd kill you for calling it porn."

"I can take her."

"Can you take Adam?"

"Probably not. But he wouldn't kill a family member."

"You bet your life on that?"

His laugh gets louder. "Then don't tell her."

"I can't promise anything."

His smile widens. "Whether it's erotic photography or hardcore anal. Or something suggestive. A fully dressed woman. An explicitly written sex scene."

"When have you read an explicit sex scene?"

"There's some crazy hot shit in the books Opal reads."

Of course. "And that's the one part you read?"

"Hell yeah. But whatever it is, it's missing something. It's not real. I can't smell it, taste it, feel it."

"But you can with memories?"

"Or fantasies."

"The boss roleplay?"

His eyes flit to my chest. "Yeah."

"How does that go?"

"The usual shit."

I arch a brow.

"My smoking hot assistant comes into my office, calls me Mr. Pierce, talks about how she's desperate to fill every one of my needs."

"Selfish of you."

"What if I need to make her come?"

"Is that how it goes?"

"It varies."

"This is something you… use?"

"I try not to."

"Who do you imagine?"

"Bri—"

"Oh."

"It's not—"

"It's fine. I have plenty of fantasies about you."

"Hurting me?"

"Not in the way you'd like."

He smiles, but it's not easy. It's charged. The joke isn't enough to defuse the tension.

It's in the air.

It's everywhere.

He wants to fuck me.

I want to fuck him.

And, just like before, I can step back, go to sleep, run to some promise of normal.

Or I can move forward.

"I uh… think I'm going back to bed," I say.

"I'll walk you."

"It's not far."

"Then it's not a far walk." He motions to the door. *After you.*

I turn. Step through the frame. Toward my room.

His fingers skim my back. The silk tank top.

Then under it.

Liam's hand on my bare skin. The brush of his fingers. The pressure of his palm.

He leads me back to my room.

I turn. Look up at him.

Then I say the stupidest thing in the world: "Do you want to come in?"

Chapter Twenty-Five

BRIAR

Do *you want to come in?*

We're not at my front door.

We're in his apartment. In front of the spare bedroom. In case someone stops by to check if we're officially together.

This is crazy.

I'm crazy.

Liam's eyes fix on me. They bore into mine. Ask for something deep inside of me. Need, love, affection, desire.

All of the above.

"Briar." My name is a whisper. A promise.

"If you don't—"

He cuts me off with a kiss. It's hard, fast, intoxicating.

My hands go to his hair. My groan vibrates down his throat.

He tastes so fucking good, like Liam and mint and the promise of everything.

For two years, I've wanted to slap him and kiss him in equal measure.

And this is it. Our first real kiss.

It isn't for practice. It isn't for show.

It's solely and completely ours.

And it's perfect.

The wool of his slacks brushes my bare legs. He's wet, but I don't care. I need him closer. I need all his warmth.

I pull back with a sigh. "You're soaked."

"Not yet."

"Liam."

He smiles and presses his forehead to mine. "I want to, Bri. I do. But only if you're sure."

"Take off your clothes." I tug at his tie. "Now."

"You want it bossy?"

"Don't joke—"

"I'm not." He undoes the knot of his tie. Tosses it aside. "Is that how you like it? You want to boss me around?"

"No."

"How do you like it?" He does away with his suit jacket. "I've been wondering for the last two years. Wondering exactly what pushes your buttons." He brings his hands to my hips. "I want every fucking detail."

Shit.

My cheeks flush. My chest too.

He's a dirty master. Of course he is.

He's great at bullshitting dirty talk. Why wouldn't he be great at the real thing?

"Do you take other women to your room?" I ask.

"I have before."

"The spare?"

"No."

"Then there." I turn the handle.

He lifts me and holds me against his chest. Then he carries me into the room, lays me on the bed, pulls something from the dresser.

A condom.

He tosses it on the soft sheets. Steps out of his socks and shoes.

I climb to the edge of the bed. Undo his belt. The button of his slacks. The zipper.

He pushes the pants off his hips. Then he climbs onto the bed in his boxers.

His hand goes to my neck. His lips go to my lips.

This time, his kiss is hard, deep, hungry. His tongue swirls around mine, claiming my mouth, claiming me.

Only for tonight, maybe.

But for tonight.

I climb into his lap, my legs around his thighs, my pelvis over his. He's hard against me.

And, fuck, it feels good.

I need it. All of it. All of him.

He pulls my top over my head. Runs his fingers against my collarbone as he looks me up and down. "Fuck, Bri—"

My blush deepens.

"Fucking perfect." He kisses me hard as he brings his hand to my chest. He teases with brushes of his thumb. Up and down. Left and right. Back and forth.

I groan against his mouth.

He toys with me again and again, winding me tighter and tighter, until I'm sure I'm going to break.

Then he moves to my other nipple and he teases me just as mercilessly.

I rock my hips, grinding against him. There are three layers of fabric in the way. It's three too many.

I need to wrap my hand around him. I need to taste him. I need to feel him inside me.

"Please." I rock against him again. "Please, Liam. Fuck me."

"Not yet."

A whine falls from my lips.

"Bri, baby, you have no idea how badly I can tease you."

Baby. He's said it in jest before. But this—

Fuck.

"I won't if you don't like it. Well-" He presses his lips to my neck. "Not this time."

"Liam."

"I've been dreaming about this." His lips brush my collarbone. "For too fucking long." His thumbs hook into the waistband of my shorts. "Off."

I raise my hips.

He pushes the shorts off my ass.

I kick them aside.

Then I do away with my panties.

I'm naked, in bed, with Liam Pierce.

I'm out of my fucking mind, and I don't care.

"Every time you wear a skirt." He kisses a line down my stomach. "I think about diving between your legs, peeling your panties to your ankles, licking you until you're groaning my name."

"Me too."

"Greedy."

"I am."

"Bad girl." His voice is a purr. All approval. All desire. "I'm going to have to punish you for that."

"Liam—"

"Later. Right now, you need to come on my face." Liam pushes my thighs apart and lowers himself between my legs.

He presses his lips to my inner thigh.

Then higher.

Softer.

So soft I can barely feel it.

Closer and closer and closer.

His lips brush my clit. A whisper of a touch.

Then harder.

The flick of his tongue.

A groan falls from my lips. It's been a long time. Too long.

"Fuck, you taste good." He pins my thighs to the bed. Then he brings his tongue to my clit.

He licks me with steady strokes.

Soft to start.

Then harder.

Higher.

Right.

Left.

There.

"Fuck." My nails scrape his shoulders. His back.

He groans against me.

I find the back of his head. Knot my hand in his hair.

He goes to that perfect spot and he works me with steady strokes.

Again and again.

Every flick of his tongue winds me tighter.

Tighter.

His nails scrape my inner thighs.

I tug at his hair.

Almost.

Almost—

There. I groan his name as I come. My sex pulses against his lips. Pleasure spills through my pelvis, stomach, thighs.

All the way to my fingers and toes.

Every part of me feels awake and alive.

He works me through my orgasm, then he presses his lips to my inner thigh. "Better than I imagined." He reaches for something. The condom. "So much better."

"Fuck."

He tears the wrapper with his teeth. "Spread your legs."

"Lose the boxers."

He half-smiles, still Liam, still ridiculous, even here. "Help me."

I sit up. Bring my hands to the waistband of his boxers. Push them off his hips.

Fuck.

No wonder he's cocky all the time.

That's—

Fuck.

Liam groans as I wrap my hand around his cock.

He feels so good in my hands. Thick and warm and hard.

I run my thumb over his tip then I pump him with a steady stroke.

"Fuck, Bri—" His eyelids flutter closed. "On your back. I need to fuck you."

I need him to fuck me. I pump him one more time, then I release him, lower myself onto my back.

He does away with his boxers, then he rolls the condom over his cock.

Liam lowers his body onto mine.

Chest, stomach, pelvis.

The weight of his body sinks into mine. Hard and safe and strong.

Then his cock brushes against me.

Fuck.

My eyes close.

My fingers dig into his back.

He fills me slowly, one sweet inch at a time.

He feels so good inside me.

Too fucking good.

He stays there, for a moment, then he pulls back and drives into me again.

Slowly to start.

Then faster.

Harder.

I wrap my legs around his hips. I rock to meet him, pushing him deeper, pulling him closer.

"Fuck." It falls off his lips like poetry. "You feel good." His lips brush my neck. "I'm going to be fast. I've been dreaming about this too long."

"You have hands."

He smiles. "I like you greedy." His teeth scrape my neck. "Don't dare me, baby. I'll do it. I'll wear you out. I'll make you come until you're begging me to stop."

My nails dig into his back. "Liam—"

"Let me take a minute." His voice lowers to a purr. "Let me savor this."

There's no pretense.

No bullshit.

None of the walls he normally throws up.

Right now, there are no walls between us.

Only pure, honest need.

And I need him.

I really fucking need him.

I wrap my arms around him, then I rock my hips against him.

He matches my rhythm, filling me with slow, steady thrusts.

Again and again.

He stays there, pressed against me, filling me again and again, driving me closer and closer.

The tension in my sex winds tighter and tighter.

Until it's almost too much to take.

Then it's too much, but somehow it's not enough either.

Liam's teeth scrape my neck, and I go over the edge.

My sex pulses as I come. I groan his name into his ear, rocking my hips, digging my nails into his back.

He works me through my orgasm, then he moves faster.

Deeper.

His breath speeds. His groans run together.

He holds me close, scraping his teeth against my collarbone. His cock pulses as he comes.

There's something so satisfying about it.

Some primal need I've ignored for far too long. Some primal need only he can fill.

After he finishes, he untangles our bodies, takes care of the condom, rejoins me in bed.

I relax into the sheets, spent and sweaty.

He rolls onto his side. Looks me up and down with equal parts pride and satisfaction. "You want more?"

I shake my head.

"I remember dares."

"Warnings not to dare. I didn't dare."

"You sure?" He smiles. "'Cause I'd really like to see how many I can hit."

"It's all about you?"

"How many we can hit."

I can't help but smile. "Tomorrow. I'm exhausted."

"Is that a promise?"

"Absolutely."

"Okay." He presses his lips to mine. "I promise to make you come tomorrow."

Chapter Twenty-Six

LIAM

This isn't the first time I've woken up in another bed.

But it's the first time I've wanted to stay.

Briar West is sound asleep next to me.

Briar West is naked under the white sheets.

Briar West slept naked, next to me, last night.

Everything else—the complications, the wedding, the fate of my father figure—drifts away as I watch her chest rise and fall with her breath.

I've never watched someone sleep before. Not on purpose.

But this feels right.

She's never this serene. That's what I love about her. She's all fire and purpose, even when she's holding a perfect poker face.

I never see her with her guard down.

She stirs. Rolls onto her side. Blinks her eyes open.

"Hey." Her voice is soft. Gentle.

"Hey." Mine is too.

"I like this look for you." Her gaze flits to my bare torso then moves down it.

"Right to the dick?"

"That's what you're here for." She does nothing to hide her stare.

"You're using me?"

"You didn't realize?"

"Why do you think I'm naked?"

Her smile lights up her eyes. "Smart man."

"I have my moments."

"You really are…"

"I am…"

"Do you need me stroking your ego?"

"It's my second favorite thing for you to stroke."

A laugh spills from her lips. "Really though? Would your ego actually grow if I said, 'Liam Pierce, you have a massive cock.'"

"My ego. And my favorite thing for you to stroke."

Her smile widens. "How can you make obnoxious so adorable?"

"Skill."

"It is a skill." She stretches her arms over her head as she yawns. "Do I need to get up?"

"If you don't want your boss to reprimand you."

"What if I do?"

Fuck, the ideas that fill my head. I'm not usually into the whole punishment thing. I'm not opposed, but it's not where I go when I need to cross the finish line.

Right now, the thought of Briar bent over my desk, purring about how she's a bad girl?

Fuck.

"I guess you were right." Her eyes stay glued to my dick. "It is growing."

"Baby, you have ten seconds. Stop or I'm going to fuck you."

"What if I take all nine?"

"Might fuck you anyway."

She props herself up on her elbow. "What time is it?"

"Time to get dressed."

"Hmm…" She taps her chin. "Quite the predicament. Since my boss is the most annoying person on the planet."

"I've heard that."

"Seriously. He thinks the entire world revolves around him."

"Massive ego?"

"Oh yeah."

"But he backs it up?"

"How did you circle back to your dick so quickly?"

"I told you. Skills."

She laughs. "Can we be late?"

"Yes."

"Then let me brush my teeth first."

"It's been more than ten seconds."

"I know. You do it too."

"Bossy," I say.

"If you think this is bossy, you should try working for Liam Pierce."

I can't help but chuckle. "I'll put coffee on."

"Coffee?" Her nose scrunches in distaste. "Not tea?"

"Would you rather fuck me or have your tea?"

"Why is both not an option?"

"Go. Now. Or I'm fucking you right here."

She smiles and shifts out of bed.

Fuck, she has a fantastic ass. Those round hips, the thick thighs—

I want to die between them. I really do.

I wait until she closes the door, then I use the bathroom in the master, fill the kettle, set it to boil.

Briar steps into the kitchen in a black silk robe.

"You trying to drive me out of my mind, baby?"

"Is it working?"

"What do you think?" I motion *come here.*

She shakes her head. Returns the gesture.

"Bossy."

"No."

"Never?" I raise a brow.

"Sometimes." She undoes the sash of her robe.

"This time?"

She shakes her head.

"Next time?"

"Maybe. Or maybe next time I'll call you Mr. Pierce and find out what happens."

Fuck me.

"Are you going to stand there and stare?"

"Fuck yes."

She pushes the sides apart. "You could come closer."

"I'm enjoying the show."

"In that case—" she takes a step toward me. Then another. Another.

I meet her halfway.

Her hand curls around my neck. She looks up at me with need, affection, desire.

My heart melts.

My body roars.

My head—there's no blood left in my fucking brain. My head isn't in the picture.

I wrap my arms around her, pull her body into mine, kiss her hard.

Her lips part. My tongue slips into her mouth. Dances with hers.

There's no other way to explain it.

I lead her to the counter. Pin her to the hard surface.

She groans as my hard-on brushes her stomach.

I bring one hand to her chest. Toy with her as I kiss her. Slow circles around her nipple until she's so on edge she has to pull back to groan.

"Liam." Her nails sink into my neck.

"Say it again."

"Liam."

It's music. The only thing better is her groan.

"You need to fuck me now."

"Need a condom."

"Did you mean it? What you said about not being with anyone else?"

"Baby, I'm not coherent enough to follow you."

"Since Toronto." She looks up at me. "Have you really not been with anyone else?"

"Yeah."

"For five months?"

"Yeah."

"The story about the girl in the closet, that happened?"

"Might have."

"When?"

"At that gala for STEM in school."

"The blonde with the fake tits?"

"Baby, you want to talk about some other woman's tits?"

"They were huge."

"So?"

"Did she have them out?" She steps back. Pushes the sides of her robe apart. "Like this. Unbuttoned?"

Fuck.

"Or was she naked?"

"Bri—"

"You've thought of me?"

"Of course."

"How does it go?" She places her hand on my chest. "Do I walk into your office in my clothes. Drop to my knees behind your desk?"

"Sometimes."

"Do I take anything off?"

I nod.

She drags her hand down my torso. "What?"

"Depends what you're wearing that day."

"Last time?"

"Yesterday?"

She smiles with victory.

But I can't say I feel defeated.

"Yesterday."

"You came in. Unbuttoned your shirt to show me your tits. Like it was our secret."

"No bra?"

"No bra."

"I was wearing one."

"I wasn't worried about the logic."

Her fingers dip below my belly button. "Maybe I took it off in the bathroom."

"Bri—"

"What then?" She wraps her hand around my cock.

My eyes flutter closed. Her hand feels good. Too good. "I need to fuck you."

"Then order me." She runs her thumb over my tip. "What then?"

"You saw I was hard. Came behind my desk. Sucked me off with the blinds down. Even though someone might catch us."

"I like that." She pumps me. "Maybe later."

"You are bossy."

"Sometimes." She's daring me.

I think. It's hard to hold on to conscious thought.

The stroke of her hand feels too fucking good.

She pumps me again.

Again.

Fuck. I'm going to come if she keeps this up.

I can't exactly complain, but I want to come with her.

"Baby, I need to fuck you—"

"Like this. This time." She lowers herself slowly. Presses her lips to my stomach. The spot just below my belly button.

Then lower.

Lower.

Her lips brush my cock. Softly. Then harder.

She takes me into her mouth.

I bring my hand to the back of her head.

She wraps her arm around me. Digs her fingers into the flesh of my ass, using the grip for leverage as she takes me deeper.

She does it slowly.

So fucking slowly. Like she's savoring every inch.

My free hand goes to her shoulder. Her chest.

I cup her breast, running my thumb over her nipple.

She groans against my cock.

She toys with me. Tests soft swirls of her tongue. Hard strokes. Fast flicks. Slow ones.

When she finds it, she teases me again and again.

I toy with her as she toys with me.

It's a perfect circle of torture. Well, almost. As soon as I make her come.

Then she takes me again, and I don't give a fuck about anything but her soft, wet mouth, her sweet lips, her perfect tits.

Briar West on her knees in my fucking kitchen.

Demanding to suck me off.

I've died and gone to heaven.

I really have.

I take in the perfect sight of her for a moment, then I close my eyes, press my palm against the back of her head, guide her deeper.

Deeper.

So deep she almost gags.

But she takes it.

Then she pulls back and she does it again.

She finds that rhythm. Works me again and again. With soft, sweet perfection.

I toy with her, rubbing her harder and harder, until she's groaning against me.

The perfect vibration pushes me over the edge.

"Fuck." I tug at her hair, holding her head in place as I rock through my orgasm.

The world goes white.

An entire universe of bliss.

Every part of me feels awake and alive.

And every part wants the same thing—her.

I groan her name as I come.

She waits until I've spilled every drop, then she pulls back, swallows hard, wipes her mouth with the back of her hand.

"Fuck," I say it again.

She looks up at me with pride and victory.

But I'm pretty sure we're both winning. I offer her my hand.

She takes it. Lets me pull her to her feet.

"You think you can get away with that, baby?" I ask.

"Away with what, Mr. Pierce?"

I pin her to the table, kiss her hard, slip my hand between her legs.

She groans against my lips as my fingers find her clit.

I rub her with slow circles.

Then faster.

Faster.

Until I find the speed she needs.

I rub her as I toy with her breasts.

Again and again.

Until she's there, groaning against my mouth, rocking against my hand, raking her nails across my chest.

She pulses against me as she comes.

Then she melts. Her entire body goes slack.

I catch her. Hold her close. Soak in the warmth of her body and the sweet sound of her strained breaths.

"Better." I brush her hair behind her ear. "Much fucking better."

She nods into my chest.

"You should get dressed." I press my lips to her forehead. "We're gonna be late."

"Do you care?"

"No."

"Me either."

My entire body fills with pride. More pride than I've felt in a long fucking time.

Chapter Twenty-Seven

LIAM

I shower, dress, meet Briar in the kitchen.

"I liked your old outfit better." She turns to me with a smile.

"Can't complain about your current look."

She smooths her sheath dress. A forest green with a square neckline and a snug skirt. "I thought about the skirt and blouse, but I wanted to leave a little blood in your brain."

"Merciful."

"That's what they say about me." She strains her tea into a mug of milk. Stirs in honey—the fancy lavender honey I bought for her—and brings the spoon to her wine red lips.

"You plan that?"

"Plan what?"

"Earlier?"

"Did I plan to suck you off?" She licks honey from her spoon. "Not exactly."

"You were wearing lipstick."

She shrugs, feigning innocence. "If you didn't like it…"

"You know I did."

She smiles, victorious.

"I checked our schedule."

"Our schedule?"

"Is it not ours?"

"It's usually *your* schedule."

It is *my* schedule. And, usually, she's the one in charge of it. But, soon, it will be ours. Hers, even. She's going to run her own fucking business.

She's going to soar.

I'll be there, working with her, but not the way I am now. Not night and day. Not every business trip and conference and crisis.

I'm happy for her. I'm incredibly fucking proud. But I'm going to miss this too.

"It's ours today," I say. "And we don't have a meeting until eleven."

"We don't?"

"So sit the fuck down. I'm making breakfast."

"Since when do you cook?"

"I'm an excellent cook."

She shoots me an incredulous look.

"I can toast bread."

"Immense skill."

"And fry eggs."

"And not overcook them?"

"We can go out if you want."

"No. I want to see you fry eggs in your suit jacket." She smiles. "Then take your own clothes to the dry cleaner."

I can't help but laugh. "You think I'm incapable?"

"I think it's impossible."

"First step." I shrug my suit jacket off my shoulders. Drape it over a dining chair.

She watches as I roll my sleeves to my elbows. "Good first step."

"Brutal."

"You love it."

I do. I really do. "I guess I'm a masochist."

"Back to that, again?"

"If I am?"

"You think I won't hurt you?"

"I know you'll hurt me."

She laughs. "You shouldn't bait."

"I'm not smart enough to realize that." I warm a pan, find eggs, toast bread.

Briar surveys the counter. "Do you have avocados?"

"Why?"

"Why? You can't eat eggs and toast without avocados."

"I can't?"

"Of course not." She stares at me with surprise. "It's wrong."

"Californian."

"I don't deny that."

"You don't claim it either." I check the fridge. Find an avocado in the fruit drawer. Hold it up to her. "Is one acceptable?"

She makes a *hmm* motion. "For both of us?"

"It's all yours if you want it."

"No. One is fine."

"But one for yourself would be better?"

"I wouldn't turn it down."

"You can have it."

"No." She shakes her head. "You need to experience the avocado too."

"I've had it before."

"With the eggs and toast."

"Back seat cook."

She bites her lip. Plants in her chair. "I am, aren't I?"

I motion *a little*. Draw out my fingers until it's *a lot*.

"I'll stop."

"I'll believe it when I see it."

"Do you have cilantro?"

"See."

"It's good with the avocado."

"Sit."

"I'm sitting."

"If you hate it, we can go out."

"Okay. Deal." She takes a sip of her tea. Lets out a soft groan.

It's different than the sound she makes when she comes, but it's close. It's really fucking close.

I focus on cooking for long enough to warm oil, crack eggs, plate avocado halves, find hot sauce.

The eggs cook fast. I scoop them onto plates. Fix my coffee. Bring everything to the dining table.

Briar looks me over carefully. "I think you made it."

"Made it?"

"Without staining your shirt."

"What about this?" I grab the sriracha.

"That's dangerous." She scans the counter, looking for something.

I can't help but laugh. "Have you always been this picky?"

"I know what I like."

"I like that about you." I haven't had many breakfasts with her. I don't have any idea what she does at her apartment when she's alone. But I know Bri. I find the Cholula.

Her eyes light up. "Perfect. Thanks, Liam. Really."

I join her at the table.

"You don't want to help me find what I like?"

"Is this about sex?"

"Maybe."

"Whatever it is, yes."

"What if it's something freaky?"

"Especially if it's something freaky." I brush her hair behind her ear. "I want to be the only guy who's game."

"You mean that."

"Why wouldn't I?"

"I don't know. I'm not used to you this sincere."

"Me either."

She pours hot sauce on her eggs. Scoops them onto toast. Piles avocado on top of it.

Then she cuts a slice.

She's eating her toast with a fork and knife.

"What?" She stops mid bite. "You're giving me a look."

"Who eats toast with a fork?"

"Everyone if it's French toast."

"That's true."

"It's good this way. Try it." She picks up the hot sauce. Motions *may I?*

"Go for it."

She covers my eggs in hot sauce, then she takes a bite of her food, lets out a soft groan, follows it with a sip of tea and another groan.

Pure. Fucking. Torture.

"You're not eating," she says.

"Doing something better."

"Eat. Please."

Fuck, the way she says please. I need to hear it on her lips again.

I copy her technique. Cut a slice, bring it to my mouth, bite half.

Crisp toast, warm eggs, creamy avocado. And the hint of heat.

It's good.

Not the greatest meal in the world. But pretty fucking good. "Not bad."

She nods. "You do have skills."

I'm not the world's greatest cook. I wouldn't claim that. But I tired of living on pizza and take out after a semester at school. I learned enough to feed myself—for breakfast and dinners at home, at least—my sophomore year. "I know how to take care of myself."

"You do."

"You say it with surprise."

"You project a different image." She takes another bite. "On purpose, I think. But you sell it well."

"I don't get much fancier than this."

"It's good food. It doesn't need to be fancy."

"I keep forgetting that."

"You really think people like you because you're rich?" she asks.

"That might not be all they like about me. It might not be their favorite thing about me, but you've seen people. The way they act when they recognize my name. Or learn I'm a CFO. They're different."

"Even when you're in a suit?"

"More when I'm wearing jeans, yeah. But men in suits are a dime a dozen in the city."

She nods *true*. "Is it hard? Not knowing if people want you or your money?"

"Sometimes. I don't usually think of it that way."

"How do you think of it?"

"Everyone projects an image. We all have some choice in it. More, these days, with social media."

She nods.

"You wear combat boots and thick eyeliner."

"And the hair." She whips a purple strand.

"And the hair. People see you and they think bold,

edgy, confident. Maybe a little intimidating. Which is what you want, right?"

"Partially."

"It's who you are. Just like I'm a rich asshole sometimes. But it can't begin to describe you. You're smart and thoughtful and willing to call people on their shit, even if it might hurt you. You're guarded, sure, but you know it. And when you let your guard down, fuck… your smile lights up the entire room."

Her cheeks flush.

"When you laugh, even if it's at me, not with me—it's the second best sound in the world."

"What's the best?"

My eyes flit to her chest.

"Oh. Right." Her blush deepens. "You say stupid things on purpose. Just to make me laugh."

"Of course."

"It's sweet. Obnoxious, sometimes, but sweet."

"I know."

She smiles. "You really do. You know who you are. You know what role you play."

I nod.

"But sometimes… sometimes I think you don't know, Liam. Sometimes I wonder if you see the guy I do. Or if you see the guy you try to convince everyone you are."

"Who do you see?"

"Someone loving, sweet, who will do anything for the people he loves, who wants intimacy and connection but can't bring himself to admit it."

"Is that what you want?"

She swallows hard. "Sometimes. I don't know. I don't want to get hurt."

"Who does?"

"Some people are better at it than others." She takes

another bite. "I just… I do see you. I don't know what the fuck we're doing here, but I want you to know that. I see the guy you are. And I like him."

"I like you too."

"Is that where we are? High school crushes?"

"If you'll make out with me behind the bleachers."

She laughs.

"I missed out. All boys school."

"How did you survive?" She takes another sip of her tea. "An entire semester without sex."

"There were weekends off."

"Five whole days? Impossible."

"I made it five months."

"You really did?"

"You think I could lie under those circumstances?" I motion to the counter where she had me under her thumb. So to speak.

"Some guys will say anything."

"I'm not some guys."

"You're really not." She looks at me curiously, considering something. "Have you thought about this? Us?"

"No." I take a long sip of my coffee. Savor the sweet, creamy warmth. The domesticity.

I've never had that before.

I've never wanted it before.

But I want to wake up next to her tomorrow. I want to fall asleep next to her tonight.

Will I feel the same way after this ruse? In six months? A year?

I don't know. It's hard to imagine feeling otherwise.

"I've been too busy trying to convince myself not to touch you," I say.

"Me too," she admits.

"I've never done this before. I have no fucking idea how it goes."

"But you want it to go somewhere?"

"Yeah." I know it's true the second I say it.

"What if it's too complicated with work?"

"Then it's too complicated with work. I can bow out."

"End this…"

"Find someone else to advise you."

"Oh." She swallows hard. "You'd do that?"

"If that's what you want. I want you in my life, Bri. As much as I can have."

"That almost sounds like a commitment."

"A letter of intent, maybe?"

"Should we draft something official?" She laughs.

It's a joke, but I don't fucking care. I'm ready. "Let's do it." I stand. Grab a paper towel. Find a sharpie in the drawer.

"Really?"

"Fuck yeah."

She laughs. "Okay. Well, it's your letter of intent. Go."

Normally, these are advanced versions of cover letters or pre-contract promises. They have a lot of fluff about work experience and qualifications.

Too much to fit on a paper towel.

I keep it simple.

Dear Briar West,

I, Liam Pierce, am interested in the role of your paramour. I promise orgasms on demand, stupid jokes, and all the avocado you can eat.

Yours,
Liam Pierce

WE ROLL INTO THE MEETING FIVE MINUTES LATE, HOLDING takeout coffee, smiling like idiots.

Simon eyes us suspiciously—of course—but he sticks to the meeting script. Even says congrats on his way out.

It's bullshit, but I can't bring myself to care.

Life is blue skies and sunshine and the sound of Briar's groan.

Work passes in a blink. The night is even faster. A perfect blend of talk and takeout and Briar coming again and again.

Life is good.

Easy.

Until Simon knocks on my door Thursday and asks if I'm ready for the bachelor party.

Only it's not just Simon.

Preston is next to him, and he's wearing his exhaustion like a cheap suit.

Simon knows something is wrong.

He knows I'm keeping a secret of my own.

But he doesn't know what. Not yet.

I have to keep it that way.

Chapter Twenty-Eight

BRIAR

A h, sweet relief. The server drops off our tray of drinks.

Brandy for Preston—I swear, he's a character out of a movie.

A very expensive Japanese whiskey for Simon—ditto. The same for Harrison.

Then Liam's bright green appletini and my pink grapefruit martini.

We stand out. Not that I mind. I rock purple hair and combat boots on purpose. Usually, I enjoy it. Okay, I still enjoy it.

But the weird silence between Simon and Liam—the one that's been growing tenser every minute, for all ten minutes of our walk, then another ten of our wait—

It has me on edge.

They're trying to keep it from Preston, but they're not fooling anyone. Liam and Simon have many modes of engaging. Irritated stares. Loud arguments. Jokes at the other's expense.

Silence?

Not so much.

"Thank you so much." I nod to the server and pounce on my drink. Grapefruit and gin and St Germain and a release from the voice in my head, wondering what the fuck is going on.

Who cares? I have a martini.

I have a… whatever I should call Liam. Boss, boyfriend, fake fiancé. Potential paramour, I guess.

Does he really mean it?

I, Liam Pierce, am interested in the role of your paramour. I promise orgasms on demand, stupid jokes, and all the avocado you can eat.

Liam as my boyfriend. That I can handle.

But fiancé? Husband?

I care about him. I want him in my life.

But saying *I do?*

The thought still makes me sick.

But, hey, we're at a pre-bachelor party dinner (since when is that a thing?). This is the time to say, "are you really sure you can be with one person forever?"

"Are you going to the party?" I ask Preston.

"I don't think anyone wants their father watching their night of debauchery." Preston holds up his drink to toast. "To your wedding, Harrison."

"And your last night living it up as a free man," Liam says.

Simon shoots him a cutting look. "Aren't you engaged?"

"To Briar." Liam winks at me. "That's a prison I want to inhabit."

"Was that a compliment?" I ask.

"Was it not?" Liam asks.

Preston chuckles *silly boy*. "Stop while you're behind, son."

"The point is, I want to be tied to you for the rest of time," Liam says.

"I think Simon is pointing out the discrepancy between the claim you adore me and the claim this is Harrison's last night of freedom." I take another sip. Let the sweet, tart liquid warm my tongue.

"It's you," Liam says. "How is this not clear?"

"He's an idiot. I'm used to it," Harrison says.

Good enough for me. "Are you excited to revel in your freedom, Harrison?" I hold up my drink. "To debauchery."

"The end of debauchery." He raises his drink. "I've been waiting for this day for a long time. Lee is going to be my wife." He beams. "If I have to watch Liam throw money at strippers for one night, I can do that."

Preston chuckles.

Liam too. "You have no idea what you're in for, kid." He raises his glass.

"To your last night dealing with Liam's bullshit," Simon offers.

Liam shoots him a fuck you look, then he toasts, smiles, sips. "Refreshing."

"How do you drink those?" Harrison asks.

"They're good. Strong. Stronger than brandy." He motions to Harrison and Preston's matching glasses. "You sure you don't want to come, Preston? This is fun for all ages."

"Children?" Preston.

"Maybe. Maybe not." Liam mimes zipping his lips.

"You should come, Dad," Harrison says. "Keep an eye on Liam."

"I'm afraid I'm relinquishing that duty for the night." He smiles at his son. "It will be practice for when you have kids of your own."

"Was he always this difficult?" Harrison asks.

Simon actually chuckles. "Worse. But I'll keep him in check tonight."

Liam shoots Simon a *fuck off*. It's not his usual *fuck off*. There's something between the two of them. But no one else seems to notice.

They shift into banter, finish their round, wish me and Preston good night.

I stand to say goodbye to Liam. "Are you okay?"

"Just Simon being an asshole." His frustration disappears as he brushes my hair behind my ear. "You look so fucking beautiful tonight, baby."

"Thanks." My cheeks flush. "You look handsome too."

He runs his fingers over my chin. "Will you be okay with Preston?"

"What?"

"He wants to have dinner with you."

"I thought—"

"I know. Will you?"

The two of us? Alone? Again?

I barely survived last time.

But there's something in the way Liam looks at me. A promise I have to answer. "I'll do my best."

"You'll be perfect."

Chapter Twenty-Nine

LIAM

T he elevator is slow. This is a new building. How is the elevator this fucking slow?

Simon regales Harrison with a story about Lee. An old one, from his days dating her sister.

Finally, we arrive, walk through the lobby, find the limo outside.

Harrison's best friend, Jimmy, pops out of the moon roof. Right on cue, he yells, "Wooh," and pops a bottle of champagne.

Foam spills over the sides. The man might as well scream *look at me, I'm coming*. He's as obnoxious as I am. Or as I was, five, six, ten years ago.

I'm an idiot, sure, but I'm not desperate to party. He spent the last three years bragging about banging escorts. *It's so efficient, Liam. You don't get it. No complications. No worrying they'll work for a competitor. No promises of cuddles after.*

The girl comes to my office and blows me right there. Then she leaves.

It's the perfect relationship.

She wants to stay, sure. She adores me. But I don't have time for that.

Last year, he "graduated" to sleeping with sugar babies.

Now, he brags about the tuition he pays for his college girlfriend. And the apartment he bought for her. It's nice. In her neighborhood. So they won't run into each other by accident.

And she's Asian, so no one ever wonders if I'm her dad.

I feel an intense need to text Briar. To head back upstairs, drag her down here, beg her to save me from this pointless expression of masculinity.

Harrison doesn't want to mourn his lack of future pussy.

Jimmy doesn't want to keep it low key.

Simon doesn't want to tell me shit.

All we need is Adam teleporting from the mansion, exuding social anxiety and an intense lack of desire to touch dancers, and we'll really have a party.

How can guys with access to anything they want be such a miserable time?

"Last time you'll have the chance for that." I try to step into my role, but I'm not feeling it.

I want to take Briar home.

I want to fuck her senseless then hold her all night.

Sex.

It's still the only thing that makes sense.

Only it's more than that. Her laugh and her smile and her groan and her joy.

What would she say about Jimmy?

I wait until we're in the limo, and Jimmy is bragging about how he knows all the best strip clubs, and the strippers really do like him too, they don't just pretend, then I pull out my cell.

I text Briar.

Liam: How long until Jimmy brings up his sugar baby? Five minutes? Or less?

Briar: I'm having dinner with your surrogate father.

Liam: And?

Briar: It's rude to stop to text.

Liam: Then why are you doing it?

Briar: I'm in the bathroom.

Liam: And I'm rude?

Briar: Am I supposed to wait to pee now?

Liam: You can come.

Briar: In the bathroom? I'll pass.

Liam: To the party. I'll hold the limo.

Briar: And give Harrison that lap dance he's dreaming about? I don't think so.

Liam: What if you give me the lap dance I've been dreaming about?

Briar: Have you?

Liam: It entered my mind.

Briar: I'll think about it.

Liam: Really?

Briar: I said think. Not do. What's in it for me?

Liam: Me fucking you senseless.

Briar: Strong case.

Liam: I can reserve a private room.

Briar: Covered in creepy dudes' jizz? No thanks.

Liam: I love that you said that.

Briar: It's true. Are you actually going to a strip club?

Liam: It's that or a hotel room.

Briar: Talk about a space covered in jizz.

Liam: Fuck, Bri, I travel three months a year for work.

Briar: I know.

Liam: You're killing me.

Briar: Because you're so turned on right now?

Liam: That's it. The thought of creepy dudes' cum makes me rock hard.

Briar: You like the nasty space. It's a rich boy rebellion.

Fuck, she's right. The thought of bringing Briar to some dive in midtown, reserving a private room for the two of us, eating her out on the stage—

I'm going to be hard if I keep thinking about it.

Too hard for this fucking occasion.

Briar: He's probably already talking about his new sugar baby because the last one kicked him to the curb. Now, go back to your party, and only text me if it's an emergency.

Liam: An emergency need to come?

Briar: If you're in a space where such things are possible… then maybe. After I'm done with this task you dumped on me.

Liam: You like Preston.

Briar: I do.

Liam: He'll turn into a pumpkin soon. Offer to walk him out at nine. Trust me. You'll be home by ten.

Briar: Home, naked, fucking myself on the couch.

Liam: Baby.

Briar: Sorry. Thinking out loud. Until then.

She's pure evil.

She really is.

Someone makes that whip sound. One I haven't heard since high school.

Huh?

I look up.

And there's Jimmy, repeating the sound, adding a whip gesture.

"Never seen you pussy-whipped before," he says.

What the fuck do I even say to that? It's too stupid to dignify with a response.

"Yeah, I guess I'm a pathetic asshole who likes talking to my girlfriend," I say.

"Fiancée?" Simon offers.

"That one," I say.

Simon shoots me an incredulous look. Then he… smiles.

No.

He's not smiling.

That's not possible.

Simon smiles at victory. At destruction. At pain.

Not at… whatever the fuck this is.

"Were you really texting Briar?" he asks.

"Yeah…" What's his point?

"You just left," he says.

"I had something to tell her," I say.

Simon chuckles. "You're that inseparable."

"Rather hang with her than you assholes," I say.

"We won't fuck you," Simon says.

"But that doesn't mean you have to go home empty. Know what I'm saying?" Jimmy winks.

"Wouldn't I go home empty if I came tonight?" I ask.

Jimmy catches none of my irritation. He raises his hand for a high-five.

Right. Up-top. I high-five him back.

He passes out champagne flutes. Announces a toast to making sure Harrison's suit needs dry cleaning tomorrow.

It's muddled, yeah, but it's almost clever for him.

We drink. He returns to bragging about strip clubs. And, oh, Bri was right, his new sugar baby, who works as a dancer, who gets so hot at work when he shows up at her club she fucks him in the backroom.

For a second, I cringe at the mental image. Then it shifts, and it's Briar in some sexy scrap of black mesh, grinding against my lap, begging me to fuck her.

Bam, I'm ready to go.

A dingy strip club isn't her scene. But a nice place, with private rooms, an exclusive club even—

Can I convince her to go?

No, can I do better?

Liam: One more thing.

Briar: Oh my god, Liam! It's been five minutes.

Liam: It's a hard-on emergency.

Briar: Really?

Liam: It's really hard to keep a straight face on around Jimmy.

Briar: Now you know how I feel all the time.

Liam: No laugh?

Briar: It was good.

Liam: Clever for me?

Briar: It was.

Liam: Does it get you off? The thought of a lap dance in a private room?

Briar: Maybe.

Liam: Taking off your sheer mesh as you grind against my hard-on. My hands on your tits. You watching everything in the mirrors. Me, promising you whatever the fuck you want if you release me from the agony of how badly I want you?

Briar: When you say it like that.

Liam: Is it hot to you? The thought of me wanting you so badly I'll pay you for it?

Briar: There's something about the capitalist power exchange.

Liam: You know I get hard when you use big words.

Briar: I do.

Liam: I want to try it.

Briar: You don't say.

Liam: But I'd rather try something you've been dreaming about. Something you've always wanted to do that you've never shared with anyone.

Briar: Tonight?

Liam: If you've got the energy.

Briar: I'm already wiped.

Liam: Then soon.

Briar: Can we do yours first?

Liam: We did mine last time.

Briar: Most of my fantasies of you involve duct taping your mouth so you can't talk.

Liam: Could be an interesting start.

Briar: They don't end the way you hope.

Liam: I'm open minded.

Briar: I'll think about it.

Liam: You really dream about hurting me?

Briar: Not dream, exactly, but it's entered my mind.

Liam: Nothing sexy?

Briar: With you?

Liam: With anyone. I'll pretend I'm Chris Pine. I don't care.

Briar: I can't believe you're using that against me.

Liam: I'm inspired by your patriotism.

Briar: See, this is where the fantasies of duct tape come up.

Liam: And handcuffs, so I can't text?

Briar: Absolutely.

Liam: Would be easier to sit on my face. And it would shut me up.

Briar: Win-win.

How can she make me laugh at the same time she makes me hard?

It defies reasoning.

Liam: I can wait. But if there's something you want to try, I want to try it with you.

Briar: I really need to get back to Preston.

Liam: Then promise.

Briar: Okay. I promise.

"You done, Liam? Or should we send the limo back to the restaurant?" Jimmy laughs at his own joke. "Maybe leave you alone in here for, say, three minutes."

All right, that's not bad. "Only need two, but no thanks." I slip my phone into my pocket. "I'll save it for tonight."

"Get amped on other ladies and bring it home. Classic."

All right, sure. What do I know about monogamy? Maybe guys get amped on strippers and bring the energy to their wives.

Maybe that's a perfectly healthy relationship.

It's not one I want, but maybe it will work for the poor woman Jimmy convinces to marry him.

"Not exactly." I shoot him a coy smile.

He cocks his head, not following. Then he shrugs it off, slams a glass of champagne.

The limo parks.

The driver pulls the door open. Helps Harrison out. Then Jimmy.

"He has no idea?" Simon asks.

"Huh?"

"What you've planned?" he asks.

"You're talking to me?"

"I've been talking to you."

Right. I'm the one ignoring him. Because he's a secretive asshole.

But I'll know soon.

So it doesn't matter. Simon is Simon. He can't help it.

"You shouldn't keep secrets," I say.

"And yours?"

Yeah. That's where we always land. I've got no high ground. "You're an asshole."

"I'm aware."

"But this isn't the time. Let's truce."

"Truce?"

"Yeah. Until after the wedding. I'll pretend I don't know you're keeping shit from me."

"And I'll do the same?"

"Yeah." I offer my hand.

He shakes. "Until then." He motions *after you*. "Does *Harrison* have any idea what you've planned?"

"Maybe. But Jimmy… can't wait to see the look on his face when he puts it together."

"He's as bad as you."

"Ten times worse."

He nods. "The kind of guy you could have become."

"What, without your expert brotherly advice?"

"You deny it?" It's true. I'm not a delusional chauvinist. I'm a reasonably-in-touch-with-reality man who respects women.

Is that thanks to Simon's seriousness, Adam's studiousness, Preston's softness?

Losing our parents?

I don't know.

I don't care.

"I'm just glad I'm not as bad as that asshole," I say.

"Me too."

"That's the nicest thing you've said about me in a while."

"Don't get used to it."

———

EXCEPT FOR BRIGHT PINK LETTERS SPELLING MANHATTAN, the venue resembles any other dive bar. A bouncer stands in front of a red velvet line, checking the IDs of a giggling group of girls.

Jimmy notices the short white dress one of them is wearing, but his attention goes straight to her ass. He misses the sash reading *Bride to Be*. Or maybe he doesn't care.

The girls giggle as they enter.

Jimmy moves to the bouncer. Presents his ID. "I don't usually see ladies at places like this."

The bouncer shrugs with disinterest. "We get all types."

"Right on." He turns to me. "You think your girl would show, Liam? I heard she promised Harrison a lap dance."

Simon chuckles as he shows his ID, moves past the velvet rope. "There's really no good response here. You insult Liam's fiancée either way."

"He suggested my fiancée is some kind of prison warden." Harrison takes his turn.

"You did say that," Simon agrees.

"I thought that was your kink." I wink at Harrison. Show the bouncer my ID. "Love is love. I'm happy you're happy. All that shit." I turn to Jimmy. "You ready?"

"I was born ready!" He fails to catch on.

Perfect. I pat his back. "Let's go."

He enters the venue first.

Smiles as he notices the crowd of women. The big, black stage. The stocked bar.

The bartenders—two built guys wearing only bow ties and hot pants.

The similarly dressed dudes at go-go poles.

The letters spelling out MANhattan Hunk City.

"This is a male strip club?" he asks.

"It is," I say.

Jimmy's entire face deflates. He eyes the room again. "All right, I can work with this. Lots of ladies here. They're gonna get amped and then…" He makes a thrusting motion with his pelvis.

Yuck.

Harrison takes in the scene with a smile. "Of course." He chuckles. "Liam. It's perfect."

"I thought you'd say that… just wait." I turn to my brother. "Simon, your assistance?"

He nods *of course*, grabs Harrison's right arm as I grab the left.

We guide him to the bar. Announce his status as the groom.

The bartender—the one in a purple wig—undoes Harrison's tie and shoves it in his pocket. Then he drapes a sash over Harrison's shoulder reading *Groom to Be* and places a penis-tipped tiara on his head.

"I can't wait until you're married and I can get you back for this," Harrison says.

"Me either." I smile. I expect some resistance to build but none does.

I mean it.

I really fucking mean it.

Chapter Thirty

BRIAR

"How is it going?" Preston asks. "Is Liam torturing my son?"

"Sorry." I set my cell on the table. But it's face up. The screen is still beckoning me. Promising teasing and dirty talk and maybe even a picture.

Oh god, I don't have my privacy settings on. The image will show up on my cell screen without warning. I don't think Liam will send an unsolicited picture, but—

I slip the phone into my purse, just to be safe.

As much as I enjoy mocking Jimmy—seriously, chasing teenagers and making a whip sound—I don't need the constant updates.

I need to be here, to stay present.

Preston lets out a hearty laugh. "Did Liam drop the reveal?"

"Huh?"

"The all-male revue?"

"What?"

"Are you all right, Briar?"

No. I'm thinking about calling Liam and demanding he

287

swing the limo around for a quickie. Or at least a hotel room interlude in the middle of his party.

I'm sitting next to this nice older man, thinking about mounting the fake fiancé he sees as a son.

What the hell is wrong with me?

"He took the guys to a male strip club?" I ask.

Preston nods.

"He didn't tell me that."

"He knows how to keep a secret."

He does.

"No one wants to hear that about their fiancé." He takes a sip of his brandy. "I was never a very good wingman."

"No? You don't rack up phone numbers saying, 'Hey, have you seen how hot my friend is? He won't cheat on you, but if he did, he'd keep it under wraps really well.'"

"I haven't tried."

"Next time."

He laughs, but it's loaded.

Or maybe I'm projecting. Liam and I are keeping a secret from him. And the whole subject of cheating. Total no-go zone. I take another sip. Try to think of an appropriate response. Say the worst thing possible instead. "Was that what happened with your wife?"

"Did a wingman win her over? No, I was charming back then. Handsome too."

"You're still handsome."

His smile is genuine. "You don't have to flatter me."

"I'm not." Preston is still a handsome man. Older, sure, but he wears it well. He's not trying to hold on to his youth the way some people do. He's a little thin, and pale too, but he looks good. Distinguished.

"What would you say to flatter me?"

"I don't know. I'm not good at flattering. Probably

something about how smart and interesting you are. Men want to hear that."

"My fantastic taste in film, perhaps?"

"Or opera."

"Have you seen *La Traviata*?"

I shake my head. "I haven't seen anything."

"Tell Liam to take you. He'll argue—he's not one for 'stuffy' culture—but you'll love it."

"You think so?"

"It's transcendent."

I might be with Liam on this one. Sure, it would be hot to make out on the balcony. If the opera happens to be in the background, I don't mind. But I don't see the appeal of old tragedies.

"I have a box. Take my tickets for the show in September."

"Okay." Not thinking about Liam's hand between my legs. Thinking about the beauty of music. The climax. The opera climax. What's that called? An aria. Something like that. Something that isn't about riding my fake fiancé. "But I want my money back if I don't like it."

"For the free tickets?"

"For the dress I buy for the occasion."

He offers his hand.

I shake.

"Have you spent time pretending you find boring men interesting?"

"Only for work." I take another sip of my martini. Cut a marinated beet in half. We're mostly done with dinner, but I'm still picking at my roasted spring vegetables.

"I imagine it's the most difficult place to do it. People with power and money are used to fawning."

"Usually. What about Liam?"

"He's used to fawning."

"But he's interesting."

"I'd hope you think so."

"Even before I liked him… I thought he was annoying when we met."

He smiles. "He grew up trying to irritate his brothers."

"Maybe that's it. A younger sibling's need for attention." I take a bite of my beet. Mmm, the earthy flavor of the root mixes with the sweet citrus marinade. A perfect melody. "Simon never tries to be interesting."

"He doesn't."

"I think he is. He just doesn't want to share that with people."

"Do you?"

"Not usually," I admit. "I didn't have great luck with guys when I was young. I didn't pretend they were interesting. But I had a lot of the same interests. I used to spend a lot of time with my dad. I loved his favorite movies and the steak he barbecued and the Springsteen records he played."

"And men didn't like talking Springsteen?"

"They did at first. Then I had an opinion, and that challenged them. But Liam… he's not that way."

"No?" He motions to the beets *may I?*

I nod *go for it.* "No. He loves hearing me talk. I think he might be tuning out and staring at my boobs, but he doesn't interrupt me."

"He adores you."

"Yeah." He does.

"And you adore him. You miss him already."

"Maybe." In the last week, we finally kissed, touched, fucked. But I can't tell him that. "It's strange, being so close to the wedding."

"Bringing up thoughts of your father?"

"Yeah."

He pauses. Considers what he's about to say. "I never strayed. As far as I know, Ella didn't either. But I wouldn't have blamed her if she did. We were drifting. I wasn't there. I worked too much. I left my energy at the office. She was alone. That's why she left. She didn't want to be alone anymore."

"I'm sorry."

"It was my doing." He traces the rim of his brandy glass. "We all make mistakes. Even when we try our hardest. I thought that was what my family needed. I thought I was supposed to be a provider, I did, but it was more than that. I wanted to prove something to my father, to myself, to the entire world."

"Did you?"

"Yes. There was a sweetness to that victory. I won't claim otherwise. But when I saw the damage it had caused, when I realized what I'd given up, the years I'd missed of my son's childhood… it was bittersweet."

"Would you do it differently now?" I ask.

"Of course. But that's easy for me to say now."

"It is." Would I do anything differently? I'm still young, but I've made plenty of mistakes. Dating John for too long. Attempting casual arrangements too many times. Falling into long depressive phases and failing to claw my way out of them.

Sometimes, I couldn't help it. Sometimes, I didn't have tools. But, sometimes, I did. Sometimes, I knew what I needed to do, and I had enough good days I could do it—

"We all make mistakes." It's generic, but it's true.

"Shall we put that on our kitchen poster?"

"You remember?"

He nods.

"No, it needs to be a little more Pollyannaish."

"We all make mistakes. That's why pencils have erasers."

"Perfect." I laugh. "You're good at this."

He raises his glass.

I raise mine. Sip. Swallow. Savor.

"Your father, he wasn't faithful to your mother?"

Fuck. We're back to that already. "He wasn't."

"And you worry the same thing will happen with Liam."

"Not exactly."

"Then what?"

"I see these flashes of the woman she used to be. Someone vibrant and bright and bold. She was an artist. A painter. She crafted these gorgeous floral close-ups. Very Georgia O'Keeffe. She had write-ups in local papers. A scholarship at a prestigious school. Then she got pregnant with me and she married my father and she just stopped."

"She doesn't paint anymore?"

"No. She's there sometimes. Present, sometimes, as a mother. I still remember this summer she went to every swim meet. Took us to the beach nearly every weekend. She had this fabulous one-piece swimsuit and a big floppy hat. Both were bright pink. And the way she wore them… she didn't care that her thighs were thick and her arms were soft. And that's hard in California."

"Here too, I imagine."

"It's different here. A different standard. I guess it's hard everywhere. But easier, now, in some ways. All these brands giving up photoshopping. Women like Danielle presenting their bodies as they are. She's gorgeous, and she has curves in all the right places, but she has cellulite and stretch marks too and… I've lost you, haven't I?"

"A little," he admits.

"Sorry. I get caught up in ideas. I forget I'm talking to someone on my side. Or that there aren't sides. I just—"

"Don't apologize for your passion, Briar. Promise me you'll stop doing that."

I'm compelled to answer honestly. "You really want me to promise?"

"Of course."

"Why?"

"You're my future daughter-in-law. Not technically, maybe, but you're the woman who's going to be with my most difficult child."

"He is difficult."

"And you're a smart young woman. You're going to change the world for the better. I only wish… I only wish I'd be able to see all of it."

"None of us do."

"No. I suppose not." He stares at his brandy glass. "But now I'm the one off track. What happened with your mother?"

"You really want to talk about that?"

"I do."

"Okay." I take my last sip. Hail the waitress.

"Is it that bad?"

"A little."

He smiles softly. "You don't have to tell me. It's none of my business."

"No. It's okay." I want to tell someone. I want to tell him something true.

The waitress appears. Somehow senses my needs. "Another round?"

"Yes, please," I say.

Preston nods *of course*.

Thankfully, the waitress is quick with our drinks.

Again, I pounce on mine.

I take another sip. Swallow hard. I can do this. Really.

Confronting my fear of commitment with the man who thinks I'm committed to marrying his son—

No fucking problem.

I take a deep breath and I start.

Chapter Thirty-One

BRIAR

"**I**s it obvious I'm uncomfortable about marriage?" I ask.

"You hide it well." Preston listens carefully, as if he wants to hear everything I have to say.

It shouldn't feel unusual—isn't this how conversation goes—but it does.

With my dad…

It's not that he doesn't listen. He did. When I was a kid, I was daddy's little girl. I loved spending time with him, and he loved spending time with me.

He listened when I rambled on about the stingray I saw at the aquarium or the swim meet on Saturday or the action on my current cartoon.

Even when I was older, when I was talking about the bad music at middle school dances, or the books in Honors American Literature, or the guy who asked me to homecoming—

He always listened. He always knew how to make me feel like daddy's little girl.

When did I realize it? Realize he was cheating on Mom? Leaving her alone, with her pain, all the time?

I knew, deep down, for a long time. Somehow, I managed to ignore all the signs. Somehow, I convinced myself it was something else.

And not him abandoning her.

And even when I realized it, I didn't follow him to a hotel room and tell him off. I didn't announce his affair at his office. I didn't do anything except pull away.

Fall into the same depression my mother did. Follow the same patterns my mother did.

That wasn't my fault, but it was fucked up.

How do I explain that? Where do I even start? I barely understand it myself.

"I really do wish Harrison the best," I say. "I don't know him that well, but he seems like a great guy, and he's happy."

"You don't like Lee?"

How did he pick that up?

"It's all right. I wasn't sure, at first. Harrison wouldn't be the first man to think with his—" He nods to his crotch.

It's absurd, this kind, distinguished man imitating a lewd gesture. I can't help but laugh. "She's beautiful."

"That feels important when you're young. Maybe always. He… he hasn't always been the wisest in matters of the heart. But he adores her. Even the things others don't like about her."

"Oh?"

"I thought she was… what do you call it, a mean girl?"

"That's it."

"I thought she was a mean girl when I met her," he says. "Maybe she is. She needs to learn to treat people more fairly. More kindly. I worried about Harrison, because he's not strong in those areas. He isn't the type of man who stands up for himself. Certainly not to beautiful, powerful women."

"He's quiet."

"Yes. I thought she was manipulating him, but she wasn't. He knew she needed to work on treating others better. But there was another side to that behavior. A positive."

There was?

"She is ruthless, yes. For him. As part of his team. He needs someone with that power. The ability to push her feelings aside and seize what she wants."

"I didn't consider it that way."

"You don't need to like her. You don't need to approve. I'm not sure I do. I wouldn't choose her for him, but it's not my choice. He's making his choice with open eyes. He sees her. He sees who she truly is, and he accepts her. That's all I can ask of him."

"It sounds romantic that way."

"Maybe it is." He takes a long sip of his brandy. "That was where I faltered with Ella. Where we both faltered. There was more. Work. Putting my own goals first. Not understanding what it meant to be a team. But now I'm interrupting your story."

"We're here to celebrate your son's marriage. It's okay."

"And you'd rather put it off?"

"No… Yes." I take another sip. "I'm just trying to find a way to say it."

He nods. "You told me, last time, about your parents having a rocky marriage."

"There were good times. Trips to the beach and Magic Mountain and New York." The ones Mom attended. "But there were other times. My mom, that vibrant person who painted flowers and loved art and wore bright pink—I only saw bits and pieces of her. She was depressed. I didn't realize it when I was younger. I didn't realize it until I got help myself…" My stomach drops. I might as well rip my heart out and put it on the table.

I've talked to Liam about some of this. Not all of it. He knows my… history. Six months after I started working with him, I had a bad depressive phase.

I didn't even realize I was in that phase until he asked me what was wrong. Warned me my performance was slipping. Not in a mean way, though I'm sure I thought he was an unrepentant asshole at the time.

He pushed me. I resented it, at first, but I needed it.

When I realized what was happening, I had to march into his office, sit down calmly, explain my depression as if it was any other health condition. As if my repetitive stress injury was acting up and I needed a brace and a week of rest and a little physical therapy.

And not like my brain was broken, the same way my mother's was.

I told him what I'd noticed. I made a list of action items. As if it was any other project. I started going off about them, saying I was back in therapy, and I was looking for a psychiatrist to talk about medications, and I was exercising every day again, even though I barely had the energy to get to work.

I went on and on about how I was going to fix this problem and I wasn't going to cost him productivity and I wasn't going to be difficult. He wouldn't need to fire me.

He let me finish, then he looked at me and he said I didn't have to fix everything right now. I could take time off if I needed it (I needed routine) and I didn't have to share if I didn't want to share (I didn't) but he needed to know if he should look out for anything.

And then he hugged me.

It was probably inappropriate. Really inappropriate. But it felt so warm and safe and accepting.

I didn't have to pretend anymore.

Liam saw me.

I didn't want him to see me, but he did.

It was terrifying but it was freeing too. I didn't have to hide anymore.

"I've had the same problems too," I say. "Since I was a teenager, on and off. I first got help in college. That was when I realized my mom went through the same thing. Still went through the same thing. I tried to talk to her about it, but she... I don't know. There's this gulf between us. It's hard."

Preston nods.

"I don't think it was the right time. I try to be gentle with her." The way I'd want someone to be gentle with me. The way Liam was. "Sometimes, I'm too stuck, too still, and any sort of movement is abrupt. It sends me back into my shell. So I still try, I still try to be soft with her when she's in another phase, but it's hard."

"It's not fair to you, having to take care of her."

"Who else will do it?"

"Your father?"

"He does. In some ways. That's the strange thing. He sleeps with other women. He has affairs. Some are short. Some last years. And they always send her into a depressive cycle, when she finds out. But he still makes sure she has a safe place to stay. He still gives her space and takes her out to dinner and keeps food in the fridge. He's not there to make it. I had to do that. I was cooking dinner when I was eight. First, frozen chicken tenders in the microwave. Or cans of soup. Then, sandwiches. Tacos. Spaghetti and meatballs."

"You father?"

"He was never home early enough. He'd take us to dinner on the weekends. He'd dote on us on the weekends. He was there. He was an attentive father. Until I pushed him away."

"Because of the affairs?"

I nod. "I couldn't forgive him. I thought he abandoned Mom. Abandoned us."

"It's normal to feel hurt."

"She had phases. The way I do, only much worse. But when she was on the upswing… when she is on the upswing, you've never met anyone so loving and bright." I almost smile at a memory of Mom taking us to San Diego. Then I remember two weeks after. Her locked in her room. Me signing a permission slip for a field trip, my sister crying because she didn't have lunch for school, the long, silent nights at home. "I guess I blamed my dad. Marriage. Kids. Maybe that wasn't all of it, but it was a big part. And I don't want that. I don't want to lose my vibrancy." I blink and a tear catches on my lashes.

Preston offers his hand.

I take it. Squeeze tightly. "Thanks, I… I don't think I've said this out loud. It's just fucked up."

His laugh is sad. "It is. Children shouldn't take care of their parents."

"Not when we're young, maybe. But when we're older… isn't that what people expect?"

"Some. But that isn't fair either. I wanted to have a child. I wanted three or four, but Ella and I were only able to have one. We adored Harrison. We wanted him more than anything. He loves us too, but he didn't ask to be born. He doesn't owe us anything."

"He would want to take care of you though."

"Maybe. But as his father, I owe it to him to take care of myself."

Maybe. I don't know. Everything is running together. "I haven't told anyone this."

"Liam doesn't know?"

"He does." Sort of. He knows about my depression, but we haven't really talked about it beyond the practical.

He knows my parents have a fucked-up marriage.

He knows I don't believe in love.

Not bad, what with us kissing for the first time last week, but he's supposed to be my fiancé, so, uh…

Shit.

"Why did you say yes?" Preston asks. "When he asked you to marry you, you said yes?"

"I did." Technically.

"Why?"

"I trust him."

"But you still worry?"

I nod. "That I'll feel trapped. Or end up like my mom. Or see him with other women."

"You doubt his faithfulness?"

"It's not that I think he'd cheat. I just can't see marriage in that light. It feels like a prison. I… I'm sorry. I'm really bringing down the wedding mood."

"Don't be sorry. I asked. And I want to know."

I nod.

"Don't apologize for your feelings, Briar. Even if it's to a nice old man who rambles about his kid."

"I don't, usually."

"Then don't make an exception for me."

"I'm just…" I'm not used to sharing my feelings. My thoughts? Sure. My ideas? Yes. But actual feelings? It's horrifying. "I, uh… I might not have noble intentions."

"With Liam?"

"Yeah."

"He's a handsome young man."

"He is. But it's more about my business."

"Using him for his money?"

No. It's a deal. But I can't say that. I can't say anything. "My app. For mental health support. It will help a lot of people. People like me. My mom. He knows it's my first priority. He knows I want to make it a big thing. And he… he's going to be a really good partner."

"That's why you agreed to marry him? So he'll blow up your app?"

"Not exactly." Yes, exactly, but there's a way to explain this. "But it helps."

"You're ignoble, wanting to help people?"

"When you put it like that…"

"Isn't it?"

Is it? Maybe. "I'm using him."

"Does he know?"

"Liam? Of course."

"Does he care?"

"No. He appreciates being used."

Preston smiles *I know you mean that in a dirty way*. "You understand each other."

I nod.

"He sees you. And you see him, don't you?"

"I like to think so."

"That's what you need in a marriage. It's not all you need. It's hard work, sometimes. Not usually. But sometimes. You need commitment, respect, conflict resolution. But you need to understand each other too. The rest… you two will figure it out."

"You really think so?"

"I do."

"And if we don't? If we get married and it gets fucked up and I leave him?"

"There are many things in my life I regret. The failure of my marriage is one. But the marriage itself? Never."

"Why do you always sound so wise?"

"I'm in a thoughtful mood these days." He looks at me like he's considering adding to his statement, but he doesn't. He finishes his brandy, he hails the waitress, he pats my hand. "What do you say I walk you home?"

"How about to a car?" I show off my heeled sandals. "I don't want to walk all the way home in these."

"Deal." He offers his hand.

I shake.

Then I let him pay, I collect my purse, I follow Preston to the elevator, the lobby, the cab waiting out front.

"Liam loves you. I know he doesn't seem capable sometimes, but he will take care of you if you let him. If you tell him you need that. Please, do it. For me."

"I'll try."

He nods and pulls me into a hug.

It's strange, paternal, this affection I used to feel from my own father, that I blocked a long time ago.

The tension in my shoulders releases. My back. My jaw. My legs.

When he releases me, I stumble. I take careful steps, slide into the car gently.

The driver asks where I want to go.

But I don't ask him to take me home.

I crash Liam's party instead.

Chapter Thirty-Two

LIAM

"Hell yeah!" Jimmy claps his hands together. "About time." He slides one arm around the lady on his left—the one in the *Maid of Dishonor* sash. "You ready?"

"She's already topless." The maid of honor giggles as the dancer on stage shimmies.

The dancer is, in fact, topless. She's wearing some kind of pastel pink thong covered in rhinestones. It matches her glittery pastel pink heels.

With the long blond hair and the big fake tits, she's got a real old school *Playboy* aesthetic. I was raised on those particular magazines—among others—but I'm uninspired by her hip thrusts.

Even as she hooks a leg around the pole, spins, turns upside down.

It's a cool trick, sure, but what's the nudity add to the equation? I've never minded strip clubs—naked women, why not—but I've never been into them either.

I prefer a little privacy in these situations.

I guess that's why some guy invented the champagne

room. And, honestly, I get why douchebags like Jimmy enjoy the setting.

A hot chick, taking off her clothes, grinding on my dick, pretending she finds me fascinating?

I see the appeal.

I even appreciate the transparent transactional nature of the situation.

Jimmy doesn't need to worry that Candy here is using him for his money. He doesn't need to worry about breaking her heart or giving her the wrong impression.

He deludes himself into believing she likes him, sure, but, deep down, he knows what he's getting.

For four hundred dollars an hour, she'll twist herself into any angle he likes. She'll pretend he's the most fascinating, sexy man on the planet and she'll do it without her clothes.

It's all on the table. Much like her bra and the bills lining the stage.

The guy wants to get off without getting involved. He pays for the privilege. Good for him for knowing what he wants.

I considered professional help a few times. After a string of particularly painful endings. I'm an asshole sometimes, but never on purpose. I don't want to break hearts. It doesn't feel good.

I didn't know what to do to change the situation. I thought I was being upfront. I thought I made things clear.

Somehow, I didn't.

But I couldn't convince myself to add a few hundred dollars to the equation, even if it somehow removed the heartbreak. No matter how many times I told myself there was no shame in paying, I couldn't shake the ick factor.

Was I really going to become one of those men?

A man like Jimmy?

When did he cross the line into unrepentant douchebag? It wasn't when he started paying for it.

He had the same attitude before; that sex started with his erection and ended with his orgasm.

Has the guy ever eaten pussy in his life?

Doubtful.

But then he'd still be an asshole if it was his favorite activity in the world. Somehow, he'd fuck it up, and make it all about him.

Simon is right. Maybe I was never on Jimmy's exact path, but I was close.

Where did we verge?

When did I swing left?

I don't know, but I know I need to get the fuck away from this guy. Yeah, he was surprisingly game at the male revue. Everyone had a good time. Mostly thanks to the screaming women in the room and their extreme sexual energy.

But Jimmy kept it pretty contained. He invited another party to join a second club with us, paid for their entry, bought everyone drinks.

Sure, we're not at a traditional club filled with naked babes, but Jimmy is showing the bridesmaid a good time.

I shouldn't be so desperate to leave. It's early. It's Harrison's night. If he wants to watch a blonde twist around a pole topless—

Oh, there go her panties.

Who gives a fuck?

"Is that a dancer with purple hair?" Harrison raises a brow.

"The bartender wasn't enough for you?" I try to tease him, but I don't sell the enthusiasm.

"He didn't give me a lap dance," he says.

"He offered."

Harrison chuckles *you're ridiculous*.

"You want to bail?" I can't bail before the groom—that's a failure of duty—but I need to get out of here soon.

"After we talk to her."

"No way you're getting a lap dance from her."

"Maybe I am."

"Bullshit."

"We'll see." He turns to the dancer. "Hey, can you come over here?"

And she emerges from a group of bros.

Not a stripper in six-inch heels.

Briar in the dress she wore to dinner. "Hey."

Harrison doubles over laughing. "Did you set this up?"

"No." I turn to Bri. "Are you okay?"

"Yeah, I just, uh… well, I thought you were still at the male dancers club. I thought I'd crash. When I asked Simon for the address, he didn't mention that it was for a new venue. Full of naked women."

She surveys the place. Mirrored walls. Two stages. One with a single pole, with Candy here, and the other with two poles and similarly styled dancers.

It's the look here.

"Jimmy's idea?" she asks.

"How did you guess?" I ask.

"How about…" Harrison laughs. "I can't even ask. Sorry, Briar. You're a beautiful woman, but I'm not interested."

"No offense taken." She offers him a smile. "Congratulations. I'm sorry to crash your party."

"Don't be. I'm leaving." Harrison nods goodbye to Jimmy. "Where is Simon?"

"He walked a bridesmaid home." Yeah, he claimed he was going to check on Opal after that, but I didn't buy it. If he really did send Briar here…

The timing would have to be pretty specific.

Did he make me think he was getting laid so I wouldn't call him on bailing on the party?

Asshole is copying my moves.

"Take the limo home," I yell to Harrison.

He shakes his head. "It's too purple. You take it. That is your color." He winks and he moves through the cloud of douchebags.

He's gone.

And Jimmy is still cheering at the blonde, pulling the maid of honor closer, barely aware of our presence.

"Do you want to stay and watch him make a fool of himself?" I ask.

"Book a private room for a dance?" She half-smiles.

"Baby, if you want, I'm fucking game. If not, I'm ready to get the fuck out of here."

"You don't want to stay, watch the dancers?"

"Are you okay, Bri? You're not a party crasher."

"I, uh, I think so. It was just a lot. Dinner. And I was thinking about my dad, and…" She throws her arms around me and pulls me into a kiss.

It's fast, hard, hungry.

And like *that* I'm ready to go in every sense of the word. I need to touch her, taste her, fuck her. I don't care as long as I hear her groan.

"You want to stay, we stay." It's too loud to talk, so I bring my mouth to her ear. "We can debate whether or not Jimmy has ever eaten out a woman."

"Once. He wasn't immediately good at it, so he didn't like it. Now, he claims 'he's just not into it.'"

"Generous assessment."

"You think never?"

"I have my doubts."

She laughs. "I won't argue with them."

"I want to be where you are. If it's here, it's here—"

"No, I wanted to see naked guys."

"The second show is sold out tonight."

"No."

"And it started an hour ago."

"Terrible."

"Yeah." My fingers curl into her neck. "It was really something. A spectacle."

"Were they really…"

"Naked? No. They were wearing bow-ties."

She laughs. "But the dick?"

"Swinging in the breeze."

"Oh god. And Simon and Harrison stood there and watched?"

"I wouldn't say they watched, exactly. They were at the bar, talking about some museum in Paris, but they saw plenty."

"And you?"

"Gotta stay with the groom."

She rests her head in the crook of my neck. "Did you… did you get a dance here?"

"No."

"Oh. Good. I… wouldn't be okay with that. I know some women don't mind. Maybe, if we did it together. I don't mind you watching, but I don't want anyone else touching you."

"I don't want anyone else touching me."

"You promise?"

"I do." I pull her closer. "Now, can we get the fuck out of here?"

"Yeah, but I still want to see some dick."

"Some? Or mine?" I turn her around. Press my palm into the small of her back.

"I was hoping for multiple dicks, but I guess I'll take yours."

"You guess?"

"One is less than many."

"You want quantity over quality?"

"I want quality and quantity," she teases.

"I should punish you for that sass, baby."

"You should."

I lead her out of the club.

Finally, we hit fresh air. Quiet. At two blocks from Times Square, I can see the bright neon if I look to the right. Kind of quiet, but bliss, compared to the club.

I've never been a strip club guy, but I've enjoyed it before. That was fucking torture.

Was it all Jimmy?

Or is it something else? Only wanting her?

It's strange, new, intoxicating.

"You want to take the limo home?" I ask.

"You meant what you said about five months? Without another woman?"

"Yeah."

"And you've been tested recently?"

"Last month. Why?"

"Me too. At my last checkup. It's been a while. And I have the IUD…" She looks up at me. "Should we?"

"Should we?"

"Try it without a condom?"

"Where the fuck is that limo?"

Chapter Thirty-Three

BRIAR

L iam pulls the door closed behind him. He slides onto the bench next to me, rolls the partition, connects his cell to the sound system. "Requests?"

"Do you usually play music?"

"The divider only works so well."

"Considerate."

"Are you teasing me, baby?"

Am I? I'm not sure. I'm nervous. I'm not usually this nervous around Liam. We've been together.

Why are my hands sweaty?

Why are my palms shaking?

It's desire, yes, but it's more.

Liam sees me.

I see him.

Does he love me? Do I love him?

I don't know. I don't even know what it means. Does my dad love my mom? He stays, he makes sure she has food in the fridge and a roof over her head. When she's well, and he sees her smiling, he lights up like a pinball machine.

Does she love him? She stays, even though she knows. She accepts him abandoning her to other women.

But maybe she's doing the same thing too. She isn't abandoning him in favor of other men, but she's still pulling away, locking him out.

It's different. She can't help it. But she's not leaving him a choice either.

Which is worse?

Following in her footsteps, staying with someone who strays?

Or following in her footsteps, pushing away the people who love me, refusing to accept their help?

"Where are you going, baby?" Liam picks a classic R&B hit. He motions to his cell. "All slow jams."

"What if I want fast?"

"I'll play at double speed." He smiles, but there's a weariness to it. He's as worn as I am. "Do you?"

"Want fast? No." I want to feel him, all of him, all of his body against all of mine. The other details don't matter. "This is perfect."

"Good." He scoots closer. "Do I smell like a cheap club?"

"A little."

"This should help." He does away with his suit jacket. Then the tie.

My hand goes to his collar. I undo his top button. The second. The third.

"Are you okay, Bri?"

"I don't know." I press my palm flat against his chest. He feels so good. This simple, gentle touch feels so good. Vibrant and alive. "It's weird, lying to Preston." And not lying to him too. "He loves you."

"I love him."

"I've never heard you say that."

"Maybe." He pulls me into his lap. Looks up at me. "We don't have to fuck."

"Yes, we do."

His laugh is pure delight. "We do?"

"Lose the pants."

"You're still dressed."

"I was promised dick."

He pulls me closer as he laughs.

It's so strange and wonderful, the way his body shakes against mine. The feeling of his joy flowing into me.

Maybe I do love him.

That means something.

I need to stay.

Or I need to leave.

One of the two.

But I can't contemplate that now. I can't lose anything else or suffer any other insights. Not tonight.

Tonight, I need to melt into him. To fall apart in his arms and let him put me back together.

Am I capable? I'm not sure, but I have to try.

No, I have to stop thinking. I have to feel him, feel this, savor every fucking second.

"Do you want to talk?" Liam cups my neck with his palm.

I shake my head.

"You're not here, baby. I want to fuck you, but only if you're here."

"What if I want to imagine someone else?"

"Then pick a location with fewer mirrors."

"You want to pretend I'm in the zone?"

"It's been a week." He pushes my dress up my thighs. "If you want to imagine other guys already… that's going to be a blow to my ego."

"Is it?"

"Yeah. In a few months, maybe, when we've exhausted other options for novelty."

"It will only take a few months?"

"If I fuck you three times a day."

"Can you even go three times a day?"

"What did I say about dares?" He pushes my dress a few inches higher. "You're riding the line."

"What are you going to do about it?"

"You think I won't punish you?"

I'm not sure. I dare him anyway. "I don't think you want to."

"Not now, no." He slips his hand under my dress. Presses his palm flat against my sex, over my panties. "But I will tease you." He runs his thumb over me, pressing the fabric against my clit.

"You will?"

"Yeah." He does it again. Again. "Are these silk?"

I nod.

"Feels like heaven." He presses his lips to my neck. "At first." He runs his thumb over me again. "Then it's torture, not having my hand on your skin."

"Is it?"

"Yeah." He kisses my neck again. Softly. So softly I can barely feel it.

Again and again, as he runs his thumb over me.

My eyes flutter closed.

My fingers curl into his chest.

My breath hitches.

He teases me, again and again, soft kisses and soft touches.

Winding me tighter and tighter, but not close enough, never close enough.

A groan falls from my lips. "Please."

"Please?"

"Please, Liam." I shift my hips, rocking against his hand, increasing the pressure of his touch. Better. But not enough. "Touch me."

"Not yet." He places another kiss on my neck. "I'm torturing you, baby."

I shake my head.

He nods. "You dared me."

"Please."

"Never thought I was into begging." He teases me with another slow, soft stroke. "But *please* sounds so fucking good on your lips."

"Liam."

He runs his thumb over me again.

"Please."

Again and again and again.

I'm putty in his hands. So, so, so close to where I need to be, so desperate for release, too full of bliss to move.

All I can do is say "please" again.

Liam doesn't release me. He teases me again and again and again.

Until I'm wound so tight, I'm sure I'm going to break. And then he does it more. That perfect slow brush of his thumb, back and forth, again and again.

Until my hips act of their own accord. I rock into his hand again, demanding more pressure, taking it from him.

Fuck.

I nearly come on the spot.

I have to tug at his shirt to stay upright. And I'm sitting.

"Bad girl," he purrs with approval. "Impatient." He places a kiss on my ear, shoulder, collarbone.

Liam repositions me in his lap, then he brings one hand to my chest, pushes my straps off on my shoulders.

"Fuck." His breath hitches.

He wants to relent as badly as I do, but he holds strong. He runs his thumb over me again, teasing mercilessly.

Then he cups my breast, teases me with his thumb.

Again and again and again.

My eyes go to the mirror on our right. The beautiful image of Liam, still in his button-down, the same Liam I've seen at work every day for two years, toying with me again and again.

He's in his shirt and I'm topless in his lap.

I've never been an exhibitionist, but being on display for him sets me on fire.

Maybe I do want to put on a set of sheer mesh and dance for him in a room full of mirrors.

No, I do.

I want that. I want this. I want everything.

All of Liam's creativity and drive, all focused on blowing my fucking mind.

"Please." It falls off my lips.

He toys with me again.

"Please, Liam."

Again and again.

"I need you inside me."

"Fuck." He presses his palm flat against my sex. "You have any idea what that does to me, baby?"

"Yes."

He shifts his hips, so I feel his hard-on.

"Please." I pull my dress up my thighs. "Please, Liam." I look down at him. Savor the desire in his blue eyes. "Fuck me."

"Fuck." His fingers hook into the sides of my panties. "Off."

I raise my hips so he can pull them off my feet. It's torture, shifting off him for long enough to undo his zipper and push his boxers aside.

Fuck, he's beautiful. I've never thought of a cock as beautiful before, but his really is. Long and thick and hard and—

"Sit on my cock, baby." Liam brings his hands to my hips. Guides me into place.

Slowly, I lower my body onto his.

His tip strains against me.

A sweet fucking tease. And it's all him. No barrier between us.

Nothing between us.

I rise, tease him one more time. Then one more, for good measure.

Then, slowly, one sweet inch at a time, I lower my body onto his.

Fuck. It's been a long time since I've had sex without a condom. Since I felt all of someone against all of me.

All that trust and intimacy flowing between us.

Has it always been this overwhelming?

Or is it Liam?

I've only done this with John. I was with him for a long time. In some ways, I knew him well, and he knew me well.

But it wasn't like with Liam. He didn't see me, accept me, love every broken part of me.

I didn't see him, accept him, love every broken part of him.

Fuck.

I love him.

I do.

I think I have for a long time. But this is different, deeper, more intense.

All of him against all of me.

It's possible here. But everywhere else?

I don't know.

"Fuck." His breath hitches in his throat. "Fuck, Bri." His fingers curl into my hips. "You feel so fucking good."

I barely manage to nod.

He presses his lips to my neck. No teasing this time. His kiss is hard, aggressive, needy.

He kisses a line down my chest. Then he takes my nipple into his mouth. Toys with soft flicks of his tongue. Slow swirls.

The soft brush of his teeth.

"Fuck." My nails dig into his chest. It's not enough. I need more of his bare skin.

I push the sides of his shirt apart. Press my hand to his stomach. Curl the other around his neck.

Then I raise my hips and I drive down on him.

Slowly, the first time.

Then faster.

Harder.

As deep as I can take him.

Fuck, he feels so good inside me. Hard and warm and mine.

Is he really mine?

Can I even handle that?

Everywhere else, I don't know. But here?

Here, I need every fucking molecule.

Liam toys with my nipple as I drive onto him again and again.

My eyes go to the mirror. I watch him take my breast into his mouth. Watch his fingers curl into my back.

Watch mine curl into his hair.

Watch my body raise and lift as I take him again and again.

My dress is in the way. I can't see the explicit action. But watching his mouth close around my nipple is enough to push me to the edge.

Maybe I am an exhibitionist. I need to test it. To watch more of him, me, us.

But right now—

My eyes flutter closed. I'm too close. Watching is too intense.

I drive down on Liam as he toys with my breasts.

Again and again.

So, so, so, fucking close.

Then he brings one hand to my head and pulls me into a slow, deep kiss.

He brings the other to my clit.

He draws slow circles as he kisses me.

With the next brush of his thumb, I come. I swirl my tongue around his, kissing him hard, driving down on him again and again.

My sex pulses around him.

Pleasure spills through my stomach, my thighs, my breasts.

All the way to my fingers and toes.

Every part of me unravels. There's no spool. I'm a mess of thread on the floor and it feels so fucking good.

His lips stay locked to mine. His hands go to my hips. He guides me over him. A little slower. A little deeper.

Then he's there, groaning against my mouth as he comes.

I can feel every pulse, every drop, every groan.

It's different.

More intimate.

After he works through his orgasm, he pulls me close, holds my body against his.

It's not quite every inch of me against every inch of him, but it's close.

It's really fucking close.

———

THE DRIVE PASSES IN A BLUR OF SLOW JAMS AND SOFT SKIN.

Liam helps me out of the car, kisses me in the elevator, carries me into the fucking apartment.

We go straight to the shower, strip each other out of our clothes, step into the warm water.

The glass shower is massive by shower standards, but it's still a tiny space, still too small for all the feelings flowing through my veins.

I don't know how to explain them. I never do.

So, I kiss him, and help him soap, and wrap my hand around his cock, and pump him until he's groaning my name.

This time, he holds me close as he enters me, every inch of my skin against every inch of his.

I come twice.

He follows.

Then, finally, we clean properly, slip into our pajamas, collapse in his bed.

I don't know what the fuck this means, how I'll feel in the morning, what I'll do after the wedding.

But right now, I'm exactly where I want to be.

In his bed, in his heart, in his life.

Chapter Thirty-Four

LIAM

B riar West is naked in my bed.

An angel in the soft morning light.

A vixen in the crisp white sheets.

Holding me together.

Tearing me apart.

What was it she said about that Japanese pottery? Finding broken pieces, filling them with gold, gluing them back together.

It's beautiful, but it means breaking.

Right now, that's not an option.

But then, right now, I can't think about the world outside this room. Only Bri. Her serene expression, her soft skin, her sweet groan.

I want to spend the day here.

The weekend.

The month.

The rest of my life.

The two of us, tangled in the sheets, sweaty and out of breath, only breaking to eat, sleep, shower.

What could be better?

She stirs, blinks her eyes open, stretches her arms over her head. "Hey."

"Hey."

"What time is it?"

"Early." I brush a hair behind her ear. "Go back to bed."

"Are you leaving?"

"Gym."

"Do you have to?"

"No." I don't want to go. I want to stay here. I want to hold her close. I want to collapse in her arms.

It's too tempting.

It's dangerous.

The wedding is a week away.

That's it. I have to keep this shit together, my shit and Preston's, until the happy couple heads to the honeymoon suite.

Then it's his problem.

Then, I can soak in the weight of the situation.

I want to stay.

I want to stay forever.

"Okay." Briar nods into her pillow, rolls over, falls back asleep.

A laugh spills from my lips.

Perfect. Fucking. Response.

I watch her sleep for another minute, then I climb out of bed, get ready, head to the gym in the building.

When I was a kid, my dad made sure we exercised. He thought running laps around the house built character. Even though the boarding school I attended was focused on academics, there was no question.

Of course, I was participating in athletics.

Water polo in the fall, swimming in the spring. Not the sports he'd choose, but sufficiently exclusive.

Pools are expensive. Especially in New York.

The routine is drilled into me. Five mornings a week, I rise early, run or lift weights or swim laps. Today is leg day. There's too much time to think between sets.

I shift from the warmth of Briar's laugh to the sweetness of her groan to the desperation of Preston's expression.

Like I'm the only thing between him and oblivion.

No, oblivion is coming for him, fast, whether he wants it to or not. We're all in the same fucking boat there. But the thought of adding *memento mori* to my list of cliché tattoos isn't doing shit to soothe me.

I don't want to consider oblivion. I don't want to lie for Preston. I don't want to watch him die.

But I don't have a choice there. Yes, I can speak up, I can refuse more bullshit, I can even run away.

He'll still die.

I'll still lose him.

I'll still be a thousand pieces on the floor.

For one more day, I want to forget. I want to lose myself in Briar's laugh, smile, groan.

She's not an angel here to save me, but, fuck, sometimes it feels like it.

I hold on to the warm, soft feeling of her body against mine as I finish, head home, shower, dress, fix coffee.

A knock on the door interrupts any possibility of peace.

A courier with a sealed package.

My information from Ian.

Whatever the fuck it is Simon is hiding.

The ugly truth, in all its glory.

The one thing I can't handle.

"Hey." Briar's voice startles me. "Did you join the CIA?"

"Huh?" I slip the package under my arm as I turn to face her.

"That looks serious." She cinches her robe. "Is it?"

Very.

I offered Simon a truce. It didn't specifically include these terms. Technically, I'm in the clear to look, but…

"It's nothing you need to worry about," I say.

"Do you need to worry about it?"

"Not right now."

"You sure?"

I watch her teeth sink into her lower lip, watch her expression shift from curious to *then how about you fuck me now* and I am.

One more fucking day of peace.

The whole week even.

Then, I fall apart.

But now?

Now, I fuck her senseless.

———

I SPEND THE WEEKEND TANGLED IN BRIAR. I FIX HER breakfast. I convince her to watch *The Matrix*, then I fuck her on the couch.

We order lunch, eat Caesars on the balcony, talk about the future of robots taking over and raves going underground.

Then she takes me to the bedroom and fucks me and we spend an eternity tangled in my bed, in the sheets, warm and safe and far away from the rest of the world.

Over brunch and eggplant parm and Death Cab for Cutie and an entire afternoon in my bed.

It's perfect.

On Monday, I wake, I hide the sealed file in my suitcase. I wake her up, fix her tea, head to work to face the world.

The week moves fast. She's training her replacement. I'm setting up her team, her tech, her support.

Before I know it, we're sitting in a limo, on the way to the mansion, for the all-day rehearsal dinner.

My last sliver of heaven before I charge into battle.

Chapter Thirty-Five

BRIAR

I thought Liam was being metaphorical when he said Adam locked himself in his castle, but the Pierce mansion is straight out of a fairy tale.

Steep roof, sweeping vistas, wrought iron gate.

An actual castle at the very end of Long Island.

Even on a warm May day, surrounded by blue skies and puffy clouds, the place looks ornate and ominous. If anything, the blue sky is a stark contrast to the mansion's untouchable vibe.

The scent of salt and roses fills my nose as I step out of the car. The lull of crashing waves—we're on a cliff—underlines the silence.

We're secluded.

The most secluded I've been since I moved to New York.

Liam wraps his hands around my waist, pulls my body into his, presses his lips to my neck. "You smell good."

"You didn't notice in the limo?"

"I noticed." He nips at my ear. "I notice now."

And, now, he's face-to-face with this symbol of his

childhood, his father's death, his late brother, and he's desperate to escape.

Not that I mind. I want to race to Liam's bedroom and fuck him senseless. But I want to be here for him too. For this. Whatever this is.

He slides a hand around my thigh. Runs his thumb over the fabric of my jeans. "Aren't you hot in these?"

"No. Are you?"

"Yeah." He rocks his hips, grinding his cock against my ass.

Fuck. That feels good. I need to be here. I need to fuck him senseless.

"You look good." He nips at my ear again. "But I need these on my floor."

The driver shoots us an irritated look. He shakes his head *damn rich people* and drops our luggage by the front door.

I've been that guy. I've been the assistant, the one people ignore and talk around. I'm not going to make his life harder by making out in front of him.

I take Liam's hand. "Shall we?"

"Fuck in my room? Or on the dining table?"

"Don't you have a housekeeper?"

"She won't watch."

"Isn't Adam home?"

"He won't watch. But Danielle…"

"Obviously."

"Is that a yes?" He's teasing, but it's lacking his usual zest.

Do I really know him that well now? That's terrifying. "Later."

"Later." He squeezes my hand as he leads me along the walkway, up the steps, to the massive oak door.

He pulls a key from his pocket and presses it between

his palms, soaking in the weight of the gesture, then he opens the door and motions *after you*.

The place is even grander inside. A foyer leads to a living room. The staircase on our left curls along the walls, disappears into a hallway in one direction, turns into mezzanine in the other.

There's a ballroom, an actual ballroom, past the living room. With high ceilings and massive windows.

It's straight out of *Beauty and the Beast*.

I want to step into a gown and take to the dance floor. Immediately.

"Do you have a library?" I ask.

"Of course."

"Can we go?"

An older woman in a simple black dress interrupts us. "You must be Ms. West." She smiles and meets me in the middle of the room. "I'm Trish."

I offer my hand.

She pulls me into a hug instead of shaking. "Mr. Pierce has told me so much about you."

"Liam?"

"Yes." She looks me over with affection, the way Preston did, like she's so happy her son has finally found love. "He's enamored."

"It's true." Liam greets her with a hug. "Keep playing my wingwoman?"

"I'll consider that," she says.

He whispers something in her ear.

She laughs. "Of course."

"You look good. I knew there was something going on," he says.

"I look good for myself," she says.

"Really? You do all that if you're alone?" he asks.

"I do," she says.

"Come on. If you're home, alone, it's pajama time, hair down, makeup off," he says.

"You buy silk pajamas for all your *friends*," she says.

"That's Simon's thing," he says.

"Have you tried them yourself?" she asks.

"I have a pair," he says.

"And…" She raises a brow. "You don't need company for sensual experiences."

"Are you telling me to fuck myself?" he asks.

She shrugs *am I?*

"He does take it as a suggestion," I say.

"Was that a request?" He turns to me and he lights up. Like he's home. Like he's safe from the danger of his actual home. "The living room isn't the most sensual environment, but I aim to please."

"Not the living room," I say.

"The library?" he asks.

My cheeks flush.

He smiles, victorious. "Right now?"

"Aren't Adam and Danielle here?" I ask.

"Mr. Pierce and Ms. Bellamy live here," Trish interrupts.

Right. She's here.

I'm flirting in front of her. Liam grew up with Trish, sure. She's used to his nonsense. She probably realizes he's playing up his nonsense because she's here.

But still—

I'm not going to subject her to PDAs.

Trish must notice my horror because she smiles and places her hand on my shoulder. "Don't worry, Ms. West. I know Liam acts out around authority figures."

"Authority figures?" he challenges. "Fuck. Proving her point already."

"A new record." She laughs, softly. "Wait until Simon is here. Then…" She shakes her head *he's ridiculous*.

"That, I've seen," I say.

"Wait until you see it here," she says.

"You know I'm right here?" Liam folds his arms, feigning offense. "If you're going to talk about me like I'm in the other room, make it dirtier."

"Liam, you're like a son to me," she says.

"Then say one of those weird mom things. Compliment Briar's body inappropriately," he says.

She chuckles. "What would I say?"

"What would you say? Look at her." Liam motions to me.

"What about her?" she asks.

"She has a great ass," Liam says.

She just laughs. "Yes, you look wonderful in your jeans, Briar. Will you be wearing them for the party? Or do you need to change?"

"Do I need to change?" I ask Liam.

"For dinner." He taps his jeans. "I will too." He's in casual gear today, jeans and a t-shirt.

He looks just as good in the outfit. Maybe better.

That's not surprising—jeans are sexy, period—but it's amazing how natural he looks. Like a guy who lives in jeans.

Liam Pierce rocks every outfit he wears. He's not as stylish as I am—like he said, he's constrained by the standards of fashion for men—but he looks at home more often than I do.

I feel awkward in a pencil skirt and heels. Like I'm playing a secretary in a bad porno.

It's not that I need casual—even in jeans, I'm wearing a top with mesh paneling and a lot of makeup—more that I can't stand the corporate dress code. I need flair. I need to find a way to bring flair to business attire if I'm going to run my own company.

"Are you staying in Liam's room?" she asks. "Or do you want the spare?"

"You have rooms to spare? Isn't everyone staying here?" I ask.

"Only Mr. Pierce, and he has his room," she says.

"Simon," Liam explains.

"How long do we have? Until guests arrive?" I ask.

"A few hours." Trish motions to the dining room. "Make yourself comfortable. I'll bring drinks. Liam tells me you enjoy London Fogs."

"I do," I say.

"Strong, with a little honey." She looks to me. "Is that right?"

"Yes, thank you, Trish."

She nods *of course* and moves into the kitchen.

Upstairs, a door opens. "Is that you?" Danielle emerges at the top of the stairs, her wavy hair messy, her marigold sundress slightly askew. "Hey." She fixes her top button. "You just got here?"

"You just got laid," Liam says.

"Maybe." She moves down the stairs with grace, aware she's making an entrance.

She looks hot. She always looks hot—between her curvy frame, her dark eyes, and her long hair, she's a babe—but she's glowing today. That sex glow.

Or maybe it's a love glow.

Maybe I'm still underestimating the power of love.

"Who calls sex in a relationship getting laid?" she asks.

He shoots me an *is that right* look.

"It's rare," I admit.

"How long have you two been dating again?" she asks.

"I don't care what you call it, as long as I can make my

girl come." Liam wraps his hands around me. "Right, baby?"

"Uh…"

Danielle laughs.

Liam winks at her. "You can go back up there for round two. I'm not going to c-block you."

"C-block? That's tame for you," she says.

"No. Equal opportunity. All the c's," he says.

"Are there more than two?" she asks. "You know what, don't tell me. I don't want to know the depths of your depravity."

"Good call," I say.

She steps onto the main floor. Crosses the room to us.

Liam looks at her hand with curiosity. "You wash up after?"

"Would you care if I hadn't?" she asks.

"Fuck no." He accepts her hug. "But Adam… he's a possessive guy."

"Is he always this difficult?" She releases Liam and pulls me into a hug.

He's not, no. He's ramping it up now that he's here. It's as clear as day. A few months ago, I might not have seen it. Right now, it's easy. I know him. I see him.

"You look great." She releases me. Gives me a quick once-over. "You always look like a rock star."

"I do?" My cheeks flush.

"Oh yeah. Even in your sheath dress. It's effortless," she says.

"Does that make me your groupie?" Liam asks.

"Depends how often you dispense sexual favors," she says.

"As often as possible," he says.

She laughs *oh, silly Liam* and motions to the dining room. "Trish is making tea?"

Liam nods.

"Then let's go, sit, catch up before the drama starts," she says.

"You think so too?" he asks.

"Of course," she says.

"I told him. Simon and Vanessa. It's combustible," he says.

"No." Danielle laughs. "Simon and you."

"What?" He looks at her dumbfounded.

"I've never seen the two of you go more than five minutes without fighting." She laughs as she takes in his confused expression. "You really don't notice that pattern?"

"He starts it," Liam says.

"Uh-huh," she says.

"Bri, baby, back me up," Liam says.

"You're on your own this time," I say.

"Am I going to have to torture it out of you?" he asks.

"Absolutely," I say.

"Now, that I want to see," Danielle says.

Liam chuckles. "Is there anything you don't want to see?"

She just smiles *ah, Liam, silly boy.*

The same as Trish's. As Preston's.

I've even seen Adam look at Liam this way.

Has Simon? I don't know. I don't know him well, but I can tell he loves Liam.

Liam and Danielle trade teases about her voyeurism as we move to the dining room. She likes to watch. And show. It's the focus of her photography.

And, well, Liam is right. If we start making out in front of her, she'll probably whip out her camera.

After we take our seats, Liam helps Trish bring out our tea, snacks, water. Then he sits and slips into his role.

"Adam is still upstairs?" he asks.

Danielle nods.

"You wear him out that well?"

"Maybe," she says.

"Are you blushing?" he asks. "I can't tell."

She shrugs.

"When did you get so easygoing?" he asks.

"Wouldn't you like to know?" she teases.

"I would. And I bet you would too." He raises a brow. "The two of you have all sorts of freaky details to share."

"And why would I tell you?" she asks.

"'Cause you're an exhibitionist. You want to," he says.

"I thought I was a voyeur."

"Both. You're a real freak," he says.

She laughs. "What do you propose?"

"I have the perfect trade. I'm happy to propose it. But you have to promise to give it a chance."

She looks at him incredulously. "I do?"

"Oh yeah." He offers his hand. "Promise?"

She shakes. "Game on."

Chapter Thirty-Six

BRIAR

L iam stands dramatically. He places his hands on the table with utmost seriousness. "Never. Have. I. Ever."

"Never have I ever?" Danielle laughs. "Are you kidding?"

"Do I kid?" Liam asks.

"All you do is kid," she says. "And you didn't even ask your fiancée if she wants to play."

"Uh…"

"See." She motions to me. "Never have I ever is for high schoolers. Why not play truth or dare?"

"Why not?" He raises a brow. "I'm game."

"Let me guess. You pick *dare* and your first dare is streak in the backyard," she says.

"Danielle, I can't pick dare and then pick my own dare. Now, if you want to dare me to take my clothes off… well, that's on brand for you," he says.

She laughs. "I dare you to step in front of my camera?"

"Truth comes out." Liam turns to me. "If you think it's

339

too high school, fine. But I went to an all-boys school. And the game is not nearly as fun that way."

"No?" she asks.

"You ever read *Catcher in the Rye*?" he asks.

"Have you?" she asks.

"I did," he says.

"You did? Really?" I ask.

He nods. "Only book I read in four years. About a kid who goes crazy because all boy's boarding schools are hell."

She laughs. "It doesn't end well in *Dead Poets Society*."

"It's terrible. You have to resort to naming magazines. Never have I ever borrowed Jimmy's Playboys."

"You went to school with Jimmy?" I ask.

"Why else would I talk to him?" Liam asks.

"Was he more obnoxious than you back then?" I ask.

"No. We were equally obnoxious. But he became Jimmy. And I…" He pulls his shirt down low enough to show off the Latin quote on his pec. "I may be a tool, but I'm not Jimmy."

"What compliments. To yourself," I say.

"Thanks. One of my better works, I agree."

A door upstairs opens.

Danielle lights up.

Liam notices. Chuckles. "You didn't wear him out that well." He places his hand over his mouth and stage whispers, "Quick. A dirty detail."

"About what?" she asks.

"Never have I ever let my fiancée tie me up." Liam holds up all ten fingers.

"What if we take fiancée out of that sentence?" Danielle holds up her two hands. "Then?"

"All right. No fiancée." He drops a finger.

She does too.

They look to me to participate in their game.

"This is very high school." But I guess that makes sense. We're at Liam's childhood home. We're seeing family. We're attending his high school friend's wedding. I hold up all ten fingers.

"Really? No one?" Danielle asks.

"Danielle, the point of the game is not to shame the inexperienced," Liam says.

"There's a point to this game?" she asks.

"To embarrass your friends," he says.

"Sorry, Briar. I'm not trying to embarrass you. There's no shame in not being into something," she says.

Oh god, talk about embarrassing. My cheeks flush.

Danielle drops her hands and turns to her fiancé.

Adam steps into the dining room with a serious expression. He looks every bit the Adam I recognize. Tall and broad and brooding.

It's easy to picture him as a beast, sulking around his castle, locking people out. He's not angry, at least, not on the surface, but he wears his pain all over his face.

I guess he can't help it, with the scars. But it's not the scars, really. It's the way he holds himself. His expression.

He looks strange in jeans and a t-shirt. Out of place.

Then he looks into Danielle's eyes, and the pain disappears. He's exactly where he wants to be.

He's in heaven.

He pulls her into a tight hug.

She buries her head in his chest. Even in her wedge sandals, she's quite a bit shorter than he is.

They really are an adorable couple. Similar and opposite in so many ways.

"Danielle was just explaining about how much she likes when you tie her up," Liam says.

Adam ignores him. "Do you?" He cups her cheek with his hand. "We can do it more often."

She leans into his touch.

I think she blushes, but with her light brown skin, it's hard to tell.

Liam recognizes defeat—she's not going to play the silly game in front of Adam—and turns to me. "You really haven't?" He picks up his creamy coffee. Takes a long sip.

Already, he's shifting into the Liam I know. The one only I see. Leaning into sex the way Danielle is leaning into her fiancé.

Is that all it is? Liam reaching for the closest comfort?

Or is he reaching for me because he loves me?

Maybe it doesn't matter. He needs comfort. I want to comfort him.

"When would I?" I take a sip of my London Fog. Mmm, it's perfect. Strong and creamy with that sweet hint of bergamot and honey. "With John?"

"There were other guys." He takes another sip. "A handful."

"Hey."

"I'm not judging based on quantity, but I figure there were enough you got the chance."

"I'm not going to let a stranger tie me up," I say.

"A friend with benefits?"

I shake my head.

"Because you're not into it?"

"No." My cheeks flush. Liam and I have had these discussions before, but never in a *let's try this now* kind of way. "I'd try."

"You'd try? Or you're into it?"

"I'm into it."

"Yeah." His voice perks. "Right now?"

"Liam!" I reach for a tea sandwich. "We're in front of your brother."

"And look at them." He motions to Danielle and Adam, still embracing. "It will be an orgy."

"I'm not into orgies."

"Never?"

"Never."

"I'm not into sharing."

"Me either."

He places his hand on my thigh. Motions to Danielle. "Not sure you can keep her from watching though."

"I know."

"You ever want someone to watch?"

"I did think about your idea."

His eyes bore into mine. "Which one?"

"The club."

"Oh?"

"It would be interesting. Maybe not in an actual club, but…"

"I'll make it happen. What else?"

"I didn't prepare a list."

"Bullshit, Bri. I see you at work. Drifting off, daydreaming. You have a rich inner life."

That is true.

"No way it's bereft of sexual fantasies."

"Did you just say bereft?"

"Hell yeah. Don't try to distract me."

"There are some."

"Well…" He drags his hand up my thigh. Closer, closer, closer. "Tell me—"

"On the balcony in front of the city."

Closer, closer, closer—

"In the middle of a meeting. One of those dinner meetings we have to attend. You start like this. Then I excuse myself and I head to a private room. Maybe I even tease you with some pictures."

There. He presses his palm against my sex, over my jeans.

Fuck. My eyes flutter together. That's intense. Too intense. And completely inappropriate. "Then you join me. And it's our secret."

"You think of it during any of our meetings?"

"I have."

"When was the last?"

"A few weeks ago. The startup dating app. The guy was going on about matching preferences. You kept teasing him about sex. Then you'd look at me like you were picturing me naked."

"I was."

"Inappropriate."

"I know."

"Liam—"

"I know." He runs his finger over the seam of my jeans. "One more." He leans in and presses his lips to my neck. "Then I'll wait until we're alone. So enjoy it, baby." He does it again.

One slow, perfect brush of his thumb against me. Then he pulls his hand back and invites his brother to join our conversation.

It takes me a few minutes to catch my breath. I nod, sip milky Earl Grey, nibble on a hazelnut butter and plum jam sandwich.

After half a mug and three tea sandwiches, plus a chocolate-walnut cookie, I'm able to think something besides *must mount Liam now*.

I watch Liam spill stories of Adam's youth, trying to embarrass him, delighting Danielle.

Adam repays the favor with his own stories about Liam and he's just as unable to make Liam blush.

They're too used to this. Liam is too shameless. Adam is too expert in his poker face.

For an hour, they trade escalating stories, Liam with all his usual energy and enthusiasm, Adam with his typical quiet confidence. Bigger and better embarrassment, until they catch up to last year, to the last party Bash attended—

They hit that detail and all the joy dissipates.

The room quiets. The mood dulls. Danielle talks about her latest art project and asks about my business, but nothing fills the space with color.

Even when Simon arrives with Opal. And, as usual, Opal races to us, pulls us into tight hugs, enthuses over our outfits, jobs, presence.

"You promise you'll hang out with me during the party?" She looks at me and Danielle, deadly serious. "Because I seriously cannot get pulled into another conversation with Lee. Or Jimmy." She sticks her tongue out in horror. "And it's so awful hearing adult after adult say 'wow, eighteen, you're so young.' Or 'college next year, your life is ahead of you.' 'That will be the best time of your life.' Seriously, I can't stand it."

"I promise," Danielle says.

Opal looks to me.

"I promise… I'll make sure you're talking to Danielle before I disappear to fuck my fiancée," I say.

Opal laughs. "Honest. The best promises are." She hugs me and Danielle again. Releases us to pull Simon from his conversation with his brothers.

They look civil, but Liam knows how to make hostility look civil.

His eyes lock on mine. He raises a brow *should we?*

I nod *we should*, excuse myself, meet him in the upstairs hallway.

He leads me to the room at the end. I expect to see his bedroom, all the signs of teenage Liam, but I see shelves of books, a massive window, a view of the ocean.

The library.

"Do you need a minute with the books?" Liam presses the door closed. "Or you ready to come on my hand now?"

Chapter Thirty-Seven

LIAM

Briar looks around the room with wide eyes. She takes in the endless view of the ocean, the blue sky, the afternoon light falling over the oak furniture.

Then the bookshelves.

She's in heaven, surrounded by three walls of bookshelves.

"Did I cock block myself"—I wrap my arm around her waist—"picking this room?"

"No." She brings her eyes to mine. "It's perfect."

"Yeah?"

"Yeah." Her cheeks flush. "I always wanted to have sex in a library."

Thank fuck. I need to be inside her and out of my head. "Against a shelf?"

"Won't the books fall?"

"Can you think of a better way to die?"

"No. But I have an app to launch." She wraps her hand around my waist. "Between the stacks." She looks to the one bookshelf jutting from the wall.

It's not a library stack, but it's something.

"In high school, I dated this guy who loved manga. We'd hang out in the graphic novels section."

"You read manga?"

"We didn't get to the actual reading."

I press my palm into the small of her back. Lead her to the space between the bookshelf and the wide-open window.

She looks out at the backyard. The aqua pool, the rose garden, the massive lawn stacked with tables.

Already set up for the party.

So much like the house I grew up in. Like this is another one of Dad's parties. To celebrate the start of the season, or woo an investor, or impress a client.

Massive house, outdoor dining room, well-behaved children.

Simon, nearly old enough to step into his role. Adam following in his footsteps.

Then me and Bash, already troublemakers, in that *boys will be boys* way.

Between boarding school and weeks with Preston, I didn't spend as much time here. But there was enough. More than enough.

When Bash was here, the place was *alive*.

Now, it's not.

"We'd make out." She turns to face me. Slides her arms around my neck. "Sometimes, he'd feel me up."

"In the bookstore, in front of everyone?"

"Are you jealous?"

"A little."

"I never see you jealous."

"I never cared enough to be jealous." I pin her to the wall, slip my hand under her shirt, cup her breast over her bra. "Like this?"

She nods.

"Just this?"

"No."

I rock my hips against hers, slip my thumb into her bra. Her shirt is tight. I don't have a lot of room to move, but I still manage to run my thumb over her again and again.

"Liam." Her hips rock against mine. "Fuck."

I tease her again and again.

Her eyelids flutter closed.

"You like the tease?"

She barely manages to nod.

"Like this, in your clothes, 'cause I want you too badly to wait until they're off."

"Yes," she breathes.

"Me too." I press my lips to hers.

She melts into me, legs putty, lips parting, tongue dancing with mine.

She is mine.

It feels so fucking good, knowing how to play her, to push her to the edge, to take my fucking time with her bliss.

I've never claimed a love of control before. I've never been into issuing orders or tying women to my headboard.

But the way Briar melts into me feels so fucking good. The pleasure, the trust, the need.

Every fucking bit.

This strong, sarcastic, tough as nails woman putty in my hands.

Mine.

The rest of the world is a mess. This makes sense. This is music.

I don't know shit about music.

But I know Briar. I know what makes her laugh, what makes her ache, what makes her groan.

I kiss her hard as I tease her.

Her hips buck against mine. Her hands find my hair.

She kisses back, hard, claiming all of me, claiming something deep inside me, something only I can give her.

I tease her until she's panting, then I slip my other hand under her blouse.

The thing is skin tight. There's no room. I roll it up her stomach, over her bra, all the way to her collarbones.

She looks up at me, her grey eyes wracked with need, her expression hazy with pleasure. "Liam."

I push the cups of her bra aside. Replace them with my palms.

She groans as I draw circles around her nipples. Again and again. Until she's tugging at my hair.

Then more for good measure.

She rocks her hips against mine. She's wearing jeans, the same as I am. It's too much friction. And not enough.

I need her skin against mine.

I need every inch of her against every inch of me.

This room isn't private, but it's a big fucking house, and we have time.

I pull her shirt over her head.

She does away with her bra. Tugs my t-shirt over my head.

I wrap my arms around her and pin her to the wall.

Briar kisses me hard, her tongue swirling around mine, her hand knotting in my hair.

I want to stay here forever, locked with her in this place that makes perfect sense, on the precipice of an ocean of pleasure.

But my body is impatient. Too fucking impatient.

"Turn around." My voice drops to something low and demanding. A tone I rarely use. It's too honest. Too vulnerable.

With anyone else, it would be terrifying.

With Briar—

It's still terrifying. Free fall.

But staying still is scarier.

I can't lose her. I can't lose this. I can't lose anything else, but I really can't lose her.

"Don't make me ask twice, baby." The demand feels strange on my tongue. Too fucking right and too fucking wrong.

Her breath hitches in her throat. She barely nods. Turns. Puts her hands on the wall.

Reading my fucking mind.

I place my body behind hers. For one perfect moment, I soak in the feeling of her ass against my cock, her body arched into mine, the two of us on the precipice.

Then I undo the button of her jeans, roll them to her thighs, push her panties off her ass.

I slip my hand between her legs. "You always get this wet, baby?"

"No."

"Only for me?"

"Yes." She rocks against my hand.

I slip two fingers inside her.

Briar lets out a soft gasp. Her fingers curl into the wall. Her back arches, pushing me deeper.

She's ready—wet and pliable—but I warm her up anyway. I push my hand deeper, pull back, do it again and again.

"Liam—" She drops one arm. Wraps her hand around my wrist. "I need you inside me." Her fingers curl into my skin. "Please."

Maybe a stronger man could resist her, but I can't. Not with all the need in her voice. "Say it again."

"I need you inside me." She holds my hand in place as she rocks against it. "Please."

"Hands on the wall."

She returns her hand to position slowly.

I undo my button. Push my jeans and boxers from my hips in one swift motion.

My hands go to her hips. Slowly, I pull her into position.

She groans as my tip strains against her. "Fuck." Her fingers curl into the wall. "Please."

I need to hear it again. I need to soak in every letter. I dig my nails into her hips, pull back, tease her again.

Again.

Again.

"Please, Liam." Her voice drops to a whine. "Please fuck me."

In one swift motion, I drive into her.

Her breath hitches.

My fingers curl into her skin.

This is right. Where we both belong. Where the entire world makes sense.

My thoughts disappear.

My body takes over.

I bring my lips to her neck. Tease her with soft flicks of my tongue. With one hand, I hold her against me. I bring the other to her chest, toy with her nipples as I drive into her.

She rocks her hips to meet me, driving me deeper, pulling me closer.

She feels too fucking good. Warm and sweet and mine.

It fills the space.

The only warm, safe, beautiful thing in the fucking house.

Briar West's body joined with mine.

Briar West under my thumb.

Briar West coming on my cock.

Fuck. I need her coming on my cock.

I bring my lips to her ear. "Touch yourself, baby." I draw a circle around her nipple. "I want to feel you come."

She responds with a groan. Her hand slips between her legs. Right to the spot where she needs it.

She rubs herself with steady circles.

I drive into her again and again.

Again and again.

Until her groans run together and her nails scratch the fucking wall. Then she's there, groaning my name as she comes, her cunt pulsing around my cock, her bliss filling the room.

The entire world perfect and pure.

She pulls me over the edge with her. With my next thrust, I come. I work through my orgasm, groaning her name into her neck, spilling every fucking drop.

Pleasure spills through my senses. Everything is bliss. The air, the ground, the sound of her groan, the feel of her skin against mine.

I hold her close as I catch my breath.

"Fuck." She reaches back. Runs her fingers over my thigh. "Fuck, Liam."

"Yeah."

Slowly, she untangles our bodies. Slips back into her panties and jeans.

I fix my jeans, then I pull her into a tight embrace.

She's still mine.

This still makes sense.

When we leave the room, I don't have a clue.

But here and now, this makes perfect fucking sense. It's the only thing that makes sense.

———

I offer Briar my bedroom, but she insists she needs a full mirror. She showers, dresses, fixes her hair and makeup in the bathroom in the hall.

After a quick shower, I slip into my suit. It's strange, fixing my tie in my childhood bedroom. Familiar.

I've stood here, in front of the mirror, a thousand times.

But only once since Bash died.

This house has always been cold and sterile. But when the four of us were here, when Bash was alive—

We didn't fill every nook and cranny with laughter, but we came close. We came really fucking close.

Even in the middle of winter, with Dad's death looming over us and the high ceilings inviting draft, we filled the space with warmth.

He was alive.

There's no other way to describe it.

He was as alive as I was before I lost him. No, more. We were both bright and vibrant, but he loved with his entire heart.

He fell headfirst.

Then he died.

I don't live in a cave. I heard the foul play rumors too. A car accident, really? Because of some dysfunction in the engine? It's hard to believe.

Of course, Simon looked into it.

But maybe that's all it was. A little too much suspicion. Some bad luck. An engineering failure.

Is that what I'll find in the folder at the bottom of my suitcase?

A confirmation of Simon's inability to move on.

What else could it be?

If it was intentional, if someone else was responsible—

There's no fucking way Simon would let that go.

The asshole would already be in the ground.

But then maybe he is. Maybe my brother already murdered the asshole and disposed of the body and everyone shrugged *ah, well, he was about to go away for insider trading. I guess he flew the coop.*

Fuck. I need to get out of here. Away from the mirror, my reflection, the truth at the bottom of my suitcase.

That's a metaphor if I've ever heard one.

But I can't contemplate it for another second.

I slip into the hallway. Knock on the bathroom door.

"Liam?" Briar's voice is soft. "Is the party starting?"

"Almost."

"I'll be out in five."

"Want to make it ten?"

"Ten… oh." She laughs. "Only five minutes? That doesn't speak well of your abilities."

"You doubt me?"

She unlocks the door.

I step inside. It's just as strange, being in this familiar space. The clawfoot bathtub on the left. The giant mirror. The double sink.

And Briar, standing on the marble floor barefoot, already a vision in her short black cocktail dress.

"You look fucking amazing."

"Thanks." Her eyes flit to my tie. "You too."

I don't usually complain about the suit, but it's too much today. I need it gone. I need all this shit gone. "I won't fuck up your makeup." I press my lips to her neck. "Or your hair."

"You promise?"

"I promise." I slip my hand between her legs.

"Well." Her breath hitches as I rub her over her panties. "If you promise."

I slip between her legs, roll her panties to her ankles, lick her until she's groaning my name.

She tastes like heaven.

And the sound of her groan bouncing around the room?

There's nothing better.

It's perfect.

A few minutes in heaven.

Then I stand, clean up, and prepare to walk into hell.

Chapter Thirty-Eight

BRIAR

"I'm going to steal your fiancée for a minute." Opal hooks arms with me. "Thanks, Liam." She blows him a kiss.

"Did I say yes?" he asks.

"Did I ask a question?" She raises a brow exactly the way he does. "Briar is her own person. Not your property."

"You're the one claiming you're stealing her."

She shoots him a *please* look. "I am taking Briar away from this location with or without your permission." She turns to me. "If you don't mind. And even if you do. You promised."

"I did." And I didn't promise Liam I'd stay by his side. Not exactly. But I promised something, and he needs someone.

"Go for it, Bri. I'm fine." He fails to sell his statement.

The party is in its early stages—two dozen people, mostly on the patio, watching the sun begin its descent into the horizon—and Liam is already antsy.

"You want a drink?" He looks to me. "Grapefruit martini?"

"Thanks." I need to relax a little. There's too much in my head. I'm too overwhelmed by my desire to stay by his side.

I want to drag him back to his bedroom and fuck him all night.

And I want to snuggle in a blanket and watch the stars and talk about life.

It's a clear evening. Are the stars as bright as Liam claims? I can't remember the last time I saw a sky full of stars.

Those perfect specks of light against the darkness.

I need to see them. To see them with him.

The sun is starting to set. That means, what, two hours until a brilliant sky? I can survive two hours of small talk.

"Can I have one too?" Opal presses her palms together. "Please, Liam."

"Simon already wants to kill me," he says.

"You're taking his side?" She pouts. "I can't believe that."

"You think that's going to work?" he asks.

She nods.

He chuckles. "Yeah. I'm pretty fucking obvious, huh?"

"Sometimes." She releases me to throw her arms around him. "Thanks, Liam. You're my favorite."

"What's the qualifier this time? Favorite brother who lets you drink?"

"We'll go with that, sure." She releases him. "I promise I'll take good care of her."

Uh…

She leads me to the patio. There are a dozen people I don't know here, but my eyes go straight to the table next to the rose garden.

Harrison is sitting with his father, laughing and sipping champagne.

They share the same mix of exhaustion and excitement.

Opal watches Liam grab our drinks. Meets him at the bar. Gets pulled into a conversation with him and Simon.

I keep my attention on the groom and his father. There's so much pride in Preston's eyes. And Harrison is meeting it with his own. They both want to see him married. They both appreciate the importance of the occasion.

And not in a solemn way.

With joy.

When was the last time I felt that? My family flew out for my graduation. They toured the city for days, clapped as I accepted my diploma, took me to dinner three nights in a row.

Dad was proud. I saw it, but I was too hurt and angry to accept it.

Mom was there, but she wasn't *there*. It was like she only had so much energy and excitement to give, and the second it ran out, she was in free fall.

I know that feeling. I've been there.

But it still hurt. It still hurts.

"Simon is such a buzz kill." Opal interrupts my train of thought. "But Liam distracted him." She holds up dual pastel pink cocktails.

Grapefruit martinis. Yum. I take mine. Let the sweet mix of citrus and gin warm my lips and ease my shoulders.

The world is a fucked-up mess.

The West family is a fucked-up mess.

Hell, the Pierce family is a fucked-up mess.

But we're here to celebrate love, dammit. Even if the word terrifies me and the thought of an actual engagement ring makes my throat close.

Harrison is happy.

I'm celebrating that.

Carpe fucking diem.

I raise my glass. "Cheers."

Opal smiles as she raises her glass. "Cheers." She takes a long sip. Lets out a soft sigh. "That's really good. The last thing I drank was…" She looks back to the bar, where Simon and Liam are talking. "Very cheap vodka and even cheaper orange soda. This is a big step up."

"Really?"

"You don't believe me?"

"Aren't you a Park Avenue Princess now?"

"A princess locked in her tower. Simon is the most overprotective person on the planet. He gave me a curfew."

"Really?"

"Yeah. Me, a grown adult, starting college next year, and he thinks he can give me a curfew."

"Why do you follow it?"

"He gets so worried." She looks back to him. "I know he means well."

"It's what we do, as older siblings. We worry."

"And you boss your younger siblings around?"

I nod.

"We did negotiate. Two a.m. on weekends."

"That's not enough time to party?"

"That's not the point! I'm an adult. I should be able to spend the night at a guy's house."

I can't help but chuckle.

"What? Not you too, Briar. If you tell me some bullshit about how young I am, I'll throw this drink in your face."

"That's not a mature move," I say.

She raises her drink. "You've been warned."

I can't help but laugh. "You're so much like Liam."

"So I hear." She looks to her brothers again. "I love

Simon. I hate how worried he gets. I just wish… I wish he wouldn't always throw down this my way or the highway thing."

"He's not used to having a young woman in his apartment."

She taps her chin with her index finger. "Dangerously close to the line, but I'll allow it."

"Has he ever lived with a woman?"

"No."

"It's different, but…"

"He knew to stock tampons."

A laugh spills from my lips.

"What? Guys don't always know."

"They don't."

"And… god. He's so paternal. He took me to the Museum of Sex. The Museum of Sex with my brother! Can you believe that?"

"I can."

"And, after, we go to the gift shop, and he tells me I should explore my sexuality with whatever device I see fit, as long as I do it alone. I almost died of embarrassment."

God, I can imagine that. It's hilarious. Poor Opal.

"You're laughing at my pain."

I motion *a little*. "What did you buy?"

"Is this a thing? When I hit twenty-one, will I be legally allowed to drink and suddenly obsessed with other people's masturbation?"

My laugh gets louder.

"It's not funny."

"It kind of is."

"Briar West, you're cruel!"

"If you ever want to shop with a friend." I place my hand on my heart. "I'm available. And I won't discuss any of your brothers."

"I appreciate that, but I'm set. Plenty of tools."

I raise a brow.

"Not you too? Danielle is already lecturing me about self-enjoyment. Like she invented masturbation because she takes pictures of it."

Oh god. I double over, laughing. I nearly spill my drink.

Everyone looks at me.

"Why is that funny? Why do older people think it's funny, telling younger people things we figured out years ago?" Opal shakes her head. "I've had a vibrator for a long time now. I don't need Simon buying me one."

Oh my god. I can't stop laughing.

"Fucking grown-ups." She shakes her head and takes a sip. "You're all terrible. Your generation didn't invent masturbation!"

"Aren't we the same generation?"

"Whatever! The point stands."

A woman in a long wine-colored dress looks our way. She stands tall and proud, the way Simon does. Regal, powerful, gorgeous.

She stands out. Not just because she's *wearing* that dress. And not just because she's the only Black woman at the party, besides her mom. Because she magnetically attracts attention.

The way Simon does.

Her dark eyes meet mine and she looks away to Opal.

Opal notices. "Vanessa, hey! How are you?"

"Busy." She offers her hand.

Opal pulls her into a tight hug. "You look amazing."

"You do," I say.

She turns to me. "Briar, right?"

I nod and offer my hand. We've met before, but only in professional circumstances. Never family events.

I've seen her around. She's Lee's step-sister, but they're as close as any biological sisters. She's at most family events.

But she's usually with Lee.

And Lee is…

Well, Lee is Lee.

She shakes with a friendly nod. Looks to the bar, where Simon and Liam are still in conversation, still maintaining an air of civility.

There's something in her eyes, but I can't tell if it's yearning, curiosity, or hatred. She's rocking an excellent poker face. As good as Simon's.

"Did you say hi? He'd love to hear from you," Opal says.

"I don't think he would." She looks to me.

"He would. He talks about you all the time," Opal says.

Her laugh is knowing. "I can imagine."

Can she?

She's staring at him like she wants to tear his clothes off. Does she hate him as much as Liam claims?

Or is there something else there?

"What's it like, being the sister of the bride?" Opal asks.

"Exhausting. But good exhausting," she says.

"You'll be relieved tomorrow evening?" Opal asks.

"Very." Vanessa turns to the ballroom—seriously, there's a ballroom—as Lee enters.

Lee spins until her dress twirls, then steps onto the patio. She looks gorgeous, her long blond hair in neat waves, her chiffon dress blowing in the breeze.

She spots her sister with a smile. "Vanessa. You're already here." She squeezes her with a tight hug. "And Briar. What a fabulous dress. I wish I had the guts to pull off that hairstyle."

Opal's lips curl into a frown. "She looks hot, right?"

"Very sexy, yes. I wouldn't expect anything else." Lee smiles with her usual evil glee.

Or maybe that's my hate. Maybe she means it as a compliment. There's a universe where that's a compliment.

If Liam whispered it in my ear as he slid his hand under my dress—

That would be hot as fuck.

But this?

Whatever.

I'm happy Harrison is happy.

"I know. I wish I was more like Briar. I care too much about what people think. There was this mean girl at my school. You know the type?" Opal pauses for a split second, to let the implications land, then she continues. "She would always insult my hair or my makeup or my clothes. And we wore uniforms, so that took a lot of effort. I let it get to me all year. Even at the prom. Then, when the night was winding down, I saw her in the bathroom crying. And I thought, yes, finally, I can get my revenge, and take her down, right?"

"Of course." Lee nods.

"I opened my mouth, ready to destroy her, but I didn't. I didn't want to. I asked if she was okay. And she just started bawling. Her boyfriend—this older guy, a college guy—didn't show up, because he didn't want his friends to know he was dating a high school girl. He was dragging her around, using her, making her feel like shit. And I hadn't been there, exactly, but I understood. I told her it was okay. I even gave her a hug."

"Really?" I ask.

"Yeah. And she still insulted my dress at graduation. But I didn't care," Opal says. "I saw through her. I saw that it didn't matter." She directs the words at Lee, specifically.

But Lee doesn't seem to see herself in the story. "It's good of you to take the high road." She squeezes her sister's hand. "It's a hard thing to do."

Uh… okay. I guess that's good advice. Or it would be from someone else.

"Thanks." Opal smiles.

"Do you have a picture of the dress?" I ask.

"Why? Do you want to critique it too? I swear, Briar, if you insult my dress *after* asking about my masturbation habits, you're going to be my least favorite sister-in-law."

"Below Danielle?" I ask.

"Way below. She always compliments my outfits." She stage whispers. "I know you're way more fashionable, but still…"

"That's why I want to see."

"You'll be nice?" she asks.

Vanessa's eyes flit from us to Simon's.

He catches her staring.

She turns to us, turns her back to him, but he does nothing to hide his attention.

He watches the four of us gather around Opal's cell to look at her dress.

Opal looks cute in her crimson cap and gown. And she looks hot in her crimson dress. It suits her long, narrow frame, and it brings out the blue in her eyes.

But she looks like a high school girl.

Today, she looks grown up.

"Briar, I know that expression! You're trying to put it gently." Opal shakes her head. "I live with Simon. I don't need gentle."

"You'd look great in a paper bag," I say. "With those legs and those eyes."

"And the hair." She flips her hair behind her head. "Don't forget the hair."

"The guys go crazy for it?" I ask.

"Of course. But now we need another drink, yeah?" Opal asks. "Nice to see you, Vanessa. Congrats on the wedding, Lee."

"Thank you." Lee beams, then she spots her fiancé, and somehow, she gets even brighter.

She may be a bratty mean girl, but she loves him.

That's as clear as day.

And maybe it's the only thing that matters too.

"I know, I know, no drinks. Whatever." Opal rolls her eyes as she takes Simon's arm. "Your crush is staring at you."

"She isn't my crush," Simon says.

"Yeah, she hates him," Liam says.

"Those things aren't mutually exclusive," Opal says.

"Probably why he likes her, huh?" Liam asks.

"Or maybe because she's smart and successful and gorgeous," Opal says. "She runs a non-profit."

"She is hot." Liam nods.

"Why do you make it crass?" Opal groans. "She's beautiful."

"I'm making it crass? Your favorite brother is staring like he's about to rip her clothes off," Liam says.

He's not wrong.

Simon's stare is intense. Packed with a mix of lust and loathing. No, not loathing. Something closer to frustration.

He wants her.

He doesn't want to want her, but he does.

"She probably doesn't think about him at all," Liam says. "Sad."

"She does," he says.

"Do you really think you're that important?" Opal asks.

"Of course he does," Liam says. "What kind of question is that?"

Simon's eyes flit to us. Then back to Vanessa.

This time, she catches him looking. But he doesn't look away.

"He's going to say some bullshit about how he's not into her," Liam says.

I don't think so. Simon isn't the type to deny his desires. And his stare isn't just lust. It's something deeper.

I never really believed Liam's claims that Simon was hung up on his high school crush slash rival, but there's something between them.

Something big.

"Simon? You gonna argue your case at all?" Liam asks.

"Not with you." Simon returns to the conversation, not at all aware of what we're discussing. "Have a drink if you want one, Opal. We're celebrating."

"Really? Thank you." She motions *get me a drink* to Liam.

"I'm talking to you right now," he says.

"Your fiancée needs one too," she says.

He chuckles. "You're as bossy as Simon."

"I am not," she says.

"Yeah, you're worse. And he's all pent-up sexual frustration. It's like that book you gave me," he says.

"Oh my god, Liam! Did you read the book? It was extremely explicit about the older man's uh… I don't want to think about my brother's dick!"

"Then why are you?" he asks.

"Drink. Now." She folds her arms.

He chuckles *too easy.* "For that, I will." He blows her a kiss. After she waves it away, he laughs and heads to the bar.

"How do you deal with him?" she asks.

"You won't like my answer," I say.

"His dick? Ugh, he talks about it enough. Why are you talking about it too?" she asks.

"Was it strictly sexual when it started?" Simon asks.

God, the way he asks is terrifying and hot at the same time. No wonder all the women at work spread rumors about his predilections. I've heard everything from monastic self-deprivation to sex clubs every weekend.

What does Simon like?

He is pent up, but he never explodes. He must release the tension somewhere—

"Are you willingly asking about Liam's dick?" Opal's nose scrunches. "Gross."

"I thought so." My eyes go to Liam. "But now, I'm not so sure. I knew him then. Not as well as I know him now, but I… I've cared about him for a long time."

He turns to me. Motions to the line at the bar *you believe this shit?*

I laugh and nod *I do*.

This is easy.

Fun even.

I'm a part of the family. A dysfunctional family, sure, but one where everyone loves each other and wants to be together.

Liam returns with our drinks.

He proposes a toast to the bride and groom.

Everyone cheers. People start to dance.

Even Preston joins on the dance floor.

It's almost silly. By uptight rich people standards. I have another drink, relax, melt into Liam's arms.

The stars come out.

The night is beautiful, perfect, peaceful.

Until Preston collapses in the middle of the dance floor.

Chapter Thirty-Nine

BRIAR

I t's twenty minutes to the nearest hospital. An ambulance will take too long.

Simon leaps into action. He helps Preston and Harrison into his car. Instructs someone to call for a room.

Somehow, I jump into action too. Find someone sober enough to drive. Climb into the back seat of their car with Liam and Opal. Squeeze their hands on the way.

The second we arrive at the ER, I see it.

All the guilt on Liam's face.

He knows something.

He's known something.

For all this time, he's known something.

Is that why he asked me to participate in this ruse? He said it was about Preston moving to London. I didn't look closely at his claim. I was too busy contemplating the complications of playing Liam's fake fiancée.

I was too busy negotiating points on my business.

What does it matter if he has six percent or seven or ten if this is—

I can't say it. I can't even think it.

He didn't tell me.

How could he not tell me?

Simon is already here, with two rows of teal chairs reserved, ready to explain the situation in a calm, even tone.

Preston is dehydrated. Nothing serious, for a man without health problems, but with his medical condition, mixing alcohol with his meds—

It's in every word Simon utters. Even with his calm tone of voice, it's clear: Preston is dying.

The way their father died. A slow decline, one easy to miss, then boom—

Gone.

Simon stays still. Liam paces around the room. Opal hugs her shoulders, barely attempting to hold in her nerves. She's not close with Preston, but she lost her mom the same way.

I ask if she wants to take a walk. She accepts gladly. We circle the courtyard, making small talk about the last book she read, a dirty story of domination and submission.

"There's a scene like this, actually," she says. "The heroine is overwhelmed by what's happening with her family, and sex is the only way she can escape. So they sneak off and find some empty room and he uses his tie as a blindfold. And even though it's weird, it works, it helps her center herself."

"It sounds romantic."

"Yeah. But I… I forgot how horrible hospitals feel. The smell of them. It's not sexy. It's just…" She shakes her head as her voice fades.

I pull her into a tight hug, then I change the subject to her plans for her summer trip to Europe, and we continue our slow circles.

It's easier, focusing on Opal, on making sure she's okay.

I've never lost a parent. I've never sat in a hospital room, waiting for test results or news from an operation, wondering if this is the last time I'm going to see someone I love.

Preston is fading.

I've seen the signs. I told myself they were something else, but some part of me knew. The talk about legacy and love and death—

Of course, he's thinking about his mortality.

We walk in circles for a long time. Until Simon interrupts us.

"I'll take you home." He offers his sister his hand.

She looks to me, her blue eyes wide with concern. "Are you going to be okay here?"

"We're staying at the house," Simon says. "I can bring you home now or come back later."

"You're not staying?" she asks.

"It's fine. I'll catch a ride," I say.

"Liam is inside." Concern drops into Simon's voice. "He… he'll appreciate your company."

"Yeah. Of course." I'm his fiancée. That's still our story. Is Simon still suspicious or is that just Simon? The guy isn't exactly the world's biggest believer in love. Not that I can talk.

I just—

I can't face Liam. I can't look him in the eyes and demand an explanation.

How could he lie to me?

Why am I so desperate to collapse in his arms? To catch him when he falls?

It's too dangerous.

I need to go somewhere else, somewhere safe.

"I'll walk you out, Opal," I say.

Simon shoots me an *are you sure that's a good idea* look, but he still nods and leads us to the parking lot.

I hug Opal and help her into the passenger seat.

He stands there, at the driver's side, all tall and broad and imposing. "He didn't tell me either."

Huh?

"Liam. He knew. You didn't?"

"No."

"Secrets are a burden," he says. "He's trying to protect you."

Maybe, but is that really love? Isn't love about sharing your burdens, sharing your secrets, letting someone help you?

How the fuck am I supposed to know?

"Good night, Simon," I say.

"Call me if you need anything." He slips into the driver's seat, turns the car on, pulls out of the parking lot.

I watch the luxury car turn onto the main road, then I return to the waiting room, find Liam sitting in one of the teal chairs, the same guilty look on his face.

He turns to me and his expression shifts.

Fear. Relief. Something I can't place.

I don't know what to say. I don't know how to say it.

"You didn't tell me." My voice is a whisper. "You knew, and you didn't tell me."

"Bri—"

"Did you know?"

Guilt fills his eyes. Then fear. The realization of what this means. What I'm here to do.

I can't look at him.

I can't watch his heart break.

He knew.

He knows I know.

And he knows what I'm about to do.

I just have to do it.

"You weren't supposed to lie to me," I say. "You promised."

"I know," he whispers.

I can feel it, feel his heart breaking, but I can't bring myself to look at him. "I… I can't do this. I'm sorry." I slip the engagement ring off my finger. Press it into his palm. "I'm sorry, Liam. I can't."

I can't pretend.

I can't not pretend.

I can't love someone who locks me out.

My father and my mother—

I can't walk down that path. I can't do it.

"Bri, please—"

I don't give him a chance to ask me to stay. Or let me go without protest. I can't handle either. "I'm sorry, Liam." I don't give him a chance to respond.

I turn, leave, call a car, find the nearest hotel.

It's a cheap place, but it's clean and conveniently located. I shower, change into the plush robe, climb into bed, fail to find sleep.

Secrets are a burden. Simon is right about that. But he's wrong about Liam protecting me.

He's protecting himself.

I can't blame him, but I can't live with it either.

I need all of him.

Every broken part.

Every need.

Every burden.

Chapter Forty

LIAM

I give Harrison time with his father. Give Preston time to explain. It's awkward as fuck, standing in the hallway, across from the window to the room, pretending I'm not watching their conversation unfold.

Is the truth setting him free?

Or trapping him in a cage?

My whole life, I've craved freedom. From my dad, from boarding school rules, from the expectations thrust upon me.

For the last few months, I've cursed Simon for hiding shit from me, all while keeping my own secrets.

Was Preston's confession the truth, setting me free?

Or is this?

There's weight to a secret. The heaviness in my shoulders is easing.

But without Briar here—

Will anything be easy again?

Harrison leaves in a huff. I slip into the room, pull up a chair next to Preston, offer him my hand.

He looks at me, weary and worn, the weight of his secrecy written all over his face.

"We don't have to talk," I say.

"You're able to go without conversation?"

"For a few minutes, max. Make the most of them."

He nods and takes my hand.

Everything is a fucked-up mess.

But he's here.

And I'm here, honoring my promise to him, repaying him the only way I can.

Chapter Forty-One

BRIAR

One downside of running away? I'm lacking attire. I slip into my cocktail dress, fasten the straps of my heels, debate the merits of wearing last night's underwear or skipping underwear entirely.

Neither option appeals, but going commando to see my ex fake fiancé's father figure—

That's a no go.

I slide into last night's panties, call a ride share, stop at the pharmacy on my way to the hospital. I slip into the waiting room, ready to find a bathroom and change into a pair of cotton briefs, but it's not necessary.

Simon is already here, with my purple overnight bag on the chair next to him. "Liam's out, grabbing coffee for Harrison."

"Oh."

He taps the chair. "Trish packed it."

"Thanks."

"He'll be back in twenty minutes."

Okay. That's good information. Twenty minutes to say hey, sorry you're dying, did you realize I lied about my

377

engagement to Liam? No. Then never mind. It was all real. Totally.

"He loves you."

What?

"That isn't always enough. I won't ask you to ignore the other factors. But don't ignore that."

What can I say? *No, he doesn't, we're just pretending we're in love.* If this is really over, and this is the end, then Liam's family is no longer any of my business.

We're coworkers.

That's all.

I can handle that. Absolutely.

"I know." It falls off my lips easily, but it's not true. I don't know. I wonder, I hope, I suspect, but I don't know.

Simon nods. "Room one fifteen."

"Thanks." I grab the overnight bag, change into jeans, a t-shirt, and a fresh pair of panties in the bathroom. And, yes, flat shoes. Much better. I check my outfit for anything that screams *I slept in a hotel and not in Liam's bed*, take a deep breath, and find Preston's room.

He's half asleep, an opened paperback on his chest, his son asleep on the chair across from his.

He stirs as I enter, motions to his sleeping son, presses his fingers to his lips. "Shall we take a walk?"

"Can you?"

"Who's going to stop me?"

"The nurse? Your son?"

"Then let's stay quiet."

"Okay." I offer my hand.

He uses it for leverage as he slips out of bed. His IV is already on a cart, and he's wearing pajamas under his gown.

Rich people perks or modern hospital life? I'm not

sure. I'm lucky. I haven't had to spend much time in hospitals.

I can see why so many people hate them. They're strange and sterile. A place to fall, fade, die.

It happens to all of us. But it's close for Preston. And I—

Fuck, I don't want to see it happen. I don't know him well, but I don't want to lose him. I don't want the world to lose him.

Harrison must be reeling.

It's supposed to be his wedding day.

Once Preston is standing, he takes my hand and moves into the hallway. I lead him to the courtyard where Opal and I paced last night.

It's different in the morning light. Bright and beautiful. A place to live, breathe, bloom.

"It's sweet of you to visit me," he says.

"What do you mean?"

"Your ring." He motions to my left hand. "You're not wearing it."

Shit. That's obvious.

"Liam didn't tell me, but I could see it in his eyes. This sense of loss."

"How do you know it's me? And not... your condition?"

"I was looking him in the eyes when I told him this news. It was different."

"Oh."

"This is my fault, Briar. I asked him to keep this a secret. It was selfish. It wasn't fair to Liam."

Maybe, but Liam said yes. He kept this from me. He had a million chances to tell me, but he chose to keep it to himself every time.

"Is it over between you two?"

"It's complicated."

"I didn't want to burden my son. I told myself that and it's true. But it's more. I don't want people to look at me like I'm dying."

"Am I?"

"Yes." He pats the back of my hand. "But I understand. It's surprising news."

"I'm sorry. I just…" Fuck, I can't put this on him. It's my problem. He's not my actual father, however paternal he is. "It is surprising."

"Liam needs you."

"I know." I need him too, but not like this. Not if he's going to keep secrets, lock me out, keep his scars to himself.

"He loves you."

"You're the second person to say that today."

"Simon?"

I nod.

"Everyone can see it."

"How?"

"The way he looks at you. He adores you."

"Maybe."

"Absolutely. And you feel the same?"

"I do."

He's quiet for a moment. "You're afraid of ending up with your parents' marriage."

It's not a question, but I nod anyway.

"It's okay to be unsure, Briar. To be scared. I'm supposed to be brave in the face of death, but I'm not. I don't want to miss my son's wedding. I don't want to miss meeting my grandchildren. I don't want to miss seeing you and Liam work through your problems."

Fuck. "Do we really make your list?"

"Liam is like a son to me. My most difficult son."

"He's difficult."

"Does he need your certainty?"

"No. He didn't ask for anything. I just... I need more of him. I need all of him. His secrets too."

"I'm the one who asked him to lie. Be angry with me."

"I'm not angry." I wish I was. I know what to do with anger. I know how to handle it. This empty feeling in my chest? This desire for all of Liam next to this fear I'll have it? It's awful.

"Then be disappointed in me."

"I... I can't."

"The perk of dying."

My laugh is sad. "You didn't know me. Liam did." And I'm still lying to him, but maybe it doesn't matter. I'm not pretending. I do love Liam. Maybe I wouldn't agree to a marriage proposal, but Preston knows my feelings on the matter. "You've been kind to me. You've listened. The father I never had. I just..." A tear catches on my lashes. "Thank you for taking care of him."

"I can't accept that thank you."

I blink and my eyes are cloudy.

"Not if it means you're giving up on him."

"I don't know what I'm doing."

"That's the most honest thing I've heard all day." He smiles.

I try to smile back, but I only get halfway there. "I do... I do love him. I just... I need all of him. And I'm not sure he can give me that."

"Try. As a favor to me."

"Okay." How can I turn down a dying man's request? "I'll try." I'll try really fucking hard.

Chapter Forty-Two

LIAM

The takeout cup is heavy in my hands. How can a sixteen ounce cup feel this fucking heavy?

Damn Simon. Is this his idea of being a wing-man? I'm not exactly in prime condition in yesterday's suit on two hours of sleep.

The automatic doors slide open.

Briar steps outside. She's wearing casual clothes, jeans and a plain top, and she's nearly bare-faced, but she still looks like Bri.

The woman who's tormented me and accepted my torment for the last two years.

She can't leave like this.

I can't let her.

I try to think of some appropriate introduction. Fail miserably. "Hey."

"Hey." Her voice is soft. Hurt. "Are you okay?"

"No. You?"

She shakes her head. "I'm sorry you're losing him. He's a great guy. He… the world is going to miss him."

"He's not in the ground yet."

"I know, but…"

"Yeah." Fuck, this isn't charming. Where's my fucking charm? I offer her the takeout cup. "There's no lavender, but I watched them make it. Made sure they brewed the tea first, then added the milk."

"Annoyed them so much they spit in it?"

"Absolutely, but that's spit with a great London Fog attached."

She laughs and my heart sings. For a split second, the world is a big, beautiful place.

Then the stupid doors slide together and the aura of hospital infects everything.

"Thanks, Liam." Her fingers brush mine as she takes the cup. "I, uh, I should get back to the city."

"Stay."

"I—"

"For the wedding."

"It's still happening?"

I nod. "Here, at the chapel, instead of on the beach."

"Lee agreed to that?"

"Seemed happy to step up, actually."

"She really does love him."

"Yeah, she does. And she still wears the dress."

"It's a nice dress."

"Intimate this way," I say. "Friends and family only."

"I'm not family."

"You're always family."

She holds my gaze for a moment, then she looks to the ground, hides behind her takeout cup.

"Same time. No dress code."

"I can't wear jeans to a wedding."

She can, but she won't. I know her that well. "Opal's at the house. She'll be glad to see you and I won't…" I don't know what to call it. "I'll be here for a while."

"Thanks, Liam. Really." She looks at me like she's not sure how to say goodbye, then she offers her hand.

"If you think I'm shaking you're out of your fucking mind."

"I am?"

"Yeah. I don't know how I'm going to fix this. I don't know how I broke it. But I'm going to figure it out. And I'm going to do it."

"You didn't break anything."

"Are you coming in the supply closet?"

"That's not sexy."

"Then I did."

"It's not like that. It's… I just… I want all of you. The secrets, the pain, the burdens. I can't settle for anything less."

Then she turns and leaves.

Like it's that fucking obvious she doesn't have all of me.

Like it's that fucking obvious she'll never have all of me.

———

FOR A FEW HOURS, I JOIN THE SOCIALIZING IN PRESTON'S hospital room. We talk around the elephant in the room for a while.

Eventually, he tires of the eggshells, insists we owe it to him to talk about his son's wedding day. Even though Harrison is sitting right there, awkwardly discussing delaying the honeymoon.

Simon and I send Harrison home to get ready. We stay with Preston for a while.

Then Simon takes his turn and I head to the mansion.

The house feels bigger without Briar. Emptier. There's no sign of her stuff in my bedroom. No sign she was ever here.

No sign she ever loved me.

A shower does nothing to clear my head. I dress in the suit I packed, the emerald green tie Harrison requests of his groomsmen, an old pair of cufflinks my dad gave me.

The last gift he gave before he died.

I wander the house, trying to find the warmth Briar took with her. It's not here. It's missing. It's been missing for a long time.

Since we lost Bash.

And before that too. Did a little leak with every loss? Or has it been pouring from the place for my entire life?

Maybe there is a leak and it's up to us to make enough to compensate.

To fill the space with joy, laughter, groans.

I find Opal in the library, in a long fuchsia dress, reading a folded paperback.

She looks up at me and shakes her head. "You're going to fix things with her, right?"

"Nice to see you too."

"Are you leaving?"

"You don't have to come."

"I know." She stands. Sets the book on the shelf. Crosses the room to me. "But you need me."

I expect to prove her wrong, comfort her, at least play up the bullshit for long enough to keep her distracted, but she's right. The second I step into the hospital, my limbs are jelly.

A teenage girl is the only thing holding me together.

It's pathetic.

And it only gets worse when I step into the chapel. See Briar standing next to Lee's sister.

It's a fast wedding, with barely any pomp and circumstance. A chaplain officiates. Lee walks the aisle in a fancy dress. She and Harrison light up the second they lock eyes.

Like the rest of the world—and the ugly realities of the day—are gone.

Like they're the only two people who've ever been in love.

I see it. I believe it. I almost understand it.

But after they kiss, and pop champagne, and I try to find Briar, to find some way to articulate the shit running away in my head, I lose it.

She's gone.

Back to the city, to her life, to a life that doesn't involve me.

Chapter Forty-Three

LIAM

fter the ceremony winds down, I drive Opal home. I set her up in the library, take a shower, debate whether I'm staying or going.

I'm too worn to argue, even with myself. I don't want to be here, but I'm not sure how I'll make it to the city coherent.

I finish, dry, wrap myself in a robe.

Find Simon in my bedroom, sitting on my fucking bed, like Dad, waiting to deliver an important speech.

He's in his suit, not a thread out of place, his hand on the folder from the bottom of my suitcase.

The one with every secret he's hiding.

The one I'm yet to read.

"You mind?" I motion to the clothes on my bed.

He turns, so his back is to me.

Whatever. I don't give a shit what he sees. I slip into clean clothes. Easy clothes. Jeans and a t-shirt. Not his stuck-up suit and his designer tie.

He waits until I stop moving, then he says, "Did you read it?"

"Not yet."

He turns and looks me in the eyes. "What's it say?"

"I didn't read it yet. How the fuck should I know?"

"Who did you ask?"

"What's the difference?"

He stands and turns the folder over. "You could have asked."

"I tried."

"Did you? Did you ever sit me down and say, Simon, please, it's killing me you're keeping secrets. I want to know what happened. I want to know why you're hiding things."

"I'm too tired for this argument."

"Are you claiming the high road? Really? After keeping Preston's condition a secret?"

"He asked."

Simon says nothing.

"Who asked you to hide things from me?"

"I'm trying to protect you."

"That's bullshit. You're not wiser. You're not special. You're not more capable of handling burdens."

"I'm your older brother."

"Fuck you. You think I can't carry my own burdens? You think I shrugged it off when Bash died? When Adam was in critical condition? He took all the space for grief. And that was fine. He almost died. He was closer to Bash than anyone. He needed the space. He never claimed superiority for it. But you—you act like you're the only person who cares about this family."

"Liam."

"Whatever it is, I don't care. Fuck you for shielding me. I'm not a child. I haven't been a child for a long time."

"You're right."

"What?"

"You're right. I'm sorry."

Am I hearing things? There's no way my older brother, Simon Pierce, is admitting he's wrong and apologizing.

What.

The.

Actual.

Fuck.

"I won't shield you anymore. If you want to know, it's here." He taps the folder. No longer sealed. Now, seen by his eyes. "It's your decision, not mine."

"What's in there?"

"Secrets I've kept to shield you."

"And Adam?"

"He did his own research."

Like brother, like brother. "He knows everything?"

"No. There are things his PI didn't find. Things I had to dig to find." His eyes flit to the paper. "Things not in this report."

"Are you going to tell me?"

"I want to keep this from you, Liam. I want to protect you from it. But you're right. You deserve the truth, if you want it. Everything in here. And everything else I know." He places the folder on the bed. "I love you, Liam. You're my brother. You infuriate me and you always will, and I'll always love you. I'll always protect you."

"I love you too." It's been a long time since I've said it with this tone. All sincerity. No promise or threat or high ground.

Then Simon does the last thing I expect.

He pulls me into a fucking hug.

He pats me on the back. "Get some rest. We're going back to the city tomorrow."

"We are?"

"Yeah. I promised Preston I'd make sure you win Briar back."

Chapter Forty-Four

BRIAR

Every part of me is exhausted, but I still can't sleep. I keep thinking of the hurt in Liam's eyes. The pain in his voice. The desperate desire to erase all of it.

No, I don't want to erase it. Not exactly.

I want to be there for him. Sit with him, listen, hold him, help him.

I'm not good with feelings. I've never been good with them, never wanted to learn how to deal.

With Liam, I want that.

I want everything.

I wake to the warmth of the sun. The soft hum of the air conditioner. The cheap cotton sheet covering my tiny twin bed.

My room, my apartment, my life.

It's not as grand as Liam's, but it's mine, all mine, and I understand it.

I know where I stand. I know who I am.

Briar West, lover of literature and London Fogs. Stylish, witty, smart.

No lies, no compromises, no desperate need to hold someone together.

I'm safe here.

No one can hurt me. No one can abandon me, break promises, force me to become a shell of myself.

No one can lock me out, pull away, force me to watch them fade.

I'm alone. I'm safe.

Only I'm not, not anymore.

My heart isn't mine anymore.

It's Liam's.

I don't want to miss him. I don't want to need him. I don't want to feel this desperate ache without him.

That's how my mom fell apart. My dad's abandonment. He promised to help her hold herself together, then he left, and she couldn't do it on her own.

That's part of it.

But maybe it wasn't all of it.

He broke his promise to her, yes. Nothing absolves him of cheating.

But she broke her promise too. She stopped showing him her ugly parts; she stopped letting him in, stopped accepting his love.

It wasn't her fault she suffered from depression. But it wasn't his either.

It certainly wasn't mine.

So why am I the person carrying the weight of it?

All this time, I've been afraid of becoming my mother, losing my spark, watching my husband abandon me.

But I'm just as scared of becoming my father, watching my partner lock me out, keep me away, abandon me emotionally.

I'm fucking it up on every fucking level.

I don't want to hurt. But the alternative is worse. Locking everyone out, hiding all my ugly parts, refusing to embrace love—

That isn't a life.

It's not the life I want.

I don't want to keep everything to myself anymore. I want to have someone there. To be there for him.

Can Liam do that?

I don't know.

But I know I have to ask. I have to try.

I promised Preston.

I sort through my thoughts as I shower, fix tea, make toast. The raspberry jam is a far cry from the fancy stuff at the Pierce manor, but it's mine, and it feels good, being in my space, taking care of myself, believing in this future where I let someone take care of me.

Maybe it's not Liam. Maybe it's someone else.

But, fuck, I really want it to be Liam.

I need to say something, do something, somehow explain.

At least, I need to find him.

I pull out my cell, but I chicken out. I text Danielle instead.

Briar: Did Liam come back to the city?

Danielle: He and Simon left early this morning.

Briar: Thanks.

Danielle: What happened?

Briar: Love is complicated.

Danielle: It is.

If he's on his way, I need to get dressed. I need to do something. I find a simple outfit. A black sundress and sandals.

My phone buzzes with a string of texts.

Danielle: He's downstairs. He asked me to say that.

Briar: How are you involved?

Danielle: Opal is texting me.

Briar: I have an audience?

Danielle: Apparently. Should I tell them to step off?

Briar: I prefer one on one.

Danielle: She says no promises.

Briar: Tell her I'll buy her a bottle of gin if she does.

Danielle: She says you're not good for it unless you stick with Liam.

Briar: Is she really doubting my word?

Danielle: Sounds like it.

There's a knock on my door.

Danielle: Shit, I think it's happening. Good luck, Briar. We're still friends, no matter what happens.

I take a deep breath. Let out a slow exhale.

Easy breaths.

Steady breaths.

It's six steps to my door.

And there's Liam, standing in the hallway, a vase in his hands.

Not any vase. One that's been broken and repaired with gold lacquer. Kintsugi.

"I know, it's cheesy." He traces a gold line. "But I figured the best presentations have a visual component."

"What about taking off your shirt?"

"That's plan B."

"No A?"

"Gotta save some of my good material."

Fuck, I miss him. How can I already miss him so badly?

"And if that doesn't work, just imagine what else I'll take out."

A laugh spills from my lips.

He smiles. "Can I come in?"

"You ask now?"

"You can say no."

"I know." I pull the door a little wider. "Come in."

He steps inside. Sets the vase on the kitchen counter. Presses his palms to his thighs, suddenly awkward. "I'm sorry I lied to you. I wanted to tell you, but Preston… fuck, that's bullshit. He asked me to keep that secret, but it wasn't just for him. It was for me too, because I couldn't say it out loud."

"You didn't want to tell me?"

"No, baby, I was desperate to tell you. It wasn't you. It was me. I didn't want to face it. I didn't want to look at it. I didn't want to look at you and see what a fucked-up mess I am. I know that's no excuse. And that's not what you want. You want it all. Everything." His eyes meet mine. "You deserve that. You deserve someone who gives you every part of himself. I want that, too. I want to be your everything."

"Liam—"

"I don't know how. I don't know if I'm any good at it, but I want to try. Briar West, I love you."

"I love you too."

"I know I'm a fucking mess. I'm still going to be a mess tomorrow. And next week. Maybe forever. I can't promise I'll figure my shit out, but I can promise to try. I can promise to love you better every fucking day."

"Yeah?"

"Yeah. I want to be the person you need. I want to help tape together your broken pieces."

"And to let me tape together yours?"

"Yeah. The tape thing isn't working with my vase metaphor here."

A laugh spills from my lips.

"I'm ruining the moment with this metaphor pedantry, huh?"

"No." I wrap my arms around his waist. "It's perfect."

Epilogue

LIAM

I double check the mirrors. The mood lights. The music.

This is it.

My promise to Bri, to deliver on every one of her dirty fantasies.

Starting with this one.

I need to nail this.

For her.

I need to be what she needs, the one person who gets this side of her.

This is still where we make the most sense. Where I know how to fill every single one of her needs.

I make her breakfast; I fix her tea; I hold her close.

I get Bri, I do.

But I don't know what the fuck she's going to say about my offer—

The other one—

She doesn't talk marriage. She doesn't use the word girlfriend. She doesn't faint when people ask about her fake engagement ring (she still wears it, supposedly to ward off douchebags, but I like to believe a part of her loves the idea of marriage and commitment), but she doesn't rush to discuss it either.

She might never come around on making it official, but she's figuring out her shit, on her own time, in her own way.

She even wants to go to Los Angeles this Christmas.

For three days, staying in a hotel, driving a rental car, yeah—

But she's still willing to spend the day with her parents. That's fucking progress.

It's not as fast as I'd like, but—

Who the fuck am I kidding? Preston was right. I'm all in. I want to fly to Vegas and marry her tonight.

I can wait.

I don't fucking want to wait, but I can. I will. I'll wait a thousand years if that's what it takes.

This, what I want to do tonight—

Well, what I want to do tonight, after I do her—

Will she say yes?

I don't know.

I check the bottom drawer. It's still there, adorned, ready, waiting for my question.

And there's something under it, something I haven't seen in weeks—

My folder of info on Simon. The secrets he's hiding. The skeletons in his closet.

All sorts of shit that isn't any of my business.

It's been sitting here for months.

I want to know, I do, but not like this.

I don't forgive Simon for keeping secrets, but I under-stand. I appreciate his intentions.

Sometimes, I even admit he has good intentions.

Not out loud. Not to anyone else. Certainly not to Simon.

But I see it. I do.

Simon respects me enough to leave this with me. He respects me enough to offer me the truth.

My older brother actually respects me. I've always known he loves me, but this?

It's hard to wrap my head around it.

And I respect him, respect his intent enough to wait.

I'm going to ask, talk to him, trust him when he says I'm better off not knowing.

Soon.

Really fucking soon.

We're not there. Not yet.

But we're on the way. It's going to be a long fucking journey, but this is a big start.

Now, why the fuck am I still thinking about my brother?

I grab my gift for Briar. Put it in the top drawer. Do one last check of the room.

Lights.

Music.

Action.

I open the door a crack. My signal to her.

I want this for her, to make it happen for her.

But it's not in my hands anymore.

It's up to her.

―――――

BRIAR

.   .   .

A FAMILIAR MELODY FLOATS INTO MY EARS. A SOFT GUITAR riff. Steady drums. Moody vocals.

The second verse, already.

How long have I been standing here, in the bathroom, staring at my reflection?

My makeup is in place, my hair is neat, my outfit is fire.

There's no reason to wait. I don't have an excuse.

I apply another coat of lipstick anyway. Moshpit. The perfect plum.

Liam's favorite.

Not that he can tell the difference between plum, berry plum, berry, and wine.

He sees purple-red and his thoughts go straight to the gutter. *I need your lips on mine, baby.*

It's my signature. I guess that will make it hard for him to have an affair. I'll catch the shade on his collar like *that*.

Not that I think Liam would cheat. I know he wouldn't. I do. I trust him.

It's just the word marriage still sends my thoughts straight to affair.

Not as fast as it did a few months ago. But fast enough.

The whole commitment thing—

I swallow hard.

I'm not here to contemplate forever. Or discuss marriage. Or think about the future.

I'm here to drive him out of his fucking mind.

And I'm doing it.

Liam pushed for this. And he was, well, pushy. In a Liam kind of way. But it wasn't for him.

It was for me. It is for me.

He wants me to feel free and uninhibited and completely in touch with my inner freak.

I'm ready to do this.

Mostly.

I take a deep breath. Exhale slowly. This is it. As soon as the song ends.

The chorus fades into the outro.

For a moment, the hum of the air-conditioning fills my ears. Then it's the slow, sultry intro.

Deep breath. Steady exhale.

I step into the hallway. Slip through the open door. Into Liam's bedroom.

The room is every bit the club scene he promised. Red-purple lights, silk sheets, mirrors everywhere.

And Liam, sitting in a plush chair, staring at me like I'm the only thing he's ever wanted.

Fuck.

My heart thuds against my chest. My stomach flutters. My sex clenches.

How can I be turned on, nervous, and impossibly in love with him at the same time? It defies explanation.

But that's Liam.

"The room." He barely forces the words from his lips. "Good?"

"Good." Somehow, I'm less tongue-tied than he is.

It's strange and wonderful, leaving silver-tongued Liam Pierce speechless.

Fuck.

The desire in his eyes—

I'm going to burst into flames.

I suck a breath through my teeth. Take another step toward him.

His eyes pass over me slowly, from my spiked heels, to my sheer panties and bra, to the purple strands falling at my chin, highlighting the plum shade of my lips.

"Fuck." His eyes stay glued to me.

"This is my song." I motion to the Bluetooth stereo in

the corner. "My set. Three songs to do whatever I want with you."

He nods.

I close my eyes. Let my thoughts drift to a dirtier scenario. The two of us, at an actual club, in an actual private room (he offered to make it happen, but I wanted to try this first).

On the balcony at an exclusive bar.

In his office, after hours, him reprimanding me and ordering me onto my knees.

But Liam doesn't reprimand.

And I'm the one in charge here.

Maybe another time. Maybe next time. Maybe tomorrow, fucking tonight. I don't know.

Right now, I want to sink into this.

Right now, I'm the one driving him out of his fucking mind.

I take in the desire in his eyes, then I bring my gaze to our reflection: The back of the arm chair. His messy hair. Me, standing in my heels and lingerie, commanding the attention in the room.

It's hot as fuck, but it's not enough. I need to see him. To see us.

I take another step toward him.

Then another.

Then I'm close enough to touch him.

He reaches for my hips.

I take his wrists. Press them to the chair. "Not yet." I undo the hook of my bra. "Not until I'm done with you."

His pupils dilate.

Fuck, I want to feel every inch of his body against every inch of mine. But I want this more. I want to toy with him the way he toys with me.

I want to push him to the brink of what he can take.

Or past it even.

I slip the bra off my shoulders. Toss it on the floor behind me.

I haven't seen a lot of lap dances in person, but I know what I want—to see my body against his, to see him out of his fucking mind.

And *then* I'll feel his hands on my skin, his lips on my lips, his cock driving into me again and again.

I bring my hands to his shoulders and slide onto his lap.

He presses his palms into the chair, equal parts patient and desperate. Usually, I'm the one patient with him. When he teases me. When he drives me crazy. When he says stupid shit to make me laugh.

But with this, him drawing out my fantasies, pushing just enough, delivering everything I want?

He's endlessly patient. Like he really can wait forever.

Can he?

Right now, I almost believe it.

Even as I roll my hips against his, feel him hard against me.

I roll in time with the music, slow and steady. Not patient, but biding my time, drawing *him* out, making *him* wait.

My eyes flit to the right. To our reflection. Him, sitting up straight in the armchair, staring up at me with wonder and need.

Me, topless in his lap, grinding against him.

He's in his clothes.

I'm in control.

Who has the power? I don't know. I don't care. I don't care about anything but driving him out of his mind.

I grind against him until the song shifts, then I undo

the knot of his tie, unbutton his shirt, run my fingers over his chest.

His hands slip from the chair. He reaches for me. Stops himself.

I grind against him one more time, then I shift onto my feet. I lock eyes with him as I slip my panties off my hips, kick them aside, turn to show off my ass.

To see the two of us in full view of the mirror.

Fuck.

When I slip onto his lap, he reaches for me.

I grab his hands again, but I don't put them on the chair. I place them on my hips. "Not yet."

His breath hitches in his throat.

I grind against him again and again, rocking against his cock.

His slacks are in the way, but I still feel him, hard and thick and ready for me.

I want that. I really fucking want that. Like it's the first time. Like it's been a million years. Like I'll die if I don't have him inside me.

He's the one driving me out of my fucking mind.

His fingers dig into my hips.

I slide back as far as I can, so I'm completely pressed against him, so I'm wide open, on view for him.

A groan falls from his lips.

Then another.

I spread my legs a little wider, take his hands, bring them to my chest.

His lips brush my neck.

He kisses softly as he cups my breasts. Then it's harder, rougher.

The scrape of his teeth. The pressure of his thumbs.

I rock against him as he toys with me.

Through the verse, the chorus, the breakdown.

Until the chorus fades into the outro.

Three songs to toy with him.

One left.

This feels so fucking good, but I need more. I need him completely at my mercy.

I take his hands. Press them to the chair again.

I slip off him. Onto my feet.

My eyes go to our reflection. Then I turn to face him.

He looks up at me like I'm heaven sent.

It's better than last time. Better than every time. Better than anything.

I bring my hand to his thigh.

He shudders as I unzip his slacks and push his boxers aside.

Fuck, he feels so good. He always feels so good. But this isn't enough. I need more. I always need more with him.

He watches as I lower myself to my knees.

I run my thumb over his tip, then I wrap my hand around him and pump.

Again.

And again, for good measure.

He groans as I bring my lips to his tip.

A soft brush.

I'm not patient enough to tease him.

But I need to see this. I take one moment, soak in the sight of me on my knees, my lips around him, his hand on my chest.

Then I take him into my mouth.

He knots his hand in my hair. "Bri, fuck." His words are strained. A tone I recognize.

He wants to insist he fucks me.

But his body is begging him to relent, to surrender to pleasure now, and here, and come in my mouth.

I press my palm into his thigh.

He tugs at my hair, pulling me over him. Then his hand is cupping the back of my head, pushing me forward.

He groans again.

I flick my tongue against his tip.

Then he's tugging harder, pulling me off him.

"Song's over." His breath is ragged. "Please, baby."

Fuck, that sounds good on his lips.

And I want him inside me. I really fucking do.

He offers his hand, to help me up.

But I don't take it. This is still my fucking game. And he's still under my fucking thumb.

I make him wait. For stopping me. For trying to take charge. Because I love watching him wait.

Then I slide onto his lap.

His hands go to my hips.

His cock brushes my sex.

His lips go to my nipple.

He pulls me down, onto him, as he flicks his tongue against me.

Fuck. My eyes close. My hand goes to his neck. The back of his head.

I work with him, driving down on him again and again.

I'm already wound so tight.

I'm already so fucking close.

My eyes flutter open. My gaze goes to our reflection.

Me, naked in his lap, his lips around my nipple, his cock driving into me again and again.

Fuck.

With the next rock of my hips, I go over the edge.

My sex pulses around him, pulling him closer, taking him deeper.

Pleasure rushes through my thighs, but I don't stop. I

move faster, trying to take more of him, to take him over the edge with me.

He scrapes his teeth against my nipple.

He runs his nails over my back.

Then he's groaning against my skin, digging his fingers into my hips, driving me over him again and again.

He shifts his hips, so my clit is against his pubic bone, that perfect fucking pressure.

Again.

And again.

Exactly what I need to fall over the edge.

I groan his name as I come.

This time, I pull him with me.

He pulses, spilling inside me, groaning into my chest as he works through his orgasm.

It's fast. Intense. Almost too intense.

I work through his orgasm, then I collapse in his arms, catch my breath.

Fuck.

It's the only word I have.

He presses his lips to my neck, then he untangles our bodies, helps me to the bed, does away with his clothes, climbs in next to me.

He pulls my body into his. "Fuck, baby." He presses his lips to my shoulder. "You're perfect."

"Yeah?"

"Fuck yeah." He kisses me again. "Was it what you wanted?"

"Could you not tell?"

"Couldn't take my eyes off your tits."

"Really?"

"It was a struggle." He pulls me closer. "I can tell. Still want to ask."

"It was."

"Everything you wanted?"

My cheeks flush. How can I be nervous to tell him this? I just demanded his attention for a three-song set?

And then some.

I push past my embarrassment. "The club next time. And we'll… roleplay it."

"Oh?"

"Yeah. I'm a dancer who plays by the rules. But you want me so bad you convince me to break them."

"Sounds fucking hot."

It does.

"Tomorrow?"

I laugh. "You're ready that fast?"

"I can be ready in twenty minutes."

"Should I count?"

"Fuck yeah. Get dressed. I'll get into my suit. It will take an hour to clear a room, but I'll make it happen."

"In a few weeks."

"Tomorrow?"

"The office."

"Fuck yes."

Yes. I can do that. I've wanted to fuck in his office for a long time, but I haven't found the nerve yet.

"This is the time to ask, huh?"

I nod.

"I'll get a yes to anything?"

"Your odds are good."

He smiles. Then something strange happens.

He blushes.

Liam Pierce blushing.

Fuck.

It's adorable and sexy and smooth all at once.

"I had this whole thing planned," he says.

"To get me to fuck you in your office?"

"With a key in a jewelry box." He turns me around. Brushes my hair from his eyes. "In the dresser."

"This dresser?"

"Yeah. I can grab it if you want, but I don't want to wait."

I know what he's going to ask, but I don't know what to say. So I find the nearest thing. "You're naked."

"Yeah."

"Playing to your strengths."

"Always." He doesn't take the bait. He smiles, that charming, confident Liam. Then his eyes meet mine, and he's nervous. "You know what I'm asking."

Fuck, he's really—

"If you're not ready, I get it. But I want you here. Every morning. Every night. Every fucking day."

"It's early."

"I know."

"What if I annoy you, leaving my tea everywhere?"

"You do that already."

"Or you annoy me?"

"I do that already."

Right. He's very annoying.

But I—

He—

Fuck.

"Are you sure?" I ask.

"I'd marry you right now."

"Right now?"

"Right now."

"Because I'm naked?"

"Because I love you."

"And I'm naked."

"Doesn't hurt." He cups my cheek. "But it's a lot more than that."

"I'm not ready."

"I know."

"Not for that." I can say the word. "Not for marriage."

"I know. I'm not asking. I want you here every day. I want this to be our place. I want this to be our life." He runs his thumb over my temple. "If you're not ready, that's okay."

"No. I want to."

"Are you sure?"

"No. I'll never be sure, but I—"

"I love you too," he says.

"I didn't say it first."

"You thought it."

"I did. I do love you."

"And you're going to move in?"

I take a deep breath. "Yeah. I am."

He presses his lips to mine. "You're my roomie now."

"Not your… girlfriend?"

His eyes light up. "You're ready to say it?"

"Sometimes."

He nods. "Yeah. My girlfriend."

"Is that how you think of me?"

"Yeah, but it's more than that. You're witty, gorgeous, sexy as fuck. And with your company expanding, you're the queen of New York."

"What does that make you?"

"The luckiest guy in the entire fucking world."

Want More?

Get another taste of Liam and Briar in this exclusive bonus scene.

New to the Pierce Family? Check out *Broken Beast* for Adam and Danielle's story.

Ruthless Rival, Simon's story, is coming soon. Turn the page for a preview.

In the meantime, get to know mysterious billionaire Ian Hunt in *Dirty Desires,* a smoking hot virginity sale romance.

Ruthless Rival

SPECIAL PREVIEW

Chapter One

VANESSA

Tere's never enough money.

That's true for most people. Even the CEOs schmoozing in the ball room.

For a non-profit? It's practically the company motto.

Asking for donations is the cost of doing business.

I spend my days helping domestic violence victims start over.

In exchange, I spend my evenings and lunches begging rich men for money.

Tonight is no different. A party for a tech company. Hosted by a friend of a friend of our organization.

And, finally, after two hours of adopting my best *I love asking for money because I believe in the cause* smile, shaking hands, ignoring men staring at my chest as I talk—

Finally, I'm done.

I slip away from the party, fix my makeup in the bath-room, find the bar in the corner of the lobby.

It's a Moyer tradition. We celebrate a job well done. No matter how miserable and exhausted we are, we hold our heads high and proclaim victory.

This is a nice spot for a party of one. Wood furniture, crystal chandeliers, wide windows with a gorgeous view of the Financial District.

New York City at night. The soft blue of the sky, the spots of yellow light, all that steel and glass.

Even after thirty years in the city, I love the sight.

I put my phone on silent and hail the bartender.

He looks at me funny, unsure what to make of the combination of my silk gown and skin tone. "What can I get you, miss?"

"An aviation, please," I say.

"On me." A deep voice interrupts. Simon Pierce.

The richest man in any room.

Bossy, difficult, cold as ice.

A million years ago, we went to the same private high school.

He had the world at his fingertips and he shrugged it off.

He's the same now.

He has everything he wants and he doesn't care.

He offers me a half-smile. Amused and above it all. The Simon Pierce signature.

Unfortunately, it's also hot as fuck.

His deep blue eyes fix on me as he places his credit card on the table.

My knees threaten to buckle.

Which is ridiculous. Sure, Simon Pierce is hot as hell, but he's basically the devil. If anything, he makes Lucifer look like an amateur.

I swallow the words that rise in my throat. *Fuck off. Fuck me.* "Thank you."

The bartender looks between us *ah, they're meeting here to fuck, of course.* "For you, sir?"

"Bourbon, neat."

418

The bartender nods. Turns his attention to the drinks.

Bourbon, really? "Are you going to smoke a cigar too?" I ask.

"If you have one."

"Smoked my last cigar on the balcony."

"Next time."

The bartender places my cocktail glass on the bar. Then Simon's short glass of amber liquid.

Simon wraps his fingers around his drink. Raises his glass. "Cheers."

I copy the gesture. "Cheers."

He watches as I bring the drink to my lips.

Gin and lemon and flowers. The perfect mix of herbaceous, tart, sweet.

"And you?" he says. "Ordering an Aviation?"

"Maybe I like purple."

His eyes flit to my wine lips. "I've never seen you in purple."

"You keep track?"

"A color-coded diary."

Is that a joke? I'm too surprised to laugh. "The color of my outfit?"

"What else?"

Another joke. What the fuck. I actually smile.

We've known each other a long time. Since the ninth grade.

We talk sometimes, sure, when we're stuck together on an elevator. Or shaking hands at a gala. Or hiding from festivities at a family party—my sister is married to his kid brother's best friend.

But it's polite hellos.

An occasional tease—he thinks it's cute how hard I try to save the world.

No jokes.

No lingering stares.

At least, not from him.

I can't help myself sometimes. He's evil, sure, but he's also extremely handsome. Tall and broad, with short dark hair, intense blue eyes, an extremely chiseled jaw.

Impeccable style.

He *always* wears a suit. A perfectly fitted, sleek designed suit.

"Do you really drink it because it's purple?" he asks.

"I drink it because I like it."

"You drank gin in high school," he says.

"You brought five hundred dollar bottles of bourbon to parties in high school."

"You noticed."

His eyes fix on me.

They're so dark and intense. Like the deepest parts of the ocean.

Dangerous.

Inviting in their danger.

He watches as I take a sip. Watches my lipstick mark the glass. "You don't like me."

I swallow hard. "No. I don't."

"What was it you called? The Prince of Darkness?"

How did he hear that? "The King."

He smiles. "An upgrade."

"You wouldn't stop until you had the throne."

"I wouldn't." He takes another sip. "Is that how you see me?"

I take another sip. "Yes."

"But you're here, having a drink with me."

"You sat with me."

"I can leave. If that's what you want."

Yes. Get the fuck out of here. Before I tell you what I really think of you. Or tear your clothes off. "You're a useful ally."

"Is that all you want from me?" His eyes flit to my lips, chest, waist. "Contacts?"

"What are you offering?"

"You know what I'm offering." Intent drops into his voice.

He turns to me. Brings every bit of his attention to me. Fuck.

My stomach flutters. My thighs shake.

My brain tries to cut in. To remind me Simon Pierce is a spoiled rich boy who stands for everything I despise.

I need to hold my head high.

I need to make my father proud.

I need to slip my panties in Simon's pocket.

"I have a room upstairs," he says. "A suite."

A suite. Because he has all the money in the world. Because he has everything he wants and he doesn't even notice.

For some reason, I can't bring myself to focus on the injustice of it all.

I'm too lost in his deep blue eyes.

"We can stay here. Talk about my resemblance to Beelzebub. Or we can go somewhere private." Desire drips into his voice. "It's up to you, Vanessa. Do you want to stay? Or do you want to go?"

Chapter Two

VANESSA

"*I*
t's up to you, Vanessa. Do you want to stay? Or do you want to go?"
My fingers curl into the cool glass.

My thighs shake.

My legs struggle to stay upright.

Simon Pierce is inviting me to his place.

No, not his place, a hotel room.

He's not inviting me into his life. It's sex. That's all.

But that's better.

This what I need to do. One night. One time.

The thrill of my life.

Or a total let down.

Either way, he's out of my system.

Our unresolved sexual tension is resolved.

Fourteen years of lust and loathing… finished.

That's possible.

"You can say no." He finishes his bourbon. "I won't be offended."

"You won't?"

"No. I know you want me." His eyes stay fixed on me.

"You might hate me, but you want me. You've wanted me since ninth grade."

"I—"

"I want you too."

"You've never said anything."

"You either."

That's true. But I'm not the one making the offer. "Why now?"

He hails the bartender. "You want the truth?"

"As opposed to what?"

"A lie."

"Has anyone ever said, yes, I want a lie?"

"No. But they did."

"And you're kind enough to give it to them?"

"Yes." He holds strong and sure.

I don't agree with him, but I can't argue with his conviction. "What's the lie?"

"You don't get both."

"Why not?"

He chuckles. "You're a demanding woman."

"Thank you."

He nods to the bartender, orders another round, closes his tab.

He's leaving after this. With or without me, I guess.

My heart thuds against my chest. I'm a thirty-one year old woman. Almost thirty-two.

How am I this nervous around a boy? A man, a man with all the power in the world, yes.

But it's not about that. It's not about Simon's money or status or company.

It's about how much I want his hands on my skin.

How terrified I am to feel his hands on my skin.

How terrified I am I'll miss the feel.

Or miss out on the feel.

I don't want to want him.

I really don't.

I finish my drink. The bartender takes my glass. Drops off another round.

Simon motions to the balcony. "It's more private outside."

It is. And it's nice today. By August in New York City standards. Only eighty and barely humid.

No one is out there. Anything can happen.

I nod. Take my drink. Follow him onto the balcony.

The view is better outside. And with the breeze, well, it's still hot, but, somehow, I don't mind.

We find a couch around the corner. A blue leather loveseat far from prying eyes.

He sits across from me.

I focus on my drink.

"I made someone a promise," he says. "To ask you."

"For sex?"

"Yes."

"Really?"

"Really." He looks to his drink. "My brother saw us together. Saw the way I looked at you." He takes a long sip. "He made me promise I'd size the day."

"Those were his exact words?"

"In Latin." His smile is sad. "Carpe diem."

Simon Pierce saying carpe diem. It's absurd. Beyond absurd.

He's calculating, patient, still.

He seizes opportunities, yes.

But he's not living in the moment. He's not living life to its fullest.

Not that I can talk.

I love my job. I don't mind the way it consumes me, but it does.

Am I really here, listening to Simon Pierce claim an interest in seizing the day?

I'm drunk.

Or dreaming.

I pinch myself.

Still here. Still awake. Still sitting across from him, with the offer hanging in the air.

"When did you promise?" I ask.

"Awhile ago."

"Then why now?"

"I had a deadline. Midnight."

"It's ten-thirty."

He nods.

"Cutting it close."

"I know."

"Will you tell him?"

"No." Something slips into his voice. Something I can't place. Then he shakes it off. "But I'm a man of my word."

He's hurt. It's there for a second, then it's gone.

It's strange on him.

I know he's human. I know he's subject to normal human frailties. I even know he's suffered horrible loss.

But he just—

He never shows it.

Even when we were kids, even when his father died—

He's always that same aloof, above it all guy

"Is that all it is? A promise," I say.

"No. That's why I asked today." He turns towards me. "I asked because I want to fuck you. I've wanted to fuck you for a long, long time."

"I hate you."

"I know."

"You don't mind?"

426

"I do." He brings his hand to my cheek. "But I still want to fuck you."

"Oh."

"We don't have to go upstairs." He runs his thumb over my temple. "We can stay here."

"Fuck, here, on the balcony?"

"Talk."

No. I don't want to talk. I want to mount him.

"Or fuck, here, on the balcony." He brings his lips to my ear. "Is that what you want?"

Yes. Here. Now. Everywhere. Why are you still wearing pants. "Upstairs."

"Now?"

"Not yet." I reach for my drink. Bring it to my lips. Try to find some sort of conscious thought.

The gin isn't helpful.

It's a sledgehammer to my inhibitions. That voice, the one whispering *how will you feel in the morning* is long gone. Replaced with a neon light flashing *Fuck. Simon. Now.*

He's sure and steady as he sips his bourbon. Settles into his seat. Watches me down half my drink. "You're nervous."

"You're unnerving."

"Why?"

"You're always in control."

"I like it that way."

"I do too."

He raises a brow.

"I do. But I didn't meant that. It's your demeanor. Nothing affects you."

"It does. I just don't show it." He peels my fingers from my glass. Sets my drink on the table.

He brings his hand to my cheek. Runs his thumb over my temple.

His other hand curls around my neck.

He pulls me into a soft, slow kiss.

A light brush of his lips. The taste of bourbon. And, under that, something all him. Something equally masculine.

He pulls back with a sigh.

"You taste good." He runs his thumb over my temple again. "I've wondered for a long time."

He pulls me into another kiss.

His lips close around my bottom lip. He sucks softly. Then harder.

The light scrape of his teeth.

My fingers curl into my thighs. The smooth silk of my dress.

It's too much fabric.

I need it gone.

I need his hands on my skin.

I don't care what happens tomorrow as long as I fuck him tonight.

He releases me. Brings his eyes to mine. "Better than I imagined."

He pulls me into another slow, deep kiss. He keeps one hand curled around my neck. Brings the other to my skirt. The slit of my dress.

He slips his hand under the silk fabric.

His fingers brush my skin.

The top of my thigh.

The inside.

Higher and higher.

"Spread your legs." His voice is heavy. Breathy.

In any other circumstance, I'd curse his bossiness, but the way he purrs is intoxicating.

I part my knees.

He slips his hand higher, higher, higher.

Until his fingers brush the silk fabric of my panties.

A groan falls from my lips.

He runs his first two fingers over the fabric, pressing the silk against my clit.

The friction is intense. So much I have to close my eyes.

Too much.

And not enough.

Not his hands.

He runs his fingers over me again and again.

Winding me tighter and tighter.

Giving me so much, but not enough.

Again and again, tighter and tighter, until I'm sure I'm going to break.

"Simon." It falls off my lips. "Touch me."

He pulls me into another slow deep kiss, then he brings his lips to my ear. "Come on my hand."

He pushes my panties aside. Runs his thumb over my clit as he brings his lips to my neck.

Soft kisses.

Soft brushes of his thumb.

Then harder.

The scrape of his teeth.

The perfect amount of pressure.

Again and again.

My hand finds his skin. The back of his neck. Soft, exposed, vulnerable.

Mine.

Only for tonight.

But mine.

I dig my nails into his skin.

With the next brush of his thumb, I come. The tension in my sex winds so tight I can't take it.

Then it unravels.

My sex pulses.

Pleasure spills through my pelvis.

Every part of me feels awake and alive and perfectly in bliss.

And every part wants the same thing.

More of him.

He rubs me through my orgasm, then he pulls his hand from my thighs, rights my dress, returns to the version of Simon Pierce I know well.

In control, intense, impossible to ruffle.

Only there's something in his eyes, something I recognize:

Desire.

He finishes his drink. Stands. Offers his hand.

I take it. Ignore the rest of my drink. Follow him through the bar, the lobby, up the elevator.

All the way to the presidential suite.

This is it.

One night with Simon Pierce.

I'm going to use it wisely.

Author's Note

Adam's book was difficult.

Simon's book is impossible (like the man himself).

But Liam's book, much like Liam, felt easy. Natural. It flowed. Right away, I knew Liam and Briar, their dynamic, what they needed.

Liam is my favorite kind of guy-- a troublemaker who hides his vulnerability behind his seemingly effortless smile. And Briar is the kind of girl I want to see in romance (especially romances featuring rich guys)-- an ambitious bad ass who marches to the beat of her own drum.

It reminded me of one of my favorites, *Play Your Heart Out*, not just because of the fake relationship, but because of the dynamic between Liam and Simon (it's almost a personality swap. Liam has Pete's steady approach to life and Tom's manic front. Simon has Pete's stoic personality and Tom's high strung approach to life. Only, Liam & Simon have about 100x the tension that Pete and Tom do). Actually, the entire series reminds me of Sinful Serenade, my first successful series, and my favorite.

There's the same dysfunctional family dynamic. The

same central mansion. The same focus on grief and family. The same mix of bad boy vibes & all the money in the world. Sure, these guys lean a bit more traditional billionaire, but Liam really is a playboy prince. He grew up in this world of money and manners. He knows how to play his part. But he follows his instincts too. He plays as hard as he works. (Plus tattoos. Always tattoos).

Sinful Serenade will always be my favorite series--it was my first--and I'll always answer "the one I'm working on now," when you ask my favorite book.

But this series, the Pierce Family, is special.

I didn't go in knowing I was going to write a tightly connected family series, but by the time I finished my first draft of Adam's book, I knew. And it feels damn good! The last time I started a new, tightly connected series was *Tempting*! That was nearly four years ago.

Don't get me wrong. I love the Inked Love spin-off and the newer Dirty Rich books (I wrote book one in 2015! And book six in 2020!) but I was ready for something new.

I almost forgot how much I love getting lost in a new world, with a new mix of dysfunctional characters. This was the first totally new thing I did after my mom passed and, well… it's obvious what's been on my mind if you're reading these books.

This series might not be exactly what readers expect of classic Crystal Kaswell, but this book is: a tortured bad boy hero, a smart, sassy heroine, a lot of heat, a dysfunctional family, even a few too many (for some) mentions of tea.

These are the things I love to write: tortured heroes, three dimensional characters, sharp banter, layered emotions, complicated family dynamics, all the secret, beautiful, horrible things we think but don't want to admit to others.

And it's something new too.

I'm not the same person I was in 2015. I've lived, grown, changed.

I'm sure you have too.

That's the beautiful, horrible thing about writing fiction full-time.

People expect certain things from you.

They want some things to stay the same.

But they want to see change too. They want to grow with you too.

I love music (as you might guess, from the amount of rock star books I've written). I love a lot of bands. There are bands that grew away from me. They got too poppy or too weird or too obsessed with subjects that don't interest me.

And there are bands that grew with me, that kept putting out great albums with newer, more adult concerns.

Those are my favorite.

That's what I want to be:

An artist who grows, stretches, pushes herself.

Who brings you what you want with a fresh take.

Because the only thing sadder than growing apart is not growing at all. Who wants to be the same person they were five, ten, fifteen years ago?

I want to get wiser, sharper, better.

Semper ad meliora.

Always towards better things.

It's not the pretentious Latin tattoo I have (mine is *memento mori*--perfect for this series), but it's one I respect.

(And maybe it's time to add it to the canvas).

Acknowledgments

My first thanks goes to my husband, for his support when I'm lost in bookland and for generally being the sun in my sky. Sweetheart, you're better than all the broken bad boys in the world.

The second goes to my father, for insisting I go to the best film school in the country, everything else be damned. I wouldn't love movies, writing, or storytelling half as much if not for all our afternoon trips to the bookstore and weekends at the movies. You've always been supportive of my goals, and that means the world to me.

A big shout out to all my beta readers. And also to my ARC readers for helping spread the word to everyone else in the world.

To all my writer friends who talk me down from the ledge, hold my hand, and tell me when my ideas are terrible and when they're brilliant, thank you.

Thanks so much to my editor Marla, and to Hang Le for the cover design.

As always, my biggest thanks goes to my readers.

Thank you for picking up *Playboy Prince*. I hope you'll be back for *Ruthless Rival,* Simon and Vanessa's story.

The Best Friend Bargain - Forest

The First Taste - Holden

The Roomie Rulebook - Oliver

Sinful Serenade

Sing Your Heart Out - Miles

Strum Your Heart Out - Drew

Rock Your Heart Out - Tom

Play Your Heart Out - Pete

Sinful Ever After – series sequel

Just a Taste - Miles's POV

Dangerous Noise

Dangerous Kiss - Ethan

Dangerous Crush – Kit

Dangerous Rock – Joel

Dangerous Fling – Mal

Dangerous Encore - series sequel

Standalones

Broken - Trent & Delilah

Come Undone Trilogy

Come Undone

Come Apart

Come To Me

Sign up for the Crystal Kaswell mailing list

Printed in Great Britain
by Amazon